the

MARRIAGE
SPELL

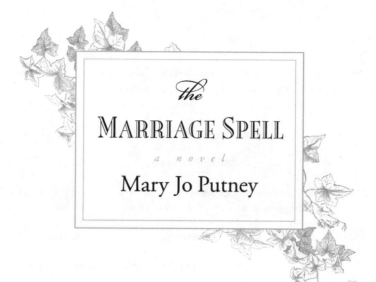

the

MARRIAGE SPELL

a novel

Mary Jo Putney

Ballantine Books NEW YORK

Published in the United States by Ballantine Books, an imprint of the Random House Publishing Group, a division of Random House, Inc., New York.

BALLANTINE and colophon are registered trademarks of Random House, Inc.

Library of Congress Cataloging-in-Publication Data
Putney, Mary Jo.
The marriage spell: a novel / Mary Jo Putney
p. cm.
ISBN 0-345-44918-5 (acid-free paper)
I. Title.

PS3566.U83M37 2006
813'.54—dc22
2005057087

Printed in the United States of America on acid-free paper

www.ballantinebooks.com

2 4 6 8 9 7 5 3 1

First Edition

Text design by Laurie Jewell

IN MEMORY OF DAVID BLUM

who was a terrific and articulate source of
information on lawyering, Judaism, and being a twin.
And who without a word demonstrated
what it is to be a mensch.

Acknowledgments

My thanks to all the usual suspects, who required particular patience with my whimpering while this book was slouching toward the finish line.

Very special thanks go to Laurie Grant Kingery for vetting all things medical on behalf of my healer heroine.

And thanks to all those nurses who use the human magic of compassion and kindness when working with suffering patients.

the
MARRIAGE
SPELL

STONEBRIDGE ACADEMY
CUMBERLAND, NORTHWEST ENGLAND
SEPTEMBER 1793

"Time to get up, rat!"

Jack Langdon's narrow bed tilted ruthlessly, pitching him onto the cold stone floor. He shoved himself to a sitting position and blinked sleepily at the young man who had invaded his room. Where *was* he?

Stonebridge Academy. Of course. The family travel coach had deposited him here late the night before after days of exhausting travel. Jack had been given a piece of bread and shown to this room without seeing anything of his new school or classmates. Today he must learn how to survive the next years.

He scrambled to his feet and asked the older boy, "Are you a prefect?"

"I am. Call me Mr. Fullerton, *sir*. And you're a rat, the lowest of the low. Get dressed and go down into the courtyard. The colonel wants to speak to the new rats." The prefect scowled. "Do I need to stand over you while you put your clothes on?"

Jack had a powerful desire to plant a facer on that smirking mouth, but he wasn't stupid. The prefect was probably seventeen, twice Jack's size and three times as mean. He settled for saying, "No, Mr. Fullerton, *sir.* I'll be right down."

"See that you are." Fullerton left for the next room.

Shivering, Jack went to the washstand. He had to break a skin of ice in the pitcher before he could pour the water. He should have guessed how cold Cumberland would be in September since they were practically in Scotland. It had taken three long days of uncomfortable travel to reach here from his home in Yorkshire.

His home. He tried not to think of Langdale Hall, where he'd lived his whole eleven years. He'd never wanted to leave. Though he'd known school was inevitable, he'd assumed they would send him to a regular place like Eton, not that he would end up at Stonebridge Academy in disgrace.

Trying to soften the blow, his mother had said the school was small and very good. The headmaster, Colonel Hiram Stark, was widely respected. Jack would learn a great deal, and each boy had his own room, not like some schools where dozens of boys slept in the same chamber.

Jack scanned his spartan surroundings. His own room? More like his own cell. Even his mother hadn't tried to convince him that Stonebridge was anything other than punishment.

Fullerton stuck his head in the door. "Am I going to have to strip that nightshirt off, rat?" There was something avid in the prefect's eyes that made Jack nervous for reasons he didn't understand, and didn't want to.

"No, Mr. Fullerton, *sir.*" Jack picked up his discarded clothing from the night before, grateful when Fullerton moved along to bully the next new student. He'd heard talk of how miserable schools were and thought maybe it was just older boys trying to scare younger ones. Apparently the rumors had been true.

When he grew up and entered the army, he'd have to put up with cold billets and beastly senior officers, so time to get used to it. He yanked on his clothes and grabbed his cloak, then headed into the corridor.

Outside in the long, gloomy hall, he hesitated. When a footman brought him to this room last night, it had been late and dark and he'd been too tired to notice the route. But he thought they'd come from the left. He turned that direction and set off at a brisk walk. It wouldn't do to be late when summoned by the headmaster, and maybe walking would warm him up.

His corridor ended at another. As he paused and tried to remember, another boy of about his age emerged from a room to the left. Jack said, "Hello, I'm Jack Langdon. Are you going to the courtyard?"

The newcomer, wiry and blond with ice gray eyes, nodded. "I'm Ransom."

Jack offered his hand. Ransom looked startled for a moment before returning the handshake.

"Do you know how to find it?" Jack asked.

"That way." Ransom indicated the corridor to the right. "There's a staircase to the ground floor at the end."

They fell into step together. Jack was glad to meet another student—a fellow rat?—and wondered what he had done to end up here. But asking questions was bad form and Ransom looked like the touchy sort.

They were halfway to the stairs at the end when Jack heard a smothered cry from behind a door on his left. He halted, frowning, and wondered if he should investigate. Uncertainty was resolved when a sharper cry sounded.

"Hang on a moment," Jack said to Ransom. The other boy scowled, but waited rather than continuing.

Jack tapped on the door. " 'Lo in there! Are you all right?"

When there was no answer, he cautiously turned the knob. The door opened easily, but he didn't find the sick boy he expected. Looking at him were three students—and the older two were tormenting a youth smaller than Jack. The tallest was viciously twisting the boy's arm behind his back while his comrade was threatening the boy's face with a candle flame.

"I say!" Jack said, shocked. "You shouldn't be doing that."

The largest boy, a redhead with a ferrety face, snarled, "Mind your own business, rat. I'm a prefect and can do what I damned well want."

The boy with the candle growled, "Leave now and you won't get hurt."

Their victim stared at Jack but said nothing. Slight and dark-skinned, he had startling green eyes and an expression of bleak resignation.

Jack teetered on the edge of fleeing. But he couldn't imagine that the boy had done anything to justify the way he was being treated, and right was right. Girding himself for a beating, he said, "It's not fair for two of you to gang up on a smaller boy. If . . . if you don't stop, you must face the consequences."

The redhead laughed nastily. "As if we can't thrash two rats as easily as one! But if that's what you want . . ." He released his victim's arm and moved toward the door.

"Not two. Three." Ransom stepped into the doorway beside Jack and gave a smile that was all teeth. "Rats fight nastily when cornered."

The redhead hesitated. Jack didn't blame him. He'd just as soon not take on an opponent who looked as fierce as Ransom.

He sensed movement behind him. A cool voice said, "A fight? Splendid! I assume we'll take on these two ugly bullies?"

From the corner of his eye, Jack saw that two more boys had joined them. Surrendering, the redhead shoved the green-eyed boy toward the door. "Go on, join your pack of rats and be grateful that they're here to save you! For now." His last words were a clear threat.

The smaller boy darted across the room and joined Jack's group. There was a burn mark on his cheekbone and he looked as if tears were near the surface, but he didn't complain. Slamming the door shut, he said, "Thank you. All of you."

"Why did that happen?" Jack asked. "Do you know each other already?"

"No. They just don't approve of me on principle," the boy said tersely. "I'm Ashby. Hadn't we better get down to the courtyard?"

"Right," said the one of the two boys who had joined at the end. Fair-haired and whip-thin, he pivoted and headed down the corridor. "I'm Kenmore and this lethal lad is Lucas Winslow."

Dark-haired Winslow was the one who had expressed that cool willingness to fight. Jack decided that Winslow and Ransom looked like a good match for each other. Tough fellows, but they'd come through when needed.

Moving at a fast trot, the five of them made their way down to the courtyard. The manor house rose on three sides, the gray stone looming over the flagstones in the yard. The academy was high in the hills, and a bitter wind slashed to the bone.

Several other boys were standing in a ragged line in front of a tall silver-haired man with a glower that would melt granite. Jack stiffened, knowing this had to be Colonel Stark, the headmaster of the academy. The colonel had achieved fame first in battle, then as founder of the most notorious school in Britain.

Against his better judgment, Jack cautiously tried to touch the colonel with his mind. Not to pry, just to get an idea of his personality. How to please the old devil and avoid punishment.

Nothing. Jack tried again, harder, and still got nothing. Queasily he realized that magic didn't work here. He shouldn't be surprised. That was the whole point, wasn't it?

The colonel's piercing gaze raked the newly arrived students. "You five are late. You're off to a bad start. No breakfast for you. Now line up with the others and make sure the line is straight."

Jack considered explaining why they were late and immediately discarded the thought. Stark wasn't the sort to accept any excuses. Even if Jack had been delayed saving his mother's life, it wouldn't matter. He sighed, his stomach growling at the thought of no breakfast.

The newcomers joined the other boys in a line. Jack stood at one end, hoping he'd be overlooked.

Stark's lip curled contemptuously as his gaze moved slowly along the line. "You all know why you are here. You are the sons of Britain's greatest families. The finest blood in the land flows in your veins. You were born to become officers, diplomats, landowners, and clerics. The one thing you will *not* become is wizards. *Wyrdlings!*"

Jack shivered at the way the old man hissed the last word. The term *wyrdling* wasn't very polite, and even though his father had despised magic, he'd not allowed his children to use the word. But Stonebridge was all about contempt for magic, so Jack had better get used to hearing *wyrdling*.

The cold gaze moved back down the line, halting at Jack. "All of you have been sent here because of a disgraceful interest in magic. A refusal to put it aside along with other childish things. Your parents want that filth beaten out of you. They chose well, for I never fail."

Surprisingly Ransom spoke up. "Why is it wrong to use magic? Everyone has at least a bit of talent. It's . . . it's amusing, and it can be very useful. Even the church says magic is no sin if it's not used for evil purposes. Why should we have to give it up?"

For a moment Stark was stunned to hear such heresy. Then he stalked forward until he loomed over Ransom. "Everyone has sexual organs, but that doesn't mean they are to be glorified or exposed for the world to see," he snapped. "Magic is for women, the inferior classes, and lazy swine who lie and cheat because they're too incompetent to succeed on their own. For a gentleman to use magic is like being in trade. *Worse.*"

"Being a merchant is honest work," someone muttered farther down the line.

Jack suspected that the colonel heard the remark but pretended not to rather than admit he didn't know who had spoken. Keeping his attention on Ransom, he said, "For your defiance you will receive ten lashes. I am lenient because this is your first day. Do not expect such mercy again."

Stark pivoted and walked along the line of boys, his back ramrod straight. "You will be kept so busy with classes and sports that you will have no chance to think about the disgusting practice of magic. No form of spellcraft works within the school precincts—that wickedness has been blocked. Those of you who have been secretly using magic must learn to do without. Any lapses of behavior or attitude will leave you subject to discipline from myself, the tutors, or the prefects. Do I make myself clear?"

Horribly clear. Not only was all magic to be suppressed, but any of those evil prefects could abuse the younger boys at will. For a frantic moment, Jack considered writing his parents and begging to be allowed to come home. He'd swear never to practice magic again to get out of this place. He faltered at the idea of never again sensing another person's emotions or finding lost objects or . . .

He cut off his thoughts. There was no point in asking to come home. His mother might soften—she hadn't been keen on sending him here. But his father would never allow Jack to leave the academy. He had said so in as many words when he'd caught his son trying to cast a spell to read the future. He'd thrashed Jack and made immediate arrangements with Stonebridge Academy.

Jack drew in a deep breath. To survive here, he would need friends. They all would. As they'd proved today, a pack of rats could face down a pair of bullies if necessary. He glanced surreptitiously down the line, wondering which of this motley crew would become friends and allies.

He'd find out soon enough.

Chapter I

MELTON MOWBRAY, LEICESTERSHIRE
ENGLISH MIDLANDS
JANUARY 1813

A telescope had many fine and worthy uses. One could study soaring birds in flight. One could admire the rings of Saturn or the timeless mystery of the stars.

Or one could use it to watch handsome young men during hunting season. Since packs of horses and hounds often raced across her father's fields, Abigail Barton thought it only fair that she be allowed to admire the splendid specimens of manhood that had turned her native Leicestershire into the heart of English hunting country. Three famous hunts were based around the market town of Melton Mowbray, so the area attracted the most dedicated hunters in the country each winter.

It was a perfect early January day. Pale sunshine brightened the empty fields and there was a not-unpleasant chill to the clear air. She swung the telescope in its mounting. Today's meeting of the Quorn was forming up across the valley. . . . Ah, there.

She focused on the seething mass of horses, hounds, and riders visible on the hilltop estate opposite Barton Grange. The hunt would begin soon, but until then the riders greeted friends and quaffed drinks and did whatever it was that men did on such occasions. Talked about horses, mostly.

Being of a practical turn of mind, Abby knew that chasing foxes across the countryside was a monstrously silly business. Hunting was an inefficient way of eliminating vermin, it was shockingly expensive, and far too many men and horses were injured, maimed, or killed outright. Yet she could understand the intoxication of speed and recklessness, and she guessed that the young men who made up the bulk of the field cherished the camaraderie of their fellows.

Slowly she scanned the broad lawn where the hunters were gathering. Some she recognized as local men or as regular visitors to the Shires. Others were strangers. No matter. She enjoyed seeing the excitement and anticipation. For the youngest men, hunting in the Shires for the first time was close to a religious experience.

The slow sweep of her telescope halted. So Jack Langdon had managed to come for part of the hunting season. Though he was Lord Frayne now, she had trouble thinking of him that way. She had first seen him perhaps ten years ago, when he was a mere stripling. Now he was a man full grown, broad of shoulder and solid with muscle.

He was splendidly at home on horseback, not surprising since he and several of the friends laughing with him were army officers. During the summer campaign season, they fought Napoleon's forces in the Peninsula, but campaigning slowed or ceased altogether during the winter. Wellington and other senior military commanders were generous in allowing junior officers furlough to return home for hunting season. Chasing foxes kept them fit and happy, ready to chase Frenchies come spring.

Occasionally she had seen Jack Langdon in Melton Mowbray. Always he was the center of a group of friends. Though he wasn't the most handsome or the most fashionably dressed, he always drew her eye. His magnetic personality compelled attention like the sun attracted flowers.

The closest Abby had ever come to Langdon was the day she was leaving the draper's shop with bundles of tied fabric and almost tripped over him. He had laughed off the incident while collecting her bundles and apologizing for being in the way. In other words, he had been a perfect gentleman, but the friendly smile he'd given her had gone beyond mere courtesy. Langdon had actually seen her as a person, not as an anonymous local female. That was rare among the Meltonian hunting set.

She had been so flustered that she hadn't done a proper reading on him, and she had never come so close again. They certainly wouldn't meet socially—a viscount would never condescend to appear in any company that included a wizard's daughter. Especially one who was gifted herself.

But he had been tall and broad enough to make her feel petite and feminine, and when he hadn't known who she was, his smile had been most charming. . . .

Across the valley, a horn sounded and the hunt was on. Hounds streamed down the hill, followed by exhilarated riders on horses bred to run. Jack Langdon and his fellows dropped out of sight behind a rise.

Smiling at her foolishness, Abby covered the telescope and returned to her still room. Time for an honest wizard to return to work on her potions and remedies and leave the idle rich to their frivolous pursuits.

It was a grand morning for hunting. Less grand was the tedium when the first fox escaped and the hunters had to wait until the hounds drew another. But Jack was enjoying the day too thoroughly to mind the wait. His gaze passed over the rolling hills, their lush contours defined by neatly hedged fields and an endless variety of fences. Though he'd hunted in Spain, no place could match the Shires. Hurling himself heedlessly after the hounds, savoring the excitement of pushing the limits of courage and common sense—in this he found freedom from the intractable problems of life.

His sense of well-being faded. After he finished his hunting holiday, he would have to return to Yorkshire. He had been cowardly for too long already.

His friend Ashby, who had dismounted, remarked, "You look like you can't wait to risk your neck again, Jack. Even if you don't need a breather, Dancer does."

"Nonsense." Jack patted his mount's neck affectionately. The dark bay was one of the largest horses in the field, which was necessary for a rider of Jack's weight. "Dancer is good for a twenty-mile run. I hope we get that. Buying a hunting box here is the cleverest thing I ever did."

Ransom, his other houseguest, said with a wicked glint, "Your cleverest act was inviting Ashby and me to Melton so we can show you the way to the hounds."

Jack laughed, unoffended. "I'll be glad when Lucas arrives. He's always the best at cutting you down to size." He glanced at the manor house that crested a hill farther down the valley. "I don't recall hunting this particular land before. The owners maintain good coverts. How are the fences?"

"There are a couple of oxers that will give even you pause, Jack. Or at least they should," Ashby replied. Not being in the army, he had hunted the area more often than his companions. He nodded toward the manor house. "The local wizard, Sir Andrew Barton, lives there. A very well regarded fellow. Maybe that's why the hedges grow with such vigor."

Jack felt the chill that came with any mention of magic and wizards. Stonebridge Academy had done its job well. He hated to think how fascinated he'd been by the corrupt temptations of magic when he was a weak-willed boy. Thank God for the academy.

A deep voice called "Halloo!" from the far side of the covert. Jack whirled Dancer around. "The hounds have drawn a fox!"

As Jack and Ransom took off, Ashby vaulted onto his horse with amazing speed, no more than a few strides behind the other two. The hunt was on again.

Jack caught up with the other leaders of the field by jumping a stiff thorn hedge with a ditch on the other side. Dancer soared over with a foot to spare, as eager to fly as his rider. The hounds were in the next field, their white and tan bodies rushing headlong across the hillside and their cries echoing through the valley.

He urged Dancer faster and they went headlong through a tall bullfinch hedge. Jack held his whip in front of his face to protect his eyes from lashing branches. It was worth the scratches to find himself in the same field with the hounds. Only two or three other riders were so close, though from the corner of his eye he saw Ransom vaulting the bullfinch half a dozen strides behind him.

The fact that they were friends made the rivalry all the keener. Dancer was equal to the task of lengthening their lead over Ransom and his chestnut. The fence at the far end of the field was an oxer—a rail fence and a ditch with a narrow landing area just large enough to collect a horse and jump a second rail fence. "Are you ready, Dancer?"

The dark bay flicked his ears back with disdain. Dancer was even keener on jumping than Jack, if that was possible. They thundered at the first fence with reckless exhilaration. Man and horse soared, free of anger, regret, and sorrow. Jack laughed aloud, wishing he could stay in such a moment forever.

Dancer came down on the narrow band of earth between the ditch and the second fence. As he landed, the soil crumbled beneath his hooves. Instinctively Jack shifted his weight to help the horse regain his footing, but Dancer was too far off balance. As the horse crashed heavily to the ground, Jack pitched from the saddle. He'd had his share of falls and knew how to relax and roll, but his right foot caught in the stirrup. His foot and ankle twisted horribly and prevented him from falling cleanly.

He slammed headfirst into the rail fence, feeling a distinct cracking of bones as he crashed to the ground. His momentum sent him rolling across the damp grass and he ended sprawled on his back. He blinked dazedly at the pale blue sky and tried to assess his injuries. No pain, only numbness, except for a stinging slash on his cheek from the bull-finch hedge. Breathing was hard, very hard, but it was usual for a fall to knock the wind out of him. Numbness was also usual after a hard fall, with pain coming later. But this felt . . . different.

He realized that a horse was thrashing wildly somewhere to his right. Dancer! He tried to push himself up so he could go to his mount, but he couldn't move.

"Jack!" Ransom's face appeared against the sky. "Are you all right?"

Jack wanted to reassure his friend, but when he tried to speak, no words emerged. No air in his lungs, no words. Made perfect sense.

But he could blink, and he did repeatedly as his vision began to fade. Ashby's voice sounded horror-struck. "My God, there's so much blood!"

"Scalp wounds bleed like the devil." Ransom gently blotted blood from Jack's eyes. "I'm more worried about an injury to his neck or back. Jack, can you squeeze my hand?"

Was Ransom holding his hand? Jack felt nothing. He tried to squeeze. Again, nothing. His whole body was numb. Lucky that Ransom was here. Like Jack, he was an officer on leave from the Peninsula, and he had rough-and-ready field experience with all kinds of injuries.

Jack flickered in and out of consciousness. Other voices could be heard, one exclaiming, "My God, Lord Frayne has got himself killed!"

Another voice said, "Lucky Jack has the devil's own fortune. He'll be all right."

The distant voices faded. Ransom's face came into view again, looking white under his Spanish tan. Ashby's face also appeared as he pressed a folded cloth against Jack's skull to reduce the bleeding. Jack felt that. It hurt.

Dancer no longer thrashed, but he was whickering in pain. Ransom leaped to his feet. "Damn that horse! I'll get my pistol."

"No!" Jack managed a raw whisper. "Don't . . . kill Dancer. Not . . . his fault."

Ashby said sharply, "Stop, Ransom! Jack doesn't want you to shoot Dancer. He just said so." There were sounds of conflict, as if Ashby was physically restraining Ransom.

"Damn you, Ashby!" If Jack hadn't known it was impossible, he'd have said that Ransom sounded near tears. "That bloody beast threw Jack!"

"It looks as if Dancer landed on a weak patch of ground, over a badger hole maybe. An accident." Ashby's voice was soothing. "Jack will never forgive us if we have his favorite hunter put down unnecessarily."

"It looks like Dancer has a broken leg," Ransom said flatly. "It's shoot him now or shoot him later. And soon enough, Jack won't care."

Jack puzzled at the words. Did Ransom mean he was dying? Surely there would be pain if that was the case. But there was the problem with breathing. . . .

Fear cut through his dreamy vagueness and he tried with all his might to flex his hands, his feet, his fingers. *Nothing.*

He couldn't move any part of his body below his neck. He was paralyzed, which meant that very soon he would be dead. No wonder Ransom and Ashby were upset.

He had flirted with death for much of his life, alarming his friends with his reckless behavior. Not suicidal—he would never deliberately cause his own death. But he had thought that when the time came, probably on the field of battle, he would embrace the Grim Reaper with a certain amount of relief. Death was simple; life was not.

Yet now that the time before his demise could be counted in minutes or hours, he realized that he didn't want to die. He had problems in his life, but who didn't? If he had tried to solve them rather than running away, they'd be solved by now. New problems would arise, but those could have been solved, too.

Instead, in the name of honor and serving his country, he had run away from the duty he owed his name and family. He'd always thought there would be time enough for duty. One day he'd settle down and sort out his inheritance, but first there were battles to be fought and foxes to be chased. Which proved he was not only reckless but a fool.

Ransom said in that flat voice, "We should notify his mother and sister."

"Not until the . . . the outcome is certain." Ashby's voice was so distant it was almost inaudible. "The wizard's house is the closest. I've heard Barton is a good healer. If we take Jack there, maybe something can be done."

Ransom laughed bitterly. "You've lived a sheltered life if you think that any damned wyrdling can make a difference with this kind of injury."

"Nonetheless, we will take him to Barton Grange. The grooms have brought a hurdle, so help me lift Jack onto it so we can carry him to the house."

Jack felt barely attached to his lifeless body as half a dozen pairs of hands moved him onto the hurdle. Bleakly he accepted that he was already dead—it was just a matter of time until breath and heart stopped. He'd spent his life heedlessly, like a gambler wasting his fortune, and now he must face the consequences.

At least he wouldn't have to return to Yorkshire except to be buried.

As he slid into blackness, his last conscious thought was irritation that he was going to die in a damned wizard's house.

Chapter II

Abby stared at her mortar and pestle, trying to remember why she was grinding cardamom pods. It wasn't like her to be forgetful, but she'd been having trouble concentrating all morning. She had the itchy feeling that something was wrong.

Unfortunately she had no talent for precognition, so she had no idea what had happened or was about to happen. She didn't even know who was affected. Not her brother, she was sure, despite the dangerous work he was doing in Spain. Perhaps her father, who was in London now? She didn't think so, but it was hard to be sure. She shook her head in frustration. There were too many possibilities.

She heard hounds baying not far from the house. Maybe her unease signaled a hunting accident, though usually she didn't notice those because they didn't affect her. Once her father had called on the master of the hunt and offered their services as healers in the event of injuries in the field. The master, a duke, had rebuffed the offer curtly. Sir Andrew had told his daughter dryly that it was clear the duke would rather see members of his hunt die than entrust their treatment to wizards.

Abby shrugged and returned to grinding the cardamom. Wizards became accustomed to the contempt of the upper classes, particularly upper-class males. Her private thought was that if they were too snobbish to avail themselves of the benefits of magic, they deserved to die off quickly and leave the world to people with fewer prejudices. Not that she would dare say such a thing aloud. She'd learned early from her parents that practicing wizards needed to be discreet.

There had always been magic, of course, but in Western Europe, the influence of the Church had suppressed it for hundreds of years. Apart from village wisewomen who delivered babies and made herbal potions, magic had disappeared from public view. Then came the fourteenth century and the black death.

As the disease devastated whole nations, wizards had broken their long silence to minister to their neighbors. Often they worked side by side with priests and nuns, struggling to save lives as the religious folk struggled to save souls. Clerics came to accept that magical gifts came from God, not the devil. A bond of trust and tolerance was forged between wizards and clerics—especially since so many priests and nuns turned out to be wizards themselves.

Though the black death killed a third of Europe, it was widely recognized that without wizardly healers, the toll would have been far higher. In England, Edward III had issued an official proclamation thanking the wizards for their work, which had saved the lives of himself, his queen, and most of his children.

Other European sovereigns had followed suit. Magic became generally accepted at all levels of society, except among aristocrats, who hated anything they couldn't control. Occasionally wizards became the targets of riots and persecutions, but on the whole, they were respected citizens. Abby's father was even a baronet, an honor granted an ancestor who had served a king. Though being known as a wizard wasn't always safe, most of the magically gifted preferred to live openly, honestly—and discreetly.

Having remembered that she was making a potion to improve physical energy, she reached next for a cinnamon stick. There were many such potions, so she figured that she might as well make one that tasted good.

She was about to add ginger when she heard pounding at the front door. *It's happened!* Her unease crystallized into certainty. Not bothering to remove her apron, she raced from her workroom and down the stairs. A footman opened the door, revealing several red-coated hunters carrying an unconscious body on a woven wood hurdle ripped from a field.

Brushing past the footman, Abby said, "Someone has had a bad fall?"

The man in front, a lean, dark fellow with compelling green eyes, said, "Very bad. I've heard that Sir Andrew is a healer. Will he help?"

"My father is in London, but I am also a healer. Bring him in."

Someone muttered, "Not only a wyrdling, but a woman. The poor devil's luck has finally failed him."

A blond man with a military air gave the other fellow a quelling glance before turning back to Abby. "Where shall we take him?"

"This way." To the footman, she said, "Bring a medical kit immediately." Then she led the men into the dining room. The parlor maid yanked the decorative epergne from the center of the table.

"Move him carefully," Abby said. As the limp, heavy body was shifted sideways onto the tabletop, she clasped the bloodied head firmly to keep it steady during the transfer. When he was settled, she used her fingertips to explore the gash in his skull. Long and gory, but not too serious, she thought.

She was wiping her hands on her apron when she got a clear look at the victim's battered face. *Jack Langdon.* Or more accurately, Lord Frayne. She must remember to think of him as Lord Frayne.

The smile was gone, the strong body broken, the pulse of his life force barely a flicker. If he wasn't such a strong man, he would be dead already. She felt a wrench of deep sorrow that his warmth and laughter had been snuffed out so senselessly.

She glanced around the room. Most of the men who had carried the victim shifted uneasily, not certain what to do. Their restlessness was distracting. "There's no need for you gentlemen to stay, and your horses shouldn't be left standing around in a cold wind. I'll know more later, after I've examined him."

Looking relieved at having permission to escape, five of the seven left. The green-eyed fellow and the blond military man stayed. The former said, "I'm Ashby and this is Ransom. We've known Lord Frayne for a long time. Perhaps we can help."

Her brows arched as she realized this must be the Duke of Ashby. She knew that the duke hunted around Melton, but she'd never seen him. He wasn't what she would have expected of a duke. "Thank you, your grace."

He gave her a twisted smile. "Ashby will do."

The footman arrived with the medical kit. As she laid several pieces of cotton gauze over the bleeding scalp wound to make a temporary bandage, Ransom asked, "Shall we cut the boot off his right leg?"

She glanced up, wondering where on earth he'd been concealing that very lethal-looking dagger. "Not yet. He's lost a lot of blood, but I'm afraid that in his present condition, any jostling might drain what little strength he has left. Wait until I've examined him so that we know what we're dealing with."

The knife disappeared. Abby hoped that Ransom wouldn't feel inclined to use it if she was unable to save his friend. She started her examination by pricking Frayne's hands and legs with a needle. There wasn't even a twinge of response. Not good. "Please be very quiet while I do the scanning."

Both men nodded. She was glad they knew enough not to waste her time with questions. She closed her eyes and drew a deep breath as she meditated. Accurate scanning required total concentration, yet also deep relaxation. Nothing less would allow her to grasp the full extent of Lord Frayne's injuries.

When she was centered, she opened her eyes and attempted to scan—and sensed nothing. All she could see was his battered physical body, the same as any nonwizard would see. A second attempt at scanning was equally unsuccessful.

"Lord Frayne must be carrying a charm to shield himself from magic, because I can't scan him." Which meant the charm was exceptionally powerful. Her magic was strong enough that most such spells didn't affect her, but this one stopped her cold. She could probably penetrate it given time, but she had neither time nor power to spare. "Do you know where he carries it? If so, could you remove it?"

The men exchanged a glance. Charms carrying protective spells were common since many people were wary of wizards, though Abby considered them fairly useless. A wizard had to have a good reason to cast spells because so much power was required—and if a strong wizard seriously wanted to bespell a person, the average protective charm wouldn't be much help. But if the charms made people feel safer around wizards, they had some value.

As a rich man, Frayne could afford the best spells and so could his friends. She was tempted to see if they were also using shielding charms, but checking would be discourteous, not to mention distracting when a man's life weighed in the balance.

Ashby said, "I'll see if I can get him to agree to your using magic."

Interesting. Either Frayne had a charm that was not easily removed or his friends didn't know where he carried the charm and were reluctant to waste time looking for it. Ashby bent over his friend. "Jack, will you grant permission for Miss Barton to examine your injuries?"

Frayne blinked his eyes open. "Wyrdling," he breathed, as if that was answer enough.

"*Please,* Jack! Try for courtesy. Miss Barton is a wizard of good reputation and gentle birth. Ransom and I will stay with you, so you'll be safe. But for God's sake, grant her permission!"

After another long, rattling breath, Frayne mouthed, "Very well."

Permission had to be freely granted to neutralize a charm, and Abby wondered if Frayne's obvious reluctance would block true consent. But when she tried scanning again, she was able to sink her awareness into his body, sensing what was whole and what was damaged. By the time she reached Frayne's neck and head, she should be well attuned to his energy.

As she slowly skimmed her palms above his legs, she murmured, "The bones in his lower right leg are broken in four places. The worst is a fracture in the large bone, and the broken bits have pierced the skin. That's what's causing the bleeding. But his knees and thighbones are undamaged, which is good."

"You can really sense that?" Ashby asked with wonder.

"Yes. Bones are easy. Internal organs can be more difficult." She continued her scan, moving slowly up Frayne's body without ever touching him directly. As a woman healer working on a man, and an aristocrat at that, she needed to be circumspect.

There were bruises in profusion and several cracked ribs, but nothing lethal until she shifted her hands to the area above his throat. Immediately she felt violent energy stabbing her palms. She probed more deeply, needing to understand in detail. When she was sure, she said grimly, "Two bones at the base of the neck are broken."

One of the men sucked in his breath, but didn't speak. She guessed that both understood that their friend was mortally injured. For the sake of thoroughness, she completed her scan, moving her hands above Frayne's skull. "He has a bad concussion," she said, "but I don't think there's serious brain damage."

"The broken neck is surely enough," Ransom said heavily.

Unfortunately he was right. Yet still Frayne breathed. She frowned as she considered the extent of his injuries, trying to remember if she'd read anything in her father's books that offered hope.

"Can you do anything for him?" Ashby asked.

Before Abby could reply, Frayne drew a harsh, painful breath—then choked and stopped breathing. For a moment, Abby felt her own heart stop at the fear he would die right now. She splayed her hand over the center of Frayne's chest. His heart still beat, though faintly. What he needed was air in his lungs.

She placed her hands on both sides of Frayne's throat, pouring in energy and praying that she might temporarily stabilize the damaged neck and throat. It took all the strength she had, but she could feel a slight strengthening of the nerves. How to get him breathing on his own?

She must prime the pump. After inhaling deeply, she bent over and covered his mouth with hers, blowing air into the injured man's lungs. His lips were cool and firm, but more like a wax dummy than a living man. She inhaled again, then bent once more to share her breath. After half a dozen times, he inhaled raggedly on his own, then fell into a labored but regular breathing pattern. She had bought a little more time, she thought dizzily as she straightened.

The two men were regarding here with fascination. "Are all wizard healers like you?" Ransom asked.

"The good ones are." She brushed at her hair, which had fallen over her face, remembering too late that she was streaking blood across herself.

"Is there any kind of treatment?" Ashby asked. "Cost is not an issue."

She beckoned the men away from Frayne so she could talk to them privately. She had long suspected that injured people could hear things even when they seemed unconscious, and bad news could become a self-fulfilling prophecy. Keeping her voice low, she said, "I've never heard of a healer saving someone so badly injured. You saw that it took most of my power just to stabilize him temporarily, and that had no effect on the underlying injuries."

"What about a healing circle?" Ashby asked. "I've heard that such a circle can sometimes produce extraordinary results."

"You're familiar with healing circles?" she said with surprise.

"As I understand it, a number of people with magical power come together and channel their energy through a trained healer. Often their combined power can cure far worse illnesses than any one healer can manage, no matter how talented."

For an aristocrat, he was surprisingly well informed. "Have you also heard that healing circles are very dangerous for the wizard who is the focal point? People have died when the power became greater than they could control." And yet such circles could indeed perform miracles—sometimes. She frowned. "I wish my father was here."

"He's a more powerful healer than you?" Ransom asked.

"Not more powerful, but more experienced. But it would take days to reach him in London and bring him home again." She nodded toward Lord Frayne's motionless body. "He doesn't have days."

"You were able to start Jack breathing again," Ransom said. "Could you keep him stable until your father can return?"

"It was a temporary measure only, and I had to use full power even for that," she said bluntly. "His condition will steadily deteriorate. If he doesn't drown in his own lungs, he will waste away from an inability to eat and drink. Probably he would die of thirst if he doesn't suffocate first."

Ransom's face tightened. After a long silence, Ashby said, "I would be willing to be the focal point of the healing circle."

Her brows arched. "That's a brave and generous offer, but unless you're a trained healer, it would be suicidal."

His gaze was level. "I am willing to take the risk."

"No!" Ransom said with barely repressed violence. "Bad enough if we lose Jack. Being a duke doesn't make you immortal, Ash."

"Perhaps someday I will find out what being a duke is good for," Ashby murmured. "Miss Barton, are there enough people with power in the area to attempt a circle? And if so, what would you charge for performing one?"

"Cost is not the issue, but feasibility. As for people with power . . ." She made a swift mental inventory of all the wizards within a few hours' ride. "There aren't enough wizards nearby to create a circle that has a chance of working. If my father was here, there would be enough power available to at least consider trying, but without him, the attempt would be hopeless. Not to mention dangerous."

Ashby and Ransom shared a glance. Apparently reaching some decision, Ashby said, "Frayne and Ransom and I met at Stonebridge Academy. From your expression, I see that you've heard of it." His mouth twisted. "The headmaster did his job well, but I've always heard that magic is inherent and can't be beaten out of a boy, even if the desire to use it is. Since I had some power then, presumably I still do. Would you be able to draw on that if I joined the circle?"

Stonebridge Academy? Intriguing. "May I scan you?"

The duke nodded. He must have neutralized a shielding charm at the same time because his aura suddenly blazed with power. Closing her eyes, she assessed him. What a very intriguing background he had. It explained the dark coloring as well as the magic. Reminding herself to stick to the matter at hand, she said, "You have a powerful gift. Perhaps it is enough to make a difference, but since you are untrained . . ." She shook her head doubtfully.

"What if I joined the circle?" Ransom said. "I also had magic. Once."

As he released his shielding charm, she closed her eyes and found that he was an immensely complicated man, spun of contradictions that spiraled down into mysterious depths that included magic. "You would contribute enough power that we might just have a chance of success if I am able to channel the energy properly."

"Then will you do it?" Ashby asked, his gaze intent.

She frowned as she looked at Lord Frayne. Lucky Jack Langdon. He probably wouldn't have smiled at her on the streets of Melton Mowbray if he'd known she was a wizard. More likely he would have sneered and turned away. Yet the man still drew her, both for her memories of him healthy and for his present vulnerability.

"I want very much for him to live," she said honestly. "It would be a tragedy for a strong young man who has such a gift for inspiring friendship to die needlessly. But . . . I don't know if I can do this. Would it be worth risking my life when I don't know if there is a real chance of success?" She bit her lip. "My father would be most disappointed if his only daughter killed herself while attempting something beyond her abilities."

"Is there anything that would make the risk worthwhile? If you wish wealth or independence . . ." Ashby's voice trailed off suggestively.

Abby studied Frayne's unconscious form, aching with frustration that his life was slipping away, and she didn't think she could save him. It was absurd to be half in love with a man she didn't even know.

An outrageous thought struck her. More to herself than the men, she murmured, "There is something that would make the risk worthwhile, but it's not a price Lord Frayne would be willing to pay."

"Souls can't be stolen," Ransom said. "Anything else is open for discussion."

She laughed at the absurdity of her idea. "Even marriage? I doubt he would do that, even to save his life." Yet as she gazed at him, she realized that she was willing to risk her life for no payment whatsoever, simply because she wanted him to live. *I'm sorry, Papa, but I must do this.*

To her shock, Ashby studied her through narrowed eyes. "Ask him. He might surprise you."

Her jaw dropped. "You can't be serious. The idea is outrageous."

Before she could say that she would attempt the healing circle without any extra incentives, Ashby said, "You may be a wizard, but you are also a lady, so it's not an unreasonable idea. Jack has said a couple of times that he really ought to be looking for a bride, but he can't face the horrors of the Marriage Mart. What could be easier than a wife who can save his life and doesn't need courting?"

Taking Abby's arm, the duke guided her across the room to where Lord Frayne lay. "Jack, we have a proposition for you."

Chapter III

Each time Jack drifted into darkness, he expected not to emerge from the shadows, for they grew steadily darker, more determined to suck him into ultimate blackness. This time he was pulled back to awareness when Ashby said, "Jack, we have a proposition for you. Miss Barton is a talented healer, and she will undertake the risks of conducting a healing circle in return for the honor of becoming your wife. It seems a fair bargain to me. Do you agree?"

Jack blinked, wondering if he was out of his head. "Are you *insane*?" he whispered, his voice rasping. "Better dead than enthralled by a damned wyrdling!"

Ashby leaned closer, his green eyes fierce. "That's the sort of thing one says when healthy. Would you *really* prefer death to marrying an attractive, intelligent, well-bred young woman?"

His friend had a point, damn him. Now that Death was rolling the dice with his bones, Jack realized that he wasn't yet ready to make his final throw. But marry a bloody female *wyrdling*? He blinked fuzzily at the figure standing next to Ashby.

Female, yes, rather extravagantly so. Tall and robust, with brown hair and a square jaw. Not the sort of woman one would notice if passing in the street. He supposed that men who liked Amazons might find her attractive, but Jack had always had a fondness for petite, ethereal blondes. Preferably blondes who didn't dabble in even the mildest, most acceptable forms of girlish magic.

And yet, his life was in the balance. He closed his eyes, feeling too weak to make such a decision. Marriage? He wouldn't want to marry a woman who was a complete stranger even if she wasn't a wyrdling. Granted, Ashby was generally a good judge of character, but maybe his judgment was warped by the sight of Jack's dying carcass.

Dying. His body seemed to have disappeared except for the tormented struggle to draw breath. He had seen enough men die in Spain to recognize the signs of mortal injury. Bit by bit, his life force was fading away.

He wasn't ready yet! Dear God, there were so many things he wanted to do, places he wanted to visit, friends he needed to see! With sudden, desperate ferocity, he craved life like a man perishing in the desert craved water.

He opened his eyes and stared at the Amazon. "If you try and half succeed, would I be left a helpless cripple? I truly would prefer death to that."

She bent over him, and suddenly she wasn't an abstract idea but a real woman, one with thoughts and feelings, whose eyes became the whole world. They were a pale clear blue with dark edges. Magical eyes, strange and compelling. Eyes that would not allow him to look away. "That will not happen, Lord Frayne," she said with compelling calm. "Either you will survive and eventually heal, or you will die. You will not be left a broken man dependent on others. I promise you that."

As their gazes met, he sensed that she understood his unspoken message. If she couldn't heal him, she would let him go. The knowledge was soothing.

But still . . . "You're a wizard. Can't marry a wizard." He almost called her a wyrdling again, but managed to change the word. Didn't want to be rude.

"Come now, Jack," Ransom drawled from somewhere outside of the narrow range of Jack's vision. "Think of how amusing it would be to horrify certain people by doing something so outrageous." The faintest of trembles sounded in his voice. "You've always rather liked being outrageous."

Jack choked out a laugh. Leave it to Ransom to make the idea of marrying a wizard sound like a delightful last way of thumbing his nose at society. Though the point of marrying this woman—Miss Barton?—was so that he wouldn't be thumbing his nose for the last time.

He focused on the lady—well, Ashby had implied that she was a lady, and if her father was a baronet she probably was—and asked, "What kind of wife would you be?"

Her dark brows drew together in a straight line as she considered. "An undemanding one. I like my independence and life in the country, so I wouldn't come to London to embarrass you very often." There was a faint, ironic note in her velvety voice.

The fact of her magic repelled him, and it would be a social embarrassment, but at the moment neither of those facts were compelling. "You propose to save my life. How would you benefit from such a marriage?"

"Doesn't every woman wish to acquire a title?" The irony thickened.

"That's all you want? A title?"

She glanced away. "I . . . I would also like to have a child."

An awkward subject. "The wife of a peer's first duty is to bear an heir." He closed his eyes, blocking out the sight of her. He had never imagined that a day would come when he must be grateful to still have control of his eyelids.

He was dying, and nothing would change that. Yet for a chance at life, he would take the gamble despite the impossible odds. "If I survive, a child might be managed, God willing. Very well, Miss Barton, we have a bargain. If you restore my life and health, I give my word that you will be my bride."

. . . . .

"*. . . be my bride.*" Abby clenched her fists, shocked speechless. She hadn't expected Lord Frayne's consent, and without that, she would be powerless. He doubted her ability to help him; she could see that in his bleak eyes. Even if he believed there was hope, she would have expected him to refuse to take a wizard as a bride. But the desire to live was obviously powerful enough to overcome his distaste for magic.

Consent came none too soon, since he was drifting back into unconsciousness. If there was to be any chance of saving him, she must act as soon as possible.

"Congratulations on your betrothal," Ashby said. "How long will it take to organize the healing circle?"

She pulled her disorganized thoughts together. "I will summon the local wizards immediately and they should be here by the end of the afternoon. But it's too soon to speak of a betrothal. Let me repeat that I will do my best, but there are no guarantees of success."

"I do understand that," Ashby said quietly. "But I hope that if I believe hard enough, it might help."

"Magical thinking," Ransom observed. "But worth a try, perhaps."

"You gentlemen might want to take some food and rest." She surreptitiously wiped damp palms on her skirt. In a masterpiece of understatement, she continued, "This will be a tiring experience."

"Perhaps later," Ashby said. "Before that, do you have any books that explain healing circles? I would like to learn what we might expect."

She nodded, impressed by his good sense. "There are several books in the library. If you'll follow me, I'll get them for you since I'll be writing my notes there." A footman had brought a blanket, so she spread it gently over Frayne's unconscious form after checking that his open wounds were no longer bleeding.

"I'll stay with Jack," Ransom said. "Will you move him to a bedroom?"

She shook her head. "Any movement risks injuring his spine still further."

"Lying on a table looks so uncomfortable." Ransom cut off his words. "But I suppose he can't feel that."

There was no need to answer. She gestured for Ashby to follow her to the library. When they entered, the duke studied the book-filled shelves approvingly. "Ashby Abbey is reckoned to have one of the finest libraries in England, but I believe you have even more books than I do."

"My father is a well-known scholar of magical history and practice." In fact, Sir Andrew Barton was an important figure in wizard circles, though she wasn't surprised that the duke was unaware of her father's name. Magicians were everywhere, at all levels of society, yet ignorance of magical life was rampant, especially among the nobility. That made it easier for them to pretend wizards didn't exist. She had to give Ashby and Ransom credit for civility, and the flexibility to ask for her help.

She stopped by one of the floor-to-ceiling bookcases and scanned the titles. Ah, there. She pulled two volumes from the shelf. "Both of these books discuss healing circles in some detail. I hope that will help you tonight. Now, if you excuse me, I must summon the others."

After he accepted the books with thanks, she sat down at her writing desk and began to write short notes requesting that her friends join her for a healing circle. Ashby said, "Do you have enough servants to carry the messages? If not, I could summon some of my own people to speed the process."

"Thank you, but that's not necessary." She rolled the small note tightly and tucked it into a lightweight tube made from a goose quill. "The messages will be carried by pigeons more quickly than a man can ride."

His brows arched. "Is this a form of magic?"

"Not at all. Pigeons have an instinct for returning home. Your friend Mr. Ransom might know about messenger pigeons, since I believe the army uses them. A number of wizards in this area keep pigeons raised at each other's homes so we can send messages quickly when it's required."

"I suppose that sometimes when magic is required, the need is urgent, as now."

"This is one kind of emergency, but there are others," she said dryly. "Even in this modern day, there are villages in England that might burn people like me given any kind of excuse."

He became very still. "I hadn't really thought about that, but I see that it's a burden you must carry every day."

"We all live with death only a heartbeat away. Perhaps wizards are a little more aware of that," she observed. When she left for the dovecote, Ashby was deeply engrossed in one of the books. She wondered if his study was entirely from his desire to help Lord Frayne, or whether there was a part of him that longed for his own suppressed magic. In her experience, those who possessed a gift yearned to use it. Of course she was no aristocrat. Perhaps a dukedom was power enough.

After giving the message notes to the pigeon keeper, she returned to the house and gave orders for all the spare bedrooms to be made up. By the time the healing circle was finished, her fellow wizards would be too tired to go home.

Domestic busyness helped her keep her worries under control.

By late afternoon, the last of Abby's gifted friends had arrived. It was time to begin the healing circle. She went to the breakfast room, where the local wizards had been taking refreshments and chatting with each other. Though the work ahead of them was serious, that didn't mean they couldn't enjoy this unexpected gathering. "Everyone is here now. Are you all ready? If so, it's time."

With scraping chairs and hastily swallowed drinks, the eight wizards rose and followed her to the dining room, where the patient waited. The group included both sexes, from fifteen-year-old Ella to Mr. Hambly, who was seventy-nine. Though he hadn't her father's power and skills, Mr. Hambly's decades of experience would be invaluable to Abby during the coming ritual.

The group also included a vicar, a midwife, and Young Will, the son of a farm laborer. When his gift had been discovered, Abby's father had begun tutoring him in magic and paid his fees to the local grammar school so that Will would have more opportunities than was usual for a laborer. Despite the diverse backgrounds, they were a community drawn together by their gifts. This was not the first time they had worked together, nor would it be the last.

Abby had kept the wizards away from the aristocrats, since their moods were so different. Expression grim, Ransom had refused to leave Lord Frayne's side. Ashby had spent most of the afternoon there also, sharing with Ransom what he had learned about healing circles.

Between receiving her friends and checking on Frayne's condition, Abby had also studied the notes she'd taken during lessons with her father. She knew the theory. She just hadn't thought that she would undertake a healing of this magnitude without Sir Andrew's guidance and support.

She was the leader of this circle, which meant she must project calm and confidence. She wiped damp palms on her skirts before she entered the dining room. Ransom and Ashby rose, looking bleak but resolute. To the wizards, she said, "Lord Frayne's friends will be participating in the circle. Though untrained, they are both gifted. Judith, will you stand at my right?"

Judith Wayne, the midwife, took her place by Abby's right hand. Using intuition, Abby assigned each of the participants a place in the circle around the table that supported Frayne's motionless body. Placement would help in creating a harmonious energy flow. She placed Ransom directly opposite her, next to steady old Mr. Hambly, and put Ashby at her left hand.

When everyone was in position, she said, "I believe that even our novices know the procedure, but I'll go over it again just in case. I will place my hands on Lord Frayne's head to channel the healing energy. All in the circle will join hands, with Judith and Ashby placing their free hands on my shoulders. When the circle is complete and sealed, the healing will begin. Please, please, do not break the circle under any circumstance, since that will be painful for all who participate and injurious to Lord Frayne. Does anyone have any questions?"

Ashby asked, "Do you have an idea how long this will take?"

She shook her head. "It's hard to say. Perhaps an hour. It's difficult to maintain intense energy for longer than that. The longer the ritual, the greater the risk that the circle will be broken from fatigue or some other reason."

She glanced around the circle. "Ella, did you have a question?"

The young girl asked softly, "He's bad hurt, Miss Abby. Do you think we have a chance of saving him?"

"If I didn't believe that, we wouldn't be here," Abby said honestly. "But success is not guaranteed. Reverend Wilson, will you offer a prayer that divine will be done?"

The vicar nodded and recited a prayer in a rich, sonorous voice. There were still people who believed that magic came from the devil, even though a substantial percentage of the clergy were gifted. Abby thought that it never hurt to invoke divine aid and to remind others that gifts of the spirit came from God.

When the vicar finished, Abby said, "Let us join hands, seal the circle, and begin."

Chapter IV

Abby erected her most powerful shields before Judith and Ashby rested their hands on her shoulders. Even so, the surging force of so many energies was disorienting. After she adjusted to the influx of power, she lowered her shields a little so she could separate out the energies of each person in the circle.

They were like musical notes, each unique, together creating a powerful chord. Ella was light and pure, Judith warm and compassionate, the Reverend Wilson deep and thoughtful, and so on down the line. There was a rawness about Ashby and Ransom, but she could feel their power and sincerity. Their magical abilities might just make the difference in saving their friend.

Once she had the flowing energies firmly in hand, she closed her eyes and gradually reduced her shields to nothing. Never had she focused so much power, and it was easy to see how the process could go dangerously awry. But she took every precaution, and even when her shields were entirely down, she felt that she was in control of the power that channeled through her.

In control, but also transformed. In a trance state, both detached and aware of the smallest details, she scanned Frayne's damaged body, able to see much more deeply than she had earlier. She must learn the full extent of his injuries, and she would probably have to make choices about what to attempt, since her supply of healing power wasn't unlimited.

She frowned as she sank her consciousness into Frayne's body. His life force was dangerously low, no more than a flickering ember. Worried that he might not survive the stress of the healing circle, she decided to give him some of her own vital force. Life force was different from magic. Though she could channel magical energy from everyone in the circle, when it came to lending life force, she had control over only her own, and that was as it should be.

Mentally she spun a golden thread of vital force from her solar plexus to his. Her power caused his flickering life to glow more steadily. The thread connecting them also allowed her to feel the pulse of his personality, deeply hidden now, like a bear in hibernation. He had great kindness and compassion. The world needed him as much as his friends did.

Returning to her scan, she confirmed that his brain had suffered only the concussion she had sensed earlier. That bruising would heal on its own.

Next she looked for internal bleeding. As she suspected, he had lost a great deal of blood from both his external wounds and his internal injuries, which included a damaged spleen. The power she commanded enabled the ruptures to mend, ending the bleeding.

She studied the badly splintered bones in his leg and decided it was worth expending some energy to ensure they would heal clean and straight. She visualized phantom bones that were solid and healthy and would act as a template for the real bones as they healed. If the broken leg had been his only injury, she would have fused the bones outright, but she couldn't afford the huge amounts of energy for that when his other injuries were so much more life-threatening.

Noting that inflammation was flaring up at several injury sites, she flooded his body with a spell designed to eliminate all feverishness. Infected wounds were often fatal, and he didn't have the strength to fight the inflammation.

Aware that she had already expended a substantial amount of the available power, she focused on the most critical injury: Frayne's broken neck. Not only must she repair the cracked bones, but also the blood vessels and the ruptured nerves that carried messages from mind to muscle. If those couldn't be fixed, there was no chance for Frayne to live a healthy, active life. Far kinder to withdraw and let him die in peace.

She moved her hands down to the sides of his throat, feeling the rasp of whiskers against her fingertips. First, the shattered bones . . .

After charting the cracks and breaks, she created a phantom template of healthy bones, as she had with his leg. Then she poured energy into the template with the force of a foundry fire.

She didn't have enough power. When she realized that, she wanted to weep with frustration. She was so close to being able to fuse the bones, but there simply wasn't enough magic available to finish the job. Surely she could do something.

Desperation reminded her that there might be one last resource available: Lord Frayne's own power. As Ashby had noted, a magical gift could be suppressed, but it was an integral part of one's nature and could not be destroyed.

Would Frayne approve of her using his magic when he didn't approve of magic at all? Well, he wanted to live, and she would rather save his life and incur his wrath than fail when she was so close to success.

Maintaining her grip on the energies of the circle, she dipped into the well of Frayne's self. There she found a deep pool of magic, long ignored but still powerful. She summoned his gift and braided it with the others, then returned to his damaged neck.

Miraculously, when she added his personal power, the bone shards slowly began to fuse into healthy wholeness. She poured magic in recklessly until the last piece was in place and firmly cemented in the whole.

Relief made her dizzy, so she paused and inhaled deeply. With her heightened awareness she heard not only the breathing of the other members of the circle but even their heartbeats.

When she was steadier, she girded herself for the final effort. Rebuilding his spinal column had required raw, concentrated power. In contrast, nerves and blood vessels called for the delicate skill of a master needle worker.

Painstakingly she traced each connection, knitting damaged fragments together until each structure was whole. At the edge of her awareness, she heard his labored breathing smooth out and become stronger.

With one last careful stroke, she melded the final nerve into wholeness. Knowing she was near the limits of her strength, she mentally stepped back for a survey of her patient. Was everything essential taken care of? Yes, the broken neck had been repaired, the spleen no longer bled, and the inflammation had been eliminated.

He was still extremely weak and would have to recover from the broken bones and blood loss at a normal pace. She frowned, then decided to leave the life force connection between them until his vitality was greater.

Swaying, she opened her eyes. Her companions appeared as drained as she, but the circle had held. With a tired smile, she said, "The healing is done, and with God's help, I believe we have saved him."

Eyes wide, Ella whispered, "That was incredible."

Mr. Hambly sighed and rolled his shoulders. "I've never taken part in such a healing circle as this. You did well, lass."

"We all did," she murmured.

On her left, Ashby made a sound perilously close to a sob. His dark skin had acquired a gray tinge, but he radiated relief. Ransom's eyes were closed, and she guessed he was saying a prayer of thanksgiving. Or perhaps he was invoking divine protection since he'd participated in the evil of magic.

Mustering the last of her energy, she said, "This circle is complete, and may God bless you all until we come together again." She released the energies and braced her hands on the edge of the table, her hands and muscles cramping painfully.

On her right, Judith said, "Are you all right, Abby?"

"I'm fine," she reassured her friend.

She didn't even realize she was collapsing until the floor rose up and whacked her.

He was floating in a boat on a still sea, drifting ever closer to the sunset. His anger and fear and desperate passion for life had faded into weary resignation.

Then the sun that had been sinking before him began to rise, burgeoning with power. Its rays changed from orange to pure gold as light poured over him. Light, life . . .

Jack surfaced into consciousness, feeling like a creature that had lived too long underground. Was he dead and reborn into heaven? Not likely, since he felt pain in every limb of his body. Of course he'd never thought heaven his likely destination.

Pain? He was feeling his body again? Startled, he tried to wiggle his fingers. They moved! So did his arms. He felt stabbing pains in his side, probably cracked ribs, but he could *move*!

He tried to stretch his legs and immediately regretted it when agony seared through his right leg. But his legs moved and his toes wiggled!

As shock gave way to joy, he opened his eyes and saw a molded medallion in the ceiling above him. This didn't look like heaven or hell, but a perfectly normal bedroom. Unthinking, he turned his head. Though his neck ached fiercely, there was no horrible crunch of broken bones.

Ransom was slumped in a chair by the bed, but he shot upright when Jack moved. "Thank God you're awake and moving!" He leaned forward, his face blazing with relief. "Even though your breathing was better, I couldn't quite believe you would survive. How do you feel?"

"Like I fell off Dancer and the whole damned hunting field rode over me," Jack said in a rasping voice. "Other than that, well enough." With effort, he raised his right arm, regarding it with amazement before letting it flop back onto the mattress. "I take it my injuries were less severe than they seemed at first?"

Ransom shook his head. "Your injuries were mortal, Jack. Your life was saved by a healing circle conducted by that remarkable woman whom you pledged to marry if she was successful."

Jack gasped. He had promised to marry some female? Patchy memories began to surface. Being carried to the wizard's house. An Amazon with startling eyes, his fear of dying, which led him to agree to her terms even though he'd believed his situation hopeless. Dear God, he really had promised to marry an Amazonian wizard!

Unthinkable. Yet he had given his word, and the Amazon had recalled him from the brink of death. He had been given a second chance, and he certainly couldn't start a new life by breaking his word. He must make the best of the situation. "I guess you'd better go to London and purchase a special license."

Ransom frowned. "Are you serious? Surely you would rather wait until you feel stronger. You still have a great deal of healing to do. Besides, maybe she can be persuaded to accept some other payment for her services."

" 'If it were done, 'twere well it were done quickly,' " Jack murmured, wondering how badly he was butchering the quote. "I made a promise, so there's no point in waiting. Weren't you the one who suggested that I would enjoy shocking everyone in the ton? Time I got started on that."

Ransom rose, a faint smile on his face. "If this is what you want, I'll leave for London immediately. I'm better at riding than sickrooms."

Jack managed to lift his hand and extend it to his friend. "Thanks for being here."

Ransom shook his hand, hard. "Ashby's here, too. We've taken turns sleeping."

"I am fortunate in my friends," Jack whispered, his strength fading fast.

"One makes good friends by being a good friend. I'll be back by the end of the week." Ransom touched his shoulder. "Sleep well, Jack."

As he slid into peaceful slumber, Jack made a mental note to ask Ashby what his bride's name was.

With a groan, Abby rolled over, aching in every muscle. What time was it? She opened her eyes and saw noon sunshine. She also found her friend Judith, the midwife, snoozing in the bed a foot away. What the devil?

Judith opened her eyes and covered her mouth as she yawned. Though she was several years older than Abby, in the light she looked like a young girl. A tired young girl. "So you're awake," Judith observed. "How do you feel?"

"Exhausted." Abby pushed herself to a sitting position and ran one hand through her loose hair. It was tangled abominably because she hadn't braided it before going to bed. Since she didn't remember going to bed, she assumed that someone had taken the pins from her hair and removed her gown and stays. "I don't wish to appear inhospitable, but what are you doing here?"

Judith grinned and sat up herself. Like Abby, she wore a chemise rather than a nightgown. "Beds were in short supply last night," she explained. "Everyone who participated in the circle was far too tired to go home and we were on the verge of toppling like trees. Your wonderful staff managed to find us all places to lie down before we fell down."

Abby made a mental count. "There should have been enough beds."

"I was worried about you," Judith said bluntly. "I've never seen anyone pour out as much magic as you did last night. I thought you should have someone nearby. Just in case."

Abby gave her a puzzled glance. "It was just a healing circle. There was no need to be concerned. We've done them often enough."

Judith smiled wryly. "I've never been in a circle which lasted for three hours, nor one which performed such a miracle."

"Three hours!" Abby stared. "Was it really that long?"

Her friend nodded. "Everyone was so drained that I was on the verge of closing the circle myself before one of us collapsed. I'm amazed that no one broke down. It was a very near thing."

Abby frowned as she thought back over what had happened. "I lost track of the time. Now that I think of it, I'm not surprised that it took hours. There was so much repair work to be done."

"Which is why a healing on this scale is so rare. Having enough power, patience, and skill almost never happens." Judith smiled. "You did well, Abby. I hope your noble patient is worth it."

"I think he is." Abby began finger-combing knots from her hair. "What happened last night after my maidenly faint?"

Judith covered another yawn. "I splinted our patient's broken leg so he couldn't ruin your good work if he thrashed about. At my suggestion, he was moved into that downstairs room that was your grandfather's after he became ill. I asked the housekeeper to provide a substantial breakfast all morning so people could eat whenever they woke. After such a long circle, everyone will be ravenous today."

"Thank you for taking care of all this." Abby made a face as she worked a large knot in her hair loose. "You must be as tired as I, but you managed much better."

"Tired I was, but not so much as you. After all, I'm not pouring life force into the patient," Judith said tartly.

She should have guessed that Judith would notice. "I won't do it for very long, but Lord Frayne needed extra vitality to survive the healing process. He'll continue to need a little extra until he regains some of his own strength."

"I suppose you're right," her friend conceded. "But don't keep this up very long. Life force energy is fragile and not unlimited. You could damage yourself. Or . . . worse."

"I'll be careful." Abby swung out of bed. "It's time I got dressed and found out what my guests are up to. I'll see you in the breakfast room."

She prepared for the day swiftly, very aware of her failings as a hostess. But before heading for the breakfast room, she stopped by Frayne's room to see how her patient was doing. From the doorway, she studied the firm planes of his face and thought how much more alive he looked today than yesterday. When he had been carried into her house, he had been a dying man. Now he was merely sleeping.

A tired, unshaven Ashby was watching over his friend. He rose at her entrance. "Jack was awake for a bit earlier. According to Ransom, he was very much his usual self. Aching and tired but sensible."

"I assume Ransom is taking his turn to rest. You look like you could use some sleep yourself."

Ashby gave a lopsided smile. "You're right, but I didn't want to leave Jack alone. With his valet seeing to Jack's house and Ransom off to London, that left me."

London? She supposed that men of the world were accustomed to tearing around like mail coaches. "Get some sleep, your grace," she ordered. "I'll stay with Lord Frayne until one of the footmen can come and stand watch. He doesn't need much nursing care at the moment. Mostly he needs the time to convalesce."

"I'll admit there isn't much I could do if he suffered a crisis except call for help, but I didn't want to leave him. I had just fallen asleep when Ransom asked me to take over again." Turning to leave, he added, "I thought you had agreed to call me Ashby."

She shrugged. "Yesterday was all turmoil. Today is a return to normality. You are a duke. I'm a country gentleman's daughter and a wizard. It is time to resume our normal places in life."

"You will always be the brave woman who saved my friend's life," the duke said quietly. "And I hope that I shall always be Ashby to you."

He meant it, she realized. And even though today was normal, she recognized there was a bond between them. She guessed it was rather like soldiers who had fought side by side in a battle. "Very well, Ashby. I shall endeavor to suppress my manners."

He smiled and left her alone with Frayne. As soon as the door closed, she moved to the bedside for a closer look. Even though he was sleeping, she saw humor and individuality in his face. His soul was firmly seated in his body again. She moved her hands above his body in a light scan. Yes, the repairs were sound.

She rested her hand on his forehead. No sign of fever. Though she had banished inflammation the day before, there was always a danger it would return. That was perhaps the greatest risk to his recovery.

Two tugs on the rope beside the bed would bring a footman so that she would be able to see to her guests. But before the servant could come, she allowed herself the indulgence of touching Lord Frayne.

First she brushed the back of her hand across his cheek, finding the masculine prickle of whiskers to be strangely arousing.

In teasing contrast, the brown waves of his hair were soft against her fingertips. "I'm glad you survived, Jack Langdon," she whispered.

She wondered how long it would take him to back gracefully out of his marriage bargain.

Chapter V

The *brush of an angel's wing . . .* Jack was drawn from sleep by a gentle touch on his hair.

He opened his eyes, and saw not an angel but the burning sun whose warmth had brought him back to life. He blinked in shock, and the sun dissolved into an Amazon with startled eyes. When she didn't turn into something else, he said politely, "Good day. I'm sorry I can't greet you properly, but I don't think standing would be wise just now."

Her surprise changed to amusement. "No, it wouldn't. But you are doing well, my lord. I find no trace of fever."

He felt obscurely disappointed that she had been checking his temperature, not giving him an angel's benediction. Though she had certainly acted the part of an angel to him. He studied her face. Wide cheekbones, a large mouth that seemed ready to smile, and those startlingly edged blue eyes. Not a beautiful face, but pleasant enough.

She seemed a voluptuous, healthy wench, with an earthy sensuality that some men would find provocative. But she wasn't the sort of female he would choose to wed. He repressed his sigh, not wanting to be insulting. "We are to be married, are we not? Perhaps you should call me Jack instead of my lord."

He had startled her again. After a brief hesitation, "It seems too early to call you by your Christian name or to discuss our marriage. First you must regain your health."

He didn't agree that it was too soon to discuss their nuptials, but he hadn't the energy to argue. "Alas—Miss Barton, I believe?—I do not even know your Christian name. I hope that in time you will give me leave to use it."

"My name is Abigail. Usually I am called Abby."

He noted that she didn't grant permission for him to call her that. Since lady's maids were often called abigails, the name wasn't popular in high society, yet it suited her. This was a woman who wouldn't be afraid to dirty her hands when a job needed doing. He could do worse, which was fortunate, given that he had no choice.

While he studied her, she was studying him. "You will sleep a great deal over the next few days," she said. "That is usual after a major healing. Don't fight it, my lord."

"I'm tired and hungry," he murmured as his eyes drifted shut again. "What are the chances of a few slices of roast beef when I wake up?"

"Nil," she said promptly. "But you will be fed, I promise that. A nice chicken broth with perhaps a bit of barley in it."

"Broth," he said with disgust. "Wake me up when I'm ready for beef." Or perhaps he only thought the words as he fell asleep again.

Ashby hadn't exaggerated that his lordship was himself again. Or at least he was articulate and individual. Though Abby hadn't known him before, his behavior fit her idea of him. He filled the room with his personality. Even when his handsome, highborn friends were present, it was Lord Frayne who compelled her attention.

Jack. He had bid her to use his name. Though she wasn't ready to call him that directly, she was glad to call him that in her thoughts, as she had done for years.

The footman arrived and Abby charged him with watching over their patient. She left the bedroom, knowing there was no need to order broth, since her excellent cook always had a pot on the hob. When Jack was awake and ready to eat, Abby would infuse the broth with extra healing energy. He would eat it while complaining that he preferred food that required chewing. He was not going to be the sort of patient who would stay willingly in bed.

Though he actually seemed willing to carry through on his promise to marry her. That bore thinking about.

On her way to the breakfast room, she heard angry voices in the front hall. She detoured and found a tall, dark man in a muddy driving coat castigating her butler. At her entrance, the stranger swerved toward her. "Are you the lady of the house? What is this bloody story about Lord Frayne being brought here to die?"

His voice was furious and his handsome face was all hard angles, but she saw the underlying fear. "You must be another of Lord Frayne's old friends," she said peaceably. "I am Miss Barton. Yes, his lordship was brought here yesterday gravely injured, but he is not dying. In fact, he is well on his way to recovery."

The man's anger drained out of him. "Thank God," he breathed. "When I stopped at an inn outside of Melton for breakfast, I was told Jack had been brought here and was surely dead already. I was so afraid . . ." He cut off his words.

"He has had two friends here with him—the Duke of Ashby and Mr. Ransom. Are they also friends of yours?"

"They are. So he has been in good hands." The man gave her a smile of surprising warmth. "Forgive my rag-manners, Miss Barton. I am Lucas Winslow. Might I see Lord Frayne? Or Ashby or Ransom?"

"Lord Frayne and Ashby are both sound asleep," she replied. "Yesterday was a very tiring day. Ransom left for London this morning. I can take you to Lord Frayne, but you must not wake him. He needs his rest, as does Ashby."

"I would very much like to see him."

"Then take off your coat and hat and prepare to stay a bit. After you've seen your friend, perhaps you would join us for breakfast?"

He smiled ruefully. "You're very perceptive. When I heard the news at the inn, I didn't stay to eat." His voice cooled. "If this is the home of a wyrdling, as they said, I suppose it's inevitable you would be perceptive. Invasive, even."

"If Jack Langdon hadn't been brought to a wizard's house, he would be dead," she said with equal coolness. "I ask that you show respect while you are under my roof."

His expression stilled. "My apologies, Miss Barton. I should not have said that."

She gave him credit for apologizing. Not all aristocrats were capable of admitting wrong. "No, you shouldn't, but you have had a difficult morning. Come along and see Jack, then have something to eat. It will do wonders for your disposition."

"Yes, ma'am," he said meekly as he followed her. When they entered Jack's room, the footman withdrew to give them privacy.

As Winslow moved to Jack's bedside, Abby said softly, "His neck was broken, but it's been repaired. There were other injuries, including a broken leg and cracked ribs. Those will take time to heal, but soon he should be as good as new."

Winslow glanced up sharply when she mentioned the broken neck. "A local healer was able to mend the spinal injury?"

"It took a dozen talented wizards working flat out to do the mending, but yes, that's why he has survived to hunt another day."

Winslow touched Jack's shoulder lightly, as if to reassure himself of his friend's continued life. In a voice so low she guessed she wasn't meant to hear, he said, "So despite your courtship of death you are still among us, Jack. Thank God for that."

He turned and moved away from the bed. "I'm ready for that breakfast, Miss Barton, and hungry enough to eat a sheep whole."

She would have loved to know what he meant by that remark about Jack courting death, but she didn't ask. Since her exertions the day before had made her ravenous, it was hard to think much beyond food herself.

Most of her wizard friends were in the breakfast room, chatting and laughing and enjoying the excellent buffet laid out on the sideboards. Mr. Hambly looked up from his tea when Abby and Winslow entered. "You're looking much better than you did last night, lass. How is our patient?"

"Doing well. Very tired, of course, but he conversed quite sensibly when I visited him." She gestured to the visitor. "Mr. Winslow is a friend of Lord Frayne's. Mr. Winslow, these are some of the members of the healing circle that performed a miracle."

From the faint tightening around his eyes, she guessed that he was uncomfortable in the presence of so many wizards, but he bowed courteously. "My thanks to you all."

She debated introducing everyone, then decided against it. Winslow was unlikely to have a social relationship with any of her magical friends.

As Abby and Winslow moved toward the sideboard to select food, young Ella entered the breakfast room and approached Abby, her eyes pleading. "Lord Frayne's horse has been brought to your stables, Miss Abby. He has a broken leg and there's talk of having him put down. Do you think you might be able to help?"

Winslow paused between the coddled eggs and the sliced ham. "If that's a huge dark bay, it's probably Dancer, Frayne's favorite mount. Four white socks."

"That's the one," Ella confirmed. "The finest bit of horseflesh I've ever seen."

That was high praise coming from Ella, a fervent horse lover. After a wistful glance at the buffet, Abby said, "I'll come take a look. We're all drained today. Does anyone have the energy left to help heal a horse?"

"I'll come," Hambly said. As he rose from the table, three of the other wizards, including Judith, joined him. Those who stayed in their chairs did so with regretful expressions. Abby knew they would help if they could, but their magical powers had been depleted in the healing circle and needed time to be replenished.

Abby grabbed a piece of toast and wolfed it down as the group walked out to the stables. Inside, Ella led them to a box stall where a large bay stood, his head hanging dispiritedly and his splinted right foreleg raised so it barely touched the floor. The glossy dark hide was marked by numerous abrasions and lacerations from his fall, and his breathing was shallow. Hertford, the head groom, watched from outside the stall with a worried expression.

"That's Dancer," Winslow said from behind Abby. "What would it cost to save him? Frayne thinks the world of that oversize beast."

"This is not about money, Mr. Winslow." Abby stepped up beside Hertford. He was a wizard himself, his gift an uncanny ability to work with animals. "What did you find when you examined this fellow?"

"The cannon bone in his right fore is broke, but it's a clean break," Hertford said. "It would be enough to have him put down anywhere but here, but I put a splint on, hoping you might be able to save him. 'E's a good beast and deserves a chance. You'll have to work fast, though. He's getting right feverish."

"Please keep him calm for me." Abby entered the stall, Hertford behind her. Usually a high-spirited hunter like this one would react to the approach of a stranger, but Dancer hardly noticed her.

Hertford laid his hands on the horse's head and murmured a string of soothing words while Abby scanned the broken foreleg. As the groom had said, the break was clean. Still, treating a large animal required a great deal of energy. The mere thought was exhausting, but she would have help. She turned to her friends. "Shall we give this a try? Healing one bone will be easy compared to yesterday."

"We're all here so we might as well see what we can do," Judith said practically. "But don't attempt more than you're fit for."

Judith made the average mother hen look neglectful, but Abby appreciated her concern. As the wizards filed into the loose box, she assigned them places, Ella on her right and Hambly on her left. Abby placed her hands on the right side of Dancer's neck while Hertford stood opposite, his hands also splayed out on Dancer's dark hide. There were just enough people to surround the horse, though if not for Hertford's soothing magic, the bay wouldn't have tolerated the crowding. Winslow was still present and he looked acutely uncomfortable, but he didn't withdraw. Nor did he offer to help. Dislike for magic ran particularly deep in him.

"Our hands are joined, the circle is sealed. Let us begin." Even though Abby braced herself, she wavered under the onslaught of energies.

After a few deep breaths, she managed to steady her mind. Her healing trance was not as profound as the day before, but it sufficed. An overall scan confirmed that only the broken foreleg was serious, but when she tried to fuse the bone, she didn't have sufficient strength and focus to do the job completely.

This time the patient didn't have a store of magic to draw on, but she managed to lay down a template and start the healing process. Though less than completely mended, Dancer's leg was perhaps halfway there. It would have to be good enough.

She used the last shreds of channeled power to purge Dancer's system of inflammation. As Hertford had said, infection was taking hold and would kill the horse if left unchecked.

Wearily she closed the circle. She was swaying on her feet and felt as if her body and spirit were not quite connected. Speaking was an effort. "With the splint and Hertford's good care, Dancer should be ready to hunt before his master is."

"Oh, thank you," Ella said, her eyes as bright as if she were Dancer's owner. She stroked the dark coat. "I'll come back later and groom him, if that's all right with Mr. Hertford. But you need to get back to the house and have a proper meal, Miss Abby."

The girl took Abby's arm and helped her from the stable. Things had come to a pretty pass, she thought ruefully, when she needed help from a fifteen-year-old. Consciousness wavering, she decided to skip the food and go straight to bed.

When Abby returned to awareness, she was in her own bed. No Judith slept beside her, but when she rolled to her side, she saw her friend reading in a chair by the bed. "I don't have much of a life at the moment," Abby said, her mouth dry and dusty. "All I've done for the last day or two is heal and sleep."

Judith set her book aside and poured water from a glass. "Drink this, you'll feel better. You need food and plenty to drink and no more healing for at least a fortnight. You're not made of iron, Abigail Barton."

Abby pushed herself up against the headboard and drank the water thirstily. "Believe me, I know. I feel ancient and feeble." She glanced at the window to judge the angle of the sun. "Has another day gone by?"

"Yes. You slept for about twenty hours. The other wizards have gone home. I thought I should stay until you were awake and functioning." She poured more water for Abby, then handed her a piece of bread with a slab of cheese and chutney on top.

Abby took a giant bite of the bread and cheese, washing it down with water. After another bite, she asked, "How is Lord Frayne?"

"Rather better than you at the moment," Judith said dryly. "Ashby is still here and spends most of his time with Frayne. I like Ashby—he's a remarkably sensible fellow for a duke. That starchy new visitor, Winslow, is staying at the Old Club in town, but he's here half the time, too. Frayne's valet has also moved in and taken over most of the basic nursing work."

Abby finished her bread and looked around hopefully, but there was no more food in sight. "There haven't been so many dashing young males in the house since Richard left to join the army. Did you stay partly to chaperone me?"

"The thought crossed my mind," Judith admitted. "With your father away and you an unmarried girl, I thought you needed an aging widow to lend you respectability."

Abby snorted. "I'm no girl, and you are no one's idea of an aging widow, but I appreciate your staying. With me dead to the world, someone needed to defend Barton Grange against the aristocratic hordes."

"Apart from the risk of eating you out of house and home, Frayne's friends are harmless enough. I'll stay until your father returns from London. I know you haven't much use for propriety, but on the whole, it's better to pay lip service to society's rules." Judith's mouth twisted ruefully. "You don't want to end up like me, after all."

The topic was a painful one, and there was no point in discussing it. As Abby swung out of bed to prepare for the day, she considered telling Judith about the possibility that she might marry Frayne. No, better not to speak of something that seemed so unreal.

At heart, she realized, she had never expected that a marriage might really happen.

Chapter VI

Abby dressed, not surprised to find that her gown was loose. Heavy use of magic used vast physical reserves. The house was quiet now that most of her friends had returned home, and for that she was grateful. Being sociable required energy, and she had none to spare.

A visit to the kitchen gave her the chance to finally eat her fill. "I feel like a swarm of locusts," she remarked to the cook as she swallowed a last apple tart. "I have descended on your field and gobbled everything in sight."

Cook grinned. "This is why I like working for wizards. You know how to appreciate food."

"You have a cooking gift," Abby said fervently. "And we are all grateful for it!"

She took another tart to eat on her way to Frayne's room, licking her fingers clean before opening the door. Ashby was sitting with his friend, who looked awake and alert.

The men broke off their conversation when Abby entered. The duke rose. "I'm glad to see you up and about again. You've had a demanding time these last days."

She made a face. "I'm hoping I'll never have to do such intense work again. Could I ask you to leave, Ashby? I'd like to examine my patient."

"Of course." The duke turned to his friend. "If you continue to recover at this rate, I may return to the hunt and leave your increasing restlessness to your valet and the patient Miss Barton."

"By all means, hunt," Jack said. "It's the purpose of coming to the Shires, after all. Though I'm laid up, there's no reason you shouldn't be enjoying your time here."

"Perhaps I shall cease my hovering now that you're recovering. Calling once or twice a day should be enough." Inclining his head toward Abby, the duke departed.

Abby scanned her patient, her hand about a foot above his body. The healing was progressing well. "If you don't mind the loss of company, it will probably be best if your friends do return to the hunting field. Athletic young men fidget madly in sickrooms. That includes you. You are going to be difficult, aren't you?"

"I'm afraid so," he said with no sign of repentance. "But I shan't vex you any longer. I'm ready to return to my hunting box. You've already done too much. My valet and friends can look after me until I'm fit again." He swung his legs from the bed, the splinted one straight out, and tried to stand. "You see? With a pair of crutches I could manage very well." He straightened to his full height—and promptly pitched over.

Abby leaped forward and grabbed his torso to keep him upright. "You're *mad!*" she exclaimed as she wrestled with his weight. Once he was steadied, she sat on the edge of the bed, bringing him down next to her. His left arm wrapped around her shoulders as he clung to her for support.

Holding him was . . . disturbing. His body was warm, and he had a fine set of muscles beneath that thin linen nightshirt. He had transformed from a helpless patient into a virile, attractive man, and that fact reminded her that she was a woman as well as a healer.

She drew a deep, uneven breath. "You are not yet ready for crutches, my lord. If you try to walk and fall, you could make a shambles of your broken leg. At the moment it's healing straight, but if you fall again, I can't guarantee how well you'll walk in the future. Or even if you *will* walk."

"Perhaps . . . you're right," he panted, sweat on his face. "I feel weak as a kitten."

He didn't protest when she stood and tucked him back into the bed, though he gasped when she carefully swung his legs up onto the mattress. His face became even paler. After pulling the covers over him, she rested her hand on his forehead. Though her energy was depleted, she was able to mitigate some of the pain.

His face eased. "Thank you. I probably deserve to fall on my face, but I can't say that I would enjoy that."

"You lost a great deal of blood, and that creates weakness. It will take a month or more before you recover your strength." She smiled as she perched on the bedside chair. "Actually, kittens aren't weak. Have you ever seen the way they race about? No human could keep up with the average kitten."

He had to smile at that. "Point taken. But I was feeling well enough that it was hard to believe that my injuries were as bad as Ashby described."

"They really were that bad," she said grimly. "Worse."

His brow furrowed. "I'm surprised you made the attempt to save me. How did you manage to mend a broken neck?"

"Essentially, it's a matter of visualizing the bones strong and whole, then adding healing energy."

"Surely there is more to it than that?"

"A *lot* of energy is required," she agreed. "It isn't only bones that need repairing, but blood vessels and organs and bits of anatomy for which I have no name. The work requires patience, some knowledge of how bodies work, and a clutch of strong, steady wizards to supply power, since I've never heard of an individual wizard strong enough to fuse a broken bone. Even with a dozen people in the circle, repairing your broken neck was a near run thing."

"Is that why such miracles are rare?"

She nodded. "It's unusual to have enough wizards ready, willing, and possessing the right kind of gift. The only reason we had enough here was because my father organized the wizards in this area years ago."

"I should like to meet your father."

"You will. He should be back from London within the next week." She sighed. "I wish he had been here to help. He would have done a better and more efficient job of leading the circle. I've never channeled so much power, and even so, I wasn't able to do a complete job. Only those injuries that were life threatening were fully healed, and everyone involved was magically depleted. It will probably be a fortnight before we are all at full strength again."

"I suspect that you did as well as your father could have." His fingers plucked at the coverlet. "How can I repay those who gave me so much?"

She hesitated, wondering if she could make him understand. "Magic is a gift and not for sale. A healer or wisewoman will charge for his or her time, but not for the magic itself. What was done for you was— extraordinary. Not the sort of thing that is done for money, but because of a desire to serve."

He gave a faint smile. "I believe you are saying not to insult your friends by offering crass payment?"

After she nodded, he said, "Very well. Rather than money, I would like to give each a token of my gratitude. A substantial gift chosen for their particular wants and desires rather than a fee for what is beyond price. Would that be acceptable?"

So he did understand. "It should be."

A few sheets of paper and a pencil rested on the bedside table. He lifted both and prepared to take notes. "What would your friends like? I assume you know them well enough to have a good idea."

Abby thought. "Ella is fifteen and loves all animals, especially horses, but her widowed mother can't afford to buy her one. Nothing would make Ella happier than to have a horse of her own."

He made a note, writing slowly but clearly. "I have a sweet-natured mare, beautifully mannered but with spirit, that would be just right for a young lady," he said. "Will that do, along with a bit of money for maintaining the beast?"

"Ella will be in alt." Knowing the value of a well-bred horse, Abby realized he was serious about the gifts being substantial. What would best please her generous friends, none of whom were wealthy? "Mr. Hambly's eldest daughter followed her husband to America," Abby said, thinking aloud. "Mr. and Mrs. Hambly would love to visit and see their grandchildren, but trips to America are costly."

He made another note. "Two tickets on a good ship to America. I presume they would also appreciate a carriage to take them from their home to a port of embarkation?"

"That would be very thoughtful." What next? "The Reverend Wilson has a lovely eighteen-year-old daughter. Her parents would like her to have a Season in London, but they can't afford that."

He made another note. "My sister is a grand society hostess and fond of company. I'm sure she would be willing to sponsor the young lady during the next Season. Would that be acceptable?"

She stared. "More than acceptable. It's incredibly generous."

He shrugged. "My sister will enjoy the company, so that is easy."

"Perhaps, but it takes consideration to think of such things in the first place," she said warmly. "You are a true gentleman, Lord Frayne."

He looked a little surprised at her praise. "That's a judgment that would shock my parents. Let us continue divining what your wizard friends would like."

"Judith Wayne is a midwife. She would like to own a cottage of her own. One that has enough space for her to look after patients who need special care."

He made another note. "A spacious cottage, preferably free of rising damp. Next?"

Apart from two of the wizards she didn't know as well, it took only a few minutes to complete the list. When they were done, Jack set the paper aside. "Which brings us to you, but you made your price clear from the beginning."

His words were like a slap in the face. What he said was justified—

she had indeed said that marriage was her price. Yet hearing that from him made her feel like a fortune hunter. "Saint Augustine said that it is better to marry than to burn. Would you have preferred burning? Though you might have gone to a pleasanter, cooler place."

"I would definitely have ended among the flames," he said dryly. "My feelings about magic are . . . complicated, Miss Barton. But no, I would rather not be burning for my sins now. Few men receive a second chance. I hope to use this one wisely." He shrugged. "As for marriage—I've never been betrothed before. Much less to a stranger. It will take time to become accustomed. Forgive me if I fail at the courtesies."

"My experience of betrothal is also lacking, but no doubt we can manage to sort matters out," she murmured, wondering why she was putting them in such an awkward position. She was being a fool, but when she was with him, she couldn't bear to give up her foolishness.

"Were you waiting for a peer of the realm to come your way?" he asked with cool curiosity. "Many of them come to hunt the Shires, so I suppose it was just a matter of time until one had a bad accident and ended up on your dining room table."

"What a clever idea," she said tartly. "I wish I'd thought of it."

Given that he was well enough to be difficult, she decided to stop giving him part of her life force. She hesitated a moment, realizing that she enjoyed the secret intimacy of being connected to him. But it was time to return him to his own resources.

Gently she closed off the flowing thread of energy. She immediately felt stronger, more alert. Her gain was reflected in Jack's loss. He shoved the pillows behind him away so that he could lie down again, his face tired. "Perhaps you're right about the crutches. I feel a sudden need to sleep the clock around. But I wonder why these miracles of healing aren't done for more people? I have friends who died in the Peninsula from wounds less serious than mine. It . . . isn't fair."

She stood to adjust the pillows under his head. "There will never be enough of us with healing gifts to take care of all mankind's physical ills. Even a dozen talented wizards didn't have the energy to restore you to perfect health. While we were able to fix the mortal injuries, we couldn't have achieved such good results if you hadn't been an ideal candidate for healing—a healthy adult in the prime of life. If you were old or less strong to begin with, we probably couldn't have saved you."

"Can healing be used to make a man immortal?"

"The deterioration of old age can't really be reversed. If an elderly person has a specific health problem, it might be fixable, but with age, the whole body declines. We can't cure that. There are also diseases that damage the whole body. They are very hard to cure." She thought of the insidious disease that had killed her mother. "The healing gift is limited. We may be able to give some people extra life, but there are very real limitations."

"Is this why it is not generally known that miracles are sometimes possible—so that people won't ask more than you can give?"

She nodded. "If our best work was common knowledge, every healer in the land would be besieged by desperate people. Their anger when they learned how little we can do would be . . . terrifying. It is better if people come expecting only small healings. Those can usually be managed."

He nodded, curiosity satisfied. "How soon do you think I can return home? Surely I will heal faster there, and it's just across the valley."

"Perhaps a week. It depends on how quickly you regain your strength." She sympathized with his distaste for lying in bed—she was a restless patient herself. "My grandfather was unwell the last years of his life. This was his room, to spare him from climbing stairs. He also had a wheelchair so he could move around the ground floor. It's up in the attic, I believe. Shall I have it brought down for your use?"

"Oh, please," he said fervently. "I am already tiring of this otherwise attractive room." His eyes drifted shut.

Tenderly she tucked the coverlet around him. Then she forced herself to step away, hands clenched against temptation. She wanted to run her hands down those long, powerful limbs, but she didn't have a lover's right to touch him that way even though they were discussing marriage.

Though she'd known he must be weaned from her energy soon, she hadn't realized how much the loss would weaken him. Now he would probably need to stay longer at Barton Grange.

That hadn't been her intention, but she couldn't regret it.

Chapter VII

More cautious than the evening before, Jack didn't try to get out of bed the next morning. He did insist on sitting up against pillows and asking for reading material; then he chased Morris away. He no longer needed a full-time attendant, and it was unnerving to have Morris sit there watching all day.

He was going to have to return to Yorkshire. The one clear advantage of death was that it would have removed the obligation to sort out the problems at the family estate. A second cousin he barely knew would be the next Lord Frayne, and perhaps the sorting process would have been easier for someone less closely connected.

He'd rather be alive and heading north than dead. But it was a close call.

Frowning, he forced himself to concentrate on the week-old newspaper. It was a relief when Ashby and Lucas Winslow stopped by for a visit. Despite their mud-splashed hunting pinks, they were a welcome sight.

He set the paper aside gladly. "Tell me about what great runs you've been having so I can suffer the torments of envy."

"You will be pleased to hear that it was a bad day's hunting," Lucas said cordially. "The hounds had trouble finding and we spent much of our time sitting around on our horses in the rain and trying to remember why we do this."

Ashby brushed droplets from his well-cut coat. "Worse, now that the hunt has ended for the day, the sun is coming out."

"I'll try not to gloat over your bad day," Jack promised. "Shall I ring for tea? My jailer allows me certain privileges."

Before his friends could reply, his chief jailer entered, pushing a wheeled chair in front of her. Jack felt his usual ambivalence at her presence, an uncertainty about whether to think of her as a compassionate female who had saved his life, as a wizard whose work was utterly repugnant to him—or a woman with a threatening degree of sensuality. The wheelchair definitely added weight to the view of her as compassionate.

"Good day, gentlemen," Miss Barton said cheerfully. "Lord Frayne, I thought you might enjoy a roll around the house. My grandfather's chair has been retrieved from the attics and still seems serviceable. I had the estate carpenter build a support for your splinted leg. Would you like to give it a try?"

"Yes!" He was already pushing the covers back.

"I'll send Morris in to prepare you for this grand excursion. It might well take three men to transfer you safely to the wheelchair." She withdrew from the room.

To Jack's disgust, she was right. Ashby and Lucas steadied him while Morris helped him into a robe, then moved the chair behind him so he could sit down. Jack felt huge and ungainly as everyone worked to arrange him in the chair. Morris's careful hoist of the broken leg onto the long, padded support caused excruciating pain.

By the time Jack was settled, he was sweaty and exhausted. For a moment he thought longingly of his soft bed, but he was not going to waste this opportunity to move beyond his cell.

Miss Barton reappeared with her arms full of folded blankets. He hadn't realized how tall she was, only an inch or two shorter than Ashby.

She shook out the fabric, revealing two lap robes. "It's drafty around the house," she explained as she tucked one of the robes around his legs. Her gentle touch didn't produce more pain.

As she wrapped the other robe around his shoulders, he protested, "I'm not an invalid!"

Her blue eyes sparked with amusement. "You most certainly are. Not for very long, I think, but it will be good for you to discover what it's like not to be bursting with rude health. You will learn sympathy for those less fortunate."

"You might even learn to be more careful so you won't break your neck again," Lucas said acerbically. "Are you ready to roll, Jack?"

He used his hands to shift his splinted leg a little, trying without success to make it ache less. "I am, and as excited as the first time I crossed the channel and set foot in a foreign country."

"I can't promise you the exotic delights of France or the Low Countries," Miss Barton remarked, "but at least here everyone speaks English. Mr. Winslow, beware the sill between the bedroom and the hall. It's necessary to go slowly from room to room, or your passenger will be jostled."

Lucas slowed, though not quickly enough to prevent a painful jolt. "Sorry, Jack," he apologized. "I hadn't realized that there was an art to pushing a wheelchair."

"The kingdom of illness is a whole different nation from the land of the healthy," Miss Barton said musingly. "One that most of us enter sooner or later. Turn left at the end of this hall, Mr. Winslow. That will start us on a circular tour of the ground floor."

As Lucas pushed him along, Jack studied his surroundings, absurdly delighted by the change of scene. It was a gentleman's house, attractive and well furnished with a mixture of graceful new furniture and old pieces that had obviously been in the family for generations. Nothing proclaimed that Barton Grange was the home of ill-bred wizards.

What had he expected—dried bats and newts hanging from the ceiling? Perhaps he had. It was strange trying to reconcile this peaceful oasis with the queasy darkness of wizardry.

As they rolled through the drawing room, he realized that he must come to terms with his deep distaste for magic. Out of cowardice and fear of death, he had accepted magical aid rather than die in accordance with his principles. Which meant that now he must accept a wizard wife and her wizardly family.

He hadn't thought of any of this when he gave her permission to try to save his worthless life. The prospect of death tended to narrow one's viewpoint dramatically.

The next room, a handsome library, revealed many books, a fair number of them scholarly treatises on magic, but still no dried bats. Jack made a mental note to visit the library at a later date so he could explore further.

Lucas swung the chair to enter the main drawing room. Misjudging how far the splinted leg stuck out, he banged Jack's right foot into the door frame. Jack gasped with agony, his hands clenching the arms of the chair.

Lucas swore. "I'm so sorry, Jack! I'm a clumsy brute."

"There really is an art to pushing a wheelchair," Miss Barton said as she gently rested her fingertips on Jack's right leg where the pain was blazing. Within moments, the pain receded to a manageable level. She continued, "Perhaps I should take over. I often wheeled my grandfather around, so I'm something of an expert."

"I yield to greater experience." Lucas stepped away with an exaggerated bow.

With Miss Barton doing the pushing, Jack's ride immediately became smoother. She stepped on a foot lever on the back of the chair to slightly raise the front wheels whenever they crossed a sill or moved onto a carpet. There really was an art to living in the kingdom of the ill.

Abigail Barton might be a wizard, but she also had a gentle hand with the infirm despite her own robust health. He was very aware that she was right behind him, her fingers on the chair handles just inches from his shoulders. She was a powerful presence—and despite her wizardly calling, a comforting one.

They entered the dining room. "I remember looking at that handsome chandelier hanging directly over me, and hoping it wouldn't fall and produce still more damage," he said wryly as he recognized the dining room table where he had nearly died.

"You were not the first critically injured patient to lie on that table and the chandelier hasn't fallen yet," Miss Barton remarked. "With a long table and a good light, this makes a decent operating theater. Note the splendid red and black carpet, carefully chosen to conceal bloodstains."

He tried to turn and look at her to see if she was joking, a movement that did his leg no good. "Is that true?"

She grinned. "Somewhat. The rug has been in the family for many years. I was the one who suggested that the dining room was a particularly good place for it."

Ashby moved to the mahogany table, his fingers skimming the polished surface. "It looks so peaceful now, after the high drama of life and death." His expression was abstracted as he remembered Jack's accident and the healing circle.

"I prefer peace to drama," Miss Barton said ruefully. "But we seldom have a choice." She resumed pushing the wheelchair.

The morning room was in a rear corner of the house, the comfortable furniture splashed with late afternoon sunshine. She pushed him to a position in front of the windows. Outside lay gardens to the right and outbuildings to the left. Largest of the buildings was the stable block. Jack regarded it wistfully. "Will I be able to hunt again?"

"If you wish. Though you will take longer to recover than Dancer."

His head whipped around, and this time he didn't care about causing pain in his leg. "Dancer is *alive*?"

Her brows arched. "Didn't anyone tell you?"

Lucas, who was ambling along behind with Ashby, said, "I'm sorry, Jack. I assumed you had been told by someone else. We all must have assumed that."

Jack drew a deep, unsteady breath, painfully close to tears. He had been so sure his magnificent, loyal horse was dead, killed by his rider's heedlessness. "I knew his leg broke in the accident. I . . . I assumed he'd been put down."

"Ashby wouldn't allow it, so we arranged to have him brought to the stables here. Miss Barton, her excellent head groom, and those of her wizard friends who weren't completely depleted did a healing circle for Dancer the day after they healed you," Lucas said. "It was most extraordinary. The broken cannon bone is splinted and well onto its way to being sound again."

Jack turned awkwardly to look up at Miss Barton. "Please, is it possible for me to go see him?"

Ashby frowned. "Trying to carry you down several steps to ground level would be difficult for us and painful for you, I think."

"Actually, we had a ramp built from a small side door down to ground level for my grandfather's sake. He hated being trapped inside," Miss Barton said slowly. "The pathways were made as smooth as possible for the same reason. But it will still be an uncomfortable trip."

"I don't care. I promise I won't complain." Jack would also do his best to avoid gasping with pain, since his friends found it unsettling.

She studied his face. "Very well. I suspect that you and Dancer will benefit by seeing each other."

He had to smile. "You're a practical woman."

Under her breath she murmured, "Practicality—the spinster's compensation for being plain," in a voice so low he guessed she hadn't meant her words to be heard.

She thought herself plain? The comment made her sound more vulnerable than he would have guessed. Though she was not a classic beauty and not at all his type, neither would he call her plain, not with that sensual, tantalizing body. He studied her richly curved figure and wondered how he would react to her if he was at full strength. Even in his present state of weakness, he was disturbingly aware of her. She had the kind of provocative allure that might destroy a man's control. It was a disquieting thought.

While his thoughts were wandering, his entourage followed him to the exit that was ramped. Miss Barton turned the chair halfway around so his back was facing the door. "It's safest to take a chair down backwards," she explained. "I'll ask one of you gentleman to take over. I don't know if I'm strong enough to control it on the ramp."

"Allow me," Morris murmured. Jack guessed that his valet thought he'd do a better job than the aristocrats would. Morris was not only a good valet but a big, strong fellow. Jack had once accused him of taking the post because Jack's cast-off clothing was such a good fit. Morris had smiled imperturbably and not denied the charge.

As Miss Barton had said, going outside wasn't comfortable, starting with an instinctive feeling of panic that he would fall over backward as the chair descended the ramp. Facing forward might have been less alarming, but falling out of the chair would have been a real possibility. It was a relief to get off the ramp onto level ground.

The pathway to the stable was also much rougher than a hardwood floor, and the gravel wasn't improved by puddles from the recent rain. None of that mattered. Neither did the painful jolt when the chair had to be manhandled over a high sill to get into the stables.

What did matter was Dancer's familiar whickered greeting when Jack approached. Morris pushed the chair up to the box stall, and Dancer immediately bent his head over and butted Jack's chest with enough impact to knock the chair back. Morris caught the chair and moved it closer again.

The position was awkward, but Jack managed to hug the horse with one arm while scratching between his ears with the other. He hid his face against the glossy neck, near tears. What did it say about him that he'd felt more true grief at the thought of Dancer's death than he had when his father died? Of course Dancer was much better company. "I don't even have any sugar for you, old boy."

"Here's some." Ashby offered several irregular lumps chipped from a sugar loaf. "My horse can do with less."

"Thank you." Jack offered the sugar a piece at a time. Dancer slobbered the lumps up greedily.

Jack smiled, feeling more normal than he had since the accident. He and his horse both had broken legs, but one day they would ride together again. He glanced up at Miss Barton. "I knew I owed you my life, but this is. . . . even more. Not everyone would go to the effort to save an injured beast."

"Credit goes to young Ella," she said. "To be honest, I didn't even know your horse had been brought here."

"She may have been the messenger, but you were the one who led the healing." He rested his forehead against Dancer's neck, thinking that marrying a wizard who took horses seriously was no bad thing.

Miss Barton's soft voice said, "It's time for you to return to the house, Lord Frayne. You've had enough frolicking for one day, I think."

It was a measure of his fatigue that instead of arguing, he just gave Dancer a last pat. "I'll be back tomorrow, old fellow." And he'd bring his own sugar.

Now that the excitement of seeing Dancer was past, he was so tired he could barely remain upright in the wheelchair. He'd never dreamed that sitting up and being wheeled around could take so much out of a man.

Being transferred from chair to bed was another awkward, painful endeavor, but sinking into the mattress was bliss. As Miss Barton drew the coverlet up to his chin, he said, "Thank you for letting me go outside. Now, all of you go away, please. You, too, Morris. Find yourself some supper and smoke your pipe and flirt with a housemaid before you return. I'll be fine for a couple of hours. In fact I'm going right to sleep."

His visitors all left without argument. An advantage to being convalescent was that all he had to do was claim fatigue to get privacy. He closed his eyes gratefully, hoping that sleep would claim him soon.

But despite his fatigue, sleep eluded him. Now that his mind was active again, it hopped as restlessly as a pond full of frogs. On the deepest level of his being, he sensed a profound irreversible shift. He suspected that it was called growing up, and that the changes were being triggered by his close brush with mortality.

Two complicated challenges confronted him. One was the knowledge that he was pledged to marry a wizard, a prospect so unnerving that he still hadn't looked at it clearly. He owed Miss Barton a great debt, but the fact that she was a practitioner of magic gave him chills. He could feel them now. Or was that chills and fever?

He supposed he could learn to deal with Miss Barton; she seemed a sensible woman and she didn't affect mysterious airs as some wizards did. She had also said that she would not be a demanding wife, so they should be able to find a way to get on tolerably well. Since she preferred the country, she could stay on at his hunting box across the valley, close to her family. She'd made it clear she wanted a child. If that happened, she would probably be content to stay here forever.

The other great issue was returning to Yorkshire to face his mother and stepfather. Would it be worse to confront his mother, whom he loved, or his stepfather, whom he hated? Unfortunately, the two could not be separated. Yet he had a responsibility to the people of Langdale, and it could no longer be denied.

Something hit the bottom of the bed with a thump and started walking firmly up the mattress. Startled, Jack opened his eyes and saw a large black cat moving through the darkening room. He knew black cats were traditional for wizards, but he wasn't so sure about the white feet and luxuriant white whiskers which curved out from the round black face. It was hard for a feline to look menacing with white socks and whiskers. "Hello, cat. I'm Jack. Who are you?"

The cat didn't reply, but it placed its forepaws on Jack's chest and leaned forward until their noses touched. The feline nose was pleasantly cool and moist against Jack's heated skin.

Regarding the cat cross-eyed, Jack asked, "Are you the wizard's familiar?"

The cat made a huffing sound that sounded suspiciously like disdain. Then it curled up against Jack's side and began purring loudly. Jack stroked the silky fur. He'd always been a dog lover, but there was something soothing about a cat's purr.

Very soothing indeed.

•   •   •

Abby's restless sleep was disturbed by a tapping at the door. "Miss Abigail?" It was the worried voice of the housekeeper.

Yawning, Abby swung out of bed and opened the door. "Is something wrong?"

"Lord Frayne's valet asked me to wake you. He's concerned."

"I'll be right there." Frowning, Abby pulled on a heavy robe and slippers and followed the housekeeper downstairs. Though the winter days had been fairly mild, nighttime was bitterly cold and drafty. She heard the tall drawing room clock strike three as she descended to the ground floor. Three in the morning, when vital spirits were at their lowest ebb and death drew near. She quickened her pace.

Morris greeted her with relief. He had made up a pallet in Jack's room so he could sleep near his master, just in case. "I'm sorry to disturb you, miss, but I don't like the way he's breathing."

"You did the right thing by summoning me." Even before she reached the bedside, she could hear Jack laboring for breath. What was wrong? In the lamplight, his face looked gray and he seemed diminished, as if he was fading away. Her cat, Cleocatra, was sitting beside him. Had she thought Jack needed watching? Like most cats, Cleo was preternaturally sensitive.

She inhaled slowly, trying to focus her mind while silently cursing the fact that her magic was still so depleted. If something was seriously wrong, she wouldn't be able to do much without help.

When she was centered, she laid her hand on his forehead. It was heated with fever. Inflammation must be flaring up again.

She scanned him and found hot spots in his spleen and where the bones had broken in his leg. The infections weren't out of control yet, but they would be soon. Summoning all her energy reserves, she suppressed the inflammations, struggling to dissolve the hot red energy with cool white light to quench the fever.

As she finished her work, Jack rolled restlessly to one side, on the verge of falling off the bed. Abby and Morris both leaped to catch him. As they eased Jack's overheated body back toward the middle of the mattress, his nightshirt dragged down, exposing his left shoulder. Branded into the skin was the spiral shape of a serpent.

Abby gasped, recognizing the symbol. "I see that it isn't enough for Lord Frayne to carry a charm against magic. He must have it burned into his flesh."

"My lord is very concerned about being a victim of magic," Morris said apologetically. "He's had that banishing mark as long as I've known him."

Repulsed, Abby tugged the nightshirt back over the symbol. The narrow line of the serpent's body spiraled inward seven times with the head in the center and the twisted tail on the outside. It was a common charm for banishing magic, but she had never heard of anyone branding himself with it.

Was branding the custom at Stonebridge Academy, or was Jack unusually fearful of magic even by aristocratic standards? She remembered that when he'd been brought in after the accident, she'd asked his friends if they could remove any anti-magic charms Jack carried. Instead of searching his pockets, Ashby had concentrated on getting Jack to grant permission for Abby to work on him. Obviously the duke had known about the brand. Did he and Ransom and Winslow carry the same mark on their shoulders?

Mouth tight, she said to the valet, "I've taken care of the fever, but he's still very weak. He hasn't yet recovered from losing so much blood after the accident. It was a mistake to let him go outside today."

"Maybe so," Morris said softly. "But being happy helps a man heal, and he sure was happy to see that horse."

"Maybe I should have had the horse brought in to him," she said wryly as she turned back to her patient. Though he had certainly enjoyed his expedition, she would attempt to persuade him not to attempt another one until he was stronger.

And to make him stronger, she must give him some of her life force again. She rested her hand on his solar plexus. Though it wasn't necessary, she liked touching his warm, masculine body. First she visualized a thread connecting them. Then she imagined life force flowing through it.

Her vitality dimmed, but the positive effect on Jack was immediately obvious. His face smoothed out, peaceful in normal sleep. It was not a classically handsome face, but it was . . . very dear.

When she was sure he had been stabilized, she wearily returned to her room. By morning, he should be cool and on his way to recovery.

As for Abby—she would sleep late. She needed it.

Chapter VIII

As Abby had expected, the next morning Jack was free of fever and more energetic. His improvement came at the cost of tired circles under her eyes, but she could spare some vital force until his recovery was less tenuous.

Ashby and Winslow made a habit of stopping by to visit Jack after the day's hunting. The first time it happened, Abby escorted them to his room and rang for refreshments. When she started to withdraw after ordering food, the men invited her to stay, and asked her to invite Judith as well.

The three men and two women made a convivial company. Jack was at his happiest with his friends around him. Judith also enjoyed the tea parties, laughing with a lightness Abby had seldom seen in her friend, who had been widowed too young.

On the second day, Abby let Jack sit in the wheelchair in his bedroom when his friends came. On the third day, he was strong enough to wheel the chair into the library without help, so his friends joined him there. The Barton Grange cook, pleased to have hungry young gentlemen who appreciated her craft, happily made tempting arrays of sweets and savories and fresh bread with local cheese and relishes. Ashby and Winslow, famished from the day's hunting, fell on the platters like wolves.

The first rush of hunger was fading when Ransom entered the library, his boots and breeches spattered with mud and his expression weary. "Miss Barton, Mrs. Wayne, my greetings. I do hope you greedy fellows have spared some food for me."

"Make yourself comfortable, Mr. Ransom," Abby said as she rose to greet him. "You're just returned from London?"

"Aye." Ransom paused in his piling of delicacies on a plate to reach into his coat and retrieve a folded paper. "Here's the special license you requested, Jack. Shall I hunt down a vicar so you can be married today, or will tomorrow be soon enough?"

Jack accepted the license, his expression unreadable. "That is up to Miss Barton. I bow to her wishes."

Abby froze, too shocked to respond. A special license. Dear God, he really did intend to marry her!

Judith's eyes narrowed as she studied Abby's face. "How exciting! I should think Abby would like to wait for her father to come home, which he will be within the next few days." She stood. "Abby, let's withdraw and leave the gentlemen to catch up on their news. We can decide which of your gowns to wear at the ceremony."

Judith grasped Abby's arm as she said under her breath, "Take your leave before you faint."

It was good advice. Abby rose and managed a smile. "There's much to be done. Don't tire Lord Frayne out, gentlemen."

She and Judith left amidst a masculine murmur of farewells. Wordlessly the women passed through the dining room, where Judith snared a decanter of brandy and two glasses before they climbed the stairs.

Once they reached Abby's small sitting room, Judith closed the door and said firmly, "Sit."

Abby obeyed, still struggling with her shock. Judith poured brandy into a glass and pressed it into Abby's hand. After pouring more for herself, Judith sat in the chair opposite. "What is going on? I assume that the subject of marriage must have been discussed between you and Lord Frayne, yet you looked as startled as if he had just turned into a frog."

"He did agree to marry me, but I didn't think he actually *would*." Abby swallowed a mouthful of brandy, grateful for the enlivening burn.

"Did you ask him, or did he ask you?"

"I . . . I explained that it could be dangerous to lead a healing circle, but I would risk it if he pledged to marry me if the healing was successful. This happened when he had just been brought in, broken and barely alive."

Judith stared at her. "Abby, how could you! It's immoral to coerce someone who is mortally injured."

"I know." Abby looked away, ashamed. "I didn't really mean it."

"Yet you said it." Judith cocked her head. "What, pray, *did* you mean?"

Abby frowned as she tried to reconstruct her tangled thoughts and emotions in the midst of crisis. "Frayne was half out of his head and rejecting the idea of healing magic. Ashby and Ransom were urging him to let me try. I didn't know if he could be saved, but for some reason, asking for marriage seemed like a good idea."

Judith gulped at her brandy, expression pained. "That makes no sense at all."

"I know it doesn't," Abby admitted. "But I never really believed he'd go through with a marriage. I thought that even if we saved him, he would politely withdraw. Since he agreed under duress, I wouldn't have held him to his word."

"How was he to know that? A gentleman's word is his bond, Abby," Judith said, exasperated. "A man of honor would not break his promise, even under such circumstances. It's not as if he could read your mind and learn you weren't serious. And if he *could* read your mind, your thinking is so tangled you'd give him a headache!"

"My thoughts are giving me a headache, too." Abby toyed with her brandy glass, swirling the richly colored liquid. "In fact, I've avoided thinking about the situation, since I don't understand myself why I did what I did. It's been easier to concentrate on Lord Frayne's injuries and recovery. I never thought he'd send Ransom to London without once discussing marriage with me!"

"He's a man of action, for better and worse. At least Ransom's journey kept him from fidgeting around here all week. Two anxious men were more than enough." Judith sipped her brandy again, this time more slowly. "Since a woman can break an engagement with no loss of reputation, it will be simple enough to end this. You made your point and persuaded him to allow his life to be saved. You certainly don't have to spend the rest of your life with him."

What Judith said was perfectly logical. That being so, why didn't it make Abby feel good? Instead, the knowledge that she could walk away from the marriage left her profoundly depressed. She set her brandy aside and began pacing the room. "You're quite right."

Watching her, Judith said, "Abby, do you *want* to marry Lord Frayne? I can't imagine that his title interests you. For that matter, I've never known you to show much interest in acquiring a husband at all."

Abby paused at the window to gaze at the winter-bare fields. There had been men who had showed flattering signs of interest. She had never reciprocated. "Jack Langdon is the only man who has ever really caught my attention. At first I didn't know he was heir to a title; it was he himself who was appealing. He never noticed me, of course, except once we almost ran into each other outside a shop. He had a . . . nice smile. I never imagined we would meet, much less have any kind of relationship. I just admired him, like a sunset or a fine spring day. Then suddenly he was right there, dying on my dining room table."

Abby turned from the window to face her friend. "I knew it was unlikely that he could be saved, but his presence sparked those vague thoughts I'd had for years into a kind of recklessness. I was frightened of leading a circle for the first time. Perhaps asking for marriage was a way of giving me courage by making the reward worth the risk." Her mouth twisted. "Or perhaps I was just greedy and selfish and wanted him, so I forgot every ethic ever taught me and asked for marriage in return for his life."

"When the man you'd always fancied turned up in desperate need of your skills, it's not surprising that you became a little reckless," Judith said thoughtfully. "Do you think marrying him is meant to be?"

"I'd like to think so," Abby said morosely. "Divine inspiration sounds much better than selfishness and ambition. But I heard no angelic voice telling me that Jack Langdon is my destiny. I just . . . wanted him." Dear God, how she'd wanted him. Only now would she admit to herself how true that was.

"There are worse reasons to marry," Judith said wryly. "I've never known you to be selfish and insensitive, so acquit yourself of that, at least. I find it interesting that Frayne not only agreed to your terms initially but has made no attempt to wiggle out."

"As you say, it's a matter of honor. He gave his word and hasn't thought about it since." Abby cast about for a suitable analogy. "Rather like placing an order for a pair of boots. Even if he decided he didn't want them, he would take delivery because he said he would."

Judith laughed. "You're hardly a pair of boots, Abby! If he genuinely didn't want to marry you, I believe he would have made that clear by now. Perhaps he rather likes the idea. None of his friends seem too horrified, which is a good sign."

"You have some ability to see the future, Judith. Can you see us together?"

Judith's eyes drifted out of focus. "I think you'd suit each other very well. He's a good-natured fellow who is kind but . . . driven by inner demons. He needs a strong woman who can help him master those demons."

For the first time, it occurred to Abby that Jack might need healing of the spirit as well as of the body, and she was better qualified than most to provide that. "It makes me feel better to think I might be of service as a wife."

"Don't marry him thinking to be his maidservant," Judith said tartly. "The man would be very lucky to have you. You're attractive, intelligent, agreeable, and one of the best healers in Britain. What more could a man want?"

"In this case, a woman with no magical ability at all. He hates and fears magic." Abby thought of what she had seen the night Jack was feverish. "I don't know if he would ever be able to accept me as a woman instead of a wizard."

Judith's eyes crinkled. "Daily life takes the mystery out of magic very quickly. One could live with the handsomest man in the world and hardly notice his beauty after a month. What matters is the small acts of life. Is he considerate? Does he know how to laugh? The same will be true of your magic. Very soon, it would be less important that you're a wizard than whether you know how to find and keep a good cook."

Everything Judith said made sense. Feeling more hopeful, Abby sat down again. Cleocatra materialized and stropped Abby's ankles, then leaped into her lap. Abby began to stroke the silky black fur. "So you think I should go ahead and marry him?"

Her friend hesitated. "For both your sakes, I think you must offer him the chance to end the betrothal. Otherwise your devil's bargain will always be between you."

Abby listened to Cleo's rumbling purr. She would end up an old spinster with cats. There were worse fates. "Very well, I shall do so. It was never more than a strange, fleeting dream that I might marry Lord Frayne."

"Don't assume that he won't want you, Abby. Show some confidence."

Abby laughed without humor. "You have a vivid imagination, Judith. This has also been a strange dream for him, I think. Soon he will be well enough to return to his own home. By spring, he will be able to rejoin his regiment in Spain, as good as new. I hope he takes better care of himself in the future."

Would he ever return to the Shires to hunt? She suspected not. One didn't return to the scene of a bad dream.

Jack's friends helped him back into his bed before they left. He wondered what it would be like to always be as handicapped as he was now. If that ever happened, he would have a lower bed built. He was learning a great deal. As he sank back into the pillows and bade his friends good-bye, he wondered when he would be himself again. He was learning too many things he didn't want to know.

He sent Morris away to find supper, then slipped into a doze. He came awake instantly when the door opened. Glad that his battle-sharpened instincts hadn't disappeared entirely, he looked up to see Miss Barton.

She hesitated in the doorway. "I'm sorry, were you sleeping? I didn't mean to wake you. We can speak in the morning."

She must want to discuss the wedding. "I'm awake now, so there's no need to wait." He struggled up in the bed, shoving pillows behind him and wincing when he jarred his broken leg. "Have you set our wedding day?"

"That's what I want to talk about." She moved to the bed to adjust the pillows behind him. As always, her touch and presence were soothing. After turning up the flame of the bedside lamp, she chose a seat where he could see her clearly. He realized that she always quietly acted for his maximum comfort. His friends might love him, but they didn't think to choose seating for his convenience.

"Very well, we shall discuss the matter," he said agreeably. "But first, I've been meaning to ask you why I'm so tired. I broke my leg once before and I never felt as tired as I do now. It's absurd that a visit to the library in a wheelchair should be so fatiguing."

"Some fatigue results from the healing process itself. Much of your natural strength was used in the healing circle," she replied, seeming glad of the digression. "But blood loss is the real culprit. You bled so much, inside and out, that it might have been enough to kill you if your wounds hadn't been treated promptly. Now that blood must be rebuilt, and that takes time."

"Is it possible to create more blood through magic?" he asked curiously. "I would have thought that would be easier than repairing a broken neck."

"Actually, it isn't. The fragments of bone in your neck were all present. The trick was bringing them together and fusing them into solid bone again. While that took a huge amount of power, it was relatively straightforward. Rebuilding your blood would mean creating something from nothing, which is much harder."

That made sense. "So I shall have to recover my strength at the same speed as a soldier who was wounded and bled badly."

"Precisely. You should recover your usual vitality in a few weeks. About the same time that your broken leg is sound again."

He nodded, happier now that he understood. "Shall we be married the day after your father returns from London?"

She brushed at her immaculate hair, her face cool and pale. "You agreed to marry me when under great duress. I cannot hold you to that. You are free to go about your business unencumbered by a wife, Lord Frayne."

He felt a rush of shock, relief, and—disappointment? "The circumstances were extreme," he agreed. "But why did you ask for marriage if you didn't want it?"

"It was an odd impulse," she said slowly. "You were half out of your mind. I needed to . . . to capture your attention. To make you realize how high the stakes were. Love and death—there are none higher." She gave a ghost of a smile. "It worked, too. The thought of marrying a wizard shocked you into greater awareness. Perhaps you decided that if I was willing to risk my life in the hope of an . . . an advantageous marriage, there was a chance that you might survive. That life was worth fighting for. Whatever your reasoning, you granted me permission to attempt healing magic, and for that I was grateful. And now that is behind us, and you are free to go."

Struggling to sort out what he felt, he asked, "If you don't want marriage as a reward for your efforts, what would you like instead? A horse, a house, or a trip to America, as your fellow wizards will receive?"

"Nothing." Her hands locked together, consciously calm. "As I said before, magical work on this level is rare and not for sale. I was privileged to be the focus of great power, and to enjoy the satisfaction of success. You owe me nothing. Go freely and live generously. That is enough."

Go freely. Wasn't that what he had always wanted? Freedom from the responsibilities of his inheritance. Freedom from the impossible demands of family. Freedom to ignore the starch and rules and irritations of daily life in favor of the stark realities of war.

But he had already recognized that his form of freedom was a boy's running from responsibility, and he was ready—compelled, even—to put that behind him. He was a grown man who must stop avoiding the challenges of his life. That meant selling his commission, managing his property, taking his seat in the House of Lords, no matter how little he wanted those things. It also meant finding a wife and starting a family.

He thought of lovely Lady Cynthia Devereaux, the exquisite blond sylph who had captured a bit of his heart when he'd met her the previous spring before his return to Spain. He'd thought at the time that when he was ready to settle down, he'd find a wife like her. If he was ready to marry now, why not Lady Cynthia? She was still unattached— Winslow had said as much in a passing comment. She had not seemed averse to his attentions, and she fulfilled his ideal of the perfect woman.

And yet there had been something unreal, or at least artificial, about their brief flirtation. She had been all trilling laughter and coy, fluttering lashes. He knew very little about her character. Would she risk her life in an attempt to save a stranger? Would she be serene in the midst of chaos? Would she tell the truth with eyes clear as water and deep as the sea?

Yes, Abigail Barton was a wizard, and he found that profoundly disturbing. But his accident had made him viscerally aware that he was not immortal. There was much to be said for having a gifted healer in the household.

He studied her, wondering how that ripe womanly body would feel in his bed. The thought triggered the shocking realization that he hadn't had a really sexual thought or dream since his accident. Good God, was that why she didn't want to marry him? "Will I recover in all ways, including . . . including . . ." He blushed and tried again. "Will I still be capable of . . . of marital relations?"

Her eyes lit with what might have been laughter, but she was polite enough to keep her voice grave. "If you were capable before, you will be again. Blood loss has many effects. A temporary inability is one of them."

He sighed with relief. He also wondered if there was another woman in England with whom a man could be so frank. In that spirit, he said, "You claim it was an impulse that led you to ask for marriage, yet in my experience, impulses are seldom born out of thin air. Did you think that you might like to become Lady Frayne, and now you are dismissing the possibility as a point of honor?"

Her face became even more pale. "You are perceptive, my lord. Yes, the thought of marrying you has appeal, but coercion would make a poor foundation for life's most intimate relationship. Marrying a wizard would complicate your life in numerous ways, and that in turn would complicate mine." After a moment of silence, she said tentatively, "Perhaps we could remain friends?"

The vulnerability in her words struck him to the heart. What had it been like to grow up as a wizard, needed by some, disdained by others? And a voluptuous wench like her wasn't the fashionably slim sort whose looks would compensate for her magic. Most men were drawn more to girls like Lady Cynthia Devereaux. But he was a great strapping wretch himself, and there was something to be said for bedding a woman whom he wouldn't have to worry about accidentally breaking.

He needed a wife, and he didn't want to endure hunting among the ton for girls who might be very different from their polished public appearances. Miss Barton had already proved herself kind, honest, and honorable. He might do better in London, but more likely he would do a great deal worse, given his general incompetence with women.

And despite her willingness to set him free of obligation, he was still in her debt. Honor was a sterner taskmaster than the lady herself.

He spent a last moment considering. His family and a good number of his friends would be appalled at his marrying a wizard. He also risked introducing wizardry into the Langdon family, though there must be a dash of it there already or he wouldn't have ended up at Stonebridge.

Honor mattered more than the considerable problems he would experience by marrying her. He must throw himself into the breach. "Miss Barton, I've done a great deal of thinking in this bed, and I have resolved that it is time to take up my responsibilities. That includes finding a wife."

He searched for words that would honestly describe how he'd felt. "Would you consider marrying me? You are a woman of strength and character, and I think you would make an admirable wife." Honesty compelled him to add, "I am by no means sure that I will make an admirable husband."

Her eyes lit up. "You truly wish to marry me?"

"Truly. I've just realized that I know you better than any woman except my sister. Surely that is a good start to a marriage." He smiled wryly. "I suspect that you know me a great deal better than most women will ever know their husbands. I'm not sure if that's good or bad. But since you've said you prefer your independence and life in the country and my responsibilities will keep me in London a good part of the year, we shouldn't rub each other wrongly too often."

She gazed at him for a long time, her startling eyes seeming to see right through him. Drawing a deep breath of her own, she said, "If you genuinely wish this, then I am pleased and honored to accept your offer."

He knew he had done the right thing. He just hoped he didn't come to regret it.

Chapter IX

"*Would you consider marrying me?*" Frayne's proposal was hardly the stuff of a maiden's dreams, but it was a proposal nonetheless. Abby had been sure he would retreat from marriage like a bolting hare, yet here he was, asking for her hand in all seriousness. It was what she had wanted, though depressingly matter of fact. Clearly he wanted her because she was convenient, a known quantity—and he'd given his word.

She found it significant that even though he'd been near death when marriage had first been discussed, he'd remember her saying that she would be an independent and undemanding wife, which implied an acceptance of them living separately for much of the time. Though she had wanted a marriage of close friends, like her parents had had, she would rather have Jack Langdon some of the time than any other man all of the time.

It would be easier to stay in her safe, comfortable world. But when she looked at Jack's powerful body and craggy, honest face, she felt a blaze of sensations that had nothing to do with safety. She had been safe long enough. If she wanted more from life, she must take risks, and Jack Langdon was a risk worth taking.

Their marriage might not be a success. He didn't love her now and he might never do so, but they were on their way to being friends. Perhaps that would be enough.

And if not—well, life was about change. Her father would not live forever, her brother would someday marry and take over the estate. Richard would never turn her out of Barton Grange, but she didn't want to dwindle to a maiden aunt. She would rather be a sometime wife, and know that she had had the courage to reach for what she wanted.

Holding his gaze, she said, "If you genuinely wish this, then I am pleased and honored to accept your offer." Despite her measured words, she found herself breaking into a beaming smile.

His smile was slower, but it seemed genuine. "I do believe this will work out well." His smile faded. "Perhaps I should tell you more about my family while you still have time to change your mind."

Wondering what made him worry about his family, she said, "We all have some dirty dishes among our relatives. I will forgive you yours if you do the same for me. But I am wondering about how we will arrange our lives. I said before that I would not be a demanding wife. Do you wish me to live with you? If you are rejoining your regiment when you recover, it might be best if I stay at Barton Grange until you return."

He looked startled. "Of course I want my wife to live with me. I intend to sell my commission. I've been a competent officer, but my presence isn't required to defeat the French. It is time to take over the management of my inheritance and claim my seat in the House of Lords. Those tasks will be enhanced by my being a married man."

She tried to imagine him in ermine and velvet. It would be like decorating a lion: absurd and unnecessary. "You will bring refreshing common sense to the position."

He rolled his eyes. "You are more confident than I, but I'll worry about Parliament later. As soon as your father returns, we can use the special license Ransom went to such effort to procure. I've imposed on the hospitality of Barton Grange long enough, so after the ceremony we can move across the valley to my hunting box. After I'm fit, we can go up to London to buy you a trousseau and enjoy the pleasures of the city. I should be ready to travel soon, I hope?"

"Unless you break more bones, you should be well in a few weeks." She hesitated. "Are you sure you wish to take me to London? I fear I will be an embarrassment to you there."

His jaw set stubbornly. "There may be a certain awkwardness, but that will pass. Traditionalists must accept that the new Lady Frayne is a wizard. Even if you choose never to go to London again, it's important to let society see you at least once."

"It is brave of you to be willing to face them down." She was silent for a moment. "I'm not sure I'm a crusader."

"This won't be a crusade, but a campaign to shape how you will be accepted for the rest of your life," he said seriously. "The best way to begin is with all banners flying, as if you care nothing for the opinion of the beau monde."

"All banners flying—and avoid doing anything too embarrassingly magical," she said wryly. "Since I am not a famous wizard, no one is likely to already know about my tawdry occupation, and I will not make a point of mentioning it."

He looked relieved. "You're right, there's no need to attract censure unnecessarily. You are a woman of good birth and breeding, entirely suited to be my wife. That is all anyone need know."

She guessed there would be some surprise that Lord Frayne had married a country girl of modest birth and fortune, without the outstanding beauty that would make such a choice understandable. But that was less scandalous than marrying a despised wyrdling. When the full story came out, she would be suspected of ensorcelling him when he was injured and weak. As he'd said, she must go in with pride and confidence, for it was unlikely that her wizardry would pass unnoticed for long.

In the Shires, she and her magic were known and accepted, but London would be different. She wondered what it would be like to enter a ballroom and have everyone present give her the cut direct. The thought made her stomach clench.

It wasn't too late to change her mind. Would retreat be the wiser part of valor? *No.* When she looked at Jack, she knew that wisdom wasn't part of this transaction. Only desire. And if London proved impossible, she wouldn't visit there in the future.

Realizing that her betrothed looked exhausted, she rose and crossed to the bed. "Thank you, Jack." Leaning forward, she pressed her lips to his forehead. The skin was healthily warm, not feverish. "Now you must rest."

He caught her hand, then relaxed into the pillows, looking tired but happy. "The more I think of marrying you, the better I like the idea." Too tired to raise his head, he pressed her hand to his lips. "Thank you for accepting me, Abby."

She stood stock-still. Surely a simple kiss shouldn't scald her fingers like fire!

The door opened, and a solid, familiar figure entered. The silver-haired man arched his brows. "Ah, so this is where you're hiding, Abigail."

"Papa!" Delighted, she threw herself into Sir Andrew Barton's embrace despite the rain dripping from his cloak and hat. "You're back sooner than I expected!"

"I had a feeling I should come home." He stepped back and held her shoulders, eyes intent. "You're looking happy. I assume this is your noble patient, Lord Frayne?"

"He is both my noble patient and my betrothed, Papa."

"Indeed?" Sir Andrew pivoted and studied Jack with piercing intensity.

"Sir!" Jack struggled to sit up in the bed, his fatigue forgotten and his eyes slightly panicked at being unexpectedly confronted with his future father-in-law. "It's a pleasure to meet you, Sir Andrew. Perhaps I should have waited and asked you for Miss Barton's hand, but . . . but I didn't really think of that."

"My daughter is her own mistress, and I know better than to argue with her." Sir Andrew stepped forward and shook hands with a firm grip. "When I arrived, I was told that you'd been severely injured while hunting and were brought here?"

"Yes, sir. Miss Barton summoned a group of her wizard friends and held a healing circle to cure me," Jack said. "I owe her my life."

Sir Andrew swung around to stare at Abby. Even for his daughter, he had a gaze that could cut through solid granite. "You led a full healing circle? That was a huge risk, my girl!"

"I know. But . . . we succeeded." She was grateful for Jack's presence, which reduced the likelihood of a scolding. "And nothing else would have been enough. I'd watched you often enough that I thought I could manage."

"And you did." His mouth quirked up. "Sooner or later you had to take the risk. I only wish I had been here. But I gather there was no time to waste."

"Your daughter was very brave, sir," Jack said. "I don't remember much, but my friends were truly amazed."

"Abigail is one of the most talented healers of her generation. Do you fully understand what that means?"

Jack's gaze didn't waver. "Having been healed of a broken neck, I have a personal appreciation for her abilities."

"I suppose you do." Sir Andrew turned toward his daughter. "Being married to an ungifted husband will not bother you?"

"He attended the Stonebridge Academy," she said quietly.

"Did he now!" The baronet examined Jack with alarming intensity. "So I see," he said slowly. "You will have an interesting marriage, I think."

"That is not a comforting statement," Abby said tartly.

Her father laughed. "It wasn't intended to be. Marriage always requires adjustments. Neither of you are children, so I assume you've thought about what you're getting into. When do you intend to marry?"

"Since you're home now, perhaps tomorrow?" Abby said hesitantly. "Or the next day. A friend of Jack's procured a special license, so there's no need to wait. We could be married right in this room."

Jack cleared his throat. "I would prefer a church, if that can be arranged. If we're going to move across the valley to my house, perhaps there is a church on the way?"

"Actually, our parish church is more or less in that direction," Abby said. "I'll make the arrangements for the day after tomorrow."

Jack nodded, looking gray with fatigue.

"Lord Frayne, you appear tired," Sir Andrew said. "I shall see you tomorrow. Abby, will you join me?"

It sounded as if she would be unable to avoid that scolding. "Of course, Papa." She tugged the covers up around Jack and indulged herself in a gentle brush of his hair. "Sleep well, Jack."

His eyes closed wearily. She guessed that he was asleep before she left the room. Her father was waiting outside the door. "Are you sure, Abby?" he asked quietly.

Her smile was wry as they fell into step along the corridor. "Sure that I'm doing the right thing? No. Sure that I want to marry him? Absolutely. I've never had any interest in marrying anyone else, you know." She hesitated, then added, "Jack has always caught my eye whenever I've seen him around Melton. It's not reasonable, but at least this way, you won't have me on your hands forever."

Her father's eyes were warm. "I've always known that someday a man would come and carry you off. I'm glad he took his time about it, since I'll miss you dreadfully when you're gone. Just remember that if the marriage doesn't work out, you always have a home here." He led her to the morning room, where a tray of food had been placed for the returned traveler.

Frowning, Abby helped herself to a small slice of ham as she took the chair opposite her father's. "Do you think this is going to be a disaster? I've considered the possibility, but no man could hold a wizard who wanted to leave." She grimaced. "He is more likely to be sorry he wed me than vice versa."

Her father ate a few bites of ham and cheese before replying. "Not necessarily a disaster. That young man may seem easygoing, but only a small part of him is visible. Though it's suppressed now, he has a great deal of magic."

"I know. I had to draw on it during the healing circle, or there wouldn't have been enough power to fuse the broken bones of his neck."

Her father's brows arched. "Using his power might have activated it, you know. He might find that disconcerting."

"There seemed no other choice. His two friends who brought him here, a Mr. Ransom and the Duke of Ashby, met him at the Stonebridge Academy. They voluntarily joined the circle, or I wouldn't have tried it." Cleocatra appeared and looked up hopefully, so Abby gave her a shred of ham.

Her father's expressive brows arched even farther. "They participated in the healing? It will be interesting to see how matters play out."

Abby made a face, knowing her father's broad definition of *interesting*. But he was accepting the idea of marriage calmly, which he wouldn't if he foresaw catastrophe. She fed a sliver of cheese to the cat, who was now sitting up on her haunches and begging. "I haven't even seen Jack's hunting box. We'll move there after the wedding. When he feels strong enough, he will take me to London, then to his family seat in Yorkshire."

"London? I hope you have time to visit some of our family friends as well as the members of the beau monde that are Lord Frayne's natural circle." Sir Andrew took a meditative sip of wine. "You may need the company of friends who are comfortable with wizardry."

In other words, her father expected her to run into trouble. Well, she expected that, too. She lifted Cleo onto her lap and encouraged the cat to purr by stroking the soft black fur. Odd how even the guarantee of trouble didn't make her want to change her mind.

Chapter X

Jack was flying, swooping over the globe, arms stretched before him and the wind tugging his hair. Below were places he knew in England and Scotland, Spain, and Portugal. There was plenty of ocean, too.

His ability to fly suddenly vanished and he fell helplessly from the sky. He eyed the fast-approaching earth with resignation. He'd faced certain death after his hunting accident. Perhaps now he was better prepared.

He crashed into a meadow and bounced without being damaged. Surprised, he glanced around, trying to identify his location, but the meadow was unlike anyplace he'd ever been. The flowers, the birds, even the butterflies were different from those he knew. Brighter and more attractive, but eerie in their differences. Yet at the same time, there was an odd familiarity to the place, as if he'd seen it once long before.

He saw a familiar figure walking away from him. Scrambling to his feet, he ran after it. "Ashby, is that you? Where are we?"

The man turned and showed a face that was both Ashby and not-Ashby, but his voice was familiar when he said, "Jack?"

* * *

A hand on Jack's shoulder jerked him back to wakefulness. He opened his eyes to see Ashby, looking perfectly normal and repeating his name.

"What time is it?" Jack said groggily.

"Early. I came before breakfast to smuggle in the crutches you requested." His friend held them out proudly. "I had them made specially so they wouldn't collapse under the weight of a great hulk like you. The carpenter who built them thought to put padding on the tops to make them easier to use."

Jack came to full wakefulness instantly. "Good! I don't want to get married in a wheelchair." He sat up and swung his legs over the side of the bed, keeping the broken leg straight out. The day before, the heavy splints that immobilized his whole leg had been replaced by lighter splints bound with leather straps. It had been ridiculously exciting to be able to bend his right knee again.

He tried to raise himself on the crutches, lost his balance, and ended up sprawled on his back on the bed, swearing. His wary second attempt was more successful, and he managed to stand upright under his own power, though swaying back and forth.

"Any word yet on a wedding date?" his friend asked.

Jack nodded. The crutches were a bit short, but they'd do. Keeping his weight on his left foot, he moved the crutches forward a few inches, stepped out with his left foot, and almost fell. Not a good idea to move his foot beyond the position of the crutches, apparently. Ashby caught and steadied him. Jack was grateful that his friend was there to help, though with Jack's greater size, he might drag them both to the floor if he fell.

He took another step forward, almost falling again when he didn't allow for the height of the carpet. Amazing what a difference half an inch made.

Walking took concentration, too. He found he couldn't walk and talk at the same time. He halted to say, "Sir Andrew Barton returned home last night. For a civil fellow, he's rather fearsome—it must be the wizard eyes." Which were pale blue with dark rims, very like Abby's, now that he thought of it. "Luckily he had no objection to our marriage. The wedding is set for tomorrow in the local parish church. Abby and I will move to my hunting box directly after."

Lurching but upright, he inched forward another few steps, grimly watching his balance and where he placed the crutches. "I hadn't realized there's a knack to this, so it's good I can practice before the wedding." This would be easier if he was wearing shoes, or at least a shoe on his left foot. Damned tiring, though. He crisscrossed the room, glad to be upright again.

"How about resting in that chair?" Ashby suggested. "Walking with crutches looks exhausting."

Privately admitting that he was near collapse, Jack swung over to the wing chair, turned clumsily, and sat, half falling and jarring his leg again. Damn, it was going to be hard to get out of this deeply upholstered chair. He'd worry about that later. For now, he was panting as if he'd been running.

Ashby took the other chair. "So the wedding is set. You don't mind having to marry her because that was her price for saving your life?"

"Actually, Abby came by yesterday evening and released me from the bargain. She said she didn't want to force me, and she'd only made the suggestion in the first place to engage my attention." Jack placed the crutches together and rested them on the left side of his chair, wondering how to explain his decision to proceed. "Still, I gave my word, and apart from being a wizard, she should make a decent wife. She's no beauty, but she's good company. Intelligent. Kind."

"No, she's not a beauty," Ashby said gently. "She's magnificent, which is something quite different. I'm glad you're choosing to marry her even though you don't have to. She has a thousand times the substance of the average marriage mart miss."

Jack glanced up, startled but pleased by his friend's approval. "You won't give me the cut direct for marrying a wizard?"

"That would be rude, given that I've been running tame in her house since your accident," Ashby said dryly. "Can I help in any way with the wedding? Perhaps visit your hunting box and make sure it's ready for a new mistress? Organize a modest wedding breakfast there?"

Jack thought about what was needed. "Both those things would be much appreciated. Also, I'll need a ring—perhaps Abby's maid will lend you a ring for sizing. And if it's possible, might you find some flowers even though it's winter?"

"A duke can always find flowers," Ashby said gravely. "Anything else?"

"Would you stand up with me? Or since Winslow and Ransom are in town, maybe casting dice would be best." Reading his friend's expression, he said wryly, "You're the most likely to approve of this wedding, aren't you? So the others might prefer not to be asked."

"Ransom and Winslow both like Abby, but they are somewhat wary about seeing you marry her under these circumstances. Especially Winslow," the duke said tactfully. "I think they'll be pleased for you once they realize you're doing this of your own free will. One might dislike wizards in the abstract and still be fond of them in the particular, and Abby is very likable."

Jack was glad to hear it, because he wasn't about to change his mind even if his friends had been horrified. It was surprising, really, just how determined he was to go through with this marriage.

"There!" Judith stepped back and studied the lace veil that fell down her friend's back. "You look lovely, Abby. Every inch a bride."

"Including the nervousness?" Abby brushed the pale blue silk of her gown, hoping her hands weren't visibly trembling.

"Especially the nervousness. That's absolutely traditional." Judith's smile was a little misty. "I'm happy for you, but I'll miss you, Abby."

"Yorkshire isn't so terribly far from Leicestershire," Abby said. "You can bear me company when Frayne is in London debating the great issues of the day."

"Won't you be with him?"

Abby made a face. "I suspect that after this visit, I'll be content to keep my distance. The times I've been to London before, we stayed within the circle of our friends—wizards and those who accept magic. This will be different, and I suspect much more unpleasant than Frayne realizes."

"London may surprise you," Judith said. "The prohibition against magic has always been stronger for men than women. From what I've heard, a fair number of the ladies of the beau monde have dabbled with magic themselves, rather like their drawing and music lessons."

"If some of them are secretly practicing magic, they may be even harder on me to draw attention from their own sins." Abby lifted her prayer book and the small nosegay of orange blossoms that had been delivered that morning. One of Jack's friends must have found the flowers at the conservatory of one of the great houses of the area. Barton Grange had a conservatory, but the limited space was used for fruits and vegetables during the winter. It was a luxury to have flowers at this season. "I shall deal with criticism as it comes, and count the days until I leave London."

Judith fixed her with a stern glance. "Speaking of counting days, when are you going to stop giving your life force to Frayne? You said it was only temporary, but you're giving more than ever."

Abby sighed. "I stopped once, and he had a relapse. I decided it was better to restore the flow of energy until he is well enough to manage on his own. Today I'm giving him extra energy so he can get through the wedding and the carriage ride across the valley. I will gradually reduce the flow once he is settled in his own home."

"I hope that will be soon. You've lost weight and there are circles under your eyes. You can't keep this up much longer, Abby."

"I won't. I don't like being tired all the time." Nor did she need to look in the mirror to recognize that Judith was right about her losing weight and having tired eyes. Any beauty Abby might have today was because of her happiness, because she did look rather run-down. "It's time to leave for the church."

"You're right." Judith gave Abby a quick hug. "Be happy, my dear. Frayne is a good man, and you deserve happiness. Think of yourself sometimes, not just others."

"You give me more credit than I deserve. I'm a selfish woman, or I wouldn't have snapped up Jack when he was weak and vulnerable." Abby's smile was crooked, because she knew there was truth in her half-hearted joke.

"Nonsense. In my experience, men usually do what they want, and he would not have asked for your hand after you released him unless he really wanted you as his wife."

Hoping Judith was right, Abby left the bedchamber that had been hers since she was a small child. Most of her belongings had already been packed for transport to Jack's hunting box. She tried not to think of all she was leaving behind. She should be looking to the future, not mourning the past.

Her father waited at the foot of the stairs to escort her and Judith to the church. The ceremony would be small, just a few friends and relatives. Next summer, she and her husband—husband!—would visit Melton Mowbray and her father could host an outdoor reception for the tenants and neighbors.

He looked up and gave her a smile that came close to breaking Abby's heart. "You look beautiful, my dear girl. I wish your mother was here to see you."

She swallowed hard. "Don't get me started crying or I won't be able to stop, and that won't be at all flattering to my new husband."

"Don't worry, I came prepared." He handed her a handkerchief.

Abby laughed a little, blotted the incipient moisture from her eyes, and tucked the handkerchief away for future use. Then she donned her cloak, as did Judith, and they left the house for the carriage ride to the church.

Abby no longer looked back. It was her future that intrigued her now. A future with the only man she had ever wanted.

Jack had insisted on getting to the church early. He wanted time to recover from the effort of traveling in a carriage. He'd never fully realized just how much carriages bounced. But at least he was well dressed, thanks to the skills of his valet. Morris had opened the seam of Jack's best trousers and sewed in an extra panel to accommodate the splint on his right leg.

That leg was aching badly by the time they reached Saint Anselm in the Fields, the pretty stone church that served the Bartons' parish. Ashby and Ransom helped him from the carriage, Winslow bringing up the rear. The cold winter weather had turned mild today, with more sunshine than cloud. That was a good sign, he thought. He worked out how long it had been since his accident, and realized soon Parliament would be opening in London. He really must take his seat like a proper lord.

"Watch your step," Ransom said. "The ground is rough here."

"I'm learning that the world is full of hazards if you're on crutches." Jack clambered awkwardly up the three steps to the church and swung through the door that Ashby opened for him.

His shoulders and armpits ached from his stealthy practicing on the crutches the day before, but it would be worth it to surprise Abby. He grinned, wondering if she would smile with pleasure to see him upright or frown with concern that he was pushing himself too hard. Either expression would be charming.

Concentrating hard on the floor, which was flagstone and considerably less than even, he made his way to the front of the church. Beside him, Winslow said, "If you have any doubts, you don't have to go through with this. No one would blame you for refusing to be coerced into marriage with a wyrdling."

Jack stopped his slow progress so he could glare at his friend. "I have not been coerced and I have no doubts. If you feel you can't support me in this, you are free to leave. There's still time to join today's hunt if you hurry."

"I swear the woman has enchanted you, despite your anti-magic charm." Winslow's eyes narrowed. "You had to have given her permission to use magic to heal you. Maybe she took advantage of that to ensorcell you at the same time."

Jack was ready to explode furiously when Ransom's mild voice intervened. "Careful, Winslow, or you will find out just how formidable a weapon a crutch can be. And I might hold you down so Jack can take a few extra whacks."

The interruption gave Jack time to recapture his temper. Lowering himself into the front pew, he said, "Lucas, you're an ass, but I'll forgive you this time because your intentions are good. Wrong, but good. Abby gave me a chance to withdraw, and I found that I didn't want to. She didn't ensorcell me."

He hesitated before saying with the surprise of discovery, "The plain truth is that I *like* her. Yes, she's a wizard, but she doesn't make me feel clumsy or tongue-tied, like so many grand ladies do. She's kind and bright and down-to-earth. I think I'm damned lucky to have found her even though I did it the hard way."

Ashby added, "If you'd seen Abby in action, you would have no doubts, Lucas. She isn't at all like the bits of fluff that appeal to you, and that's all to the good."

Winslow started to snap a reply, then halted. "Very well, I . . . I apologize for doubting your choice, Jack. I shall attempt to see her as you do. As for my support—you always have that."

"Thank you." Jack grimaced. "I'm going to need that support in society, where too many people will assume I've gone mad, or that Abby used magic to steal my wits."

A man entered the sanctuary from a small side door. The vicar, by his dress. As Jack was thinking he looked familiar, Ransom stepped forward, hand extended. "Mr. Wilson. We met at the healing circle, I believe."

The vicar returned the handshake. "We did indeed. I'm glad we meet again in happier circumstances." He turned and shook Jack's hand. "No need to stand, Lord Frayne. You're looking well. You're a lucky man in more ways than one."

"Thank you, sir. I agree." Jack heard footsteps and swiveled around, wondering if the bridal party had arrived. No Abby, but half a dozen people were taking seats in the rear. A moment later, a family with several children entered and also sat down.

The door hadn't even closed before three men with similar long noses entered, two carrying fiddles and one a wooden flute. The three walked to the front of the church. While the fiddlers studied Jack with frank curiosity, the flutist said to the vicar, "Sir, they say Miss Abby is getting married today. Do you think she'd like it if we played for her?"

The vicar smiled. "I think she'd be very pleased, as long as you play when she's coming and going and not during the actual service."

The flutist bobbed his head and led his companions off to one side of the church, where they started playing softly. They were quite good, too, though Jack didn't recognize the music.

In the time that the musicians were getting settled, at least a dozen more people had come into the church. Most seemed like simple villagers and laborers dressed in plain, neat garments. Perplexed, Jack said to the vicar, "Abby and I had planned to have a very small wedding with just a few friends. Who are all these people?"

"They've all been helped by Abby and her family at one time or another," Wilson replied. "Word of the wedding obviously got out and they've come to pay their respects. Since the church is open to all, they are welcome to attend. You are a fortunate man to marry a woman who is so loved."

Even Winslow looked impressed by the vicar's explanation. With a nod of his head, Wilson moved away to speak with a woman and her daughter at the front of the church. They were placing vases of berried branches, holly leaves, cattails, and other vegetation that could be found at this stark season. The arrangements were quite pretty, too. Jack thought of the parable of the widow's mite. These were offerings of people with little money but a true-hearted desire to honor Abby.

A voice said excitedly, "The bride has arrived!"

With shuffling feet and rustling clothing, dozens of people rose as the double doors to the church opened. Sunshine illuminated the four figures who stepped inside. Sir Andrew Barton, Judith Wayne, Abby's maid—but it was only Abby that he really saw. She looked like a goddess. The sun caught golden and auburn highlights in her hair and shimmered on her ripe, womanly form. Judith removed the cloak from Abby's shoulders and his bride moved forward through the light, music swelling to fill the church with exhilarating melody.

Ashby had been right. Abby wasn't beautiful—she was magnificent.

Chapter XI

Coming out of the bright sunlight, Abby had trouble seeing inside the dim church. Good heavens, who were all these people? As her eyes adjusted, she recognized the friends and neighbors she had grown up with. News of the wedding had spread. The Mackie brothers had even come to play for her. Tom, the eldest, had recovered well from the lung disease she'd treated, or he wouldn't be playing the flute with such joyous sweetness.

Her gaze went to the altar, and there was Jack. And he was standing with crutches! He must have enlisted his friends to acquire them and watch over him as he practiced. She should worry that he was walking too soon, but she couldn't prevent herself from beaming with delight. Though he was not yet fully healed, he was once again the powerful, compelling man who had held her attention for years. And so handsome in dark formal wear that he took her breath away.

Gracefully in time to the music, Judith walked down the center aisle, nodding to people she recognized and babies she had delivered. Taking a tight grip on her father's arm, Abby followed, her gaze on Jack.

When she reached the altar, her father kissed her on the cheek, saying softly, "Be happy, my darling." Then he stepped back, no longer the most important man in her life.

Before she could shed threatening tears, Jack reached out to take her hand, almost dropping the crutch in the process. Ashby deftly stabilized it.

"You are lovely, my lass," Jack whispered, a hint of Yorkshire in his voice for the first time since they'd met. She knew instinctively that he was speaking from his heart.

She clenched his hand, hardly daring to believe they were really about to wed. They had never stood side by side like this, and she hadn't fully realized just how tall he was. Most men were near her own height, but with Jack, she had to look up. Those shoulders looked so much wider now that he was standing rather than lying on a bed.

Her gaze locked with Jack's as she listened to the ancient, beautiful words that joined them together. When Mr. Wilson said, "With this ring I thee wed," Jack accepted the ring from Ashby and almost dropped the other crutch. Ashby was a most efficient best man, for he managed to keep the crutch from clattering to the floor.

Jack might have trouble managing his crutches, but the ring was a perfect fit when he slid it onto her third finger. "With this ring I thee wed. With my body I thee worship, and with all my worldly goods I thee endow," he said softly.

After the vicar blessed the marriage, Jack leaned forward to give Abby the kiss of peace. Though the touch of his lips on her cheek was light, she almost dissolved as shocks of delight ran through her.

And then the ceremony was over and the Mackies' music soared into a triumphal march. She looked up at Jack, still beaming, and squeezed his hand. "Thank you for becoming my husband."

He gave her a rueful smile. "I wish I could walk down the aisle holding your hand, but I can't. If I had a third hand, maybe."

She laughed and placed her hand lightly at the small of his back. "This will do, I think. Come, my lord."

She saw something change in his eyes when she touched him. Then he turned, moving the crutches in short steps, and together they started to walk up the aisle.

Progress was slow because of the guests who called greetings or reached out to take Abby's hand. "We'll miss you, Miss Abby," and "God bless and keep you," were repeated over and over, along with thanks for particular healings she had done. She had known that she was liked and her healing talent valued, but this outpouring of love melted her heart. How could she leave the valley?

A glance at Jack reminded her of the answer. He was smiling and bantering with the guests, comfortable with them even though they were strangers from the lower classes. She worried a little about him keeping his balance in the press of people, but he kept his steps small, slow, and sure.

They reached the doorway and stayed there so Abby could speak to everyone who wanted to see her. Jack unobtrusively leaned against the door frame until the last congratulations and hugs were received. When only the wedding party was left, he shifted his weight onto his crutches again so they could leave. "I'm surprised they let me marry you, Abby. You are greatly valued."

"Luckily, there are other good healers in the area." She took her cloak from Judith and wrapped it around her shoulders. "I don't suppose you know if there are any healers in your family's part of Yorkshire?"

He made a face. "I have no idea, I'm afraid." He set his crutches on the step below and lowered himself. Abby winced as he swayed, grateful that his friends were hovering beside and below to catch him if he fell. Luckily there were only three steps, and he made it safely to the ground without crashing. Though it was a near thing.

The waiting coach was decorated with seasonal greens and berries. Ashby handed her in since Jack couldn't. "I wish you happy, Lady Frayne."

"Thank you for all you've done," she said quietly. "It means a great deal to me to know that at least one of Jack's friends supports this marriage completely."

The duke smiled wryly. "You see too much, Abby. But the others will come around as they get to know you better."

She hoped so. After climbing up into the carriage, she slid to the far side of the seat. A moment later Jack joined her. He took up rather a lot of the seat, and the crutches were an awkward addition. As he propped them diagonally across the carriage, he asked, "Are you going to scold me for acquiring crutches behind your back?"

"You seem to be managing well and you haven't broken any more bones, so it would be very bad of me to scold." She frowned as she saw him rubbing at his shoulder. "Are you finding the crutches uncomfortable?"

"My shoulders and underarms hurt like the devil." He made a face. "Sorry, I shouldn't use such language in front of you, but I'm afraid I will. Regularly. I've spent too many years in the army. May I give a general apology for all present and future language transgressions?"

"Of course, and I now issue general forgiveness." She chuckled. "I have an older brother, you know, so my ears are not so tender as you might think. But about those crutches. In my experience, it's best to rest most of your weight on the crossbars that support your hands. If you keep your arms straight, that will take some of the strain from your shoulders."

He thought about it. "I can see where that might be an improvement. Thank you for the hint."

Aided by Ashby, Judith climbed into the carriage and sat opposite Abby, deftly avoiding the crutches. Since she and the duke had stood witness, they were riding in the same carriage to the wedding breakfast. After Ashby joined them, they set off to Abby's new home. Conversation became general, for which she was glad. She wasn't quite ready to be alone with Jack. Until now, most of their conversations had been about his health. What would they talk about for the next few decades?

The weather had been dry, so they made good time on the journey across the valley. When they passed through the estate gates, Abby leaned forward to peer out the window. "Even though I've lived here my whole life, I've never seen Hill House. It was empty for years. How large is it?"

"Only six bedrooms," Jack replied. "The place was in need of work, and most of the repairs I've made have been useful but unexciting things like the roof." He looked wary. "You can change anything you like."

"What Jack is trying to say," Ashby put in smoothly, "is that the house is rather rough and in dire need of a lady's touch."

"Oh, good! A project." Abby smiled at her new husband. "It will give us something to talk about while we get used to being married."

"A source of conversation. I hadn't thought of that." Jack chuckled. "Hill House will provide a *lot* of conversation."

So he had been worrying about what they would talk about, too! The knowledge made Abby feel less nervous.

The carriage emerged from a lane of trees and Abby saw the house for the first time. It was perhaps a century old, a gentleman's home about the size of Barton Grange. But while the Grange showed its origins as a farmhouse that had grown over time, Hill House had been built in the graceful, well-proportioned Palladian style. It was handsome but shabby. "This is most impressive for a hunting box. I shall enjoy spending your money on it. But not too much, I assume, since this isn't your principal seat."

"Do what is necessary. I may spend a fair amount of time here, since I won't be much at the family seat in Yorkshire."

Though Jack's words were neutral, Abby picked up a flicker of emotion from him, and it wasn't happy emotion. She supposed she would learn about his family problems soon enough.

When the carriage stopped in front of the entrance, two servants emerged to greet the new arrivals. One was Morris, Jack's valet, and Abby recognized the other as a servant of Ashby's, a highly competent majordomo. The duke had obviously taken steps behind the scenes to assure that all proceeded smoothly.

With the help of Ashby and Morris, Jack descended from the carriage and settled onto his crutches, keeping his arms straight and his weight on the crosspieces. His armpits would be the better for it, but learning a new walking technique made him unsteady. Abby tried not to flinch as Jack climbed the steps. Morris stood behind to catch him if he fell, and if he did, the distance probably wouldn't be mortal. But the sooner his leg was healed, the better for her nerves.

As soon as she entered Hill House, she understood why Jack had been apologetic about the place. Though the roof might be new, signs of old water damage were visible in the entry hall. The sparse furnishings were old and worn. She guessed that when the previous owners left, they took all the good pieces with them.

But the hall had been scrubbed clean and decorated with tangy bunches of greens, a fire was roaring in the fireplace, and the delicious scents of hot food wafted through the air. Shabby Hill House might be, but it was welcoming. As of tomorrow, the house would become a most satisfying project.

Though called a wedding breakfast, the celebration didn't begin until well after noon. The duke's majordomo had organized a splendid spread, and the food, drink, and gallant toasts to the bride and groom lasted for hours. The two dozen guests were a diverse lot, but aristocrats, wizards, and country gentry mixed with surprising ease.

As the early winter dusk approached, Abby decided that it was time to end the party. Though Jack was enjoying the company of his friends, Abby could sense how low his energy was, and hers wasn't much better. She rose. "It's dreadfully rude of me, but I'm going to send you all away so you can reach your homes safely before full dark. Thank you for coming to celebrate our wedding."

Jack lifted his wineglass and surveyed the gathering, his gaze meeting that of each guest. "To friendship, which is the heart's blood of life. Thank you for celebrating with us today."

The guests returned the toast, then accepted their dismissal goodnaturedly, since Abby's point about the approaching darkness was valid. But there were enough teasing comments about being impatient for the wedding night to make Abby's cheeks red. She was just as glad that their consummation would be delayed and private.

Ashby, Ransom, and Winslow left. Ransom, surprisingly, kissed her hand. "For a while, I thought I'd never see Jack live long enough to wed. Thank you."

Ashby squeezed her hand, needing no words to show his support. Her father, who was the last to leave, gave her a farewell hug. "I'm glad you'll be just across the valley for the next few weeks. Regular visits will give me time to adjust to your absence."

She clung to him. "Just as I need time to adjust to being someone called Lady Frayne. When I was little, I never dreamed of marrying a lord. It's easier to think of myself as Mrs. Jack."

Her father laughed. "Jack is not a particularly lordly lord, and you will make him a most refreshing lady." His amusement faded. "This is the right time and the right man, Abby. That doesn't mean your marriage will be easy, but it will be worth it." Gently he detached Abby and turned to descend the steps to his waiting carriage.

Suddenly bone tired, Abby returned to the dining room, where servants in Ashby's livery were quietly cleaning up. Jack had been holding court in a wing chair with his right leg supported on a matching ottoman. He gave her a tired smile. "It was a good wedding feast."

"And we owe it to Ashby. Your friends did well by us."

"One couldn't ask for better friends." His smile was nostalgic. "As boys we swore an oath of loyalty to one another to help us survive the Stonebridge Academy. Being young and melodramatic, we decided to call ourselves the Stone Saints. There was considerable irony in the name since none of us were likely candidates for sainthood."

The Stone Saints? She imagined those young boys trying hard to seem strong rather than reveal their fears and uncertainties as they endured a brutal school designed to suppress their true natures. Poor lads—though she was sure that the grown-up Stone Saints would hate knowing that she thought of them with compassion. "I haven't seen anything of the house. Did Morris prepare a bedroom for you on the ground floor?"

He shook his head. "I'll stay in my rooms upstairs. The adjoining suite for the mistress of the house should be ready for you."

Appalled, she said, "You mean to climb that long, steep flight of stairs after such a tiring day? Surely not!"

"I've been looking forward to sleeping in my own bed," he said mildly.

"Your bed could be moved down to that small parlor across the hall."

"No doubt, but I want to sleep in my own bedchamber. I like the way the sun comes in at dawn."

She had a horrible vision of him pitching down the stairs. "You might break your neck again!"

Jack caught her gaze. "Abby, you are my wife, not my mother. I will always listen to your advice, but I make my own decisions."

She flushed a deep, uncomfortable crimson. "I'm sorry. Having been your physician, I've become rather dictatorial. I won't do it again." She thought a moment before honesty compelled her to say, "At least I'll try not to be dictatorial. I won't always succeed."

"You're a strong woman and I expect opinions," he said seriously. "As long as you don't expect me to always follow your advice, we will deal well together."

Since he seemed disposed to honesty, she said, "The reverse is also true. I shall always respect your suggestions, but . . . well, though I have just vowed obedience to you, I think I'll be forsworn rather quickly."

Instead of being angry, he laughed. "Marriage is going to be much more amusing than I ever anticipated." He put his good foot on the floor and slid the ottoman sideways before gingerly lowering his right foot. "After a good night's sleep, I look forward to our discovering the shape of our marriage. But for now . . ." He covered a huge yawn. "I need rest."

Despite his amusement, she saw gray fatigue in his expression. If the stubborn man was going to climb the stairs on his crutches, she had better lend him more strength so that he didn't break his neck again. She felt dizzy for a moment when she increased the energy flow. She was nearing the limit of what she could safely spare.

Jack was sitting up, ready to stand, but he looked uncertain. Guessing his concern, she asked, "Do you need a hand getting out of that chair? Since it's soft, it might be hard to manage."

He grimaced. "That would be helpful. It's easier to sit than to stand."

"By the time you've fully mastered the crutches, you won't need them anymore." She offered both hands. He clasped them, pulling against her grip as he hoisted himself from the chair. She shifted her feet to keep from being pulled over. He was one solid man. And then he was looming over her, and she felt like melting into him.

He reached for his crutches and knocked them to the floor. "Too much wine," he said ruefully. "Would you mind?"

"Not at all." She retrieved the crutches and handed them to him. "I broke my ankle once and had to use crutches for several weeks. They're amazingly inconvenient."

He settled himself on the crutches. "Your father couldn't heal the broken bone more quickly?"

"He could, but he thought that pain and inconvenience might teach me that I couldn't fly by building wings and jumping from my bedroom window," she explained.

"You were quite the young hellion!" he said, startled. Before his words could make Abby too nervous, he added, "I consider that a splendid attribute in a wife. So many of the London ladies are terrifyingly perfect and . . . well, ladylike."

He started walking toward the stairs, and Abby fell into step beside him. "I am more likely to embarrass you because of my wizardry than to intimidate you with my perfection."

"And I shall embarrass you by my . . ." He paused, then shook his head. "I shall let you discover that on your own."

They reached the foot of the steps and Abby was about to suggest calling Morris to stand guard as Jack climbed. Before she could speak up, Jack turned around and lowered himself onto the fourth step, his right leg held out in front of him. "I believe this will work. Will you bring my crutches up, please?"

Using his arms and good leg, he hitched himself up backwards to the next step. "Not the most dignified way to travel, but safe, I think." He lifted himself another step.

"I wish I'd thought of this when I broke my ankle!" Abby followed with his crutches, making a mental note not to underestimate her new husband. She remembered her father saying that Jack had many hidden depths. Just as she would keep Jack amused, he would keep her intrigued as she discovered those depths.

By the time he reached the top of the long staircase, Jack was flagging but pleased with himself. "Now comes the tricky bit: getting to my feet."

"It will be safer if you don't stand until you're farther from the top of the stairs."

Jack obligingly hitched his way back across the hall until he was a safe distance from the steps. Abby propped his crutches against the wall and offered her hands again. This time they coordinated better and he got to his feet fairly easily.

Ignoring the crutches, he slung his right arm around her shoulders. "Will you be my crutch to the bedroom?"

"I like to be useful." She grabbed the crutches with her free hand, then followed his lead. His solid weight pressing against her made the few steps a pleasure.

His bedroom was plain, but a fire burned in the grate and the bed looked comfortable. Morris was there, meticulously checking the state of Jack's wardrobe. He turned around. "Sir, I thought you would ring for me to help you up the stairs."

"No need." Jack hopped to the bed with Abby's help, then turned and sat on the edge. "Abby, your rooms are through that door."

A connecting door so the master and mistress could come together without the household knowing. Apparently her new husband expected her to spend the night there. She knew that made sense, but wished he had shown some desire to keep her close.

She paused with her hand on the knob to her room. "Sleep well, my dear."

Then she walked through into her new bedchamber. Like Jack's room, it was sparsely furnished, but the worn pink brocade bedspread seemed chosen for a lady and a vase of orange blossoms stood on the desk, lending sweetness to the air. She also had a fire to take the chill from the room.

A quick exploration showed that one door led to the hall and another to a small sitting room. The last door opened to a dressing room where her maid, Nell, was quietly darning a pair of stockings. Nell got to her feet and bobbed her head. "Are you ready for bed, my lady?"

"I'm going to have trouble getting used to that *my lady*," Abby commented. "But I am certainly ready for bed."

It was a pleasure to change into a flowing nightgown and robe and let Nell brush out her hair. But as Nell plaited a night braid, Abby's gaze moved to the connecting door. Surely her new husband wouldn't mind if she visited him to say good night.

Chapter XII

Jack was glad that he'd managed to climb the steps without aid, but by the time Morris had helped him change from formal clothes into his nightgown, his leg was in agony and he was almost paralyzed with fatigue. No, not paralyzed. Having experienced real paralysis, he could no longer use the word lightly, even in his mind.

Morris helped Jack into bed—convenient that he was a great strong ox of a fellow, strong enough to lift another great ox. As he straightened the covers over Jack, the valet asked, "Shall I leave a candle burning for Lady Frayne?"

"Please." Jack could see that Morris was curious about whether the newlyweds would spend the night together, but of course he couldn't ask. The servants would figure it out on their own in the morning. They always did.

After his valet left, Jack settled back into the pillows, aching and ready for sleep. Would Abby come to bid him good night? He hoped so. She must be almost as tired as he and the mild day had turned into a cold night, but surely she would want to say something on the night of their marriage.

He dozed, then awoke with a start when the connecting door to Abby's bedchamber opened. His bride stood silhouetted against the light from her bedroom. The flowing fabric of her nightclothes suited her tall figure. With her thick hair falling in a braid over her shoulder, she looked like a medieval queen.

"Are you awake?" she asked in a voice just above a whisper. "I don't want to disturb you."

"Please, disturb me," he said as he pushed himself into a sitting position. His fatigue had retreated now that he had something—someone—to engage his attention. "We haven't had a chance to be alone all day. Even if our wedding night must be delayed, surely I'm entitled to a kiss."

Her face lit up. "You certainly are. A promise of better days to come." She blushed as she moved forward. "Or better nights."

She halted at his bedside, her gaze on the shape of his leg under the covers. "Your leg is hurting rather badly, it appears. Shall I reduce the pain for you?"

"Please do." As she drew the covers back, he asked, "What do you see when you look at an injury? What does pain look like?"

Her brow furrowed as she cupped her hands an inch above his aching leg. "Pain is like a restless red energy. I don't really see it with my eyes, but with my mind. Some healers like my father actually see energy fields called auras around people. Auras are lights that glow around the body in different colors. One can tell much by reading a person's aura—whether the person is calm or worried, mental or emotional. I'd like to be able to see auras, but for healing, it's enough that I can sense the colors in my mind."

She stopped talking and concentrated on his leg. To his amazement, he saw a subtle glow of white light between her hands and his leg. No, surely he was imagining that glow because he was tired and she had talked about seeing light. But whatever she was doing worked. The vicious shooting pains in his broken leg faded to a dull ache, hardly worth mentioning. "That's much better. Thank you."

Abby straightened, and he saw how tired she appeared. Since he'd seen her every day since his accident, he hadn't noticed that the healthy glow she'd had the first day had been diminished. That had to be his fault. He moved toward the middle of the bed, then reached out and caught her hand. "Come for your kiss, lass. You've done so much for me, and no one has been taking care of you."

"I'm fine. Just a little tired." But she let herself be coaxed into sitting on the edge of the mattress.

"Closer. The bed has plenty of room for two." He tugged her hand, drawing her down beside him on the bed. She swung her legs up onto the mattress and rested her head on his shoulder. She filled his embrace naturally, as if his arms had been waiting for her forever.

She exhaled softly. "Mmm, this feels nice, but I don't want to risk hurting you."

"You won't." In fact, now that her long, lush body was lying along-side him, all aches and pains were forgotten. "You've soothed all of me, not just my leg."

Her mouth curved into a smile and her eyes drifted shut. Her lovely, clear skin was an invitation to touch that he made no attempt to resist.

Her cheek was even softer than it looked. His stroking hand continued on to her hair. Calling it brown was a disservice, for the heavy braid was shot with a thousand shades of gold and red and ginger. He untied the ribbon that secured her braid, then slid his fingers into the luxuriant waves. She murmured, "Now I'll have to braid it again before I go to bed, or it will be a terrible tangle in the morning."

"Perhaps, but it's glorious now." He lifted an overflowing handful of hair and rubbed his cheek into it. There was an intoxicating sensuality in the silky texture and clean herbal scent.

She was his wife. He was allowed to kiss her. Yet he hesitated, very aware of how little experience he'd had with women. He liked females—his sister had been his best friend before he was sent to the Stonebridge Academy. He'd learned the polite banter of society, and he'd enjoyed the physical encounters available to lustful young men of means.

But he'd never had a real romance. Admiring pretty society ladies in a detached way was not the same thing. Abby . . . made him want to be romantic. He bent and touched his lips to hers. Her mouth was soft and welcoming, and as hesitant as his own.

He kissed her again, his arm tightening around her waist. She felt marvelous, a combination of rich curves and supple strength. His heartbeat quickened. This was not a lady on a pedestal, but a woman. His *wife*.

He experimentally touched her lips with his tongue. Her mouth opened, and he fell into the embrace, intoxicated by her femaleness. He moved backward toward the center of the bed and took her with him, safe in his arms. "Stay tonight," he said softly. "I would like to have you here."

Her eyes widened. How could he have ever thought her plain? Her lashes were long and dark, a perfect frame for her stunning, expressive eyes. Shyly she said, "If you're sure I won't be a nuisance."

"Never." He propped himself up on his right elbow and stroked his hand down her body, marveling at the pleasure he found in exploring her lush femaleness. In youthful amorous encounters, he'd always been frantic with lust, too hungry for the destination to enjoy the journey. "I am going to enjoy sharing a bed with you," he murmured. "You're so comfortable."

She gave a choke of laughter. "Pillows and mattresses are comfortable, so I'm not quite sure if that's a compliment. But I do enjoy being petted like a cat."

Aroused by her encouragement, he covered her breast with one hand. The ripe weight made an intoxicating handful. She inhaled sharply as he shaped that fullness with his palm. "Anything so enjoyable is surely not allowed," she gasped.

"It is now that we're married." He grinned. "I'm beginning to understand why marriage is so popular."

He bent into another kiss that became even deeper and more languorous than the first. He hadn't known that kissing could be done with the whole body, and yet that was what they were doing. As the embrace heated up, they shifted and adjusted feverishly to find the best fit.

Her pelvis warm against his, his knee pressed between her legs, his hand sliding down her back to cup the provocative fullness of her hip. He wanted to bury himself in her, mate as nature intended.

But he *couldn't.* In the past, mental and physical desire had been so intertwined as to be one. Now his mind burned with intoxicated desire, but his damned body couldn't perform. Though he felt a shadow of physical urgency, he was incapable of the joining he craved. He wanted to pummel the pillows with frustration.

He forced himself to draw away. After several slow, ragged breaths, he mastered himself enough to stretch out beside her. "I do hope you're right that when my blood is rebuilt, I'll be back to normal!" he said unsteadily.

She opened her eyes, looking a little dazed. "You will be. Considering how much blood you lost, you've improved a great deal."

She must be right, because when he thought back to the time of his injury, he hadn't found the efficient Miss Barton at all attractive. Such blindness on his part must have been a result of losing half his blood. As soon as he started healing, he began to recognize her mesmerizing sensuality. Now touching her was driving him half mad.

Part of her allure was her enchanting responsiveness. The way her uncertainty matched his own. The way her huge blue eyes regarded him as if he was the handsomest, most desirable man on earth instead of plain old Jack Langdon.

Just looking into those eyes made him even more frustrated, but complete fulfillment would have to wait. "You're *sure* I'll recover my normal capabilities?"

She laughed a little breathlessly. "Quite sure."

"Good, or I might run mad," he muttered. "Maybe I should eat nothing but beefsteak until I'm fully cured."

"Only a few more weeks," she said soothingly.

"That's too long." He looked down the lovely length of her. Despite the softness of her voice, her lips were moist and her eyes dark with desire.

In his schooldays he would be mad for the end of spring term so he could go home. Now he was mad for her, and the promise of her ripe mouth and voluptuous body. He used his thumb to tease the tip of her breast, and felt the instant hardening even through layers of night-clothes.

She gave a shivering sigh and her eyes closed again. "That feels . . . nice. Really, really nice."

It belatedly occurred to him that he might not be able to satisfy himself, but he could do more for her. Generous Abby, who asked nothing for herself.

He untied the bow at the throat of her robe and pulled the fabric back. Underneath the soft silk was a much more delicate gauze, halfway to being transparent. The neckline was too high to pull down without ripping fragile fabric, but that needn't stop him. He bent and kissed her nipple through the gauze. She arched against him with a gasp of delighted shock.

Pleased, he sucked harder and felt the instant reaction against his tongue. He could happily taste and explore her all day, a pleasant result of being less than fully functional. Normally he would be impatient to proceed to culmination. He made a mental note to develop more patience for the future, because he loved watching her response. He nuzzled her onto her back and transferred his attention to her other breast.

Her breath was coming in sharp gasps. What might she like next? He trailed his fingers down her side and leg, then tugged her hem upward so he could stroke the satin skin of her inner thighs. She moaned, shifting her legs restlessly.

He moved his hand higher yet, to the moist, hidden folds at the juncture of her thighs. She cried out, frantic with need, and her hips began thrusting against the rhythmic motion of his fingers. Suddenly her body convulsed into long shudders.

"Jack!" She clutched him as she dissolved with mingled pleasure and shock. She had known that she wanted him, but not realized how utterly primal and physical that wanting was. *This* was why she had watched Jack Langdon from the first time she saw him. Her body had known, even though her mind had dismissed any connection between them as impossible.

No wonder she had asked him to marry her in return for healing.

Her ethical wizard self would never coerce an injured man, and she had rationalized her request as a way of shocking him to attention. But ruthless female instinct had seized the chance to win the mate she had always desired. She should be ashamed of herself, except that she was far too exhilarated for shame.

Gradually his intimate strokes diminished until the last tremors faded from her body. Her face buried against his shoulder, she said unsteadily, "How . . . interesting."

He chuckled, sounding as satisfied as she. After brushing a kiss onto her temple, he settled down into the bed, holding her close. "Don't you dare think of leaving or braiding your hair or moving as much as an inch."

She laughed as she settled deeper into his embrace. "Even if I wanted to, I wouldn't have the strength."

She slid her knee between his and rested her head on his shoulder. Had she ever felt so peaceful? Not since she was a child.

Now she wanted him healthy so they could fully consummate their marriage. As wonderful as this intimacy was, surely joining as one flesh would be even more profound. Before falling asleep, she increased the energy flow from her to him. The sooner he was well, the better!

At peace with the world, he closed his eyes. All his aches were gone, and his fatigue was now the wholesome kind that came after a satisfying day's labor. He had felt her pleasure almost as intensely as he would have felt his own. His brief affairs of the past had been with women whose goal was to please him. He had never known what joy there was in pleasing a woman so thoroughly that she forgot everything but the triumph of her body. He definitely liked being married.

Once more he was flying, soaring above the English hills like a falcon. Arrowing toward Langdale Hall, which he had not seen in far too long. The home he loved, feared, and could ignore no longer.

The hall was a rambling manor rooted in the ancient stone of the York-shire Dales, its position commanding the fertile valley cut by the swift, nar-

row Lang River. As a boy, he had looked at his home and seen it shine with a pure, clear light that was centered in the ancient holy well.

Stonebridge had killed his ability to see the inner nature of people and places. Perhaps in this dream, he would see that light again.

Reaching the dale, he swooped down, excited to be back. But his delight changed to horror. The bright, vital light that had defined the estate was now ashy black. No longer was his home a place of life and growth, but a charnel house.

He told himself that this was only because he was dreaming and his vision was clouded by his fears. Langdale Hall couldn't have burned without his being informed. Whatever the trouble was, he could fix it.

He banked over the dale, riding the updrafts and looking for signs of life. Gradually he saw that walking shadows milked the cows and tended the sheep on the high slopes. The people of the dale were still there, it was only his anxiety that made them wraiths. Yet he could not shake off his doubts. Was he strong enough to do whatever must be done to lift the shadows from his home? He had never had the strength in the past.

As he soared above the vale, mapping out a campaign to retake his home, he gradually realized that he was not alone. Another being flew in tandem with him. He couldn't quite see his companion, but he sensed her presence— he knew it was a her—and was comforted.

He was no longer alone.

Chapter XIII

Abby awoke slowly, thinking she must have become tangled in her covers to be wrapped so tightly. Then awareness returned in a rush. She was in the arms of her new husband, and she had never been happier in her life.

In the pale dawn light, she examined Jack's face at close range, blushing as she remembered the night before. He was her husband, and she wanted him also as her lover, protector, and partner. She wanted to bear his children and soothe his worries and laugh with him. Most of all, she wanted to make him happy, for as they became closer, she was able to sense that under his easygoing manner he was deeply troubled.

Though she liked directness, she thought that it would be wiser to wait for him to talk to her rather than asking him outright. She would save directness for a last resort.

Ruefully she realized that she hadn't the foggiest notion of marriage etiquette. Should she get up quietly and return to her room to wash and dress? Kiss him awake? Go back to sleep herself?

Before she could decide, Jack opened his eyes, the hazel color almost golden in the morning light. "Good morning, lass." He kissed the tip of her nose. "Marriage suits me. I feel full of energy today."

He should—he was benefiting from his own inherent energy plus a good deal of hers. But she didn't mind sharing, not when she saw that affectionate light in his eyes. So far he wasn't regretting this marriage. She ran her hand down his powerful arm, delighted that she was allowed to touch him when she wanted to. "Is it time to get up and dress for breakfast? Or shall we roll over and go back to sleep since it's so early?"

"We're on our honeymoon, so rising virtuously with the dawn can wait." He chuckled, the vibration transmitted pleasantly from his rib cage to Abby. "I've spent most of my life getting up at dawn, first as a student and then as a soldier, but I've never learned to enjoy it. And that was even without a warm, touchable woman in my bed."

She blushed, feeling good about herself and him and marriage and the world. "Then by all means, let us linger."

As his hand slid to her breast, she gave a sigh of pleasure. How quickly one could become accustomed to physical intimacy!

After rising late and happy, Abby and her husband dressed separately but went downstairs together. Jack proved that traversing the steps on his backside worked as well going down as going up.

The morning was gray and a dusting of snow had fallen during the night, but the dining room was warm and welcoming. The food was so good that Abby wondered if the duke had lent his personal cook for the honeymooners.

As they finished their meal, Jack asked, "What are your plans for the house?"

"I've scarcely had time to think about it." Her gaze roamed the dining room, which was drab despite the cheery fire. "Brighter fabric and paint and wallpaper will make a huge difference. Many of the furniture pieces aren't bad, but they need refinishing and new upholstery. Do you know if the attic has any interesting old items?"

He grinned at her. "I haven't the remotest idea. Shall we explore there?"

"Perhaps when you no longer need the crutches," she said, thinking how steep most attic staircases were. "Today I'll start by exploring the lower floors. I've seen only a few of the rooms."

A footman entered the dining room. "Lady Frayne, a young person is here to see you. He says it's urgent."

Before Abby could say she would see him, the "young person" entered the dining room after the servant. She recognized Jimmy Hinton, from a farm family near Barton Grange. "Miss Abby, I'm sorry to bother you when you're just wed, but my pa is right poorly. Could you come see him now?"

Jimmy's father was the stoic sort, so if he was "right poorly," his condition must be grave. She rose, glad she'd finished her breakfast, sorry she couldn't stay with Jack. "I'll come right now. Jack, may we take your carriage to the Hinton household?"

"Of course. It's your carriage, too." Looking less than happy, he gestured to the footman to order the vehicle.

She wondered how long it would take before she thought of herself as Lady Frayne, mistress of Jack's household. "We didn't get a marriage settlement drawn up," she said aloud. "I completely forgot."

"So did I." Jack stood, using the chair frame to lever himself up. "We probably should have one for the sake of future offspring."

She blushed in a very bridelike way. "I'm sorry to leave you, but I should be gone for only a few hours."

"It will always be like this, won't it?" he said seriously. "Emergencies that you can't ignore."

She met his gaze. "I'm afraid so. I have a gift, and with that comes a responsibility to help others."

"Having benefited by your gifts, I shouldn't complain. But I wish you didn't have to rush off." He lifted himself onto the crutches that leaned against the table and circled round to give her a light kiss on the cheek. "Until later, lass."

Glad Jack accepted her need to see her patient even though he didn't like it, she left the dining room with Jimmy Hinton. Her husband would like it even less when she was called away in the middle of the night, but at least he accepted the general principle that she had obligations beyond her own household.

Her steps quickened. The sooner she helped Mr. Hinton, the sooner she could get back to Jack. And she was glad that he was sorry to see her leave.

Jack had another cup of tea. He hated that Abby was gone, but since she was, he would use this time to test himself. He rang for Morris to bring his coat and hat. The weather was damp and devilish cold and he didn't want to freeze outdoors.

As Morris helped him into the coat, the valet said, "Shall I accompany my lordship on his walk?"

Jack laughed. "Such formality! You think I'm going to get into trouble, don't you? Perhaps I should leave you here."

"I'm sure my lady would prefer I accompany you," the valet said, poker-faced.

"Good God, are you two already plotting against me?" Jack collected his crutches and headed to the door. Abby was right that putting his weight on the crosspieces was less painful. "When have you had the time to confer? She arrived only last night."

"Lady Frayne and I have not discussed the matter," Morris said repressively. "But I assume that she wishes me to look out for your welfare."

"In other words, you've just been handed another excuse to fuss like an old hen," Jack said. "Very well, come along. I want to visit Dancer."

Morris didn't dignify that with a reply. Though he'd grown up in a London slum, he could put on a haughty manner that would suit a duke.

Jack managed to descend the outside steps without incident. This time he used the crutches to go down standing upright rather than thumping along on his backside, which would be uncomfortable on the cold stone. But he was glad to have Morris standing watchful below, just in case.

Given the bite of the wind, he was also glad the walk to the stables was short. As soon as Jack entered, Dancer thrust his head from his stall and neighed a greeting. Jack propped the crutches against the wall so he could embrace the horse properly. "How are you feeling today, boy? Are you pining for a good gallop?"

He'd always got on with horses so well that he'd been accused of reading equine minds. Though he always laughed off such suggestions, he did have a knack for working with the beasts. Dancer seemed downright ecstatic to see him. "Did you fear the worst, old boy?" Jack murmured. "I almost got us both killed. We both owe our lives to a talented lady, so always treat her well."

He had the odd notion that Dancer understood and had agreed to obey Abby as he would Jack. Or maybe the horse already had a relationship with Abby because he'd been the beneficiary of one of her healing circles. Noting the leather brace on Dancer's leg, Jack said, "I suppose he's not ready to ride yet."

"Dancer's leg is healing well, but it will be some time before he is himself again," Morris said. "He seems unhurt by yesterday's journey from Barton Grange. The Barton groom walked him over, taking his time."

"Something else I owe the Bartons." Jack gave Dancer's ears a last scratch. "Very well, saddle Wesley. He's a better choice for getting back into the saddle."

"My lord! Surely you don't intend to ride today!" Morris said, horrified. "Quite aside from the risk to you, how can you control a horse when you have a broken leg?"

"Nothing wrong with my right thigh and knee, so I should be able to manage a placid old fellow like Wesley."

Morris looked stubborn, obviously calculating how far he could go in resisting a direct order. "Lady Frayne won't like it."

"Very likely not." Jack hardened his voice to command mode. "I appreciate your concern, but I will do this. Will you saddle Wesley or must I?"

If Morris were a horse, his ears would be flattened back. Before he could reply, Ransom's familiar voice said, "Don't worry, Morris. I'll do the saddling and accompany Frayne on his ride so you won't have his likely demise on your conscience."

Jack laughed as his friend ambled into the stables. "You're in a hurry to see me break my neck again."

"I covet Dancer," Ransom said. "Morris, will you bear witness that Frayne says I could have the horse if he kills himself riding?"

"Do you think I'd let a ham-handed clunch like you have Dancer?" Jack scoffed. "He goes to Ashby."

"You're a cruel man, Jack." Ransom effortlessly saddled Wesley, a calm chestnut with white socks. Though getting on in years, Wesley was still one of Jack's favorite mounts. "If I'm not to benefit by your demise, are you sure you want to do this?" Though his tone was light, his eyes were concerned as he led the horse from the stable.

"I'm sure." Jack followed on his crutches, wondering why he felt compelled to try to ride again so soon.

He recognized the answer when he moved to Wesley's side. For the first time in his life, he was afraid to get on a horse. The mere thought made him sweat as he remembered his disastrous accident. His helpless, uncontrolled fall. The crunch of bones, agony followed by cessation of feeling. . . .

Which meant that the sooner he got back on a horse, the better, for being afraid to ride would be another form of crippling. Steeling his face to blankness, he dropped the left crutch behind him and prepared to mount. Left foot into the stirrup while most of his weight was taken by his right crutch. Damn, this was tricky, especially with his strength so reduced. But with Morris holding Wesley steady, Jack was able to scramble gracelessly into the saddle. Ransom tucked his right foot into the stirrup.

While Dancer radiated eagerness, Wesley was pure calm. Jack had the strange but comforting notion that the chestnut sensed his fear and would take care of him.

"Are you ready, my lord?" Morris asked.

When Jack nodded, the valet released the reins. Jack's leg hurt—

a lot—but with his knees and weight, he was able to signal his mount out of the stable yard and onto a bridle trail that followed the ridge. Gradually his tension faded as the riding memories of a lifetime began to obliterate the horror of his lethal accident.

He urged Wesley forward in a smooth canter, following a trail that led along the the ridge between two fields. The wind was sharp, but as he relaxed, he began to enjoy the freedom he'd always found on horseback. Though Wesley wasn't as fast as Dancer, his gaits were as smooth as silk.

A stride behind him, Ransom called, "You look ready to go hunting."

Jack laughed. "Not yet, and when I do, I suspect I won't be such a neck-or-nothing rider as I used to be."

"Good to know that you're capable of learning from your errors!"

Grinning, Jack urged Wesley to go faster. To hell with his aching leg. The wind in his face was worth some pain.

Danger exploded between one heartbeat and the next when a bird burst from a clump of dried grass beside the trail. The gelding reared in a panic.

No! Unable to grip his mount's barrel with both legs, Jack lost his seat and pitched to the left, the right stirrup falling away because of his injured leg. For a dizzy moment the ice-hard ground tilted below him, waiting to smash his bones. He *knew* he would break his neck again, this time beyond repair.

Fear dissolved into a rush of energy that melded Jack and Wesley together as if they were one. *He was himself, but also the frantic horse, panicked, yet wanting to serve his master. He had four legs, was incoherent with fear, and was also a two-legged creature equally frightened. Master your fear. Steady, you're safe, don't worry.*

Before Jack could sort out the chaos in his mind, Wesley was suddenly solid beneath him again. Amazingly the horse had leaped sideways to catch his weight. Though still off balance, Jack was able to recover and maintain his seat.

Heart pounding, he reined in hard. *Where the hell had that come from?*

That mad rush of energy that had briefly made him one with his horse had enabled him to overcome Wesley's fear and persuade the beast to make the one move that would save Jack from falling. But what was the source of that wild power? It had been . . . almost like magic.

The thought that he might have controlled the horse with magic was more terrifying than his fear of falling. Damn it, he might have had a little magic once, but he was no wizard. Nor did he want to be.

"Jesus, Jack, what happened?" Ransom pounded up beside him and pulled his mount to a wild halt. "I've never seen a horse do anything like that!"

"Neither have I." Jack used his hand to slide his right foot back into the stirrup, unsure whether he or the horse was more upset. "Wesley must have recognized that I was in trouble and did something about it. Extra oats for you today, old boy."

"What startled him?"

"A partridge took off right under his nose. It was my fault for not paying enough attention." Even the steadiest of horses would startle at the unexpected. "If my leg was sound, I could have kept my balance and controlled Wesley, but I couldn't manage that today." And he'd nearly had another disaster.

"Speaking of your leg, did you injure it again?"

"It hurts like the devil," Jack admitted. "But I don't think the bone was damaged. I'm not made of glass, Ransom."

"I know." Ransom pulled his mount around, and they started back to the stables at a walk. "But it will be a long time before I get over the sight of watching you die."

Jack felt a stab of emotion so powerful that at first he didn't realize that it came not from him, but from Ransom. Jack's tough, controlled friend had been devastated when he thought Jack was dying.

Deeply unnerved to be feeling his friend's emotions, Jack drew a deep breath before speaking. "I'm sorry that my recklessness cost you so dearly."

Ransom shrugged, his face calmer than his emotions. "We're soldiers. Death is an accepted risk. We've both danced with it many times."

Yes, but it was one thing to die serving one's country. Quite another to die a meaningless death in the hunting field simply because Jack was pushing himself and his mount to the limit. An adult accepted that his actions had consequences not only for himself, but for his family and friends. Life was too precious to waste. By galloping his horse when he wasn't yet fully fit, he had once again risked a meaningless death. "I'll keep to a more sober pace until I'm fully healed."

He'd always been in tune with his horses and with his friends. What he'd just experienced was merely an extension of that, probably a result of his heightened sensitivity while recuperating. It wasn't magic. Nothing to worry about.

He fell into step beside his friend. "Let's not tell Abby."

Before Ransom could answer, they came in sight of the stables. The Frayne carriage was pulling up. Abby swung to the ground before the vehicle stopped moving. As her gaze went unerringly to Jack, Ransom murmured, "You're in trouble now."

Ransom was right: Abby's expression had the control of Wellington at his most coolly terrifying. But as the two men pulled up in front of her, she said only, "It would of course be foolish to suggest that you aren't ready to ride yet. I should have realized that you looked too innocent by half when I left."

He was glad her sense of humor had triumphed over her worry. "You'll be happy to know that today's ride has made me more careful than mere words could."

As he spoke, Ransom dismounted and tethered his horse, then moved to stand at Wesley's head, holding the chestnut's bridle. With his mount steadied, Jack used both hands to lift his throbbing right leg over the horse, then slid clumsily to the ground, grabbing the saddle to keep his balance. Given how he ached in every muscle, he was grateful not to end in an untidy pile on the cobbles.

"I'll see to the horses." Ransom handed over the crutches, which had been left leaning against the wall, then prudently withdrew into the stables with both mounts.

As Jack adjusted the crutches, Abby's gaze moved down him. Her expression changed as she looked at his right leg. "Should I reduce the pain?"

The prospect was tempting, but Jack shook his head. "No, I think it best that I suffer the consequences of my folly, as you had to endure your broken ankle when you failed to fly successfully."

She smiled and fell into step beside him as they headed toward the house. "Pain can be educational. Let me know if it becomes unendurable."

"Speaking of which, how is your Mr. Hinton? You weren't gone long."

"He was resting comfortably when I left. He has been a patient of mine for years, so I know how to treat him. An energy healing treatment and one of my herbal compounds relieved his lungs." She shook her head regretfully. "He'll make it through this winter, I think, but every winter grows more difficult for him."

"We all must live one day at a time." He glanced at her sideways. "Why don't you just go ahead and scold me? You'll feel better if you do."

She smiled a little, but shook her head. "I know I promised to curb my managing ways, but when I was leaving the Hintons, for an instant I felt that you were in grave danger. I told your coachman to spring the horses on the ride home. It was a great relief to see you safe and sound and riding at a sedate pace."

She had sensed that near disaster? Then he had better confess. "You are a most alarming wife. I was riding much too fast when a partridge frightened my horse. He reared and I almost fell. The incident made me appreciate that I should ride with great care until I'm fully fit."

"Horses can be amazingly clever. As a child, I had a fat little pony that saved me from many falls." Her eyes glinted mischievously. "If you have truly learned caution, I'll skip the scolding. Unless you really want one?"

He laughed, thinking that he was lucky to find a woman like this. Maybe breaking one's neck wasn't such a bad thing after all.

Chapter XIV

Once they were inside and warm, Abby studied her husband with narrowed eyes. His right leg raged with red energy.

Her scan confirmed what had happened outside. *She could see auras.* No longer did she have to concentrate to imagine the energy patterns. Now when she looked at Jack she saw a visible shimmer of color, elusive but definitely there.

And it wasn't just Jack's aura that she had seen. Ransom's had been predominantly a cool, clear yellow, very mental. Jack's was greener, with a tinge of gray from fatigue. Even the horses had radiated ever-shifting energy fields.

Seeing auras was an ability she'd desired but assumed she would never have. Still, it wasn't unknown for new abilities to surface. Possibly the intensive healing she had done on Jack had developed a latent talent. She hoped that it lasted. "You've had a tiring morning. Perhaps you should nap now."

Jack looked scandalized. "I can't go to bed in the middle of the day!"

Suppressing her amusement, she said, "Think of napping as an aid to healing faster rather than as evidence of weakness."

"That does sound better," he admitted. "Very well, but only a short one." He thumped over to the stairs and turned to sit. By the time he reached the top, Morris had appeared to take charge of him.

Abby guessed that Jack would sleep for several hours, so this would be a good time to explore the attics to see if there were any usable furnishings. After changing to her oldest morning gown, she wrapped a warm wool shawl around her shoulders, found a lantern, and headed upstairs. The stairs to the attics were wide, which was promising. Large furniture could have been carried up this way.

The Hill House attic was chaotic, but interestingly so. The lantern light revealed strange shapes, intriguing shadows, and evidence of vermin. Hoping it was too cold for rats or mice to be active, Abby decided to sharpen her intuition by using it to choose which trunks and barrels and boxes to explore.

Her intuition was in good working order despite the biting chill in the attic. The first trunk she opened contained attractive blue brocade draperies. They needed cleaning, but were usable. Very likely they were cut to fit existing windows.

Intuition's next choice was a long, heavy roll of canvas secured by several tied cords. She felt the buzz of a minor spell when she untied the cords. The spell had been cast to repel moths, and it had successfully preserved half a dozen handsome oriental carpets. All they needed was a beating to remove dust.

As another test of intuition, she opened a trunk that didn't call to her, and found only clothing so badly worn that servants would disdain it.

She happily worked her way across the first attic room to the opposite door, finding more draperies and some linens as well. The door opened to a larger room stacked with furniture, pieces jumbled on top of each other with such profusion that it was hard to see shapes and condition.

She hung the lamp on a nail protruding from a rough-hewn post and shifted a tangle of wooden Windsor chairs from a long sofa. The sofa's upholstery was a disaster—generations of mice had lived long and happy lives in one end—but the lines were good and the frame was sound. After cleaning and reupholstering, it would be fine enough for the drawing room.

The bentwood Windsor chairs she'd taken off the top were also usable. The wood was somewhat battered, but the scratches would largely disappear when the wood was oiled. She dusted one off and tested it. It was as comfortable as a good Windsor chair was supposed to be. The set would do for the breakfast parlor, whose present chairs were mismatched and uncomfortable.

Pleased, Abby probed deeper into the piles. Some of the furniture was in such dire condition that it was fit only for firewood, but most of the pieces were quite decent and some were excellent.

She was shifting the lantern to another post when she heard a ghostly scraping noise in the distance. She halted as shivers ran up her spine. The sounds were—inhuman. Like some great, shuffling beast looking for prey.

The scraping sounds stopped and were replaced by a muttered curse, then tapping. Jack's crutches.

Amused by how quickly superstition reared its head in a dark attic, she lifted the lantern and went to meet him. "I'm glad it's you, not a ghost, but I thought you'd sworn off risky behavior?"

His smile was roguishly handsome in the lantern light. "Climbing steps on my rump is undignified, but the only risk is Morris's reaction when he sees the effect on my trousers." He surveyed his surroundings with interest. "I've never been up here before. Have you found anything worthwhile?"

"There are some very nice pieces of furniture and good draperies. Old, but good quality. I suspect that the previous owners disliked older furniture and moved everything up here when they took residence. We shall benefit from that. Look at this lovely walnut chest." She skimmed the silky wood with her fingertips, wondering how anyone could have buried such beauty in an attic. "It's probably from Stuart times, and good for several centuries more of use."

"Very handsome. It would look good in the front hall, don't you think?" Jack picked his way across the room to examine a barrel with spindly objects sticking out the top. "A collection of canes. I wonder if any would suit me?" He set his right crutch aside and pulled out the longest cane to test the height. "Am I ready to graduate from crutches to a stick?"

Thinking this was a good opportunity to show she wasn't always managing, she said, "You are the best judge of that, I think."

Jack set the other crutch aside and took a step with the cane. Wincing, he said, "My right leg can't take so much weight yet, but this stick is a good length." He retrieved his crutches.

"I'll have the cane cleaned so it will be ready when you are." She knelt to investigate several paintings stacked against the wall. Jack came to look over her shoulder. All were landscapes or hunting scenes. "Not great art, but pleasant," she said, very aware of his warmth at her back. "What do you think?"

"They'll fill up the empty spaces nicely. I like landscapes much better than grim portraits of grim ancestors."

The vehemence in his voice suggested that his family seat in Yorkshire had its share of such portraits. She stood, careful not to brush against him and perhaps disturb his balance. "Over here, we have a very nice clothespress, plus a set of chairs that will do in the breakfast room. There are some good tables as well."

"This attic is a treasure trove," Jack agreed. "What's that against the wall?"

"I haven't looked at that yet." Abby squeezed between the clothespress and a trestle table stacked with boxes, then announced, "It's a bedstead, from the same period as that chest, I think. They might have been parts of a set." She stroked a carved post taller than she was. "Who cares about fashion when something is beautiful?"

"It's large, too. Perhaps the man who ordered it was extra tall." Again Jack moved next to Abby. "Large enough for both of us to be comfortable."

Their gazes met, and the intimacy in his eyes made Abby blush when she thought of sharing that bed. That warmth made her forget the biting chill of the attic. She was tempted to raise her face and kiss him, but being dressed and upright made her shyer than she had been the night before in his bed. A little breathlessly, she said, "I . . . I'll order new bedding for it."

From the mischief in Jack's eyes, it was obvious he knew exactly what she was thinking and was considering a kiss of his own. After a pulse-racing moment, he moved away. "What needs to be done besides moving the decent furniture downstairs?"

Wondering if he had been deliberately teasing her, she replied, "A few pieces will need a carpenter to make repairs, but in most cases, the wood just needs to be cleaned and oiled. The upholstered pieces will require more work. More draperies will be needed, too. If we're going to London, we can visit some of the fabric warehouses." She surveyed the sofa and chairs, estimating how much fabric would be needed. "What colors do you love or hate? How do you wish Hill House to look?"

"I want it to be friendly. Welcoming. Not too formal. This is a hunting box, not a ducal mansion." He lowered himself onto the sofa, avoiding the mouse-nibbled section. "Barton Grange is very welcoming. I'd like Hill House to be its equal."

"I'd like that too." She gestured at the still-unexplored piles and corners around them. "This fine old furniture will give the feeling that the house has been a much-loved family home for generations."

"I'd like that," he said softly. "Langdale Hall is . . . not so friendly."

She was tempted to ask more, but didn't want to interrupt the playful mood. "How do you feel about battered Greek statues? There's one over here, probably stolen from a temple somewhere."

As she moved past Jack, she tripped on his crutches, which were invisible in the shadows. As she tried to catch her balance, his strong hands caught her in midair. "Careful! We can't have you broken, too."

She caught her breath as he pulled her to safety in his lap. His very, very comfortable lap. Hoping she would get her kiss, she asked, "Am I crushing your leg?"

"Since I broke the lower part, not the upper, you're not causing any damage." His arms tightened around her waist. "Don't try to leave. I like holding you."

When he touched his lips to hers, Abby responded with enthusiasm. She loved the warmth of his lips, the touch of his tongue to hers, his provocative, exploring hands, the surge of heat where their bodies pressed together.

Her eyes drifted shut as she let delight take her. Gradually she noticed that the physical pleasure of their embrace was accompanied by colors that pulsed through her body and mind. It was their energies swirling and blending together, she realized, bright red and tender pink and the delicate green of growth. "I see colors dancing around us," she said dreamily. "Passion and happiness and awakening."

His hands stilled and he ended the kiss with a frown. "I see colors, too. That's never happened before."

"Magic," she whispered. "A rainbow of passion as we come together."

"The colors come from you, not me," he said brusquely. "I'm no wizard."

"You don't have the training, but you do have the power," she pointed out. "That's why you were sent to Stonebridge Academy."

Jack's whole body stiffened. "As a boy I was too interested in magic, but I had no power myself."

"Of course you do," she said, startled that he would deny it. "I forgot to tell you, but I drew on your magic when we did the healing circle. You contributed the last, vital amount of energy. Without that, we wouldn't have had enough power to save you."

"No!" The revulsion on Jack's face spoke even more strongly than his words.

Feeling as if she'd been struck, Abby scrambled from his lap. "I knew you were uncomfortable with magic. Stonebridge saw to that. But I thought you were beginning to accept it better." Her voice became edged. "After all, you married a wizard."

His mouth tightened. "You saved my life, and I had given my word."

"I released you from that promise. Did you marry me only from your misguided sense of honor?" she asked, wondering how they had so quickly slipped from passion into their first argument.

"No." There was a long pause. "I like and respect you. But it's easiest when I don't think about your abilities."

She bit her lip. She had thought that he understood and was becoming more accepting. Obviously not.

The real problem wasn't her, she realized, but him. The suggestion that he had magic was what had made his hackles stand on end. She wondered how bad the beatings had been at Stonebridge Academy. Perhaps he'd been beaten even earlier, when he was a little boy experimenting with his first stirrings of power.

Very gently she touched his mind. It was a violation of magical ethics to probe without permission, but no probing was required. The merest touch showed the emotional scars he'd acquired when his parents didn't accept him for what he was.

Knowing that allowed her to put aside her own hurt. Voice calm, she said, "It's going to be difficult to forget about my magic. You were there this morning when I was called away to do healing. That won't change. I have been given a gift from God, and it would be wrong not to use it to help where I can. We could not stay together if you tried to forbid me from doing my work."

He shifted uncomfortably. "I wouldn't ask you to stop. I, more than anyone, understand the value of what you do. But I'd rather think that your help is like what my mother did—carrying baskets of food and jellies to ailing tenants."

"I don't think of you as a man who wishes to hide from the truth."

"In most things, I don't." He hauled himself up on his crutches, his expression forbidding. "Shall we finish exploring this room? I think I see a rather nice desk in that corner, under a pile of old cushions."

Silently she lifted the lantern and they moved to investigate the corner. It was indeed a nice desk, despite the desiccated form of a long-dead bird that lay on top. Cleaned up, the desk would be suitable for one of the bedrooms.

It was easier to fix furniture than husbands.

She spent the rest of the day supervising the larger male servants as they brought furniture down the steep steps and into the unused bedrooms. With the assistance of two maids, Abby started cleaning the pieces. By dinnertime, the handsome Stuart chest was sitting in the front hall with a bust of Plato on top. She set an old tricorne hat on Plato's marble brow. Jack was much amused.

But when she came to his room that night, hoping for another sensual night, his long body was turned away from her and he was asleep.

Or pretending to be.

Chapter XV

Abby was hanging tapestries in the front hall when Judith swept in, wearing a shabby riding habit, a hat whose feather had seen better days, and a radiant expression that made the age of her clothing irrelevant. "Abby, hello! I was all prepared to be formal and ask a footman to announce my presence to Lady Frayne. I should have realized that you would resist formality like a duck sheds rain."

Abby laughed as she stepped down from the wooden stepladder. "Welcome! What do you think of the hall?"

Her friend's gaze moved over the tapestries, the Stuart era chest, the sturdy oak settle, and the richly patterned, if slightly worn, oriental carpet. "I can't believe this is the same place where the wedding breakfast was held a mere week ago! Have you developed a magical gift for conjuring up furnishings?"

"The attics were a treasure trove of old carpets, furniture, draperies, paintings, and even these tapestries, which aren't old but are very pretty," Abby explained as she gestured around her. Though the house would benefit by new paint and paper, it looked much better than it had the week before. "I've been spending Jack's money lavishly to hire people for fixing the house. At this season there isn't a lot of work, so there was no shortage of workers to scrub and polish and wax. Some of the bedrooms haven't been touched, but the rooms where we spend most of our time are much improved."

"I'd love to see what you've done, but later." Judith was almost bouncing on the tips of her riding boots. "You must have been the one who told Lord Frayne I would love to have my own cottage. It's so incredibly generous of him! As soon as I received the letter, I thought of what might be the perfect place. Will you come look at it with me?"

So Jack was doing as he'd promised. He hadn't mentioned that to his wife. Abby hesitated. "I've so much to do here."

"And you're still on your honeymoon," Judith agreed. "I know it's dreadfully bad of me to ask, but it's such a pretty, warm day, almost like spring. And I would like to get your opinion."

Abby looked at the sunshine and succumbed to temptation. "Give me a few minutes to change into riding clothes. Jack is out riding, and I should be, too."

"He's on horseback already? He heals quickly." Judith's gaze narrowed as she studied Abby, obviously seeing that there was still an energy flow from her to her husband. Though she frowned, she said nothing.

"He's determined to regain his strength as quickly as possible," Abby said as an oblique explanation. "Have a seat in the drawing room, and I'll be with you soon."

She climbed the stairs with unladylike speed, suddenly eager for fresh air and sunshine and the company of a friend. A two-legged friend, that was. Her father had brought Cleocatra across the valley to live with her. A connoisseur of comfort, Cleo was snoozing on Abby's bed. Abby gave the cat a quick scratch, then changed into her riding habit, which was almost as worn as Judith's. Though she could have afforded better, it never seemed worthwhile to dress up for the cows and crows.

Within fifteen minutes, the two women were trotting across the valley. Abby inhaled deeply. "Thank you for luring me out. I've been so busy with the house that I've neglected everything else. Now tell me about the cottage!"

"You've been by Rose Cottage many times, but it's behind hedges and trees so you might not have really noticed. It's just outside the village. The Harrises raised eight healthy children there, which seems a good omen. Mr. Harris added a wing because of all those children, so there's space for me to keep patients who need extra care."

"Sounds just right!" Unable to resist the sunny day, Abby urged her mount into a canter. "Did Mrs. Harris die? I hadn't heard that."

Judith increased her pony's gait to match Abby. "She's still alive but hasn't been well. Her oldest son moved her in with his family. The cottage has been empty for months, and they've decided to sell."

"The location is good and you need more space. I hope Rose Cottage doesn't have the rising damp your present cottage does!"

"No damp." Judith's eyes were glowing. "Abby, it's perfect! To own my own house and not have to worry about paying the rent—it's more than I dreamed of."

Abby knew her friend hadn't been raised with rising damp, or to worry about paying her bills. She had paid a high price for the right to use her magic. Her gift for midwifery made the Melton Mowbray area one of the safest places to bear children in Britain, but it wasn't a calling that always paid well. "Will repairs be required?"

They reached a fork in the road and Judith swung her solid little pony to the right. "Only whitewashing and clearing the garden, which has run wild since Mrs. Harris's health failed. Lord Frayne said he would cover the cost of necessary improvements, so I'll be able to do what's needed."

Jack was generous with his money. That didn't surprise Abby. It was his emotions that he was wary of expending.

Rose Cottage was everything Judith had said. Most of the furnishings had been left in place and the rooms had been cleaned so that the house was welcoming. As they explored the ground floor, Abby said,

"These southern windows let in wonderful light. It will be a happy house. The rooms are also well laid out. You can put an entrance in the new wing for patients, and have your privacy in the older part of the cottage."

"That's a good idea." Their explorations brought them back to the kitchen. Judith lit the coals that waited on the hearth. "Shall I make tea? I brought some with me, and Mrs. Harris's kettle and teapot are still here."

"That will be nice." Abby settled into one of the plain wooden chairs. "We can drink to your new home. That is, if there isn't another buyer interested?"

Judith shook her head. "No, I've spoken with her son. The cottage is worth more than most people around here can afford, so I'm the only one seriously interested. We've agreed on a fair price if I decide to go ahead, and it's within the range Lord Frayne allowed. I was sure this was the right house, but I wanted someone else to see it and tell me I was right."

Abby laughed. "I'm happy to perform my part in the process. It's the perfect place for you, Judith. The energy is wonderful."

Judith took the chair on the opposite side of the scrubbed deal table. "Now that we've taken care of my new cottage, how about you? Are you enjoying more of marriage than merely refurbishing Hill House?" Her eyes were twinkling.

Abby blushed. "Jack lost a great deal of blood."

She didn't need to say more since Judith was also a healer. "No wonder he's keen on recovering as quickly as possible," her friend said mischievously. "Are you comfortable with each other? You seemed on good terms at the wedding and after."

Glad to have someone to confide in, Abby said, "We got on well at first, until he showed some signs of magical ability. He found the idea so upsetting that he has withdrawn. He's perfectly polite, but distant. I knew that he wasn't fond of wizardry, but I didn't expect his feelings to run so deep. The thought that he might have power of his own repels him."

Judith frowned. "Have you done a little gentle mental exploring? As his wife, you have the right to do so if there is cause."

"He has an anti-magic charm branded into his shoulder. For the healing, he gave me permission to treat him. He didn't rescind that until he started to see energy patterns last week. Now he's like a brick wall." Except for the energy she sent him. That went through his barriers with no trouble.

"Do you want me to take a look at this?" Judith asked.

Abby nodded gratefully. "Please. I haven't the clarity to do it myself."

Judith closed her eyes and her expression smoothed out as she mentally explored the energy around Jack and Abby. When the water in the kettle began to boil, Abby quietly made the tea, not wanting to disturb her friend.

Judith's eyes opened. "I can't get too close because of the anti-magic spell, but I sense a kind of stony knot in the midst of what is generally an open personality. Is it possible that someone spelled him to make him hate the thought of magic? Hatred beyond what most men of his class feel, I mean."

Abby frowned. "I hadn't thought of that. You may be right. He's so easygoing in most ways. He even seemed to be coming to terms with my magic. But he's almost like another person when the subject of his own potential for magic comes up. Now that you mention it, the difference from his usual personality seems unnatural. Do you think the spell was cast on him when he was at school? It would explain why Stonebridge Academy is so successful at purging their students of a desire to work magic."

"One wonders if the parents would approve of magic being used on their sons when the idea is to turn the lads away from such wickedness," Judith said tartly.

"Great lords don't mind hiring wizards when there are benefits," Abby pointed out. "The way they hire tailors and stewards and laborers."

The two of them shared an ironic glance. Even the most disdainful of aristocrats was willing to use wizards when they wanted magical results. That didn't mean they'd allow wizards into their drawing rooms. "The school might have bespelled him," Abby said. "Or his family might have had it done. I wish I could look more closely, but unless he grants me permission, it will be difficult. I don't want to use brute force to blast my way through the anti-magic spell."

"It wouldn't incline him to trust you," Judith agreed. "Give it some time. If his innate power is stirring, he'll start changing on his own. And he'll need you there if his power comes in a rush."

Abby suppressed a sigh. No one had said this marriage would be easy. She sipped her tea and reminded herself that it was early days yet. She would make no major assaults on her husband's mind and spirit.

But that didn't mean she couldn't use an old-fashioned nonmagical approach. It was time to nag him.

Jack stepped into his front hall and looked around with pleasure. Every day the house looked better, and now he thought the hall was complete. Though Abby had shown him the tapestries she'd found upstairs, he hadn't realized what a warm glow of color they would bring to a room that had been too large and drafty for comfort. Now the hall offered the welcome he had always wanted to find in Hill House. Abby had talents beyond healing.

He swung into the room on his crutches, tired from his long ride but no longer aching in every muscle. Each day he became stronger. All that was required was pushing himself just short of the point where he would drop.

Halfway across the room, he changed course. Perhaps it was time to switch from crutches to a cane.

In the corner of the hall, a tall ceramic urn from Greece held the collection of canes they'd found in the attic. He stuffed his crutches into the urn and pulled out the cane that had caught his attention the week before. Holding it in his right hand, he took a cautious step. Though his leg ached, it wasn't the acute pain that had made him fear snapping the unhealed bones. Now, he guessed, the bones were almost whole again.

Still, his right leg wasn't quite ready for this much strain. He pulled a second long cane from the urn and tried walking with one in each hand. He was pleased to find that using the canes together gave him support he needed, while making him feel more agile and less disabled. Another piece of progress!

He took a last look around the hall. His wife had created the warmest home he'd ever known, and he was doing his best to avoid her. Staying busy or asleep, or inviting friends for dinner every night, couldn't keep them apart forever. Sooner or later, he would have to come to terms with her and the magic that had invaded his life.

Let it be later.

As she did each night, Abby quietly opened the connecting door to Jack's room to say good night. A lantern turned low cast a dim light over the bed where he drew deep, regular breaths. Was he asleep? She had her doubts.

She crossed to the bed and bent to kiss his cheek. His taut skin shivered slightly, but his eyes didn't open. She had a sudden powerful desire to drag her cowardly husband from the bed and dump him on the drafty floor. But that might damage him.

After a moment's thought, she smiled wickedly and slid her hand under the covers to tickle the sole of his left foot, with her cold, cold fingers.

Chapter XVI

Jack swore and almost jumped out of his skin when icy fingers tickled the arch of his left foot. So much for pretending he was asleep.

He pushed himself up in the bed, wondering if he was up to a serious conversation with his wife. Probably not, but he didn't know when it would be any easier. "Your hands are cold."

"That's not surprising in early February." She wrapped her robe tightly around her lushly curved figure and perched on the end of the bed. The faint light revealed her expression as calm but implacable. "Are we going to spend the rest of our lives avoiding each other? If so, the sooner we move to separate residences the better. You're ready for London, I think. Go without me. I'd much rather stay here than go to town with a husband who won't talk about anything more personal than furniture."

The prospect of going up to town alone presented one small, cowardly instant of relief. Life would be much simpler if he didn't have to explain a wizardly wife.

But much greater were his regret and shame. He liked having Abby nearby, even though he'd been keeping his distance.

And in the midst of a serious discussion, he was having trouble not thinking about the night they had shared in this bed, and how warm and sensually responsive she had been. If he leaned forward . . .

Focus. He needed to overcome his cowardice and talk to his wife. "I don't want to go to London by myself. I want to go with you." He grimaced. "I've been behaving badly. The problem isn't you, it's me."

"Of course it's you," she said, unimpressed by his willingness to take the blame. "We were getting on rather well, I thought, until you kissed me and sensed the energy flow around us. You have magic, but the merest suggestion of that sent you running like a fox fleeing a pack of hounds. I don't know how long you can hide from this side of your nature, but not much longer, I suspect."

"No!" *You have magic.* Just hearing the words made his stomach knot. "I'm no wizard. Once I had some interest in such matters, as boys do. Perhaps I even have a little power, since you claim to have used it during the healing. But I lost all interest in magic at school. I want nothing to do with it."

"Lost interest or were bespelled?" Her expression was grave and perhaps pitying. "Your reaction to the thought of having power is so fierce, so different from your usual temperament, that I have to wonder if a spell was cast to make you hate your magical nature. Did Stonebridge cast such spells to ensure that its students would walk the path their parents chose for them?" She paused for emphasis. "If so, do you want to live your life controlled by what others wanted for you?"

Panic washed through him, flooding his common sense. Panic so great that underneath, the small part of him that was still rational wondered at its intensity. Abby had said nothing that should frighten him—unless she was right and someone had tied knots in his mind.

He managed to choke out, "You're only guessing that someone put a spell on me. You can't know for sure. I bear the strongest anti-magic spell known on my own flesh."

Abby's dark brows arched. "There is no spell strong enough to block a wizard of my strength for long if I truly wanted to break through, but I have not done so. It would be very bad manners."

And a betrayal so great as to end any chance they might have had at a real marriage. Thank God she was wise enough to know this, or their marriage was already doomed.

But he wanted a real marriage, and despite his fear, he wondered if she might be right about the spell. "If I were to grant you permission to explore my mind, how do I know that you won't plant a spell of your own?"

Her full lips tightened. "You would have to trust me. I suppose that is asking too much, given that we are still more strangers than not. But there is another way. You can explore your own mind. Now that I've told you that you might be the victim of a suppression spell, you might be able to find it on your own."

He frowned. Though he would rather not have his mind invaded, he doubted that he would find anything there that he hadn't noticed for the last twenty years. "Even if I could find evidence of a suppression spell, what could I do about it?"

"It is an offense against nature for a spell to block a person's deepest self," she said slowly. "Even the most powerful wizard has trouble creating a suppression spell that can last indefinitely. I doubt you could have been controlled in that way if you hadn't been a boy when the spell was laid on you. You grew up not realizing that a vital aspect of your spirit had been suppressed. Now you are a man. If you look inward and find such an unnatural barrier, you might be able to break it down. Or if you give me permission, I could help you do so."

He did trust Abby, he realized. More than he trusted Colonel Stark, who had wielded discipline at the Stonebridge Academy with such unholy satisfaction. But . . . "I don't want someone else poking around inside my mind. Even you."

"I understand." Her voice was gentle. "Are you sufficiently offended by what was done to you that you will look for yourself?"

Even the thought of probing his mind for alien magic caused another spike of panic. Which meant, he realized, that he had no choice but to look inward, no matter how painful the process. "More than sufficiently offended. But how does one study one's own mind?"

"Imagine some kind of scene," she replied. "Perhaps a place you know and find comfortable. A meadow, a familiar house, perhaps how you imagine life would be if you were a fish under the sea."

"A fish?" he asked, temporarily sidetracked.

She smiled. "What you choose is only a metaphor. Move through the scene in your imagination, and if something feels wrong, look closer."

That seemed simple enough. What to imagine?

For some reason, his thoughts went to a beech wood on the estate of a friend he'd visited several times in the Cotswold. Beeches didn't grow in Yorkshire, and he had been fascinated by the dense canopy of leaves that blocked most sunlight. Because of the deep shade, few plants grew and the floor beneath the beeches was layered with a thick, yielding carpet of fallen leaves.

The peace and mystery of the beech wood had made a lasting impression. Sometimes he'd dreamed of it in Spain, on the eve of battle. Closing his eyes, he imagined himself among the massive trees. All was as he remembered, at first. If the beech wood represented his mind, he was comfortable in it. And he walked without pain, without crutches or canes.

Then he felt a tug of wrongness. Frowning, he followed the feeling. The majestic trees gave way to crooked saplings that were jammed together unhealthily. The trunks were as close as fence railings—as if they had been designed to conceal.

Wondering if a spell might be hidden in this dark corner of his beech wood, he forced his way between the crooked saplings, shouldering trunks aside by sheer force when necessary. He would not have been able to make his way through real trees, but his imaginary world had the qualities of a dream even though he was awake.

The farther he penetrated into the rank, unhealthy woods, the colder the air, the harder it was to breathe, and the greater his fear. By now it was clear that Abby was right. The fear was artificial, created by something outside himself. That didn't mean that he didn't feel looming terror, but he refused to let himself be affected by it.

Impatient at his lack of progress, he swung his arm and knocked all the trees in front of him to one side. They fell with splintering crashes to reveal a pair of iron doors set into a steep hillside. The doors were circular, as if concealing the mouth of a cave. He recognized deep wrongness. With sudden fierce certainty, he knew that this portal was the source of the blind panic that throbbed through him like a mortal injury, urging him to flee for the sake of his sanity.

Clenching his teeth against the panic, he studied the pattern embossed on the doors. The design was elusive, an ever-shifting matrix of shadows and sinuous lines, mysterious and seductive.

Dizzily he recognized that the pattern was sucking him down like a whirlpool. As he fell into the design, he sensed horrors waiting on the other side of the door.

Swearing, he shook his head and looked away, knowing that if he continued to look into the pattern he would lose all will and determination.

Abby. The mere thought of her steadied him. As the vertigo faded, he realized that if he'd ever accidentally found these doors, that sorcerous pattern would have pulled him down into paralysis. Perhaps he had been here over and over, and each time the memories had been wiped from his mind.

But this time he had been warned, and he would not lose himself to a wizard's spell. Not here, not in the middle of his own soul.

Eyes averted, he reached out and flattened his left palm on the iron door. The jangling energy was deeply unpleasant, but he forced himself to maintain the contact while he analyzed what messages the door held.

This door—this spell—had been cast at Stonebridge, he realized, and by none other than Colonel Stark himself, with the assistance of his second in command. The old devil had set up a school to suppress wizardry while being a wizard himself!

Deep in the metal, he felt an echo of the colonel's torment. Magically gifted, the man had grown up loathing himself. Ironically, the one way he had been free to use his magic was as a tool to cripple the power of the young boys placed in his care.

Jack could almost feel sorry for him. Almost, but not quite.

Are you sufficiently offended? Abby had sent him into the darkness of his own mind to seek wrongness, and he had found it. Was she also right that he might be able to destroy the spell himself because his magical nature yearned to be free? What would be strong enough to break down these iron doors?

Anger. Deliberately he reached deep into himself to find rage.

He had learned early to let go of anger because it did him no good, but now he collected all the suppressed furies of his life. He harvested the baffled misery of the times his father beat him for no reason. The rage engraved on his soul by the cold menace of Stonebridge Academy, and the torments inflicted by the most twisted of the prefects. The anguish of a small boy being punished unjustly, and his towering rage when he'd cursed God for allowing good men to die meaninglessly.

When he had gathered his life's burden of fury and outrage, he laid both hands on the doors and let his emotions blaze through his palms like Greek fire. The doors exploded, white-hot shards flying in all directions.

He barely noticed the shattered fragments of the spell because they were trivial compared to the energy that blasted loose from the bonds that had trapped it so long. He staggered back under the cascading power, feeling as if his skin was being seared away.

His left shoulder burned like the fires of Hades, worse than the time a musket ball went through his upper arm. He clawed at the pain frantically, yet pain was matched by wild exultation. A hole in his soul he hadn't known existed was being filled.

He felt as if he were too close to an exploding shell. He was in the heart of a whirlwind, tumbling frighteningly free, uncertain where he would land. Or how hard he would hit.

Ka-bang! He smashed into a hard surface with an impact that jarred his bones. Dizzily he wondered if the fall was real or in his mind.

"Jack!" a voice called. *"Jack!"*

Abby's voice. He blinked his eyes open, and found himself flat on his back on the cold floor. His wife knelt beside him, her expression shaken. "Abby?"

"Are you all right?" She began to skim her hands several inches above his body. "I felt your energy shift. Then you began flailing about and fell off the bed. I'm so sorry I didn't catch you!"

"Even you can't catch me all the time." He pushed himself to a sitting position with one hand, grateful that Abby had laid a carpet beside the bed. Its thickness had cushioned the impact a bit. "I'm all right, I think. Bruised but not broken."

"Dare I ask what happened?" Abby asked.

He ran tense fingers through his hair. "I found a closed door that felt wrong, and blasted it open. The spell was cast by Colonel Stark, the headmaster of Stonebridge Academy." He recalled what else he had detected in the doors. "My father requested the suppression spell. I don't believe it was routinely applied to all students."

"Your father had a particular hatred of wizardry? More than the usual lord?"

"He thoroughly loathed magic, especially in his son and heir. My mother was not so adamant, though she followed his lead." He realized that those two sentences were the most he'd told Abby about his parents. He really must give her a better idea of the kind of family she had married into. *Later.*

Abby got to her feet. "Can you stand with my help? If not, I'll ring for Morris."

"No need to get him up. Give me your hand."

She stood and extended both hands. With her help he managed to haul himself to his feet without discovering any new injuries in the process. Since he was shaking, he immediately sat on the edge of the bed before he could fall again. His right leg ached, but not much considering his fall.

When he rubbed at his throbbing left shoulder, she asked, "Did you hit your shoulder when you fell? It might have dislocated."

Once, Jack had dislocated his shoulder riding, and the pain had been different from this. He pulled back the neck of his nightshirt and stared in shock at bare, unbroken skin. Though the shoulder was red from his rubbing, there was no sign of damage.

"Your anti-magic spell is gone!" Abby touched his skin with cool fingers. "The scars must have been healed when you released all your suppressed magic."

"That's possible?" He rubbed at the unblemished skin incredulously. "I suppose this is the proof, but I had no idea that magic could remove scars."

Abby frowned. "Neither did I. Perhaps the brand had to be removed in order to free your magic. Did your headmaster brand you?"

Jack shook his head, remembering the drunken night when he had received the brand. "I did it to myself. One of my friends smuggled in some brandy, and we got drunk and irrational as only the very young can. In the heat of the moment, I took a friend's iron charm and heated it in the fire till it glowed red hot. Then I rammed it against my shoulder." He'd used heavy leather gloves and tongs. The serpent symbol had hurt as much going on as it did when it burned off. He hadn't been the only one to brand himself that night, either.

Abby looked aghast. "You really did that to yourself?"

Jack straightened his nightshirt over his now-uninteresting shoulder. "It seemed like a good idea at the time. I think that must have been after Colonel Stark cast his spell on me. I wouldn't have hated magic enough to do something so dramatic earlier."

"You can create your own shields now. You don't need a serpent burned into your body."

She was right. In a matter of minutes, his whole world had changed. Energy swirled around him, buffeting his inner senses. But the chaos was less than at first, and he presumed that eventually it would settle down.

When he looked at Abby, he saw her familiar figure, but by looking in a different way that he couldn't describe, he saw a transparent glow superimposed over her. The same kind of vision revealed a small swirl of light around her cat, Cleo, who sat with her tail neatly wrapped around her paws by the door to Abby's bedroom. "I feel as though I'm trapped inside a butter churn. I presume that you don't feel that way all the time?"

She shook her head. "You're sparkling like a fireworks display, but that's only because your natural power was suppressed for so long. This will pass. Apart from being churned, how do you feel?"

"Rather well," he said, surprised. "Very well, in fact, though the first blast when I took the spell down was . . . uncomfortable."

He fell silent. Abby quietly waited, saying nothing. Finally, reluctantly, he said, "You were right that my fear of and distaste for magic was part of the suppression spell. I no longer fear what is part of me, but neither do I want it. Must I use this unwelcome gift?"

"Not if you don't want to." Abby resumed her perch at the foot of the bed. "But at the very least, you should learn to shield yourself. You should also learn how to control your power so you don't accidentally cause trouble with it. I can teach you basic techniques of control if you don't know them. Are you familiar with how to visualize a shield of white light?"

He nodded. "I learned the basic magical techniques before I was sent to Stonebridge. I'll start using them again." He concentrated on surrounding himself with white light, and was surprised at how easily the shield formed. He thought back to the days when his boyish self had ridden into the dales to learn about his talents. Those had been some of the most exciting times of his childhood.

But even with the suppression spell gone, he didn't want to use magic other than for protection. The idea of becoming a practicing wizard was disturbing. He carefully packed his magical abilities away in white light. He'd leave that sort of thing to Abby.

The local vicar, Mr. Willard, had been Jack's tutor in Latin and Greek and the other subjects he would need to know when he went away to school. During visits to the vicarage, Jack has secretly borrowed Mr. Willard's books on magic. In fact, one such book had taught him shielding and control.

Looking back, he guessed that the vicar had known of Jack's borrowings, but had said nothing. Not only was Mr. Willard a kind man, but he had magic of his own, especially the deep empathy that was so useful to clergymen.

He wondered if Mr. Willard was still vicar of the Langdale parish in Yorkshire. He'd find out soon enough. But for now, he was weary to the bone.

He studied Abby's face and saw an exhaustion equal to his. Intuitively he guessed that she had followed him on his mind-bending journey, waiting to catch him if he'd shattered. His generous wife, a quiet hero to match any he'd met on the battlefield.

He swept the covers back. "Come to bed." He hesitated, thinking of what a coward he'd been for the last couple of weeks. "Unless you'd prefer your own bed?"

She smiled like a weary Madonna. "I'd like nothing better than to join you."

As he moved to the other side of the mattress, she peeled off her robe and climbed in next to him. He rolled onto his side and pulled her close, sighing with pleasure at the warmth wherever their bodies touched.

To his surprise, he found that his exhaustion was fading. The effect of Abby's healing presence, he guessed. Though his blood was not yet fully recovered, desire was building. He cupped her breast experimentally, not wanting to wake her if she slept.

She exhaled and pressed closer. "That feels good."

Encouraged, he caressed her with increasing intimacy. Her throat was convenient, so he breathed softly against the smooth skin. Her small gasp of pleasure encouraged him to kiss his way downward to the provocative intimacy of her breasts. How nice that her nightgown buttoned—and unbuttoned—down the front.

"Oh, my!" Her nails curled into his shoulders when his mouth reached her breasts, and her head arched back. Her innocent, joyful response made him feel stronger, almost strong enough to join with her fully.

Almost, but not quite. Frustrated by his inability to harden, he reminded himself that every day he was getting stronger. His time would come. Now he would concentrate on pleasing his wife. With lips and hands and tongue, he silently thanked her for all she had done for him.

Her legs opened to his touch, and he took pleasure in the pressure of her thigh between his own legs. They began moving against each other as his caresses quickened until she cried out and convulsed against him. He felt an echo of her excitement in his own body, a small climax that mirrored hers.

Her head fell against his shoulder and their bodies stilled, quiet but still entwined. Holding her gave him the greatest peace he'd known since he was a child. Which meant it was time to move forward. "It's time to go to London," he murmured. "I'm ready to take my seat in Parliament, along with all those other lordly responsibilities."

Some of her relaxation evaporated. "You're healthy enough so there is no reason to delay. Where will we stay? A hotel, or do you own a house?"

"I do, but Frayne House is leased out. We can stay with my sister, Celeste. She has plenty of space. She looks forward to sponsoring the Reverend Wilson's daughter for the little season." It would be wonderful to see his sister—it had been too long.

"Is Celeste terribly fashionable?" Abby asked warily.

"Yes, but she's a fine lass nonetheless. You'll get on well together." He paused, then realized he'd better mention something else. "She's a duchess. But a *nice* duchess."

Abby began to laugh, her curving form shivering delightfully. "It only needed that! Sleep well, my dear. We'll need all our strength for London."

She was right. With a sigh of contentment, he kissed her hair. Tonight he'd sleep well—and hadn't he been a damned fool to avoid his wife's delicious self for so long?

Chapter XVII

As the carriage rumbled to a halt in front of a vast Mayfair mansion, Abby steeled herself for whatever might come. Alderton House was extremely ducal. A bastion of aristocrat prejudice against wizardry, she suspected. "Are you going to tell your sister and her husband that I'm a wizard? Or would the news get me thrown out of the house?"

Jack hesitated. "Celeste should know, I think, though not until she's had a chance to become acquainted with you. As for Alderton . . . he's a good fellow, but rather traditional."

Abby mentally translated that to "loathes wizards." She suspected that Ashby might be the only duke in England who wouldn't run screaming from a room that contained a wizard, but he wasn't the typical duke. "Will you tell your sister about your own power?"

"There really isn't much to talk about," Jack said. "I'm glad to have Stark's blasted spell out of my mind, but that doesn't make me a wizard."

His answer was typical of his recent behavior. Though Jack's reaction to having magic was no longer the irrational loathing that had been induced by Colonel Stark's spell, he was still vehemently rejecting his newly released power. She hoped he would come to terms with it eventually, but that day wasn't imminent. She sensed that he'd locked his power away as thoroughly as Colonel Stark had done. At least now the choice was his.

A liveried footman opened the carriage door and offered his hand to Abby. "Welcome to Alderton House, Lady Frayne."

She wasn't surprised that a duke's servant knew how to read the arms painted on the carriage door. No doubt the staff had been briefed that the duchess's brother and his bride were coming for a visit. Jack had written his sister the morning after they decided it was time to come up to London, and mail coaches traveled faster than other vehicles. Especially in midwinter. They were fortunate not to have run into really terrible weather. Instead, the trip had been merely gray, cold, and miserable.

Though most London streets were slushy and patched with ice, the section in front of Alderton house has been swept clean and the steps up to the entrance were impeccably dry. Since Jack was still using a cane, Abby was glad for this level of service.

As he stepped out of the carriage, he gave her an encouraging smile. "You'll enjoy London, I promise."

As promises went, this one wasn't very convincing. She had visited London twice before, and they had stayed with wizardly friends in a neighborhood far from Mayfair. This stay would be very different.

She used her nervousness as an excuse to take Jack's hand. Not only did that make her feel better, but he could use her as a second cane as he climbed the steps. "I shall try not to disgrace you," she said under her breath as they ascended.

She wished he would offer her reassurance that he could never be ashamed of her, but he was too honest for that, so he changed the subject. "If I know Celeste, she'll hold a grand ball to introduce you to London society," he said with a shade too much heartiness. "She loves entertaining."

This was a new and alarming prospect. Abby thought of being the object of scrutiny by London's elite, and cringed. "Can we refuse?"

Jack grinned. "Perhaps. I'll leave persuasion to you. Since she's my sister, I learned early to take orders meekly."

"Liar!" The door swung open to reveal a petite blonde. "You were the most stubborn brother imaginable. Oh, Jack, I've missed you!" She darted into his arms and almost knocked him down the steps. Abby and the footman saved Jack from a fall, barely.

"Celeste, you menace!" Jack hugged his sister back enthusiastically. The top of her head barely topped his shoulder. "You seem determined to kill me on your front steps. Shall we go inside where it's safer as well as warmer?"

"Sorry." His sister stepped back and motioned her guests into the foyer, which towered a full three stories high. Her gaze was caught by his cane and halting walk. "I thought you would have recovered from that hunting accident by now?"

"Mostly I have, but . . . well, the fall was rather worse than you were told." Jack drew Abby forward. "My friends didn't want to alarm you unnecessarily, but the bald truth is that I was badly injured and would have died without Abby."

Celeste turned to study her new sister-in-law, revealing the full force of her beauty. The duchess was exquisite, her blond loveliness so perfect that she wouldn't just inspire poetry, but launch ships. Abby saw little resemblance to Jack, apart from her hazel eyes.

At the moment, those eyes were narrowed. Abby could almost hear the duchess's thoughts as she wondered what kind of scheming wench had trapped her brother into marriage. For a horrible instant, Abby saw herself as the duchess must: too large, not graceful, not elegant, not well dressed. A clumsy country female who had somehow maneuvered an honorable man into marrying her when he was too weak to resist.

"Celeste, meet Abby," Jack said gently. "Abby, meet Celeste. I hope you will be true sisters."

Obviously deciding to give this strange creature the benefit of the doubt for Jack's sake, the duchess said, "Welcome, Abby. I have been longing for Jack to take a wife these last five years. I wish you both very happy." She produced a dazzling social smile. "Since we are sisters, you may call me Celeste."

What did one say to a duchess who was one's impossibly beautiful new sister-in-law? "Thank you. I look forward to becoming better acquainted."

A brown-haired gentleman in the most beautifully tailored coat Abby had ever seen entered the foyer. Though undistinguished in features and not above middle height, he had an air of power and authority that instantly identified him as the Duke of Alderton. "Frayne. It's good to see you."

Jack shook the proffered hand with a grin. "Piers, how do you manage to look so perfect all the time?"

That produced a faint smile. "Credit goes to my valet. I doubt he'd be able to manage in a campaign tent like your Morris does, but there isn't a better valet in Britain." The duke bowed to Abby. "It's a pleasure to meet you, Lady Frayne."

His expression gave no hint as to whether he was speaking the truth or being polite. The energy in his aura was as hard to read as his face. Abby's guess was that his words were mere civility. There was a faint air of sadness about the duke. She suspected that he was not deeply interested in meeting his brother-in-law's new wife.

She glanced from the duke to his lady. With his air of power and consequence and her beauty, they made a striking couple. They had probably taken one look at each other across a crowded ballroom and decided they were made for each other.

And yet . . . as the two couples exchanged pleasantries about the weather and the journey, Abby noticed that the duke and duchess didn't quite look at each other. There were no private glances, nor did they draw together as happy couples often did. Even Abby and Jack, who were newly married and still getting to know each other, shared a smile and stood side by side. All was not well in the duchy of Alderton.

"Piers, you'll be happy to know I intend to take my seat in the House of Lords," Jack said. "When you have time, I'd like to discuss the procedure."

"I'm going to be quite busy over the next few days, but I have some time now." Alderton turned to his wife and Abby, his gaze not touching Celeste's. "Would you ladies forgive us if we retire to my study for some gentlemen's business?"

"Of course," the duchess purred. "Abby, please join me in my private parlor for tea. I look forward to a sisterly chat."

Abby thought rather sourly that neither of the men seemed to hear the barb hidden in the duchess's dulcet tones. But she'd have to face Jack's sister sooner or later and she wanted a cup of tea, so she nodded. "Give me a few minutes to refresh myself. Can you send a maid as a guide?"

A glint of humor showed in the duchess's eyes. "I'll take you to your rooms. When you're ready, a maid will be waiting outside your door. I required guidance for weeks after I moved here."

As Celeste led Abby up the curving staircase, she asked, "Do you have a maid?"

"I did, but at the prospect of her leaving Melton, her sweetheart proposed marriage," Abby explained. "I need to find another."

"The maid I'll send for guidance can help you. She often acts as abigail to female guests." As they walked along the upper corridor, the duchess's brows drew together. "I shall have to use a term other than *abigail* for the lady's maids, I see." She opened a door. "I shall send Lettie up. If you need anything, just ask her."

The duchess withdrew gracefully, leaving Abby to explore her new quarters. The bedroom proved to be part of a suite, with another bedroom for Jack, two dressing rooms, and a private sitting room. The furnishings and draperies were lavish and the ceilings so high that most of the heat moved to the top of the room, leaving the rest of the space chilly. She found herself missing the moderate ceilings and well-used but friendly furniture rescued from the attics of Hilltop House.

A servant had already hung her gowns. The sturdy, unfashionable garments did not make an impressive sight. Abby had always been more interested in practicality than style, and she was so busy that she seldom found time to have new clothing made. Jack had said that she must indulge herself with the London modistes, but for now, Abby was going to look like the dowdy provincial she was.

There was no help for it. Perhaps feeling superior would improve the duchess's mood. By the time Abby had washed up, the promised maid had appeared. The efficient young Lettie helped Abby dress her hair and change into a plain, dark blue gown and a warm Italian shawl. Then she guided the visitor to Celeste's private parlor.

Abby would have known the room belonged to the duchess even if the other woman hadn't been present. The dainty, feminine furniture, fabrics, and carpets were the perfect setting for the exquisite Celeste. Her hostess rose from her desk. "I hope your rooms are comfortable?"

"They're magnificent. Jack usually stays with you when he's in London?"

"Yes, which isn't often enough." The duchess moved to the tea table, where a silver tea service and a plate of pastries awaited. "Frayne House has been leased out for years. My mother and her husband never come to town. How do you like your tea?"

So the dowager Lady Frayne had remarried. Wondering if that was why Jack avoided discussing his childhood home, Abby specified milk for her tea and accepted a delicious French pastry as an accompaniment. They discussed the journey from Leicestershire until the duchess replenished the teacups.

Tiring of trivialities, Abby said, "Is it time for the interrogation, Celeste? To simplify matters, my birth is respectable. My father, Sir Andrew Barton, is a baronet and owner of a neat property near Melton Mowbray, my brother is an officer in Spain, and I have a dowry that is ample by gentry standards, but doubtless would look paltry to a member of the nobility." She added an irregular lump of sugar to her tea and stirred. "In other words, Jack could have done much better for himself. I freely agree that he deserves better. Nonetheless, married we are. I hope this does not distress you too greatly, since Jack would not like you to be unhappy."

The duchess's teacup froze in midair a moment before she carefully set it back in its saucer. "You are remarkably direct, Abby. I rather like that, though you might wish to be less forthcoming in society. I presume that you would not lie about the facts you just gave me, since they are so easily checked. So I will ask you the one truly important question, and I trust this answer will also be honest. Do you love my brother?"

That was not what Abby had expected from an elegant social butterfly. She concentrated on stirring her tea rather more than it needed. "Yes. Though I know the world will regard this as an unequal match, I swear I will be a good wife to him."

"Excellent." The duchess gave a genuine smile and looked much less intimidating. "My brother is a good catch, and he's far too easygoing to defend himself against scheming debutantes and their even more scheming mothers. If he hadn't been in the army these last years, I shudder to think what kind of female would have trapped him into marriage before he knew what he was about."

She took a thoughtful sip of tea. "If he had consulted me about a possible wife, I would have told him to look for a down-to-earth woman and a relationship grounded in true affection. He appears to have done just that. Not for nothing is he called Lucky Jack." She extended her hand. "Welcome to the Langdon family, Abby."

Abby took the duchess's hand. The other woman's clasp was surprisingly firm for such a delicate creature. "I'm honored, Celeste. But to be honest, I'm surprised at your approval. Jack has responsibilities as a landowner and a member of Parliament. I don't know if I will do him much credit in society." She glanced down at her plain gown.

The duchess waved her hand. "You have presence, breeding, and intelligence, which are the basic requirements to be Lady Frayne. Town polish is easily acquired. But tell me about that accident. Did you really save Jack's life?"

The full story would reveal what Abby was, but she couldn't lie to Jack's sister. Wondering if this would destroy the duchess's good regard, Abby said bluntly, "He took a terrible fall and broke his neck. When his friends brought him to our house, he was paralyzed and on the brink of death. His friends didn't want to notify his family until his fate was certain. I organized a healing circle, and together we were able to repair the worst of the damage. He has recovered with remarkable speed. A fortnight from now, he won't need the cane."

The other woman's expression changed. "You are a wizard?"

So the duchess didn't approve of magic. At least she didn't call Abby a wyrdling. "Everyone in my family is gifted with exceptional power." Jack's magic she didn't mention. That was between brother and sister. "My gift is for healing."

The duchess leaned forward, her hazel eyes blazing. "Can you cure barrenness?"

So it wasn't disapproval that had caused Celeste's expression to change so markedly. "I don't know," Abby replied. "There are many causes of barrenness. I might be able to help, but no one can guarantee a cure."

"I know there are no guarantees." With visible effort, Celeste sat back in her chair. "I have already consulted the best physicians, and I've secretly gone to healers, too, without success. But if you could save Jack's life after he broke his neck, perhaps you can succeed where others have failed."

"I didn't do it alone, Celeste." It was easier to use the duchess's given name now that the talk had become so personal. "We had a full healing circle of talented wizards. Such powerful magic is best suited to healing great injuries or illnesses. Lesser physical problems require a lighter touch, and perhaps somewhat different magical skills."

"I know all that. But . . . please, will you try?" The naked pleading in Celeste's eyes was painful to see.

Abby had seen such desperation many times. She never became indifferent to it. "I will try. And I hope you will not hate me if I fail."

The duchess gave a crooked smile. "I haven't hated any of the others who failed. Whatever the results, I will be grateful that you saved my brother's life. And I will pray that you and Jack never suffer this particular kind of hell."

The pieces suddenly fit together. "This is the source of the estrangement between you and your husband, isn't it? The failure to provide him with an heir."

Celeste caught her breath. "You're very perceptive. I suppose that goes with your other talents. Yes, we've been married almost ten years, and I have never once quickened. It has not been for a lack of trying on our part. The physicians all said I was a healthy woman and surely it was only a matter of time." Her hands knotted in her lap, no longer elegant. "More than three thousand days and nights have passed, yet still I have been unable to give my husband a child."

"The duke cannot forgive your failure?" The thought did not endear him to Abby.

"Of course he is deeply disappointed, but he has accepted my barrenness, perhaps better than I." Celeste gazed across the room, eyes unseeing. "The estrangement between us is the result of my telling him that I would cooperate if he wanted to take a mistress and pass off any resulting child as mine. The suggestion shocked him almost senseless. He . . . he accused me of wanting him to take a mistress to justify my taking lovers. Our relationship has not yet recovered."

Abby caught her breath. "How sad that you made an offer that cost you great pain, and that his rejection has caused you even more pain."

Celeste sighed. "I shouldn't have done it. Piers is the most honorable man in the kingdom, and he takes his wedding vows seriously. But I thought after all these years, he might be grateful to have an heir that was his if not mine. Instead, he thinks I . . . I don't love him."

"Surely in time he will realize that your suggestion was an expression of great love," Abby said comfortingly.

"If he doesn't, there will be no chance for a child at all."

So the duke and duchess were no longer intimate. No wonder both of them were unhappy. "Celeste, why are you speaking so freely to a woman you've only just met? I hope I am worthy of your trust, but I find your candor surprising."

"I am not usually so forthcoming. But . . ." The duchess smiled wryly and made a quick gesture with her right hand. A glowing ball of light formed on the palm.

"Good heavens," Abby gasped. "You're a wizard!"

"Not really," Celeste said, though she looked pleased at the words. "My natural power is modest and I had no proper training. I learned early that having magic would make me despised, so I hid my ability. It was a relief to realize that with you I could be myself, for both of us have much to conceal."

So the duchess was offering a pact of silence. Abby found herself feeling sorry for the other woman, who was forced to hide a vital part of her nature. Though she was beautiful, wellborn, and titled, she had not had the freedom and support Abby had enjoyed. "I will not betray you, but the fact that I'm a wizard is likely to become public knowledge soon. My family is well known in the shires, and so many men hunt there that the news will reach London quickly."

"I suppose you're right." The duchess narrowed her eyes, but her expression was friendly. "The more people who meet you before your wizardry becomes known, the better. It's harder to cut a woman one has met. Luckily, the taint of magic has never been so severe for our sex. I shall hold a ball to present you to society as soon as possible."

Abby winced. "Please, is that necessary? I truly dislike the idea of being shown off like a prize cow."

"I understand, but a ball is indeed necessary. You've married into the beau monde. Jack is about to take his place as one of the great men of Britain. It isn't required for you to be a famous hostess or a dazzling beauty with an entourage of flirtatious gentlemen around you, but you must be known, accepted, and respected. Out of London you can be less fashionable, but here you owe it to Jack to make an effort."

Abby sighed. "I said I'd do my best to be a good wife, so I will do my duty. But I shall need your aid rather desperately. My dancing is as provincial as my wardrobe."

Celeste's gaze moved over Abby from head to foot. "Forgive my tactlessness, but do you dress so plainly because you wish to be acceptable but not memorable?"

"I'm afraid so. Partly that is because of the work I do. Too fashionable an appearance would require time and effort and might make me look unapproachable. I don't want those who need me most to be afraid to ask for help." She hesitated, then added, "And to be honest, fashion simply doesn't interest me. I like to be comfortable and to blend in. Beyond that, there are more interesting things to do than stand around having pins stuck into me."

"That's all very well for the country, but not London." The duchess tapped her fingers thoughtfully on the armrest of her chair. "You have good bones, and I suspect that under the plain dress and shawl is a decent figure. A good modiste and a corsetiere will do wonders. There's no need to go to a public salon—I shall have them come here." She grinned. "I'm quite looking forward to this."

"I'm glad one of us is!" But Abby smiled when she said it. She had gained an ally in London, and also, she thought, a friend.

Chapter XVIII

The duke closed his study door behind them, then opened a handsomely inlaid wooden box. "A cigar?"

"Thank you." Jack seldom smoked, but he and his brother-in-law had developed this ritual over the years. It gave them time to relax and get used to each other again. God knew they could hardly be more different, but they always got on well.

The duke lit the cigars with a taper, then motioned Jack to sit in one of the deep, leather-upholstered chairs. "Congratulations on your marriage. Your bride looks like a sensible woman."

"She is." Jack drew in a mouthful of fragrant smoke, then slowly released it. Piers had the best cigars in London. "She's a Barton. The family is well respected in the Midlands."

"Will you be returning to the army?"

"I'm selling my commission. Visiting a broker is on my list of tasks."

"Good." The duke regarded the glowing tip of his cigar gravely. "The sooner you take your wife north and reclaim Langdale Hall, the

better. Matters there are not good, Jack. I wish you'd given me more authority to deal with the situation."

Though a solicitor handled routine business affairs for the estate,
Piers had kept an eye on both solicitor and estate while Jack was with
the army. "The problems are mine to solve. How bad is it?"

"The income is less than half what it should be. There has been disease among the livestock and blight on the crops. Tenants have left and
not been replaced, fields are lying fallow, and I hear the remaining tenants look as desolate as plague victims." He frowned. "I don't understand why affairs are in such a state. Sir Alfred Scranton is not a stupid
man and his own estate does well. There is no evidence that he is loot-
ing the property or deliberately mismanaging it. Yet Langdale Hall
doesn't prosper."

"The estate has been cursed ever since my mother married that man."

The duke made an expression of distaste. "Surely you don't believe
in curses."

Reminded of the other man's traditional views, Jack said, "Not
a literal curse. I meant that nothing has gone right since Scranton
persuaded my mother to marry him."

"I've never quite understood that match," the duke mused.

"Whatever his other failings, Scranton adores her," Jack said grudgingly. And his mother was a woman who needed to feel adored. "The
man is a blight, but he's no thief."

It would be up to Jack to send Scranton packing, even if that meant
throwing his own mother from his house. Which was why he had
avoided Yorkshire for so many years. Once it had seemed as if he faced
impossible choices. Now that he had married Abby and dismantled
Stark's crippling spell, the choices no longer seemed impossible. Merely
very difficult. Not wishing to discuss the matter further, he asked, "How
is the world treating you, Piers?"

The duke shrugged. "Well enough."

Which was a lie, now that Jack looked more closely. His brother-in-
law appeared gray and unhappy. Older than his years. The gray was in
his face and in the faint glow of energy around him.

Since breaking down the iron door in his mind, Jack had found that he could see auras despite his conscious attempts to bury his magic. Most of the time the ability was a distracting nuisance, but he had to admit that sometimes it was convenient.

Celeste hasn't looked her best, either, though he hadn't noticed at the time because of her enthusiastic greeting. It didn't take a genius to deduce that there was trouble between his sister and her husband, but it wasn't something he could ask about. Piers was intensely private. And to be honest, Jack wouldn't know what to do about someone else's marital problems, not when he hadn't figured out his own marriage.

The duke handed over a slim sheaf of papers. "Here's a summary of your estate accounts to review before you meet with your solicitor."

"Thank you." Jack knew from experience that his brother-in-law's summary would be concise and insightful, going to the heart of any problems. "I'm fortunate that you have been willing to watch over my affairs."

"Managing property is my only talent, so I enjoy exercising it," the other man said dryly. "But now it's your turn."

Jack scanned the estate summary, wincing at the income total. Much of the income was being reinvested in an attempt to turn the estate around, so far with little effect. A good thing Jack wasn't the high-living sort. "I'm planning on spending only a few weeks in town. Long enough to take my seat, sell my commission, and introduce Abby to the ton. Then it will be time for Langdon."

"Of course you are welcome to stay here as long as you wish."

"I appreciate that. It's been so long since I've seen the inside of Frayne House that I have forgotten what it looks like. Now that I'll be in town regularly for Parliament, I'll have to take possession when the lease expires. The place probably needs refurbishing after so many years of being let out. Respectability is a lot of work. Expensive, too." He set the accounts aside. "Can you refresh my memory about how one takes one's seat?"

"You'll need to have formal robes of state made up." The duke smiled faintly. "Be grateful the weather is still cold; otherwise all that velvet and ermine is deucedly hot. After you're presented to the house by two lords who are the same rank as you, you swear an oath of allegiance to king and country."

"Do I have to give a speech?"

The other man shook his head. "Your maiden speech will come later, whenever you feel ready. It's customary to give a short, uncontroversial address that will be congratulated no matter how bad it is. This is the only occasion on which you can count on your fellow members to compliment you on your speaking."

Jack had never studied rhetoric, but he'd done his share of speechifying as an army officer. He knew how to project his voice and make his point, so when the time came, he'd be ready. To his surprise, he realized that he had opinions, lots of them, about how the country should be governed. Performing the duties of his rank might be more amusing than he'd thought.

The duke stubbed out the remnant of his cigar and got to his feet. "I'm sorry to rush off, but I have a meeting to attend. I'll see you later."

Jack retrieved his cane and stood. "I'll go up to Celeste's boudoir and see how the ladies are getting along. I'm not sure if they'll like each other or be at each other's throats."

"I hope your bride is up to the talons of the city," Piers said as the men left the study. "A girl from the country might find society alarming."

Wondering if his brother-in-law was implying that Celeste had grown talons, Jack ascended the sweeping staircase that led to the upper floors. He had become adept at climbing steps, especially when there was a solid banister to hold on to. Cane in right hand, railing in left, yes. He was going to be a dab hand at crutches and canes by the time he needed neither.

As he knocked at the door to Celeste's parlor, he heard a burst of laughter from inside. Thinking that sounded promising, he entered the room. "You two seem to be managing well."

"We are indeed." Not bothering to ask if he wanted tea, Celeste poured him a cup, added milk, and set a plate of pastries beside it.

"Thank you for marrying Abby instead of that dreadful Devereaux chit you flirted with last year."

"You didn't like Lady Cynthia?" he asked, surprised. "I thought she was the sort of young lady you approved of. Wellborn, well behaved, and pretty."

"She's a sly cat." His sister smiled at Abby. "I should have had more faith in your judgment." Abby's expression turned satiric, but she didn't comment.

"I think it was my luck, not my judgment." He took the chair between his wife and sister, laid down his cane, and started in on the tea and cakes. "Who won the battle of the ball?"

"Celeste has convinced me that a ball is necessary. Luckily, she is willing to take care of all the hard work involved." Abby glanced at her new sister-in-law. "Have you decided whether to mention that matter we discussed earlier?"

Celeste's quick alarm shifted to determination. "Jack, I never dared tell you, but I have a touch of sorceress in me." She raised her hands and a globe of light formed on her right palm. She poured the light into her left hand with liquid smoothness.

"Good heavens!" He stared at his sister. "I didn't know you could do that."

"It's not uncommon for magical gifts to run in families." Abby's voice was neutral, but he recognized the strong hint in her voice. She obviously thought it was time for brother and sister to be honest with each other, and she was right.

"Power does run in families, Celeste. Maybe you were too young to realize, but I was sent to Stonebridge because I was showing signs of magical ability."

"So that's what happened," his sister said thoughtfully. "I knew the academy's goal was to suppress magic, but since I was so small, I couldn't remember if you'd done anything magical or you were merely too interested in the subject. Sometimes I thought I'd invented memories of your doing magic to make myself feel better."

His sister had needed to feel better? He didn't like knowing that under her bright, happy surface, Celeste had been painfully concealing her talent, even from him. He should have been a better brother. Thinking she would be glad to know how much they had in common, he held out his hand and imagined a ball of light on his palm. "I wonder if I can do that?"

The effort made his temples throb, but a glow appeared.

"Oh, well done, Jack!" Abby applauded.

Jack closed his hand around the light, obliterating it. "Magic is part of me. But that doesn't mean that I want it or will ever use it."

"True, but it's healthier to accept your talent, even if you choose to ignore it." Her gaze moved from Jack to Celeste. "You've both suffered from having to suppress your abilities."

"Jack more than I," Celeste said. "Once or twice I was caught practicing magic, and while I was scolded, I was never beaten the way Jack was."

Abby's eyes narrowed. "You were beaten?"

"Regularly." Jack's voice was terse. Some memories deserved to stay buried.

And yet . . . Another long-buried memory surfaced, and without thinking he reached out mentally to lift one of the little lemon-filled pastries and send it flying toward his sister. *"En garde!"*

The pastry abruptly slipped from his mental control and reversed direction to whip back across the table toward Jack. It stopped just short of his nose and hovered. His sister exclaimed, "Good God, we used to do that in the nursery! I'd forgotten."

"So had I." Jack stared cross-eyed at the pastry, shaken that both he and Celeste were able to send it flying. "How much have we forgotten? And was forgetting natural, or were spells laid on us? Abby, can you tell?" He plucked the pastry from the air and ate it in one bite. He felt the need to eat something sweet.

Abby looked troubled. "The only way to be sure would be to enter your minds. Given your father's powerful dislike of magic, it's possible, even likely, that he had you both bespelled. It's not uncommon for people of your class to lay a mild suppression spell on children who show signs of magical ability. If that spell wasn't strong enough and you continued to experiment with magic, it would explain why Colonel Stark was asked to cast a much more powerful spell on you. If only a mild spell was laid on you, Celeste, it probably wore off after a few years so you could resume working with magic."

"While I qualified for Stark's stronger spell because I was the son and heir. Lucky me." Jack dropped his hand when he found himself rubbing the shoulder where the anti-magic spell had been emblazoned. "Celeste, do you think you were bespelled? I only remember us tossing things around the nursery when we were very young."

"We seem to have stopped and forgotten. That would fit with a mild suppression spell." His sister smiled ruefully. "Until now, my earliest memories of doing magic were when I was twelve or thirteen. But even before then, the subject interested me. I used to borrow books from Mr. Willard."

"You, too? Oh, Celeste, we've hidden far too much from each other!" Jack wondered if his life would have been easier if he'd realized he could confide in his sister. Perhaps. Maybe then he wouldn't have buried so much of himself.

"I think you were both treated abominably," Abby said crisply. "I wonder who cast the spells? Ethical wizards won't do such work on someone who is unsuspecting. But there are always magic workers who are willing to do anything that is well paid."

"There are several wizards who specialize in placing such spells on wellborn children," Celeste said tightly. "I've heard other women discuss them, and what age their children should be when they're bespelled, but it never occurred to me that I had been a victim myself."

Abby shook her head. "I thank God that I was born into the gentry class and was not subject to such wicked restrictions. Since I come from a family of wizards, I had all the support and training anyone could wish." Three tarts swooped into the air and hovered before each of them.

"You're showing off," Jack said with a grin.

She laughed. "A little. But they're lovely tarts." She pulled hers from the air and ate it. Jack and Celeste followed suit.

Abby finished her tea. "It's well known that magical gifts run in families. Both of you have significant gifts. It takes real power to lift objects without touching them. Though not impossible, it would be unusual for both of you to possess substantial abilities without having other magic in your family. So where did your power come from? Your mother or your father? A grandparent?"

Jack's gaze caught his sister's, and he saw a shock that matched his own. In all these years, he had never once asked himself where his accursed magic came from. Had that lack of curiosity also been the result of a spell?

There had been a wizard in his family home, and it had subtly shaped both of their childhoods. "Father." He licked dry lips. "It had to be him."

"That's impossible," Celeste whispered, her eyes huge. "Papa hated magic."

"Even more impossible that it was Mama." Transparent, sociable, and uncomplicated, their mother had carried no hidden shadows.

Feeling suffocated, he shoved himself from his chair and stalked across the room, stopping at the window overlooking Grosvenor Square. His mind was suddenly full of memories that were the same, yet entirely different.

You must not use magic. It is wicked. Disgusting. The beatings, his father's grim, implacable face. Though Jack had been whipped harder at Stonebridge, those beatings had never hurt as much as the ones from his father.

An arm slipped around his waist, and he realized that Abby had joined him. Wisely she said nothing. Did she use healing magic to dissolve his angry pain, or was she offering only the purely human magic of caring? He put his arm around her shoulders, drawing her close to his side.

"My father was the one who ordered the Stonebridge spell," he said harshly. "He might have been the one to cast the milder spells on Celeste and me. I can . . . almost see him bespelling me. It's like a memory that is just out of reach."

"He was shamed by the magical part of himself," Abby said softly.

"He didn't want you to suffer as he had, so he tried to remove even your knowledge of your own power. I think what he did was wrong, but it was done because he loved you."

She was right, he realized. His father had been a tormented man, particularly when the subject was magic. "I'm glad he wasn't so hard on Celeste. I don't think he could bear to hurt his angel child."

A brittle laugh sounded behind them. "I'd forgotten that he called me his angel child," Celeste said. "I've forgotten so much."

Abby handed him his cane. "And you forgot this when you stood up."

So he had, and his leg ached from the extra strain. Guessing that Abby was suggesting he go to his sister, he crossed the room. Celeste sat in her chair with her usual grace, hands folded and back straight. Only the tear tracks on her face revealed her inner turmoil. "The world just changed, Celeste," he said quietly. "Yet it's no different than it was, except in our minds."

"That's a very large *except*." She stood and wrapped her arms around him in an unhappy hug. "To think that Papa was a wizard! I never knew him at all."

"Neither did I." He felt closer to his sister than he had since they were children in the nursery. He glanced up and saw Abby standing quietly at the window, allowing him the time with his sister.

He put out one arm and beckoned her to join them in their hug. Without her, there would be no new understanding. And painful though the experience of finding out was, he was glad to find that his past finally made sense.

Chapter XIX

After Jack left, well stuffed with pastries, Abby asked the duchess, "When would you like me to examine you? Tomorrow morning, perhaps?"

"Now?" Celeste laughed ruefully. "After ten years, I know that a day more or less won't really matter, but I'd like to know what you think."

Abby recognized the yearning for a miracle. Luckily, though her healing power was still below normal because of the energy she was lending Jack, that shouldn't affect her ability to scan. "I'll do a preliminary examination. That will give me the information to write my friend, Mrs. Wayne, who has great expertise in female health problems."

"If you need help, would she come to London?"

Abby shook her head. "Not if she has patients that require special care, which she usually does. She won't leave a woman who is at risk even for a duchess."

Celeste narrowed her eyes thoughtfully. "Then perhaps I can go to her, if you think it helpful. But first you must make your examination."

"Lie down on your sofa and relax."

The other woman crossed to the elegant little French style sofa and stretched out with her head on a brocade pillow. She looked more like a girl from the schoolroom than a duchess, though she must be Abby's age or older.

Abby stilled her mind and summoned the special sensitivities needed for scanning and diagnosis. When she was ready, she studied Celeste's aura. The basic color was pink. She guessed that the shade should have the brightness that marked a tender, loving, compassionate personality, but now it was marked with muddy tones and glints of a dark, depressed blue. She looked for signs of ill-health. Despite the heaviness of her aura, overall the duchess was healthy. "Your right elbow looks sore," she observed. "Does it need treatment?"

"No, it's only a bruise from where I banged into my desk by mistake," Celeste said. "But I'm impressed that you knew that without even touching me."

"There was a red glow around your elbow," Abby explained. "Relax, and we'll see what else we can find."

The duchess obediently closed her eyes and did her best to be still, though her body was still taut. Hoping to find a fixable problem but aware that other healers hadn't, Abby slowly skimmed her hands several inches above the other woman's body. "Apart from nerves, you're in fine health," she said. "You enjoy riding and brisk walks, I think?"

"You're right again." Celeste's eyes flew open. "Might that be interfering with my ability to conceive?"

"Not at all. Healthy, active women usually find it easier to bear children." Abby concentrated harder on the energy flow surrounding the female organs, but she could neither see nor feel any wrongness. "I sense no obvious problems. Now that I've examined you, I'll write Judith Wayne. Perhaps she'll have some suggestions."

Her face a mask of disappointment, the duchess sat up. "I was expecting too much to think that you could instantly come up with a cure. Perhaps I should ask instead for a love charm to lure my husband back to my bed."

"I think your own beauty and love are more potent than any magical charm," Abby said gently.

Celeste caught her breath, tears glinting in her eyes. "I hope you're right. Strange, isn't it? Most women would think I have the best life in London, with health and wealth and a wonderful husband. I used to think that myself, and give thanks. But now it's all gone wrong."

Abby sat on the chair by the sofa and produced a clean handkerchief for the duchess. "I can make no promises about a child, but surely your marriage can be restored. You and your husband love each other. You just need to find how to resolve this temporary misunderstanding."

Celeste used the handkerchief to blot her eyes and blow her nose, looking lovely even in the midst of tears. "But how? All thoughts gratefully received."

Abby thought about what she knew of the situation. "You said that Alderton believed that you didn't love him anymore. Does he have any other reason to believe that, apart from your suggestion that he take a mistress?"

"Of course not!" Celeste looked scandalized. "Men usually flutter around me at social events, but I am never more than polite. I certainly never offer any encouragement. Piers is the only man I want." Her lips started to quiver before she pressed them tight.

Following instinct, Abby said, "You are an extraordinarily beautiful woman, while your husband's looks are merely average. Might he have trouble believing you could love him for something more than his title and wealth?"

"Piers is the most attractive man I know!" Celeste looked briefly outraged. Then her expression turned thoughtful. "But I feel that because I love him. Do you think that because my appearance is admired, he assumes I don't really care for him?"

"It's possible." Abby knew from experience that an average appearance did nothing to bolster confidence in one's desirability. In the dark of night, did Alderton wonder if his beloved wife married him only for his position and had been lying to him ever since? It was a sad thought. "Where we love, we are most vulnerable, most prey to dark thoughts. Even dukes."

Celeste frowned as she restlessly turned the wedding ring on her finger. "You are a healer of the mind as well as of the body, Abby. I shall think how best to reassure my husband of my feelings. Thank you."

Abby didn't doubt that Celeste could charm her husband back to her arms. The question of a child was quite another matter.

That night Jack was too restless to wait for Abby to join him, so he collected his cane and went into her bedroom first. "My bed is so large that I was lonely," he explained, admiring the way the small night-light sculpted her softly feminine form.

She turned from braiding her hair and flipped back the covers, smiling. "There's plenty of room here."

He leaned his cane against the bedside table and climbed in. A moment later, beribboned braid swinging, Abby climbed in on the other side. He rolled over and drew her into his arms. "Is London living down to your worst fears?"

She relaxed against him with a soft, contented sigh. "So far, so good. Celeste seemed alarmingly beautiful and perfect before I realized she's really much like you."

He laughed out loud. "And I'm neither beautiful nor perfect?"

"That's not what I meant!"

"I know." He tilted her face up with a finger under her chin and gave her a kiss. Lord, she tasted good. He pulled her closer so that her lush curves were pressed against him. To his delight, he felt stirrings in the part of his body that hadn't worked properly since his injury. Might tonight be the night?

No, not yet. He wasn't ready. It would be utterly humiliating for him and upsetting for Abby if he should be unable to complete what he wanted to begin. Better to wait until he was sure. For now, caressing her warm, sensual body and bringing her to completion would do.

With a breathless laugh, she ended the kiss and settled her head on his shoulder. "There is much to talk about tonight, most of it about your family. Did you know that Celeste and her husband are having serious problems?"

"I guessed something was wrong." He and Abby had fallen into the habit of talking about their days when they came together in bed. He enjoyed the discussions, which helped him relax and sort out his thoughts, as well as deepening the bond with his wife. But if the topic was an awkward one, there was no place to hide.

"I assume you didn't ask Alderton about it because men don't discuss such things," she said pragmatically. "Celeste was more forthcoming. While there are some superficial issues, the underlying problem is that she hasn't had a child. The reason she and I became friends so quickly was because she asked if I would treat her barrenness."

"Can you heal that?" he asked, unable to keep hope from his voice. Though he and his sister had never discussed the matter, he knew that her childlessness hurt her. She had been his most faithful correspondent when he was in the army. In the early days she talked eagerly about when she and Piers would set up their nursery and speculated about whether their first child would be a boy or a girl. Gradually optimism had faded, replaced by anguished silence.

"I can try, but I don't know if I'll be successful. If I fail, perhaps Judith might be able to help. She's particularly good at treating such problems." Abby sighed. "Sometimes healing performs miracles, but so often it doesn't. I wish I could do more."

"If you could heal all ailments that were brought to you, you'd be dead of exhaustion in a week." He stroked down her torso, thinking her ribs were more prominent than they had been, and it wasn't an improvement. "You're doing too much already. If you had greater power, you would simply burn out all the sooner."

"You're right. It's the danger healers always face. We must be caring, yet accept our limitations. I'm not good at that." Her voice was sad but resigned.

"There is always another desperate person begging you to heal barrenness or a broken neck or a lung disease. I'm no better than anyone else. I want to protect you, but I'm deeply grateful you saved my worthless hide, and I can't help hoping that you will be able to help Celeste."

"Which is why healers are usually not very public in their work. Even the best of us can never do enough." After a silence, Abby asked, "How did your father die?"

"A riding accident." Jack's mouth twisted. "He tried to jump a stone wall that was too high and was thrown when his horse couldn't clear it. Smashed his skull in. Riding accidents run in the family."

Abby sucked her breath in. "Are you sure his death was an accident?"

Damn the woman. He should have realized she would ask the unanswerable question. "I don't know. I've sometimes wondered if he was deliberately reckless, pushing himself until he went too far." Never had Jack been so starkly aware of the similarities between himself and his father. "He had a streak of melancholia. If he was suffering from one of his black spells, it's possible that he was seeking oblivion that day. I don't know, and I don't want to know."

"Maybe he couldn't live with suppressing his true nature," Abby said softly. "May his soul rest at peace."

The strangest sensation rushed through Jack as if a ghostly—or angelic—hand rested briefly on his chest. No, on his heart, the energy went right through him, and was achingly familiar. "How strange," he breathed. "I feel that he is here and is truly at peace, at long last." Was that because his father's children were learning to accept themselves? If so, it was all due to Abby. He kissed her forehead.

"You've never told me about your mother. Or your stepfather."

"Just when I'm thinking what a wonderful woman you are, you ask me another impossible question," he said, half amused and half irritated.

Her hand came to rest on his chest, right where the angelic hand had touched him. "We'll be going to Yorkshire soon. It's best if I know what to expect."

She was right, as she usually was. He'd never send his men into possible danger without preparing them as much as possible.

When he'd sorted out his thoughts, he was surprised to find it easier to discuss his family than he'd expected. "My mother, Helen, is like a shining golden butterfly. Beautiful and always ready to dance in the sunshine. Men have been falling in love with her since she was in her cradle. She has a happy disposition; I've never met anyone who wasn't enchanted by her."

He thought back to his childhood. His mother had a carelessness that had frustrated him when he was a child, but in her casual way, she had loved her children. "She was the daughter of a Yorkshire clergyman—good breeding, no dowry. But because of her charm and beauty, she had her choice of suitors. She chose my father."

"If I can ask this without being too indelicate, did she love him, or do you think she was more in love with the idea of being Lady Frayne?"

"I've wondered that myself," he admitted. "I think it was a bit of both. She and my father seemed well suited. She could make him smile even during his dark moods. She was the one who calmed him down after I bought a commission against his wishes. He didn't want his heir dying of fever or bullets in some foreign land. Which was sensible, of course, but I was determined."

"Why did you join the army?" Abby asked curiously. "It's rare for the only son of a peer to do so. Were you army mad?"

"A little, but mostly I wanted to irritate my father," he said wryly. "My mother had to work hard to persuade him to accept what I'd done. After he mastered his temper, we started to correspond. Not long after that, he died. I was glad that we had been reconciled." He had never expected his father to die in the prime of life. It had been a bitter lesson in life's unpredictability.

"He sounds like a man who wasn't easy, but who did his best to live up to his responsibilities as he saw them. If only he had been able to accept his own power." Abby slid her foot under his leg. Her toes were cold. "I gather that your relationship is not so good with your stepfather."

"I prefer to think of him as my mother's husband," Jack said, unable to control the edge in his voice. "He has never been a father to me. I would not want him to be."

"Tell me about him. The good and the bad. Surely there is some good."

Jack considered doing his best to be fair. "I don't know Sir Alfred Scranton well because he didn't inherit the adjoining estate till after I had left Langdale. But he is a respected landowner in Yorkshire, and he dotes on my mother, even more than my father did."

"When did he and your mother marry?"

"A year after my father's death. My mother took off her mourning and picked up a bouquet." He vaguely assumed that she would remarry. He just hadn't expected it to happen quite so soon.

"Did you dislike him from the beginning?"

"No, I was glad that Mother had someone to care for her. She doesn't like to be alone. It seemed a good match, since Scranton is a man of wealth and consequence. But he has turned out to be a blight upon the earth. Literally. Langdale Hall has been deteriorating ever since he moved in."

"They don't live at his estate?" Abby asked, surprised.

"My mother didn't want to leave the hall, so he moved in with her. I didn't object. Since I was in the army and Celeste was married, we were both gone from Yorkshire. A house is better for being lived in, and I certainly didn't want my mother to feel unwelcome in the home where she had been mistress for twenty-five years."

"Did you visit them in Yorkshire on your next home leave?"

"Yes. Almost as soon as I walked in the door, my mother told me I should lease Frayne House, since they wouldn't be going to London again. Which was strange, since my mother had always loved going to town in the past."

The visit had been deeply strange, and he could barely conceal his frantic desire to leave and go back on campaign. Better bullets than being close to his stepfather. And yet he could think of no good reason for why he felt so strongly. He had made arrangements with his father's trusted steward to manage the estate, and fled like the veriest coward. "I found myself uninterested in visiting Langdale Hall again, so I haven't seen either of them since. My mother and I correspond, of course."

"Of course," Abby murmured. "In other words, this marriage is so distasteful to you that you allowed your stepfather to effectively drive you out of your own home. If he is so dreadful, don't you worry that he is mistreating your mother?"

"There has been no hint in her letters that he is ever unkind. In fact, she sounds very happy." Too happy, he'd sometimes thought. She was like a child in the nursery who had never seen anything of darkness. Her present blithe self-absorption was not entirely different from the way she had always been. Or was it?

"What does your sister think about the marriage?"

"Celeste hates Scranton almost as much as I do, but for our mother's sake, she has visited Langdale. She's seen nothing to make her concerned for Mother's welfare. She says Scranton is overprotective and she suspects he wants to keep my mother to himself, which is why no trips to London. They don't even socialize with the neighbors, but my mother seems content with their quiet life. Celeste can't even get her to visit Alderton Abbey, Piers's family seat, which is only a day's journey away."

"Then why do you hate Scranton so much?"

His mouth hardened as he decided to tell the truth about his feelings. "The man is evil. Ever since he moved into Langdale Hall, the land and people have suffered. Yet he hasn't done a single thing that I can point to and prove that it was wrong."

He half expected Abby to gently say that he was being irrational, probably because he was jealous of his mother's attention, but instead she said seriously, "If your instinct says Scranton is a bad man, you're probably right. Your nature is too generous to be suspicious when there is no cause."

"You are too kind, Abby," he said harshly. "The cold truth is that I have stayed away from Langdale because I'm terrified that I might murder Scranton if I visited, and then I would be hanged, which would upset everyone." He sometimes dreamed of killing Scranton with his bare hands. Slowly. "So I've stayed away, and allowed our tenants to suffer the man's evil. I'm a coward who has avoided my responsibilities. I'm not fit to be Langdale's lord."

So there it was—his wife knew the worst of him. He half expected her to withdraw. Instead, she moved even closer, her warmth flowing through him. "You're no coward, Jack. There is something profoundly wrong at Langdale Hall, and you sensed it even when you were under Colonel Stark's spell."

He hadn't known how intensely he craved her understanding until relief rushed through him like a cleansing river. "Then I'm not going mad. Sometimes I've wondered."

"Given the way people have used magic to distort your mind, it's a wonder you're as sane as you are!" Abby shook her head, the motion agitated against his shoulder. "The tracks of malicious magic are all over this situation. If you had been left alone, you would have developed your natural magic and had good strong defenses. But you had suppression spells inflicted on you, which distorted your abilities. I suspect another spell might have been used to reinforce your reluctance to return to Yorkshire."

He rubbed at his left shoulder, which had born the serpent brand for so long. "Wouldn't my anti-magic charm have protected me from further spells?"

"Not necessarily. Your charm had the strength to protect you from everyday magic. No thief would be able to sneak up on you by casting a confusion spell, and no one would be able to get away with cheating you at cards. But a really strong wizard could have got around the charm without your knowledge or permission."

"You're strong enough to do that, but you wouldn't." Of that he was sure.

"It would be an unforgivable breach of ethics and trust." She sighed, her breath soft against his throat above his nightshirt. "Few people need worry about becoming targets of serious wizardry, but you are rich and powerful, so others have wanted to control you. If Scranton is possessive of your mother, it's quite possible he would wish you to stay away. From what you say of him, he wouldn't hesitate to hire a dark magician to plant a repulsion spell in your mind to keep you distant."

Jack unleashed a string of hair-raising curses. When he managed to get his temper under control, he said, "Your theory explains so much. Ever since my last visit to Langdale Hall, I've wondered what was wrong with me that I couldn't bring myself to go home! And I've hated myself for my cowardice."

"If Scranton did that to you, he deserves to be shot, and I'd do it myself," Abby said vehemently. "Your mind needs a thorough cleansing. Too many people have used magic to work their wills on you, and because your own power was constrained, you've been unable to defend yourself. You won't be fully in control of your life and your power until any and all spells are removed."

He thought about what she had said, and could see only one conclusion. Though he disliked the idea of using his magic, even more he hated the thought of being the victim of someone else's power. "Can you enter my mind and remove the remnants of spells that have been laid on me?"

"Yes, if you trust me." She stroked his forehead gently. "When you're ready."

Her fingers soothed the throbbing in his head. "Not tonight. I've had all the revelations I can endure for one day. But soon. Very soon."

Chapter XX

Abby woke to Jack's kiss on her forehead. "Sorry to rise so early, but there is much to be done today," he murmured. "I probably won't be back before dinner."

She blinked sleepily at the clock. "You really want to get out of bed at this hour on a winter morning? Were you unable to sleep?"

"I slept the sleep of the innocent, which I don't deserve." He kissed her again, this time on her throat, lingeringly. "But I always wake up at the time I decide on the night before."

She shivered with pleasure at the pressure from his warm lips. "That's a convenient knack. Magical, even."

He looked blank. "I never thought of it that way."

"Many magics are small." She caressed his deliciously whiskery chin, wishing he could stay longer. But she would rather not attempt to persuade him and fail at the endeavor. "Try not to push yourself too hard."

"I won't." He brushed the back of his hand against her cheek, then left.

She watched him return to his own room, ruefully aware that there always seemed to be a reason to continue lending him energy. Maybe she should withdraw it now. Yet she hated to think of him collapsing in exhaustion somewhere in London. Very soon she would stop. Yawning, she rolled over and went back to sleep.

She woke again a more civilized two hours later, when Lettie entered quietly to build up the fire. A few minutes later the maid delivered a tray with hot chocolate and a fresh roll. As Abby sipped her chocolate, she realized that she could have been waking to such luxury at home, but she was always too busy to lie about in bed. It would be interesting to have leisure time here in London.

Leisure lasted until she dressed and went downstairs for breakfast. The duchess was finishing her own meal. "Oh, good, you're awake. My modiste and corsetiere will be here in a few minutes. I thought my private parlor would be a good place to work."

Abby poured a quick cup of tea. "So soon?"

"There is no time to waste. You'll need ball gowns, morning gowns, a new riding habit, cloaks, hats, shoes—the wardrobe of a London lady."

"All that?" Abby said, unnerved.

"You must dress according to your rank. This won't be as bad as you think." Celeste grinned. "Though perhaps it is more accurate to say that you might hate all the fuss and fittings, but I'll have a marvelous time bullying you and the dressmakers."

Abby had to laugh as she settled down to her eggs and toast. "That's honest, at least. I shall have to take your advice, since I haven't the remotest idea what I'll need. I hope you won't find it humorous to deck me out like a May cow!"

"I wouldn't do that to Jack's wife even if I didn't like you," the other woman assured her. "Nor would the modiste allow it. She has her pride."

After breakfast Abby made her way to the duchess's private parlor, and found it buzzing with activity. Modiste and corsetiere had arrived with half a dozen assistants and mountains of fabrics, feathers, trims, and fashion books.

Celeste said, "Lady Frayne, allow me to present Madame Ravelle, the finest modiste in London, and Madame Renault, the finest corsetiere."

Abby blinked at the two women. Both were tall, silver-haired, and massively dignified. And they weren't just similar, but virtually identical. "You are sisters?"

"Twins, milady," the modiste said. She was dressed in blue. "Our skills enhance each other, so we work together."

Madame Renault, who wore gray, added, "Without a proper foundation, even the finest of gowns will not look its best." Her eyes gleamed as she studied Abby. "And you, milady, are in dire need of my skills."

Apparently, talented artisans were allowed such rudeness. Fortunately Abby had little vanity, because the sisters and the duchess began to discuss her appearance with hair-curling bluntness. Abby was stripped down to her shift, measured in amazing detail, draped in swaths of fabric, and analyzed as if she wasn't present.

As Madame Ravelle turned to consult a copy of *La Belle Assemblée,* Abby asked her sister-in-law, "Am I allowed any opinions about what I am to wear?"

"A few," Celeste said cheerfully. "But you will be offered only good choices, so whatever you wear will look stunning."

"Indeed, milady has a magnificent figure," Madame Renault observed. "With your height and natural form, it's a crime the way you have concealed yourself with plain garments and inferior stays."

"If magnificent means overblown, you're right," Abby said tartly. "Even when I was thirteen, I didn't have the elegance of figure that the duchess possesses."

Madame Ravelle shook her head. "There is more than one kind of beauty, Lady Frayne. Her grace is the epitome of ethereal elegance. Men and women gasp when they see her. She is like a fairy queen who is briefly visiting earth to grant mere mortals a glimpse of timeless beauty."

Celeste laughed. "That is ludicrously overblown flattery, Madame Ravelle."

"Overblown, perhaps, but essentially accurate," Abby commented.

Madame Renault turned to her. "Your beauty is of an earthier, more sensual kind, Milady Frayne. When you enter a ballroom, women will see a well-dressed woman and continue what they were doing. Men will stare and yearn and consider challenging your lord husband to a duel to win your favor."

Abby's jaw dropped. "I hope your dressmaking skills are equal to your flattery. I am not the sort to arouse jealous, lustful thoughts. I don't think I would want to be."

"Wait and see," Celeste said. "I don't think you will be displeased by the results." She lifted a bolt of blue silk and pulled several yards loose, then draped it across Abby. "Look in the mirror. What do you think about this fabric for your ball gown?"

Abby turned to the full-length mirror, then gasped. The silk shimmered a myriad of blues that emphasized her eyes. And the feel! She lifted a fold to rub her cheek. It was the most sensual, luxurious fabric she'd ever touched. "It's marvelous. Any woman would feel beautiful wearing this."

"Which is part of the magic of fine clothing, Abby," Celeste said seriously. "If one feels beautiful, one is beautiful. As a child, I was a scrappy little tomboy who always had twigs in my hair and grass stains on my skirts. I might have been considered a pretty child, but I didn't become beautiful until I set my mind to it." Her gaze became distant. "That was when my mother decided it was time to take me in hand. She is the one who taught me that beauty begins in the mind." She turned to the sisters. "We're off to a good start, madames. I look forward to what you will create."

The dressmakers and their assistants swiftly collected their fabrics, pins, measuring tapes, and other paraphernalia and withdrew. One assistant helped Abby don her old morning gown again. Never had it looked so plain.

When Abby was alone with Celeste, she collapsed on the sofa. "I'm exhausted and all I did was stand still while they treated me like a dress doll!"

"Of course you're tired—over four hours have passed. You'll feel better after we have a light luncheon." Celeste pulled the bell rope to summon a servant. "In the meantime, think of your new wardrobe as armor against the claws of society."

"I just hope I haven't bankrupted Jack," Abby muttered.

"You haven't, quite. Believe me, he'll think it's worth every penny."

Abby allowed herself a brief fantasy of Jack looking at her with dazzled, yearning eyes. She didn't believe it would really happen. But it was a lovely fantasy.

Afternoon was darkening to evening when Jack returned to Alderton House. After shaking off rain, he ascended to his room and summoned Morris to help him remove his boots. Then he went in search of his wife.

He found Abby napping under a fluffy quilt. He parked his cane, pulled off his coat and shoes, then slid under the quilt beside her.

She was lying on her side, so he curved his body around hers, her back to his front. She murmured drowsily, "You're cold."

A sensible woman would retreat from his chilled self, but she reached for his left arm and pulled it around her waist. Muscle by muscle, he began to relax. "I'd forgotten how tiring London is."

"Now that your magic has been released, it will be even more tiring. Being around so many people drains power like a hole in a barrel leaks ale."

"It's always going to be so tiring in town?" he asked with alarm.

"After a few days, one adapts." She yawned. "I always need to nap the first day or two in the city. Luckily Celeste doesn't want me to be seen in society until the ball."

He propped himself on one elbow and studied Abby's face, noting the dark circles under her eyes. She did look thoroughly drained. "Since she and Alderton are going off to various affairs tonight, she suggested that we could have dinner here in our rooms."

"What a wonderful idea!" Her eyes opened. "I really like your sister, Jack."

"So do I." She had been the most constant, reliable member of his family. The one who was always glad to see him. "I hope you or Judith can do something for her."

"I wrote Judith this afternoon. I should hear back within the week." Abby shifted, her delightfully rounded backside pressing against him.

"What did you do today that roused you from bed so early? I was so sleepy I forgot to ask."

"I started with the regimental broker to formally list my commission for sale. Then I visited a tailor who specializes in making official robes of state to get ready for when I take my seat." He tightened his hold on her waist. "You'll need a set, too. Never can tell when there will be a royal funeral or some such where peers and peeresses have to parade in full finery."

"I spent half the day being mauled by your sister's modistes and their merry crews," Abby said gloomily. "I'm sure the results will be excellent, but I can't say that I enjoyed the process."

He chuckled. "I did the same this afternoon. Ashby came back to town and dragged me to his tailor. He stayed the whole time because he didn't trust my taste and feared I might bolt."

Her laughter was soft against him. "You and I have become victims of the more fashionable."

"To be honest, I was glad to have him there, once he accepted my basic rule: no garments that I can't put on or take off by myself. What's the point of a coat that requires assistance? Nothing could make a great ox like me look like a dandy even if I was willing to wear such clothes."

"Is Ashby a dandy?"

"No, he's the epitome of gentlemanly elegance. He has the figure for it. I don't, so it's best to stick with a plain, well-cut style that calls no attention."

"I'd like to do the same, being cut on generous lines myself, but I don't know if I'll be allowed to look so sensible." She sighed melodramatically. "I'm not even sure I'll be able to breathe in my new stays. The corsetiere had a dangerous gleam in her eyes."

He laughed. "Keep your courage up, my girl. We'll survive and escape back to the country in a few weeks." He moved his hand up to circle comfortably around her breast. "But for now, we'll nap."

And they did.

Chapter XXI

The Alderton chef did as fine a job on a light supper for two as he would a banquet for the Prince Regent. Abby thought it was almost indecent to enjoy such food in her robe rather than in formal dress. If so, she was in favor of indecency.

After a footman removed the empty trays and plates from their sitting room, Abby asked, "Do you think it would be a breach of wizardly ethics if I ensorcelled your sister's chef to work for us?"

"Probably, and Celeste would cut my liver out." His brows drew together. "I know you're joking, but it makes me realize how compelling temptation can be."

She made a face. "Every day offers temptations to use magic for personal advantage. It's lucky that protective charms are so common. They reduce the temptation to try to manipulate others."

"Manipulation." Jack grimaced. "I said I'd tell you when I was ready to have my mind cleansed. I'm ready now. I want to find out who I am when no one is trying to shape me to his will."

"Are you sure?" she asked gravely. "To enter someone's mind is very intimate. Don't grant permission unless you trust me fully."

"I don't like the idea of you seeing all my most shameful thoughts, but there is no one I would trust more, Abby. Go ahead."

"I'm only going to look for spells," she said reassuringly. "Minds are complicated. It's not as if I can read your thoughts. Entering a mind is more like walking through a crowded attic looking for candles. Any glimmer of light will attract my attention, but everything else is like piles of boxes and trunks. I'll have no idea what they contain."

"As long as you don't open any trunks and look inside! What should I do?"

"Get into a comfortable position on the sofa and relax. If you like, I can describe what I find as I go along."

"That would be good." Jack moved to the sofa and sat at one end.

Abby doused most of the lights and tossed some coal on the fire to maintain the room's warmth. Then she placed a chair in front of Jack and sat so close their knees were touching. For a moment she was distracted by their closeness, for the sheer broad masculinity of him made her senses sing.

But tonight's work was more important than her discreetly lusting after her husband. "Let me know if you feel something strange or upsetting." She took his hands in hers. "I can stop at any time."

His steady hazel gaze met hers unflinchingly. "I would rather we stayed with this until you've done all that needs doing."

She closed her eyes and centered in her power before reaching out to Jack. As she had told him, entering another person's mind was like visiting a strange attic filled with murky, confusing objects. If she stopped to examine a particular structure, she could get a general sense of what it meant, and with time could interpret it rather well.

But her job was to find what didn't belong—the constraints and compulsions that had been imposed on him by others, not Jack's private thoughts.

She tuned her magic to seek what was alien. Almost immediately she discovered an angry knot of energy. She hated the idea of going near it, so naturally she made herself look more closely.

"Here's something," she murmured. "Definitely a spell that has been in place for years. Let's see what it's designed for." She frowned as she analyzed its nature. "Yes! As we speculated, it's a repulsion spell that makes you want to avoid a particular place. In this case, Yorkshire."

"Can you tell who cast it?"

"Perhaps." She touched the angry knot with her mind and flooded it with neutralizing energy. After years in place, the spell was rigid but also brittle. As she increased the flow of healing magic, the ugly pattern splintered and dissolved.

Jack swore and squeezed Abby's hands hard.

Her eyes flew open. "You felt that?"

"Yes, and I'm ready to ride to Yorkshire tonight. How could I have stayed away from my home so long?" His voice was anguished. "Underneath that spell, my soul has been hungering for my home for years. I have been like a tree severed from my roots." He took an unsteady breath. "Did you identify the source of the spell?"

She studied the remnants of energy. "Male and a skilled black magician, but I don't know the name. We probably wouldn't recognize it anyhow—black magicians prefer to avoid notice. As for going to Yorkshire—first there is business to finish here in London. But soon we'll be heading north."

"I know," he said grudgingly. "Another few weeks will make no great difference, but it will be hard to wait." His hands relaxed their grip on hers. "Is there more?"

"I think so." She closed her eyes and began seeking again. Gradually she became aware of a dark energy that pulsated with surly menace. It was certainly a spell, but not a type she recognized.

She approached the dark energy cautiously, aware that it was possible to create spells that would explode in a blaze of dangerous magic if someone attempted to break them. After careful study she decided this one wasn't a trap, merely an unusual spell. She touched it with her magic and gave a huff of surprise.

"What have you found?"

"This is really strange. I think it's a spell to . . . to make you reckless," she said slowly. "The effect would be for you to crave thrills even if the danger is overwhelming. I've never seen anything like it."

"Good God! You mean it's meant to encourage me into activities where I might die young?" Jack exclaimed. "Like going into the army?"

"Yes, though I don't know if the spell is old enough to be responsible for that." Abby poked at it mentally. "I think it was created by the same wizard who cast the spell to keep you away from Yorkshire. Scranton must have wanted you not only distant but dead if possible." She smiled without humor. "After all, few women love their husbands more than their sons, so you were competition for your mother's favor."

Jack's hands tightened again with painful force. "Could my father have been the object of a similar spell?"

"Impossible to know at this late date. But if Scranton did commission a wizard to cast such a spell on your father, he's not only a villain but a murderer," Abby said grimly.

"I acquired the nickname Lucky Jack when I charged into a melee of murderous French soldiers and managed to recover the regimental flag when the bearer was killed and the banner was captured. Everyone said I should have died, but I didn't." Jack's voice was tight. "Was my so-called courage the result of a spell meant to destroy me?"

She shook her head. "There is courage to spare in you—I don't have to look into your mind closely to know that. But the spell probably affected your judgment of the odds for survival, sending you into situations where death would seem almost certain."

He released his breath roughly. "Why am I still alive, Abby? God knows I've had no shortage of opportunities to die from my recklessness."

"Perhaps your natural defenses were strong enough to counter the spell. Or . . . wait a moment." She had continued to study the pulsing energy. "The spell is surrounded by a subtle net of magic bound so closely that it's almost invisible."

"Is it more work from the black magician?"

"No, this spell is completely different in nature. It's all patched out of little fragments of power, as if constructed by an amateur." Abby probed farther before giving a soft whistle of awe. "The net was created by Celeste, and it largely neutralized the recklessness spell. Not entirely, but mostly."

"My sister did that?" he said incredulously. "She says she has had no training and little power. How could she identify a dangerous spell cast by a master wizard and know enough to counter it?"

Abby touched one of the patchwork strands. It hummed its nature in her mind. "She didn't, not deliberately. The net is composed of prayers. There is magic in prayers, you know, for they invoke the divine. For years she has prayed for your safety, and those prayers were drawn to this ugly, dangerous spell. The power of love neutralized the destructiveness. I believe she has saved your life, probably again and again."

"I had no idea." He shook his head in amazement. "I owe her more than I can repay."

Abby drained and neutralized the sullen energy of the recklessness spell, aided by Celeste's patchwork magic. She was grateful for that extra energy, since her power was flagging. "I'll look around to see if there are more spells lurking. Are there any areas where you feel your behavior has not been in line with your natural inclinations?"

He thought a moment, then shook his head. "I don't believe so. But at this point, I'm not sure what my natural inclinations are."

"I'll make sure I'm thorough, then." Abby continued her scanning and found a clumsily made attraction spell. "It looks like a lady in Spain managed to capture your attention with the crudest of aphrodisiac spells."

Jack blushed. "She was no lady."

Abby grinned, able to be amused since the spell indicated only the most casual of connections between Jack and the dubious lady. Nonetheless, she obliterated traces of the spell to reduce the likelihood of him cherishing fond memories of the wench.

"I'll do one last scan to see if anything else looks out of place." She changed her mental focus and moved through the complex patterns of Jack's mind.

Because of the strength of the anti-magic spell he'd carried so many years, there seemed to be none of the minor spell fragments found in most minds. The Spanish attraction spell never would have worked if it hadn't reinforced an action he was already inclined to. There seemed to be nothing else.

She sensed a quiet pulse of energy that wasn't Jack. It didn't seem to be a spell, but there was enough power to influence him. She looked closer and blushed hotly when she saw a ripe, voluptuous image of herself.

When she could bring herself to look more closely, she saw that her image wore only a shift—one that was much too sheer!—and her loose hair tumbled over her shoulders. Her lips were parted slightly in a provocative smile and her eyes were languorous. Good God, were her breasts and hips so lush compared to her waist?

Knowing that he saw her like this was the most embarrassing thing she'd ever seen. And the most gratifying. It wasn't only her face that felt hot.

Her image winked at her! Even more embarrassed, Abby collected herself and withdrew from Jack's mind.

Wondering if that image was merely a sign of her fatigue, she released Jack's hands and flexed her fingers. "Your mind is your own again, Jack. How does it feel?"

After a long moment, he opened his eyes and gave a smile that touched her heart. "It feels good." He stood and arched his back, stretching his arms like a lion waking from sleep. He made a delicious sight. "Now to find out what it is to have my mind to myself."

His gaze became unfocused for long moments. Then he snapped back to awareness and said with dangerous fury, "What the hell are you doing to me?"

Chapter XXII

Abby shrank back from Jack's anger. "I don't understand what you mean."

He gestured at the subtle glowing line that connected his solar plexus to Abby's. "This *thing* connecting us. I'll be damned if I'll let you replace the spells of Stark and the black magician with your own."

She bit her lip. "It's life force energy, not a spell. Look closer. You should be able to tell that it's not magic."

He focused on the glowing line and tried to analyze it. The energy flow was from her to him, and she was right, it didn't look or feel like a spell. The warm purity made sense for life force. Transferring vital force might require magical ability, but the energy itself was not magic. "You seem to be telling the truth, but why are you doing this?" he asked suspiciously.

"Because you were so weak, I've been sending energy to you since the accident." She brushed her hair back nervously. "The one time I stopped, you suffered a relapse and I had to rush to you in the middle of the night. It seemed best to continue supplying you vital force until you were fully healed. You've been doing so many things that required a lot of energy. I didn't want you to hurt yourself by going beyond your capacity, so I augmented your strength and stamina."

He frowned, trying to understand. "So this energy is your personal vitality?"

She nodded. "All living things have life force, even the smallest blade of grass. Healers are particularly good at detecting and using it. The energy is like . . . like a glowing candle. Before your accident, you blazed like the chandelier in a royal ballroom. After, there was only the barest flicker of life force. Even after the healing circle, your vitality was dangerously low, which is why I've been augmenting it."

"Surely you need that energy for yourself!"

Her gaze slid away from his. "I gave you no more than I could spare."

Despite her assurance, he was still doubtful. He studied her, really seeing the signs of deep fatigue that had gradually accumulated. She had lost weight since their marriage. Her cheekbones were more prominent and there were dark circles under her eyes. Worse, the energy glow around her was dull and weak.

"You've been undermining your own health to help mine," he said, unable to master his anger. "That can't be right."

She brushed her hair back wearily. "Judith has scolded me about this. But I wanted you well."

She had been sacrificing her own health for his for weeks. Was that a mark of a healer? Or someone too selfless for her own good? "This cannot be allowed to continue." He closed his hand over the glowing energy line, at the same time mentally cutting off the flow. His midriff twanged like a severed bowstring.

"You're right," she said, not resisting his action. "It's time for you to rely on your own resources. You're almost fully healed now."

Her aura brightened when he severed the connection, but it still seemed weak. As for himself, he felt loss. Abby's energy had provided a warmth that he now missed. Even when he'd been avoiding her at Hill

House, on some level he must have known they were connected. Now he felt cold, empty—and angry. He wanted that warmth back, but not by stealing her very life.

He shoved himself up from the sofa and stalked around the sitting room, his cane banging the floor with each step. "Damnation, Abby, I'm tired of being treated as a child! My condition hasn't been critical for weeks. If I foolishly push myself to collapse, I'll deserve it and will recover soon enough. To prevent that, you've been slowly bleeding yourself to death." He spun around and limped toward her with a glare. "The last thing I want is a wife who's a bloody martyr!"

She met his gaze steadily, her eyes transparent as water. "I didn't intend to martyr myself, but you're right, I kept giving you energy for too long." She was silent for a long moment, the circles under her eyes stark against her pale skin. "To be honest, I think I liked having that connection with you. I was not of your class and you despised my magical talents, but by quietly giving you some of my essence, I could feel that I was vital to you. It's not an admirable explanation."

Her painful honesty caught at his heart. He frowned. He hated knowing that he had taken so much from her.

It was time he returned some of her energy. Even her loss of weight and bone-deep fatigue couldn't eliminate her innate sensuality, so he caught her hands and pulled her to her feet. Then he kissed her hard, driven by a volatile mixture of anger and desire. Desire won. He wanted her, and finally, by God, he was going to have her.

After an instant of shock, her mouth opened under his and her arms wrapped around him. The fatigue that had dogged her for weeks vanished in a blaze of desire. Since their marriage, she had done her best to suppress the passion he roused, but that was no longer necessary. He was all blazing male force, and she gloried in him.

Intoxicated by the deepening kiss, she ripped at his sash and opened his robe, then stripped the garment away so that he wore only his nightshirt. His skin was hot under the thin fabric. She kneaded his back and hips, feeling the pulse of his blood in his hard muscles. And that was not the only part of him that was hard and pulsing.

He pulled off her robe so that it pooled around their feet, tangled wantonly with his robe. They pressed body to body with only night-clothes separating them. Wherever he touched, her blood rose up to meet him. Energy flowed around and through them in shimmering rainbows of light.

He pulled at the throat of her nightgown. Buttons popped, baring her throat. He nipped the tender skin, sending dark fire burning through her veins.

The image of herself she'd seen in his mind blazed in her imagination, flooding her with a sense of womanly power. She raised his chin and captured his mouth again, wanting to consume him, to inhale his essence.

He kicked the robes away and walked her back toward her bedroom. They stumbled clumsily, banging into the door frame because neither wanted to end the fierce locking of lips and tongues.

She realized that they'd reached the bed when the back of her legs struck the frame. She yanked the covers down and they tumbled onto the mattress, lying angled across it. His groin pressed into hers as their thrashing bodies tried to mate through their remaining garments.

He tugged her nightgown down another foot, buttons popping as he freed her breasts. "Magnificent," he breathed. "Your body is as generous as your spirit. Rich and full and tempting, offering all a man could ever desire." His lips caught and tugged on one nipple. She arched her back with a sharp gasp.

His words were as arousing as his touch. She had dreamed that someday he might want her as much as she wanted him. Now his urgent mouth and taut body and harsh breathing said that he did.

His caressing hand continued down over her belly as he suckled her other breast. When he reached the juncture of her thighs, her toes curled. "You seem to be . . . well recovered?" she said, desperately hoping they could achieve full union.

"We'll find out just how well," he said with a hint of wicked laughter.

From the warm pressure against her thigh, his blood supply must be close to normal. Dear lord, she hoped so!

She moaned as his palm skimmed upward under her nightgown. How could she feel so many glorious sensations at once? She thrust against his hand when he found that place of moist, heated need. "Don't stop," she gasped. "Not even if the sky falls."

"I'm not stopping till you're limp and sated and your life force energy is restored." He stroked deeper, his fingers sliding inside to tease and expand the hidden entryway. "Now, let's see. . . ."

He raised himself to balance above her on his knees. For an instant she worried if he was hurting his injured leg, but that was for him to decide. He was a man, her husband, not her patient. Selfishly she craved all he had to give.

He used both hands to rip her nightgown all the way to the hem, exposing her whole body to his avid gaze. Though she knew the night air was cool, she burned from the urgency of his desire.

His own nightshirt came off after a swift, fevered tussle, and finally they could be flesh to flesh. Dear heaven, but he was splendid, his strong bones sheathed in hard, warm muscle! The textures of his body entranced her, and she dug her fingers into his back and buttocks and long limbs.

He raised himself on his knees again, his body limned in light. Then he lowered himself so that their bodies crushed together, his chest flattening her breasts, his powerful legs between hers. His mouth recaptured hers at the same time that his shaft settled along the heated slickness of her cleft. He rocked back and forth, the friction sending cascades of mad pleasure through her.

She was on the verge of culmination when he drew his hips back, then used one hand to guide himself into the secret entry to her body. Exquisitely balanced between excitement and pain, she thrust her hips up against him, ignoring the discomfort of being stretched to the breaking point. Now, *now* . . .

Then suddenly he was inside her, filling her with the intimacy she had longed for. She rocked her hips in astonished delight.

He gasped raggedly. "I . . . I don't know how long I can last."

"Long enough." She thrust her hips up again, stimulated unbearably in unnamed places. Her arms locked around his waist, as if they could merge into one flesh.

Madness erupted, swirling them into wild motion as he plunged ever deeper. Magic, passion, craving and fulfillment, crashed over her like waves of a rainbow ocean. She was falling into him, spinning through the layers of his spirit while sharing the most private sanctuary of her soul. She hadn't known such intimacy of body and soul were possible.

For a timeless instant they fused into one being before the blazing, transforming energy began to ebb. She spun to earth like a leaf, acutely aware of his weight, the rough gulps of her breath, the deeply satisfying ache between her thighs, and the rapturous fact that they were still gently joined.

She would have liked to have him on top of her forever, but there was the question of breathing. Regretfully she shifted from under him and pulled blankets over their exhausted bodies. The air was bitingly cold now that the heat of passion had been consumed in its own flame. She touched herself, soothing away the lingering pain and stopping the minor bleeding created by their joining. Then she cuddled up against him again, draping one arm across his broad chest.

He gave a long, rattling sigh. "I think I've returned all the energy you gave me and then some. I may never move again."

She laughed with what breath she could spare. "Are you still angry with me?"

His large hand began massaging her bare shoulder. "I haven't the strength for anything so energetic as anger. But if you're wondering if I'm still upset at your endangering yourself on my behalf, the answer is yes. You saved my life, and if you thought that I needed extra vitality at first, you were probably right. But you had no right to endanger my wife's life by giving away more life force than could be spared."

"Yes, my lord husband," she said meekly.

His chest rumbled with laughter. "Do you think I'll believe you've suddenly turned obedient?"

"No, but I agree you have a point in this case." They fell silent, drowsing, his hand slowly caressing her bare skin.

After a lazy interval, he said, "The footman left two glasses and half a bottle of that rather nice claret in case we wanted to finish it. Shall I retrieve them?"

She stretched luxuriously. "Drinking wine in bed. How deliciously decadent that would be. Don't be gone long."

He swung his feet to the floor while she admired the powerful symmetry of his muscled back. Had she left those scratches? She blushed at the thought.

"Being distracted, I left my cane in the other room." He stepped gingerly onto his right foot, then halted.

Instantly alert, Abby sat up in the bed. "Is something wrong?"

"Quite the contrary." He took another step, then walked in a quick, tight circle. "The last of the pain is gone! My leg is completely healed!"

"Good heavens! I wonder how that happened?" She studied his broad figure, which was silhouetted against the light from the sitting room. All traces of red pain energy had vanished and his aura pulsed with vitality. "You're a picture of good health."

He leaned forward and planted an exuberant kiss on her lips. "Obviously it's a result of our becoming lovers. All the wonderful energy we generated must have finished healing my leg. How do you feel?"

She considered. "Wonderful, now that you mention it. Not merely content, but in blooming good health." It was the best she'd felt since the healing circle.

"You look well, too." He scanned her critically. "The darkness under your eyes has faded and you look radiant. Your vital force has increased tremendously."

Her brows drew together. "There is an element of magic in the surrender of virginity. Perhaps doing so produced enough energy to bring both of us to the best possible health?"

"That sounds reasonable, and if it's not the right explanation, no matter. What matters is how we feel." He caught her hand and laced his fingers through hers. "Let's get dressed and take a walk. I wasn't sure I'd ever be able to walk normally again, so I want to celebrate by walking."

"It's cold out there!"

He kissed the tip of her nose. "Dress warmly."

With a laugh, she surrendered and slid out of the bed, making a bee-line for the clothespress. She yanked her heaviest flannel shift over her head, then reached for thick knit stockings. "My warm bed is looking very good right now!"

"It will look even better later." Jack retreated to his own bedroom to dress, returning in time to fasten the ties on her gown. She wrapped a soft paisley scarf around her throat, liking the silliness of their going out in the middle of a winter night.

Equally silly and enjoyable was helping each other dress, laughing at their clumsy fingers and stolen kisses. She looped another warm scarf around Jack's neck, thinking it would have been easy to ring the servants' hall for help, but this was more fun. At the moment, anything they did together was fun.

As Jack placed her warmest cloak over her shoulders, she said, "Maybe you ought to take your cane, just in case the cold makes your leg ache again."

He laughed. "You do worry, don't you? Very well, I'll take the cane even though I don't need it."

He buttoned his greatcoat and donned a hat, then offered Abby his arm. She took it with ridiculously possessive pleasure, feeling truly married.

A footman sat by the front door, waiting for the duke and duchess to return home from their activities. "We won't be out long, Williams," Jack said.

The footman bowed them out, only the faintest twitch of his cheek showing surprise that the duchess's brother and his bride wanted to go for a walk on a cold winter's night.

"It's snowing!" Abby said with delight as they walked down the steps.

"So it is." Jack gave her a slanting smile. "A magical end for a magical night."

She tightened her grip on his arm. Yes, what they had shared was magic, but it was of a profoundly human kind. And thank God for it.

Chapter XXIII

Less than an inch of snow had fallen, just enough to glaze the streets to pristine white. Reflected light made it easy to see the way, though Jack found himself glad that he had the cane to balance against occasional slipperiness. A few windows glowed here and there, but they had the night to themselves. That would change later, when carriages began returning the Quality to their homes. Until then, their footprints marked the only trail in the soft whiteness.

He couldn't ever remember being happier.

Nice that Abby wasn't a chatterer. Like him, she was content to enjoy the silence. Crystalline flakes caught in her lashes like stars and frosted the warm hat she had donned. Though the air was icy cold, their warm garments kept them cozy. It was easy to forget she was a wizard. What mattered was that she was his wife.

He linked his fingers through hers and buried their joined hands in the left pocket of his heavy greatcoat. There was a delicious intimacy in their closeness that was unlike anything he'd ever experienced with a woman. He fancied that he was learning a thing or two about what *romantic* meant.

"I calculate that with another half hour or so of recovery time, I'll be ready to make love to you again, so let's be back at Alderton House by then," he murmured.

She gave him a deliciously wicked glance from the corner of her eye. "It's merely your opinion that you'll be ready. We shall see."

"If my leg is healed, so is my blood," he said positively. "In fact . . ."

He stopped and turned her toward him for another kiss, this one deep and leisurely. They were alone in the heart of London, and he wanted to kiss his wife. She filled his arms, wonderfully satisfying.

She gave a sigh of pleasure when their lips separated, her breath a pale plume in the night. "If we walk around this block and head back, will that get us to Alderton House at the right time? Or should we just head back now?"

He chuckled. "Insatiable wench. We'll walk around the block and then return."

They ambled along two sides of the block and had turned to head back when he noticed a stealthy movement from the corner of his right eye. Instantly alert, he glanced to his right for a closer look.

Someone was behind him. Before he could react to the knowledge, a man slammed into his back, the solid weight accompanied by rank smells.

Jack staggered, almost falling. Abby's grip and the cane kept him on his feet. Releasing her hand, he stepped in front of her and spun to confront their assailants.

Two—no, three—thieves had appeared from a narrow alley and gathered in a half circle just beyond arm's reach from Jack. "Give us yer money and jewelry and you might walk away," one of the shadowy figures snarled, raising his hand to reveal the glittering blade of a knife.

The one in the center said, " 'Ware, he's a big brute! You better—"

Lightning quick, Jack swung his cane up and rammed the tip into the man's throat before the sentence could be completed. His target made a horrid gurgling sound and staggered backward. Blood spurted from his throat as he collapsed into the snow.

In one swift movement, Jack swung the cane around and knocked the knife from the grip of the other man. It spun to the ground, catching the light as it fell. Before the knife hit the cobblestones, Jack slammed the cane into the assailant behind him. A howl of agony proved that he'd hit his target.

"Bastard!" The other man scrabbled in the snow to retrieve the knife, then moved forward, watching the cane warily. Since the thief's gaze was on the cane, a roundhouse punch from Jack's left hand was enough to smash his nose with an audible crunch. As blood splattered, the thief tried to retreat, but he slipped on the snow and fell clumsily. His head hit the ground with an audible thump and he lay unmoving.

The man struck in the throat also lay still, his blood a black stain in the snow. The one who'd tackled Jack from behind was wrapped around himself, moaning horribly as his crossed hands protected his injured crotch.

Jack drew a deep breath, shaky now that the need for action was over. "Are you all right, Abby?"

"I . . . I'm fine." She stood rigid, her hands clenched. "They never touched me."

"Fortunate that you suggested I bring my cane. It made a good weapon." He watched his wife narrowly. "You're sure you're all right?"

"Sh-shaken." She collected herself with visible effort. "I hadn't really thought about your military life. You are very good at fighting."

He shrugged. "The military life doesn't involve much actual combat. There are a lot more long days slapping flies and trying to keep the men out of trouble. But when one needs to fight, there are no second chances, so it needs to be done well."

"Did you know where that man was behind you, or was it a lucky blow?"

He thought about it. "I believe I did know. I struck at him without thinking, but even so, I knew I would hit where he was most vulnerable."

"Do you always know the location of your enemies when you fight? If so, it might be a magical ability. A valuable one."

Startled, he thought back. It was disquieting to think he might have been using magic for years. "You may be right," he said reluctantly. "Usually the action is so fast I don't have time to think, but if I do know who is around me, that had to have helped me survive. But that's really not magic. More like soldierly instinct."

"Call it what you will, but seeing what's behind you is definitely a gift."

He shrugged uneasily. "Everyone has a little magic. This kind is common among soldiers who survive for any length of time." Wanting to change the subject, he studied the fallen men, their bodies dark against the snow. "Now to decide what to do with these villains. I think there's a watch station nearby."

"A watchman from there is patrolling about a block away and heading in this direction. I imagine Mayfair gets better protection than most neighborhoods." Her voice caught as she gestured at the man he'd struck in the throat. "No need to hurry for this one. He's dead." Her voice was flat.

Jack was silent a moment. "I didn't mean to kill him, but I can't say I have any regrets, either." He thought about the rage and violence he'd felt from the assailants. "They would have robbed us, maybe even killed us on a whim."

"And possibly raped me first. I know." Abby rubbed at her temples. "They are not good men. But when someone dies, especially so abruptly, I . . . feel it."

"I'm sorry." Jack wondered how death felt to someone like Abby. A painful emptiness? He had noticed nothing, but he was no healer. "I wonder if this attack was pure bad luck, or if the danger spells in my mind helped draw these men to us."

"You could be right," she said with a frown. "Those spells might have drawn these villains into your vicinity. If we hadn't walked out tonight, they might have moved on to attack others now that the spells have been removed. I certainly hope this doesn't happen again!"

The man whose nose had been broken made a bubbling sound and pushed his hands against the ground in a feeble attempt to sit up. As Jack stepped closer, Abby said sharply, "Don't hit him again. I think I can keep them asleep until the watch arrives."

"That would be good." Though Jack would do what was necessary, he wasn't keen on striking men who were down.

She knelt in the snow and placed one hand on the moaning man's temple. After a moment, he slumped to the ground again. She turned to the other survivor and did the same while Jack thought about what had happened. He'd killed before, but never had he found it so sobering. Just as well that he was leaving the army, since a man couldn't think too much about the results of what he was doing when fighting for his life.

He was not the man he had been. This was another disturbing thought. But it didn't mean he was a wizard.

The watchman appeared, as Abby had predicted. Jack waved the fellow over. "I'm Lord Frayne and this is Lady Frayne. These men attacked us."

The watchman was broad and elderly, and he had the air of competence that suggested he was a retired sergeant. He made a quick examination of the thieves. "There been other attacks 'round here lately. Looks like you put a stop to that." He rose creakily and gave Jack a curious glance. "You took all three down?"

"Ten years as an army officer," Jack said tersely. "May I take my wife home? We're staying at Alderton House. I'm brother to the duchess, and you can find me there if you need a statement about this incident."

"Go along and take care of your lady, my lord. Someone will call at Alderton House tomorrow for that statement. You've done the city a service tonight." The watchman tipped his hat, then pulled manacles from his pocket.

Jack took Abby's hand and they returned to his sister's house. Their earlier playfulness was gone. As they climbed the steps of Alderton House, Abby asked, "What will happen to the two men who survived?"

"Probably transportation to New South Wales."

"It's said the colony is warm and sunny, so they may end up grateful." Her attempt at lightness was undermined by a shiver.

He put his arm around her shoulders, not caring what the footman who let them in might think. "It's been a full day, lass."

And a day that had ended on a sobering note. They returned to their rooms, changed into nightclothes, and climbed into bed with few words. He drew Abby into his arms and felt better when she settled down with a contented sigh. There was comfort in closeness. He suspected that there might be even more comfort in making love, but he didn't need to be a wizard to know that his bride was not in the mood for passion.

Despite having Abby in his arms, his sleep was troubled. *He soared over the blighted hills and valley of Langdale, his heart anguished by the sorrow below. His mate flew with him, above and a little behind, guarding his journey.*

Abby had said, "You always know the location of your enemies."

His enemy was below, in Langdale Hall. Sir Alfred Scranton wasn't just an unpleasant family connection, but truly Jack's enemy. The battle for Langdale's soul would not end till one of them was dead.

Sweating, Jack jarred into wakefulness. He stared into the darkness, his arm tightening around Abby. Was his dream a prophecy, or an expression of his worst fears? Would it be possible to separate Scranton from his mother without breaking her heart? She adored the man, her letters were mostly about him. Yet Scranton must go.

The simplest resolution of the problem would be to evict Scranton from Langdale Hall, forbidding him to ever return. Jack's mother would presumably accompany her husband and be bitter about her son's treatment of Scranton.

Jack knew in his bones that the solution wouldn't be so simple. Too many dark influences were involved. Yet when the crisis came, he would have no choice. He was an army officer and a lord, and both of those roles required him to protect those who were his responsibility—even at the cost of his mother's happiness.

He had a swift mental image of his mother laughing as she took his hand and they ran into the house to escape a rain shower. He had been perhaps five or six years old. She had wrapped him in a shawl, then had a rainy day tea party with him and Celeste, who had been very proud to be trusted with a delicate porcelain teacup. That day had been his mother at her best.

If he destroyed her husband, she would hate him forever.

His mouth twisted. Given how estranged they had become, that would not be very different from the present situation, but at least now she didn't hate him.

With a sigh, he closed his eyes and willed himself to sleep, one hand stroking Abby's shoulder. He would do what must be done—and may God help them all.

Abby awoke slowly, so comfortable in her husband's embrace that she was reluctant to move. Too much had happened the previous day. Her cleansing Jack's mind of old spells, his loss of temper with her. The consummation of their marriage.

The first time she'd seen her husband kill a man.

Yet when she opened her eyes, he was sleeping peacefully, his face looking the same as always. Strong, good-humored, tolerant. It was her perception that had changed. She was grateful to have a husband so capable of defending her, but she felt as if one of her tabbies had turned into a tiger.

No matter. He was a soldier as well as her husband, and soldiers killed when they had to. She trusted him to do what was appropriate.

She realized that he was now watching her through lazily slit eyes. "Good morning," he murmured. "I wonder what today will bring."

She stretched like a cat, managing to move closer to Jack. "Celeste will give me lessons on surviving the ton, complete with diagrams on who hates whom and who the worst gossips are." She contemplated the prospect without pleasure. "What about you?"

"Alderton and Ashby are dragging me around the clubs to introduce me to various political chieftains." He sighed. "I'm not looking forward to it."

"Let's see, White's is Tory, Brooks' is Whig. Which do you belong to?"

"Both." He grinned. "I prefer to keep everyone guessing. Besides, I don't agree completely with either of the parties. I think I shall be independent and universally despised by both sides."

"Can I go and baffle the politicians with you? It sounds interesting."

"Trust me, it won't be."

She chuckled at his vehemence. "Did I mention that Celeste has arranged for us to have dancing lessons three days from now?"

Jack looked appalled. "I'm recovering from a dire injury! I don't have to dance."

"You're not an invalid anymore," she pointed out. "Unless you can convince your sister that you're in agony or crippled, it's dance lessons for you."

"Celeste is a tyrant," he said gloomily.

"But for your own good." Abby sighed. "I would just as soon avoid dancing myself, but Celeste says that if I do, I'll call more attention to myself than if I do take the floor. I don't have to be brilliant, merely unexceptionable. I suppose I can manage that after lessons to teach me what is fashionable so I won't appear too rustic."

"By the time we head north, we'll both be ready to flee the city," he predicted. His hand moved down her with gentle thoroughness. "As for now . . ."

When he kissed her, she returned it with interest. She was still a little shy, but that was changing fast.

To her surprise, Jack caught hold of her waist and lifted her so that she was sprawled full length on top of him. "What?"

He grinned. "Use that fine mind of yours."

She relaxed and looked down into his warm hazel eyes, and found that she quite liked having his hard male body underneath her. He gasped when she gave a slow roll of her hips. Encouraged, she began to slowly unfasten the buttons at the throat of her nightgown. His eyes darkened as he watched, until he seized her shoulders and pulled her close enough for him to kiss her breasts.

Excitement shot through her, bringing every fiber of her body to urgent life. She settled down and started using her fine mind.

Among other things.

Chapter XXIV

Every day in London was crowded with activity, but gradually Abby's strength and magical reserves recovered from the weeks of strain and depletion. She should be ready for whatever Yorkshire had to offer.

Even the dancing lessons were less fearsome than expected. Abby found that Jack was actually a capable dancer. She shouldn't have been surprised, given his athletic skills. Despite commencing the lessons with a pained expression, he was soon enjoying himself.

The lessons were one of the few occasions when they saw each other during the day, since Jack was as busy as she. Luckily they came together at night, and what nights! Abby started every day with a daft, happy smile.

So did Jack. That was a source of great satisfaction to her.

A week after the initial session of measurements and choosing fabrics, the formidable dressmaker twins returned for final fittings and took over Abby's bedroom. While Celeste perused her correspondence in the sitting room, Abby was marched into the bedroom, attended by the sisters. They started by styling her hair in a sleek, elegant tumble atop her head.

She withdrew behind a screen for modesty's sake when they told her to strip to her skin. First a chemise was handed over. Abby pulled it over her head. The soft cotton caressed her skin like silk. "How lovely! The embroidery is exquisite." Abby wasn't much for needlework herself, but she recognized quality when she saw it.

Madame Renault permitted herself a small smile of satisfaction as she moved the screen aside. "My girls make the finest lingerie in England. Now for the stays, milady." There were several forms of corset and this was a long one, designed to give a smooth line from hips to chest and to raise the breasts.

Abby steeled herself as madame personally helped her into the corset and began lacing up the back. "These stays are comfortable!" she exclaimed. "Even more comfortable than my old ones."

"Of course, milady. A properly designed corset must fit the body perfectly, enhancing but not forcing the feminine attributes into an impossible shape." She studied the garment's fit with narrowed eyes. "Many women require false bosoms to look their best, but you have been blessed with a splendid figure, milady. Finally the world will know it."

Abby was unsure how she felt about that, but there was no time to ponder since Madame Ravelle was approaching with a ball gown. Not the blue silk one for the duchess's ball, but a handsome confection of soft rose silk. With matching slippers.

As madame and her minions fussed with the hemline, Abby glanced down at the low-cut bodice, appalled. "I may die of lung fever!"

"Dancing will keep you warm, and you will never lack for partners. Not as long as you carry yourself with pride. There are short women who would kill to have your height and presence," Madame Ravelle said grandly. "Now show yourself to her grace."

Abby opened the door separating her bedroom from the private sitting room. At her entrance, the duchess looked up from the desk. "Oh, well done, madames! Abby, my brother shall be the envy of the ton for the wife he has found."

"I will settle for his not being a laughingstock." Abby gestured at the vast expanse of pale skin revealed by the gown. "You're sure this is fashionable, not vulgar?"

Celeste laughed and turned her to face the gilt-edged mirror over the fireplace. "It's the height of fashion. Look at yourself, my dear."

Abby blinked at her reflection. Though she would never be as elegant as Celeste, she did look impressive. Very . . . female. A well-designed corset certainly made a substantial difference. "I think I would prefer rustic to flamboyant," she said uncertainly.

"You look grand, not flamboyant, but you'll no longer be able to pretend you're a plain country lass. You never were, but you did your best to give that impression." Celeste cocked her head to one side. "Did you deliberately downplay your appearance? Or were you merely not that interested in fashion?"

"Some of both. I didn't want to draw attention to myself. Since there's a lot of me, that meant dressing plainly." Abby was silent before adding a deeper truth. "I reached womanhood early. The attention from men was . . . not enjoyable." She'd once had to use magic to free herself from the unwanted attentions of a drunken tinker. She had run home panting and in tears, never telling anyone because of her sin in using magic to knock a man unconscious.

"Ah." Celeste gave an understanding nod. "To be attractive to men at a young age is unsettling, especially if one's beauty is more sensual than ethereal. So you took on the plain plumage of a wren instead of the rich colors of the kingfisher."

Why had Abby never seen the connection between her lavish figure and her desire to go unnoticed? Probably because she never thought much about how she dressed. But as she studied her image in the mirror, she decided she could like more colorful plumage.

The door to the hall opened and she turned to see that Jack had returned early from his business. He entered, saying, "Hello, my dear."

Then he stopped in his tracks, his jaw dropping. "Abby?"

Celeste laughed. "Come in, Jack. And do try for some composure."

While Abby blushed, Jack circled her admiringly. "You look splendid, Abby. Not that you don't always look nice, but now! If I had my troops here, they'd give you a fifteen-gun salute."

"I'm glad you approve." The light in Jack's eyes removed all Abby's doubts about her new clothing. "All credit goes to your sister and Madames Ravelle and Renault. I'm merely obeying orders."

"Now that you've admired Abby, go away, Jack. There is much fitting to be done still, and it's no sight for a gentleman." Celeste's eyes gleamed. "Especially not a gentleman who looks as if he wishes to carry his bride off to some private place."

Celeste's comments caused both Abby and Jack to blush. After he beat a hasty retreat, the ladies resumed the fittings. The number of gowns and accessories seemed endless, but Abby found herself much more patient than she had been in the past. Patience was easier now that she realized she was going to enjoy being well dressed.

It was midafternoon by the time the dressmakers and their assistants left. Abby and Celeste collapsed in Abby's sitting room after the duchess rang for refreshments. As they demolished a selection of small sandwiches and sweets that again had Abby thinking about ensorcelling the Alderton chef, the footman returned bearing a silver tray with two small stacks of letters, one for each lady.

"Thank you, Williams." Abby accepted her letters with enthusiasm, glad for news from home.

She and Celeste sipped tea and read until Abby said, "Ah, a reply from Judith."

Celeste looked up eagerly as Abby scanned the letter. After general news of Melton Mowbray and the progress of several patients, Abby reached the information she had been waiting for: "About that matter you inquired about. I have thought and consulted my case notes and even wrote Mrs. Lampry in Birmingham, who has more experience with such problems than anyone."

As Abby continued reading, her brow furrowed. Unable to bear the tension, Celeste said, "Mrs. Wayne says nothing can be done for me?"

"No," Abby said slowly. "She said that in cases like yours, where neither physician nor healer can find anything amiss with the wife, it is logical to ask if the problem might lie with the husband."

Celeste gasped, her eyes widening. "It has never occurred to anyone that there could be any . . . any weakness in Alderton."

"Women are generally blamed when a couple is childless," Abby said dryly. "And of course one does not suggest that a duke might be less than perfect. But blame is not appropriate. Infertility is a physical problem, not a sin."

"I see." Celeste bit her lip. "Can male problems be healed?"

"Sometimes, especially if the problem is a minor blockage. Would Alderton allow a healer to examine him? As you know, there is no pain or discomfort."

The duchess shook her head. "He despises wizardry. Nor would he welcome the suggestion that he is in some way deficient. Would it be possible to examine him without his knowledge?"

Abby frowned. "That would be unethical. Also probably useless, since I imagine that the duke carries a powerful anti-magic charm."

"He does." Celeste clutched her teacup so hard Abby thought it might break. "He and I are barely talking. I can't imagine asking him to allow a healer to perform an examination to see if he's capable of fathering a child."

"There are two issues here," Abby pointed out. "If you can heal the estrangement and become intimate again, it will be much easier to talk to him about an examination."

"You're right. Heaven knows the first problem is difficult, but it's simpler than trying to solve both problems at once." Celeste's eyes narrowed. "Do you think an aphrodisiac might help?"

"I wouldn't recommend it. You are husband and wife, not an anxious girl trying to catch the attention of a local boy." Or a Spanish wench trying to catch the eye of a generous English officer. "Your relationship is deeper and far more complicated. Already trust is strained because he suspects your motives in encouraging him to take a mistress. If you try to manipulate him with a love potion and he finds out, he will be justly furious. You must solve your problems with honesty, not trickery."

Celeste sighed. "I know you're right, but I wish there was a simple solution."

Abby had learned much about men in the last few days. "What

about going to his room some night wearing sheer silk and nothing else?"

The other woman looked away. "I tried that. He . . . he has locked his door to me."

Abby winced, guessing how painful that rejection must have felt. "It sounds as if your solution must come through words."

"That man could make a rock look talkative when he's in this mood. But I'll try. He has withdrawn before, but eventually he always thaws. I shall have to wait him out." Celeste glanced down at her hands. "Though he looks the image of a duke, he was a third son, mostly ignored until his father and brothers died of a virulent fever. Perhaps he might have had more confidence if he'd been raised as the heir."

Abby reached out to the duke and did the kind of light reading that could be done even on someone who was shielded. Celeste was right. Her husband had learned to play the role of a duke, but in his heart, he was still an unnecessary son. "That explains a great deal. He needs to feel that he is loved, not merely the prize in a successful husband hunt."

"I knew that, but sometimes I haven't remembered as well as I should," Celeste said softly. "I'm grateful that you and Jack are in town to distract me. Otherwise I would be half mad with worry by now."

"Then I must be grateful for his moods, because you have been a godsend for easing my visit in London." Abby contemplated what she had accomplished so far, and what remained to be done. "All I must do is watch Jack take his seat, which should be easy, and survive the ball, which will be less easy. I'll manage."

"And then you'll both be off for Yorkshire." The duchess looked pensive. "I wonder how Jack will get on with Sir Alfred?"

"What do you think of your stepfather?"

"He's my mother's husband, not a father to me."

"That's exactly what Jack said. How am I likely to react to Sir Alfred? I know what Jack thinks of the man. I'd like to know what you think."

Celeste considered her words. "He is cold as Scottish granite, except when he looks at my mother. Then he . . . he burns. Perhaps I should find his devotion romantic, but it seems rather unwholesome."

If Scranton was so obsessed with the dowager Lady Frayne that he'd had spells cast to injure her first husband and son, he was more than unwholesome. He was a menace. Perhaps even a murderer. If so, he must be stopped from injuring anyone else.

Yorkshire promised to be interesting.

Taking his seat in the House of Lords proved more painless than Jack had expected. In keeping with his mischievous desire to avoid political alignment, he was sponsored by one Whig viscount and one Tory viscount.

When he emerged from the Robing Room with his sponsors, he surreptitiously scanned the chamber and found Abby and Celeste in the gallery, both watching with beaming approval. Abby wore one of her new gowns, this one high-necked and demure. She looked lovely and entirely at home in London. Clothes really did make a difference. In his formal robes of state, Jack almost felt as if he belonged in the House of Lords.

Alderton had orchestrated the ceremony and it went off without a hitch. Jack was unexpectedly moved when he swore allegiance to king and country. He had served both for years, could easily have laid down his life. Yet it was different to pledge his loyalty and best efforts toward governing this nation. Dying was easier than making good laws.

The Langdons of Langdale had been peers for centuries, cultivating their lands and doing their duty. The family had supplied its share of soldiers and clergymen, and even a few diplomats. In the thirteenth century, a Langdon had stood with the other barons at Runnymede to face down King John.

God willing, Jack would return to this chamber year after year to debate issues great and small. Just standing here made him feel more opinionated. But it also gave him a desire to find a middle ground. He had seen enough of war. Talk was better.

Winslow, who was one of his sponsors, murmured, "Sobering, isn't it? I took my seat at twenty-one and still haven't recovered."

Jack nodded, glad his friend understood. He shook the hand of the Lord Chancellor, then was escorted to the benches reserved for viscounts.

When they reached the viscounts' bench, there was more handshaking and congratulating and welcoming him to the House. Jack knew some of his peers personally, and many more by reputation. For today, at least, all was goodwill.

He was sharing a joke with Ashby when he heard a man behind him remark, "They say Frayne has married a rustic wyrdling."

Another voice said, "He *married* her?" There was a knowing laugh. "Wizard wenches make demmed fine mistresses, but one doesn't marry them."

Jack felt a blast of pure rage. After drawing several deep breaths to master it, he turned and asked pleasantly, "Did I hear my name mentioned?"

Something in his face caused the two men's expressions to change. "Glad to have you here, Frayne," one said hastily. "Demmed fine work in the Peninsula."

"Right, right," the other man said. "Your army experience will be useful here. Good you've taken your seat."

Formalities observed, the two peers withdrew. Jack recognized one as a baron called Worley, from East Anglia, he thought. The other was a stranger.

Not that it mattered who they were, for their opinions were common in this place. In the weeks since the accident, Jack had been among people who accepted magic. Though he was still uneasy with his own power and probably always would be, he was much more accepting of wizards in general. He'd half forgotten how many aristocrats believed magic was contemptible, an occupation for inferior people.

Not for the first time, he pondered why the upper classes were so dead set against wizardry. He suspected that it was because magic was a talent that paid no attention to class. No amount of money could buy magical ability. Most of the best wizards were of humble origin.

No wonder aristocrats despised magic. It was a power they couldn't control, so they feared it. And fear was usually at the root of hatred.

Jack wasn't sure when he would make his maiden speech. Certainly not before the next session of Parliament. But when the time came, he would not settle for a safe, noncontroversial topic. He'd make a plea for tolerance and acceptance of wizards on the grounds that they were Britons, too, and no different from anyone else. *"If you prick us, do we not bleed? If you tickle us, do we not laugh? If you poison us, do we not die?"*

He smiled as he remembered the words from *The Merchant of Venice.* Leave it to Shakespeare to say everything important first.

Chapter XXV

Celeste's personal maid tied the last ribbon in Abby's hair and carefully trained the narrow lengths of dark blue silk to curl down over her right shoulder. "There, milady. You are perfection."

Abby studied her reflection in the bedroom mirror. She was not perfection. She would never be as beautiful as Celeste, with features so exquisite they took the breath away.

But for a woman of average appearance, she looked very fine. The shimmering blue silk of her gown made her eyes electric and emphasized the cornflower shade of the embroidered underskirt. Madame Renault's corset shaped her figure into a sensual hourglass, and her shining brown hair glinted with auburn and gold highlights in a sophisticated upswept coiffure.

The maid was not responsible for the fact that Abby wore the expression of a woman about to be hanged. She reminded herself that all she need do was endure the evening without disgracing herself or Jack or Jack's family. She could manage that. "Thank you, Lasalle. You've done a wonderful job. Now go to your mistress."

The maid inclined her head and withdrew. Because she had to dress two ladies this evening, she'd come to Abby early. Now Abby had entirely too much time to make herself feel even more nervous. Needing distraction, she left her room, crossed the sitting room, and knocked on the door of Jack's bedchamber. "May I come in?"

"Of course, lass," he called. "I want to see you in all your glory."

She entered to find Jack wearing his scarlet regimentals. He was a sight to dazzle the hardest female heart. Abby caught her breath, her nerves temporarily forgotten. No wonder the wench in Spain had used an aphrodisiac to capture his interest!

Though Abby had always admired Jack's looks, now he had truly come into his own. He had accepted himself and his station in life, and the result was a powerful authority that riveted the eye. "You look magnificent! I've never seen you in uniform before. You must have left a chain of broken hearts wherever you marched."

"Hardly. Remember, all officers wore uniforms and many were better looking and more gallant with ladies." He tweaked the sash so that it lay perfectly. "Morris will miss the uniform. He says it displays my shoulders to advantage, which compensates for my lack of elegance. He was generous enough to say that while it is harder to dress a large man fashionably, at least I am not fat." Jack grinned. "He's a hard taskmaster. It was easier when we were in Spain and standards were lower."

"Celeste's maid did her best for me, but I could hear her thinking that she prefers dressing her mistress, who is a perfect showcase for a maid's skills."

Jack cocked his head to one side. "You can read minds?"

"No, but I could read her feelings. She was doing her best, and grateful that she would soon be dressing *madam*." Abby smiled wryly. "I'm duty, Celeste is pleasure, from the point of view of Lasalle."

"Nonsense. You look glorious, lass," he said warmly.

"So do you."

He smiled at her. "I was never one to wear my uniform when not on duty, but since I'm almost out of the army, I realized this might be my last chance to show my colors."

"Will you miss the army?" she asked quietly.

He gave an exaggerated shudder. "Lord, no! Bad food, worse quarters, stupid orders, and the chance of dying nastily in a strange place. I won't miss any of that."

"But surely there were some good things, too."

After a long silence, he said, "The people. My friends, both living and dead. My troops. The way war can turn a man who would never be your friend in regular life into something closer than a brother. Such things are beyond price."

She drew a deep breath before saying, "You don't have to sell your commission, you know. I would not ask that of you."

Jack hesitated, then shook his head. "Though selling out isn't my choice, it's time to take up my responsibilities." He smoothed the gold lace that trimmed his scarlet coat. "I'll regret losing the uniform, though. There isn't a man born who doesn't look his best in scarlet regimentals."

"I suspect the uniforms are designed with that in mind. It must help persuade men to join up." She regretted the fact that he would prefer to stay in the army if he could, but at least selling out was his decision. An idea struck her. "As a wedding present, I'd like to commission a portrait of you in your uniform. I'm sure that Celeste can give me the name of a painter worthy to the task."

"I'd have to look at myself forever?" he said warily.

"If you don't like the portrait, I'll hang it in my private boudoir. Assuming I have one. Long after we are gone, it will be a Langdon family treasure." She smiled mischievously. "If only because the uniform is so splendid."

"I'll agree to the portrait if you will, too. I want to have a painting of you as you look tonight."

She blushed with pleasure. "I'd like that, since I'll never look better."

He cocked his head to one side. "Why are you so anxious? In most matters you are fearless, so what do you fear in London society? This is merely a ball. What's the worst that can happen to you?"

"Burn, witch, burn!" she blurted out. She stopped, shocked at what she had said. "I don't think of such things every day, but knowing that I am going among people hostile to what I am stirs up ancient fears.

Even though wizards have been tolerated since the black death, it's still not uncommon to hear of one being killed in some benighted, superstitious corner of the country. Two hundred years ago, women like me could be burned for having a house or a piece of land some man coveted. All he had to do was accuse me of cursing his children or his cattle and I'd have to run for my life. Those fears are in my family's bones, Jack."

"I can see how that would make a person wary, but there will be no burnings in the Alderton ballroom tonight. The worst that might happen would be the cut direct." His eyes narrowed. "And anyone who offers that to you will have to deal with me."

"What happens in the future if it becomes known you have magic and the cuts direct are offered to you?" she asked, genuinely curious.

He frowned. "I haven't thought about that. Magic still seems like something other people have. But if I'm ever condemned for having some magical ability—well, bedamned to the bigots!"

Abby wished she had that sort of confidence. Would the day ever come when all men and women could live freely, without the fear of persecution if they were different? She wanted to believe this would happen, but it wouldn't be in her lifetime. "Over the years, the situation has improved. These days, the average person accepts magic and is willing to visit a wizard or healer when needed."

"Perhaps you will help bring the beau monde into greater acceptance. After all, you are one of them now as well as a wizard."

She sighed. "That is part of my fear. It's only a matter of time until it becomes known that Lady Frayne works magic. It could even happen tonight, which won't be good for your sister's ball."

"If it does, hold your head high and know that you are the equal of any man or woman in Britain." He gave a sudden wicked smile. "But for now, perhaps I can relax you since it's still too early to go down."

The midnight blue ribbons that fell enticingly from her hair began gliding sensuously over her bare skin. When they curled into the hollow between her breasts, she gasped with shock, startled by the erotic charge of his touching her magically when he was on the far side of the room. "I thought you didn't believe in using your power."

"I'm willing to make an exception for a good cause," he said mischievously. "Let's see what more I can move."

As one end of the ribbon caressed the top of her breasts, the other end rose upward to stroke her mouth with gossamer promise. Instinctively she licked her lips, imagining the taste of one of his kisses.

Her right nipple was squeezed teasingly by the quilted dimity of her corset. Then the left. She clasped her hands to her breasts, aching for his touch. "Jack! If we go to bed and I ruin my dress and hair, Celeste and her maid will never forgive me!"

"Don't worry, your gown is safe." Brow furrowed with concentration, he tightened the corset on both nipples at once. They hardened, throbbing urgently.

"Are you sure this is wise?" she said unsteadily.

"Probably not." His intense gaze moved lower on her body.

Under her silk gown, the sheer fabric of her chemise glided provocatively across her thighs. Pleasure shimmered over her skin, stimulating her body in astonishingly intimate places. "I'm not worried about the ball now," she managed to say. "Instead, I ache for you. Is that better?"

"Much better, for I can soothe that ache." He stepped close and bent to kiss her throat just above the sapphire necklace inherited from her mother.

Fire shot through her, pooling in her loins. Dizzily she reached for his shoulder to steady herself.

He wrapped one arm around her waist and raised her skirt with his other hand, careful not to crush the silk. She moaned as his hard, knowing hand slid upward between her thighs. As soon as he touched the moist heat between her legs, she began writhing against him as frantic spasms rocked her. She would have fallen if not for his support. He filled her world, his tenderness even more shattering than his passionate skill.

As her body stilled, she found that her forehead rested against his shoulder. Though he supported her, their bodies weren't crushed together. "You spared the gown," she said with a choke of laughter. "But what about you?" Her hand moved tentatively down his body.

He caught her hand and raised it to his heart. "I will collect my reward later," he said, his voice a rich rumble. "Are you relaxed about the ball now?"

"So relaxed I can barely stand upright!"

"You'll be grand, lass." He kissed her hard on her mouth. She felt strength flow from him into her, and with it some of his confidence.

She felt *ready*.

The mundane business of standing in a receiving line and being introduced to what seemed like half of London eliminated the last of Abby's nervousness. The members of the ton she met were mostly pleasant. And if a fair number of the men studied her figure with frank admiration—well, that wasn't so bad, not with Jack standing protectively beside her.

"Lady Cynthia Devereaux." The announced name caught Abby's attention. Wasn't that the girl Jack had admired? Abby kept most of her attention on Lady Castlereagh, the foreign minister's wife, who was welcoming Abby to London, but she did look out the corner of her eye at the female who was approaching him.

Lady Cynthia looked . . . just like Celeste. No, not just like her—their features and expressions were quite different. But both were petite, exquisitely dressed blondes who looked as if they belonged on pedestals. Beside Lady Cynthia was a taller, darker blonde who must be her sister, and who was almost equally attractive.

As Lady Castlereagh inclined her head and moved away, Abby heard Lady Cynthia say to her companion, "I see that Frayne decided to marry a great cow."

The other young woman tittered maliciously. "She must have a huge dowry. There couldn't be any other reason he'd marry such a creature."

The words were a stiletto through Abby's heart. She had feared such contempt for her person almost as much as she feared being revealed as a wizard.

Had the comments been meant to be overheard? She hadn't had

much experience with malice. In Melton Mowbray, everyone liked her, or they concealed it if they didn't. Welcome to high society.

"Lady Cynthia, it's good to see you. You're in your best looks, I see." Jack must not have heard the comments, for his smile was friendly. "And Lady Jane, you also dazzle. I believe I saw a notice of your engagement in the newspaper last week?"

"Yes, I'm soon to marry Lord Mortensen." Lady Jane's smile was very close to a smirk of satisfaction. She had won a major prize in the Marriage Mart and would marry before her sister. Abby wondered if Mortensen knew his intended was mean-spirited. Perhaps he wouldn't care, since she was wellborn and pretty.

More important was whether Jack still cared about Lady Cynthia. There was no sign of special interest in his face or in his aura. His greeting was what he might offer any old friend.

The line moved. While Lady Jane and Jack exchanged a few more words, Lady Cynthia stepped up to Abby.

How should she behave? *Take the high ground.* Spitting in the little minx's face wouldn't help Abby's reputation. She summoned her warmest smile. "Lady Cynthia, I've heard so much about you. I'm so glad you were able to attend tonight."

"I wouldn't have missed the chance to meet Jack's wife," Lady Cynthia purred, her use of his given name implying deep intimacy. Though her words and tone were civil, there was malice in her eyes. "I heard that he was injured in the Shires and you nursed him?" Her eyes flicked disdainfully over Abby. Without saying a word, she implied that Abby must have taken advantage of Jack's weakness to snare him.

"He was brought to my father's house after the accident." Abby added a dash of magic to her smile, wanting to project profound marital satisfaction both in and out of bed. "The way we discovered each other was like a miracle."

Lady Cynthia's mouth tightened to a hard line, and there was little civility when she said, "How fortunate for you both."

The mental energy saturating her words was so vivid that Abby understood in a flash what had happened. The previous year, Lady

Cynthia had hoped for an offer from another man, a marquess who was a better catch, but she had encouraged Jack's attentions and considered him a good second choice. She'd assumed he would be hers for the asking if she wanted him.

But she hadn't succeeded with her first choice, Jack was no longer available, and wealthy, titled men were in short supply. Though she was beautiful, every season brought new beauties to town, and her prospects were not as good as they had seemed the previous year. Of course she hated Abby.

Feeling rather sorry for her, Abby said gently, "Fortunate indeed. I hope you enjoy the ball, Lady Cynthia."

Anger flashed through the other woman's face for a moment. Then she schooled her features to superficial social charm and moved away. As Abby turned to greet the next guest, she wondered how many years would pass before that angry spirit would be written on Lady Cynthia's face for the world to see.

A few minutes later, the duchess announced, "I think most of the guests have arrived, so now we can dance!"

She was stunning in a white gown whose sparkling crystals echoed the spectacular diamonds at her ears and around her throat. But Abby noted that she and her husband still weren't looking at each other.

Alderton wore impeccably tailored black coat and breeches with a white-on-white embroidered waistcoat, but his expression was sober. Sad, even. Though he was always polite to Abby, she had no sense that she really knew him. She was unable to resist a gentle mental touch to see what she could read in his personality, but she felt only the shield of a powerful anti-magic charm. To attempt to look deeper would be an invasion of privacy, not to mention out of place at a ball.

Jack glanced down at her, his hazel eyes golden. Lord, he dazzled in that uniform! Still another reason for Lady Cynthia to resent the woman who had become Lady Frayne. "Shall we dance, lass?"

"I would love to." The set forming was for a country dance where men and women lined up opposite each other. Partners couldn't converse easily, but the dance was great fun and an old favorite of hers. Jack was light on his feet for a large man, and he gave every evidence of enjoying himself.

By the end of the set, she was flushed and laughing and full of confidence. She should have known that this ball couldn't be as bad as she'd feared. When Ashby asked her for the next dance, she accepted with pleasure while Jack left to ask his sister to stand up with him.

"Only in London could I dance with two dukes in one night," she told Ashby as the new set formed.

He laughed. "Alderton is a better dancer than I. Are you enjoying your stay here, Abby? Jack looks not only healed, but happy."

"I know," she said with satisfaction. "To be honest, I was worried about this visit, but all is well. Jack's sister is wonderful, and so is her modiste."

"Indeed." Ashby let his gaze move over her with deep masculine appreciation, the kind an honorable man shows to a good friend's wife.

The music began and Ashby proved to be a better dancer than he claimed. Later in the evening Abby stood up with Alderton, who did indeed dance beautifully. She wondered giddily if there were any other dukes present so she could try for three. Probably just as well not to hope for that—most dukes were elderly and gout ridden.

No matter. There were plenty of other men who wanted to dance with her. As Madame Ravelle had predicted, Abby danced every set and was in no danger of lung fever despite her décolletage.

She caught a glimpse of Lady Cynthia Devereaux occasionally. The petite blonde never lacked for partners. Perhaps too many balls had left her jaded, for her rosebud mouth had a petulant cast. Though she managed to make pouting look pretty, Abby could feel the sourness underneath.

The last dance before supper ended and Abby looked around for Jack, since they had planned to eat together. He wasn't in sight and the guests were milling about as they searched for supper partners, so she decided to stand still and wait for him to find her. She had a sense that he'd left the ballroom, so she sent out a mental call.

A dozen feet away, Lady Cynthia was talking with a middle-aged man. He said something that caused her to gasp with surprise and glance at Abby. Her expression of pleasure was alarming.

Abby moved away, the back of her neck prickling. Where the devil was Jack?

After another swift exchange of sentences with the man, Lady Cynthia moved forward and blocked Abby's path. In a voice designed to carry through the ballroom, she asked, "Lady Frayne, is it true that you are a wyrdling?"

Chapter XXVI

Burn, *witch, burn.* The words echoed through Abby's mind, reinforced by the expressions of the people around her. Lady Cynthia radiated vicious satisfaction while other guests showed shock, fear, and avid curiosity. Worst of all, the Duke of Alderton stared at Abby, his face appalled.

Feeling ill, Abby wondered if the duke would throw her from his house. Guests edged away and the ballroom was eerily silent as everyone waited to hear her reply.

For one cowardly instant, Abby was tempted to lie and claim that the rumor of her wizardry was wrong. She wanted to turn back the clock to the moment before, when she was an unexceptionable new bride having a wonderful time at her first London ball.

But there was no future in lying when the truth would be confirmed quickly. She would not deny what she was. "The polite term is wizard, Lady Cynthia," she replied, hoping her voice was steady. "Yes, I'm a healer."

Abby could feel the mood of the crowd, and it was volatile. As Jack had said, there would be no burnings in a ballroom, but she might never again move freely in these social circles. Where was Jack? She urgently needed him to come to her and show that he supported his wife.

Lady Cynthia narrowed her eyes, not willing to drop the subject. "Being a healer gives a woman wonderful opportunities to enchant men when they are at their weakest."

"No enchantment is necessary when the woman is beautiful, charming, and kind." Jack's voice boomed through the ballroom as he entered from the terrace and came to Abby's side, smelling of the fresh evening air. He touched the small of her back with tender possessiveness. "Abby saved my life. The fact that she agreed to become my bride was a bonus that still awes me."

Lady Cynthia wilted under his unflinching gaze, perhaps realizing she had sacrificed any fondness he might have had for her. Struggling to save face, she said, " 'Tis a most romantic tale." The words seemed to stick in her mouth. "I wish you very happy."

Abby noted that Jack didn't mention his own magical gifts. Just as well under the circumstances, since that would cloud the issue. What mattered was that he defended her.

Celeste moved forward to stand by her brother. "Isn't it marvelous that we now have a healer in the family?" She glanced fondly at Jack. "I had begun to despair of my brother taking time enough from the army to find a wife. Abby was like a gift."

The duchess's smile was radiantly untroubled, but Abby saw that her aura thrummed with tension. She was risking her own social credit by publicly supporting her wizardly sister-in-law. Would her acceptance protect Abby—or would Abby tarnish Celeste's position?

Ashby ambled forward to join them. "A gift indeed. I shall always regret that before I had time to plan a courtship, Lady Frayne was already promised elsewhere." He smiled at Abby, his green eyes warm. "Next time I meet a beautiful healer, I shall move more quickly." She knew that he was acting, he'd had no romantic interest in her, but she almost wept with gratitude at his gesture of friendship.

The mood of the crowd became less volatile. A duke and a duchess had declared their support, and as wizards went, healers were more useful than most. After tonight, Abby would probably be more or less accepted by the ton. It was damnable that it took the support of a viscount, a duchess, and a duke for that to happen, but it was a step forward for the cause of wizardly acceptance.

Jack offered Abby his arm. "Surely it's time for supper? All that dancing has given me quite an appetite."

"I ordered your very favorite lobster tarts for tonight," Celeste said indulgently. "They won't last long, so it's time to adjourn to the supper room."

She gestured at the musicians in the gallery and they began to play quiet music suitable for dining. Then she took Jack's other arm and personally escorted him and Abby into the adjoining room, where the supper buffet and tables awaited.

They found a prime table at one side and Jack headed for the buffet to collect food for them. Under her breath, Abby said, "I'm sorry your ball has been ruined, Celeste. I knew this might happen, but I didn't expect it so soon."

"On the contrary, tomorrow this ball will be the talk of London." The duchess sighed. "It was naive of me to think you would go unnoticed for any length of time, not when you're from Melton Mowbray and so many men hunt. It was a hunting man who told Lady Cynthia what you are."

"She certainly delighted in exposing me."

"Her attempt to cause you trouble had the reverse effect. You were a lady. She looked like a malicious cat, which she is." Celeste shook her head. "The thought that Jack might have absentmindedly offered for her last spring gives me nightmares. As to your power being revealed tonight . . ." She shrugged. "In the long run, it probably doesn't matter. You were wise to immediately say that you're a healer, since they are the most accepted of wizards."

A thin, elegant woman in her thirties approached the table. Though her face was composed, her blue eyes were haunted. "Lady Frayne, would you speak with me for a moment? In private?"

The woman must need healing for herself or someone close to her.

Abby was unsurprised. Whenever her abilities became known, desperate people appeared like bees coming to flowers. Since Abby didn't know this woman, she glanced at Celeste for guidance.

The duchess gave a slight nod. "You remember meeting the Countess of Roreton earlier, don't you? She has four of the loveliest children you've ever seen." For a moment, Celeste's wistfulness showed. "Go ahead, and I'll do my best to prevent Jack from eating all the lobster tarts."

Abby rose, grateful that Celeste had told her the woman's name. "Shall we go out to the terrace, Lady Roreton? I imagine that is empty now that supper is being served."

Lady Roreton nodded and followed Abby through the empty ballroom and out the French doors to the terrace. It was bitingly cold, especially for someone wearing only a ball gown. Abby shivered, but the other woman didn't seem to notice. Abby studied her aura, which was a dark orange shot with muddy blue. "You need help, I think."

Lady Roreton's thin frame began to shake with silent, wrenching sobs. "I'm sorry, this is not the right time, but when I heard you were a healer, I . . . I had to speak with you." Her hand went to her right breast. "There is a lump. My children are so young, Lady Frayne. They need me. What if I can't be there for them?"

"Not all lumps are dangerous." Abby guided the other woman to one side of the French doors so that they couldn't be seen from inside. Though the countess was right that this wasn't a good place, it was hard to deny someone so much in need. "If you like, I can make a quick examination."

"Oh, please, if you would, I'd be forever grateful. I've wanted to visit a healer, but my family was appalled when I suggested that I might do that. I would have gone anyhow if I'd known where to find a good one." The other woman bit her lip. "Don't be afraid to tell me the truth. If it is the worst kind of news, I will need time to ensure that my children will be properly taken care of."

"Where is the lump?"

Lady Roreton touched the side of her breast. "Here, though it can't be felt through my stays."

"Will you allow me to touch you in a rather intimate way?"

The countess took a deep breath. "Do what you must."

Abby centered herself, collecting her healing perceptions. When her power was in balance, she slid her fingers inside the countess's bodice. There was something to be said for deep décolletage. She found the lump easily. It was sizable, with a slight resilience. She scanned deeply, not wanting to make a mistake.

When she was sure, she stepped back. "The lump is not a cancer but a cyst filled with fluid. Though it might be uncomfortable, it will not harm you."

"Oh, thank God." Lady Roreton buried her face in her hands and wept again, this time with relief. Her aura brightened noticeably, the muddiness clearing somewhat.

"If you would like me to try, I might be able to reduce it."

"I would be grateful for anything you can do." The countess's mouth twisted. "Even if the lump isn't dangerous, its presence is . . . disturbing."

This time Abby lightly touched the outside of the countess's rose-colored gown. Scanning deeply, she found a weak spot in the wall of the cyst. With a short, focused burst of energy, she thinned the wall to nothing there. Fluid began to seep out. Soon it would be absorbed back into the body. "In a day or two, it should be gone."

Lady Roreton gingerly probed the area, then gave a gasp of delight. "Already it's smaller. You are a miracle worker. I have been living in fear for months. The family physician recommended bleeding, but that didn't save my friend when she had a similar problem. Now I can start to live again." She smiled radiantly. "God bless you for your kindness, Lady Frayne. What can I do to repay you?"

"By speaking kindly of wizards," Abby said. "I don't want my host and hostess to suffer for the crime of having me as a guest."

"I will do that." Lady Roreton's expression changed, the fear replaced by determination. "I am not without influence in society."

"I will be grateful if you exercise that influence on behalf of me and my new family." Abby wrapped her arms around herself, shivering. Jack had said that she would be embarking on a campaign for acceptance, and she knew from experience that tolerance must be earned one mind at a time. "Now let's go inside before we freeze!"

Laughing, they headed back into the house. Abby didn't know whether or not Lady Roreton would become a friend—but she was certainly an ally, and at the moment, that was even better.

Jack was relieved when Abby rejoined him and Celeste at their table, looking composed. "Are you all right?"

"Fine." Abby's gaze fell on the food. "One of those is mine, I hope?"

He set a plate in front of her. "I got a bit of everything since we haven't been married long enough for me to be sure of your tastes. But the lobster tarts are heavenly."

"It's generous of you to share." Abby took a bite of one, then closed her eyes in bliss. "Celeste, I must confess that I periodically have thoughts of casting an enchantment on your chef and stealing him away."

The duchess looked stern. "It's better not to joke about magic in this place."

"I wasn't joking!"

"That's even worse." Celeste smiled a little. "You helped Alice Roreton?"

Abby nodded while swallowing the rest of the lobster tart. "Yes, she was troubled, and I was able to relieve her mind. She has offered her aid in countering the social disaster of my presence."

"Excellent," Celeste said, relieved. "She is considered a model of chaste, respectable conduct, so she can do a great deal to smooth this matter over."

Jack was picking up a cheese puff when the Duke of Alderton came to the table.

"Frayne. Madame." His gaze went from Jack to his wife, ignoring Abby. "I would speak with you in private. Now." His voice could not have been heard more than a yard away, but it vibrated with barely controlled anger.

His granite-like expression and formal language did not bode well. Jack rose, thinking that perhaps Abby had been right in wanting to avoid this ball. The night was producing far too many consequences. "Abby?" She took a deep breath and stood also, her expression that of a woman expecting serious trouble.

"I did not invite her," Alderton snapped.

"She is my wife, and also, I suspect, the cause of this discussion." Jack's gaze was challenging. Alderton was entitled to castigate them and demand they leave his house, but he didn't have the right to act as if Abby was beneath his notice.

"Very well," Alderton said ungraciously. "But she won't like what I have to say."

As Jack and the two women left the table, he glanced at the nearly full plates regretfully, suspecting that they wouldn't return to them. He'd learned to forage in the army, so he grabbed two lobster tarts, eating one and offering the other to Abby as they followed the duke from the dining room. Her smile was unsteady, but she took the tart and ate it as they climbed the stairs to the next floor.

One of the first rules of war was to eat well when one could. Especially with a bloody battle imminent.

Chapter XXVII

The duke led them to his private study, a quiet room in the back of the house. It was well lit with candles and a fire and looked misleadingly welcoming.

Alderton closed the door behind them, then whirled on Jack and allowed his anger free rein. "How *dare* you bring a wyrdling into my home when you know how I feel about such creatures! I had thought we were friends, Frayne, yet you have betrayed me."

Jack clamped down on his own anger. "I didn't bring a wyrdling, I brought my wife. Abby is a wellborn young woman of impeccable reputation who happens to be blessed with the gift of healing. I didn't realize that bringing her to your home was a betrayal of our friendship. Or do you think it was treacherous of her to save my life?"

Alderton's mouth twisted. "If you thought it was all right, why didn't you tell me at the beginning instead of leaving me to be humiliated in front of half of London?"

The duke had a valid point. Jack had known his brother-in-law might be uncomfortable with Abby's magic. But he hadn't expected such fury, or he would never have come to stay with his sister.

Celeste spoke up. "Abby told me as soon as she arrived, Piers. Jack is my brother. Surely he and his wife are welcome in my home."

The duke's face shuttered. "So you have betrayed me again. My wife, the harlot, who yearns for other lovers and doesn't mind allowing a witch under my roof."

Celeste gasped, then flared with a rage that shimmered incandescent red in her aura. "Damn you, Alderton! You have no right to say such a thing! I have never wanted to take a lover." She drew a shuddering breath as she struggled for control. "I hated the thought. *Hated it!* Do you think I have ever done anything in my life more difficult than suggest you find a mistress to give you a child? But the first duty of a duchess is to give her husband an heir, and I have failed to do so. I was willing to break my own heart to give you what you want and need."

"What I want and need," the duke snapped, "is a faithful wife who knows better than to allow a damned wyrdling in my home!"

"Then you had better throw me out now!" she hissed. A silver chain slithered up from under the duke's shirt, powered by a blast of her magic so strong it rocked Jack and Abby. Hanging from the chain was an anti-magic charm of the highest potency.

"Do you have any idea how often this charm has burned my skin when we made love?" she exclaimed, tears rolling down her cheeks. "I am everything you despise, Piers. An untrained wizard who has been too afraid to tell my own husband what I am." The charm jerked at the chain, snapping the links, then sailed across the room to bounce off the opposite wall.

Aghast, the duke watched the charm rip away, then stared at Celeste as if he had never seen her before. "You're a wizard?"

"Magic often runs in families, Alderton," Jack said as he took a protective step toward his sister. He didn't think her husband would hurt her, but at the moment he wasn't sure. "Remember that I was sent to Stonebridge Academy because of too much interest in wizardry. They taught me to hate myself, but they couldn't change my essential nature."

He hesitated a moment before continuing. He hated claiming his magic, but he couldn't bear to let Alderton lash out at Abby and Celeste. He raised his hand and created a ball of shimmering light. "If you must rail at wizardry, aim your venom at me. It was I who married Abby and brought her here, thinking you would be at least civil, and our arrival was what persuaded my sister to accept her talents." He let his anger show. "I had thought our friendship was stronger than this, Piers."

"He is being eaten alive by his pain," Abby said quietly. "Look at his aura. His anger is based in the fear that Celeste doesn't love him, and that fear is poisoning him from the heart out. Because he fears, it is easy to hate us."

Alderton turned white at Abby's words. "This is why wyrdlings are hated," he said starkly. "Because they steal the secrets from a man's soul."

"Time and again I have said how much I love you. What more can I say?" Celeste asked, her anger fading into anguish as she stepped between her husband and the targets of his fury. "Why will you not believe me?"

"Perhaps you love the Duke of Alderton." He stared at his wife, so mesmerized by her ethereal beauty that Jack and Abby might not have existed. "But would you have married me when I was Lord Piers, a third son of modest fortune? What I have always wanted and needed is you, Celeste. Far more than I want an heir. I need a wife who loves *me*, not the Duke of Alderton. I have never been sure that I have such a wife."

"You want to be loved for yourself, not because you're a duke," Celeste retorted. "But would you love me if I wasn't beautiful? How much of your feeling for me is because of the pretty face and blond hair you prize so much?"

Alderton was taken aback. "That's not the same!"

"Close enough," she said tartly. "My beauty has shaped my life and become part of who I am. I would not be the same woman if I was plain. But neither would you be the same man if you had not become the duke."

Her voice softened. "I love all of you, Piers, and part of that is because of the dignity, fairness, and justice you exercise as the Duke of Alderton. I think I would love you no matter what your station in life, but this is the only way I have known you. Can you say the same? Would you have asked me to dance that first time if I had been plain and shy and badly dressed?"

"I . . . I don't know," Alderton said with painful honesty. "But London is full of beautiful women, and far too many try to catch the attention of a duke. Seldom did I ask one for a second dance." He reached out and touched her bright hair, his expression taut. "With you—I couldn't get enough of your company, and it wasn't only because of your beauty." As they gazed into each other's eyes, the air thickened with sexual tension.

"Can you love me even though I have magical power?" she whispered, laying her hand over his. "I can refuse to use it, but it's still part of me."

"If that's true," he said hoarsely, "then I will learn to love magic, because I truly do love you."

Tears running down her face, she stepped toward him. His control shattered and he drew her into a crushing embrace, as if his kiss could draw her soul into his. Celeste's hands bit into his back to hold him so tightly that he could never leave her.

Nerve endings tingling from the energy that scorched through the room, Jack grabbed Abby's arm and hustled her out into the hall, slamming the door behind them. "The power generated by that fight must have set all the pigeons in London flying!"

"Not only the pigeons." Abby's pupils were dark and her cheeks flushed with sensual promise. He couldn't take his gaze from the magnificent swell of her breasts.

"I shouldn't have been affected by that," he said hoarsely as his blood hammered through his veins. "She's my *sister.*"

"That room held enough passion to make monks break their vows. The source doesn't matter." Eyes blazing, Abby pulled his head down for a fierce kiss. "And I am not your sister."

Raw lust seared through him. As their mouths locked in an urgent kiss that knew no end, he braced her against the wall and fumbled with the buttons on his trousers to release himself. Mindless with desire, he raised her skirts, and this time he had no thought for saving the fabric from being crushed.

Her body was hot and ready, and she cried out when he entered her, the sound swallowed up in his mouth. She convulsed around him almost instantly. As rainbow colors rioted around them, he thrust again and again, spilling into her, trying to merge physically with an intensity that stripped away all consciousness until frantic desire shattered into a stunning release.

When the madness had passed, his forehead rested against the wall as his arms clung to his wife's richly provocative form. "No wonder people fear the power of sexual magic," he panted. "If not for the wall, I think we'd both collapse."

"Very likely." She smiled crookedly. "Much of that magic came from you, I think, for I've never been so strongly affected."

"A good thing no one came down this hall. Though I think a herd of galloping elephants could have passed and I wouldn't have noticed."

Shakily he released her and straightened, half surprised he could stand. As he buttoned his trousers, he asked, "What just happened? Apart from the obvious," he added hastily when he saw Abby's mischievous smile.

"I think that Celeste and her husband have both been suppressing their passions for quite some time." She accepted the handkerchief he offered and dried herself. "As they fought, all that suppressed desire exploded, augmented by Celeste's magic. Since we were right there and also involved in the argument, we were caught in a firestorm of desire. I wonder if others in the house felt that, too?"

Jack shuddered. "I hope not, or we're going to return to the ballroom and find an orgy in progress."

"Must we return to the ball?" She made a face. "I suppose we should, since we're the guests of honor."

"And the host and hostess are unlikely to reappear. Do I appear respectable?"

"Well enough for this stage of the evening. If you'd looked like this earlier, people would have suspected something more than energetic dancing." She smoothed her hands down her gown. "How is my appearance?"

"You look like you've been dancing *very* energetically," he said gravely. "But no more than that, I think." He offered his arm. "Shall we go down?"

She bit her lip. "I did something I shouldn't have. When Celeste pulled Alderton's charm off, she left him unprotected from magic. I . . . I did a deep scan of his body and I think I found the cause of their failure to have a child. It was a simple blockage, and I fixed it. I think."

He stared, imagining how intimate that scan had been. "That was fast work."

"Some problems are simple and can be healed quickly." She sighed. "What I did was wrong, yet I can't bring myself to be sorry. Even if the events of the evening make Alderton more tolerant toward wizardry, I think he'd be a long way from allowing a healer to examine and treat him."

She was right. For Celeste and Piers's sakes, he hoped she'd been successful. "It may have been unethical, but the rewards of success will be enormous. If you failed—well, no one but me will ever know."

"But it's not something I should do again."

"No, and especially not to me!"

"I wouldn't need to," she said. "I can talk to you and know you'll listen."

As they headed down to the ballroom, he realized that the ability to talk to each other was perhaps an even greater blessing than the amazing passion between them.

His friends were right. He was a very lucky man.

*　　*　　*

Abby woke and stretched, the length of her body rustling pleasantly against her husband's solid frame. "Do we have to get out of bed today?"

"I think so. But not just yet." He settled in closer, his arm around her waist. They'd never made it into their nightclothes the night before, so he was enjoying her delicious nakedness.

"I wonder how many flowers will arrive with notes hoping that the duchess has recovered from the illness that forced her to leave the ball early." Abby smiled as she thought of the social lies they had spun the night before to explain the disappearance of the host and hostess. "And how many women will envy the fact that she has a husband solicitous enough to sit with her."

"I doubt much sitting was going on," Jack said with amusement. "With luck, they'll have patched up their differences, but matters could be awkward today. It's not too late for us to leave rather than wait until tomorrow. Both of us are mostly packed, aren't we?"

"I don't know," Abby said doubtfully. "When is your mother expecting us?"

"She isn't."

When Abby's brows arched, he said, "It seemed better not to give Scranton a chance to prepare. It's not as if I need to give notice to return to my own home."

"I wonder what awaits us there." Abby tried to get a sense of the events that laid ahead, with little success. "I think it will be . . . complicated."

"Perhaps even dangerous." Jack's expression was grave. "If we are right, there is something profoundly wrong with Scranton."

"Between us, we can prevail over one wicked stepfather."

Jack nodded, but didn't look reassured. Changing the subject, he asked, "Can you sense the moods of Celeste and Piers?"

"I feel deep contentment, but I don't want to look any more closely. I've interfered enough already."

His circling hand began caressing her midriff. "More and more, I understand the dangerous temptations of magic. It must seem so easy to look in on people's emotions. To make little changes for their own good."

"Exactly," she said, glad he understood. "It's fortunate that so many people carry anti-magic charms. While they won't stop a powerful and determined wizard, running into the shield produced by a charm is a reminder that one is going too far."

"At which point, ethical wizards like you withdraw." The circles he made on her stomach transformed into longer strokes over her belly. "How many wizards are ethical?"

"The stronger one's magic, the more likely one is to be ethical. The most powerful spells require discipline, and the consequences of misbehavior become greater." She moved into his caressing hand like a cat. "The most dangerous wizards are the charlatans with only a trace of talent and no scruples. They give us all a bad name."

"I'm losing interest in the subject of wizards," he murmured. "And thinking how wise we were to feel we'd be too tired to travel the morning after the ball."

"Are you tired?" she asked with spurious innocence as her hand began its own explorations.

His hand settled over her breast. "Too tired to climb in a carriage and ride all day. But staying in bed—that's easy."

A shiver ran through her. Staying in bed was indeed easy, but tiring in its own delightful way.

Abby felt more than a little wary as they went down to the family dining room for a late breakfast. She and Jack hadn't eaten much the previous night, so she was ravenous. It was a relief to find that they had the breakfast room to themselves. She was finishing eggs, toast, and tea when Celeste came in. The duchess had shadows under her eyes, but her expression was radiant.

"All is well?" Jack asked.

"All is *wonderful!*" She swept down on her brother and gave him a hug, then turned and did the same for Abby. "I can't even regret the weeks of misery, since Piers and I understand each other so much better now." She plopped into the chair next to Abby, asking under her breath, "Abby, is it possible for a woman to know she's pregnant as soon as it happens?"

Startled, Abby studied Celeste's aura. There did seem to be an extra glow around the abdomen. "I've known women who have made such claims and been right."

"It's too soon to tell anyone, but in my heart, I know." Celeste lowered her voice still further. "Did you do something? I saw how intently you were studying Piers during that horrible fight."

Abby flushed. "I did a quick scan and found a small anomaly, then corrected it. That was wrong of me, but at the time it seemed like a golden opportunity."

Celeste's hazel eyes glowed with gratitude. "It was, and I thank you from the bottom of my heart for taking advantage of it."

Before Celeste could say more, the door opened and the Duke of Alderton entered. Abby stiffened and Jack rose to his feet warily. "We can leave almost immediately if you wish us to," he said to his brother-in-law.

"That isn't necessary." The duke looked directly at Abby. "I apologize, Lady Frayne. I was upset and irrational and behaved very badly to everyone, particularly to you. I hope you can forgive me."

Her wariness melted. "Of course. We all behave badly sometimes." She hoped his rudeness to her balanced her action in healing him without his permission. "You called me Abby when I first came. I hope you will do so again."

"Thank you, Abby. I hope we can begin again." The duke was a very different man from yesterday. The darkness and anger in his aura had been replaced by calm contentment. This was his real nature when he wasn't driven half mad by doubt and fear.

Jack asked bluntly, "How do you feel about magic now?"

Alderton hesitated. "Still rather uneasy, but I've realized that if I set aside the preconceptions I was raised with, there is no reason to despise everyone who works with magic. Especially since such powers are more common than I realized." He smiled ruefully. "I am working on acceptance. I'll reach that eventually."

Which was good, Abby thought, since she had a strong intuition that the long-awaited Alderton heir would have a talent for wizardry.

She looked forward to finding out.

Chapter XXVIII

"We're almost there." Jack leaned forward and gazed out the window, expression tense. "The gates to the driveway are just around the next bend."

"Time to put Cleo back in her basket." Abby transferred her drowsing cat from her lap to the cushioned, lidded basket she had bought to keep her feline friend safe on the trip. She hadn't wanted to risk Cleocatra becoming frightened and bolting from the carriage at a stop.

On the journey north, they had stopped in Melton Mowbray for three nights. Besides visiting family and friends, they collected Dancer. Jack's horse had recovered from his hunting injury and was now trotting behind the carriage on a lead.

The night before they had stayed in Leeds, the nearest city to Langdale Hall. Today the carriage had climbed into the Pennines, the chain of steep hills that divided Britain in the north.

Even on a gray day with rain threatening, the landscape was spectacular, with craggy cliffs and waterfalls that plunged down hillsides before flowing into the fertile valleys, which the locals called dales. Abby could learn to love Yorkshire, she thought. "Spring is coming early this year. Even this far north, I've seen daffodils. Soon the countryside will come alive."

They rounded the bend and the carriage halted in front of the cast-iron gates that led to the hall. Jack opened the window and called, "Halloo, Ned! Are you still here?"

When no gatekeeper appeared, Jack muttered an oath and climbed from the carriage to open the gates himself. A wizened old man shuffled out of the gatehouse. "Ned!" Jack offered his hand through the iron bars. "It's good to see you again."

The old man ignored the outstretched hand. "Ye've taken your time coming home. My lord." The title was stuck on with no pretense of welcome.

"I've been busy fighting Britain's battles, Ned," Jack said as he lowered his hand.

The gatekeeper snorted eloquently, making it clear that foreign battles mattered little to him. As he opened the gates, he said, "Much has changed. My lord."

"In what way?"

"Ye'll find out." Ned closed the gates behind the carriage and stomped into the gatehouse.

As soon as the carriage drove onto Langdon property, there was a startling energy shift. Abby had grown accustomed to the bracing Yorkshire air and a sense of sturdy upland life. Now that they had entered Langdale, there was a flat, suffocating heaviness that pervaded the atmosphere.

"Do you feel a difference?" Jack asked.

"Dramatically so," Abby replied as the carriage started up the driveway. It ran up the dale so far she couldn't see the house at the end. "Did you choose your gatekeeper to frighten people away?"

"Ned used to be a lot friendlier." Jack frowned. "You have much more experience reading auras than I do. What did you see in his?"

"He seemed like a man struggling to survive, his energy pulled tight around him."

"That was what I sensed. He felt *wrong*." Jack rapped on the panel by the driver as a signal to stop the carriage. "Everything feels wrong."

When the carriage stopped, Jack swung out. "I'll only be a minute."

Abby waited as the minute stretched to several. Nerves taut, she opened the door and climbed out. Jack stood about a hundred yards away beside a small grove of bare-branched trees. As she walked to join him, the first cold drops of rain began to fall. Wishing she had worn her bonnet, she said, "What are you looking for?"

"There was a mass of daffodil bulbs planted here, and the number increased every year. The flowers covered the ground like a shimmering golden blanket. Now there isn't so much as a single shoot breaking the soil."

He was right. Now that they had entered Langdale, all traces of spring had vanished. No shoots broke the ground, and the leaf buds on the trees were as tight and hard as if it was midwinter. Knowing that daffodils were famously resilient, she asked, "Could someone have dug up all the bulbs?"

"I can't imagine why." Jack squatted and used a stick to poke into the earth. Almost immediately, he found a bulb and freed it from the soil.

Abby peered at the wizened bulb. "This doesn't look dead, but it's like a bulb in December, not March. It should be at least sprouting by now. Maybe even blooming."

Jack got to his feet. "Proof that I'm not imagining this sense of wrongness."

Abby scanned the barren landscape. The wind moaned in the trees and the rain was coming harder. "This land is dormant. Barely alive."

"Cursed?"

"I don't think so, but I'm not sure," she said slowly. "It would take a wizard of unimaginable power to curse such a large area, and curses have a distinct, twisted feel to them. This land feels as if it has been drained of life until there is almost none left."

"Curses, draining of life, whatever. My land is near death, and I don't know how to cure it." He shoved the bulb back in the earth, tamping loose soil over it. "Ned also seemed barely alive. I had dreamed that Langdale Hall was blighted, but I didn't realize that the blight is literally true."

"Do you think this denial of life comes from your stepfather?"

"Probably. I hope to know for sure when I see him." Jack turned back to the carriage. "Does killing a man lift his curses?"

"I hope you're joking," Abby said, unnerved by his soldierly ease with violence.

"Not really." Jack's bleak gaze swept the hills. "Langdale is my responsibility. Now that I have returned, I will do whatever is necessary to restore it to health."

"Murder won't do the trick," Abby said firmly. "Even if a black magician was hired to curse this land, Scranton's death won't end the curse. Even the black magician's death wouldn't end it. If there is a curse, the cure is to counter it with powerful healing magic. So don't do anything foolish! I don't want to see you swing at Tyburn."

Jack didn't reply. With cold clarity, she realized that he would indeed do whatever he deemed necessary to lift this strange lifelessness. Trained as a soldier, not a wizard, he didn't really understand how taking life would make the land even further out of harmony. She must keep him in balance, if she could. As he helped her into the carriage, she said quietly, "Please don't do anything dramatic or criminal without talking to me first. Together we can discover the truth and find a solution."

Alarmed when he didn't reply, she said sharply, "Jack?"

He gave a reluctant nod. "I won't kill Scranton without informing you first."

"I find that faint comfort," she said tartly as she tried to neaten her wet hair.

"I hope it doesn't come to that. But my skin crawls from the wrongness here."

Abby could feel it, too, and the effect must be much harsher for Jack, since this was his home. That knowledge did nothing to reassure her. "There will be a solution. We must take the time to find it."

"I fear the solution is to throw my mother from her home," Jack said, his face tight. "How does one accomplish that?"

"Think of this as throwing your stepfather from your house," she suggested. "Your mother can stay or go as she pleases. She has choices, after all. She can go with her husband to his estate, which is right next door. Or stay at Langdale Hall without him. Or use her jointure to set up an establishment elsewhere, such as London or Bath."

"You're right. It's not like I'm condemning her to the workhouse." He frowned. "But it will be difficult to ask her to move. Will you help me, Abby?"

She had been afraid of this. "Of course. Do you want me to tell her she must go? She'll resent me anyhow, so I might as well be the villain."

"That's tempting, but it is my place to issue the ultimatum." He sighed. "Just . . . support me. Don't let me give in and avoid doing what I know is right."

In some ways, that would be even harder than giving the orders herself. "I'll do my best. But you must be sure of what you want to do. If you are uncertain, it will be difficult for you to be as firm as you will need to be."

"I am certain that I want to restore Langdale Hall. I hope that will give me the resolution necessary to send Scranton away."

"If he is the source of this blight, removing him from the estate might be a good start to fixing the situation. If we're really lucky, perhaps nothing more will be needed."

"Then I will get rid of him." Jack smiled wryly. "On the whole, it would be easier to shoot him. Guns are simpler than difficult conversations."

"No doubt. But not the best long term solution."

The rest of the ride to the house was in silence. Abby kept Cleocatra's basket in her lap, one hand resting inside on the cat's soft fur. Considering how nervous Cleo had been since they'd entered the estate, she wasn't sure who needed comfort more.

The sprawling manor house was an interesting mix of old and older styles. The carriage pulled under a portico on the right side that protected them from the now-heavy rain. Jack helped her from the vehicle. "The oldest section of Langdale Hall dates back to the thirteenth century, they say. Various Langdons have added new bits when in the mood, with never a thought for what was already here."

"It is rather a hodgepodge," she admitted. "But charming."

"You lie well," he said with a glimmer of a smile.

"I'm not lying." She gestured at the jumble of towers and mismatched facades and windows. There was a nice chunk in Tudor style, and even a Palladian wing from the last century. "Granted, the place looks like it was built by a blind tinker, but the pieces all go together. The lovely gray stone makes it look as if the hall has grown out of the bones of the Yorkshire hills."

His expression softened. "I've always thought that, too."

As they walked to the door that opened from the portico into the house, Abby held Jack's arm with one hand and carried Cleo's basket in the other. Jack rang the bell. Once more there was a wait.

This time the door was opened by a well-dressed footman in livery and powdered wig. His eyes widened as he saw Jack. "You were not expected, Lord Frayne."

Jack arched his brows. "Is the hall in such a state that a warning is necessary before bringing my bride home?"

"No, my lord." The footman bowed after a quick glance at Abby. "It's good to see you again, my lord. Welcome to Langdale Hall, my lady."

"You're Young Jenkins, aren't you? The eldest son of the butler?"

"Yes, my lord." The young man's face was touched with shadow. "My father passed away two winters ago."

"I'm sorry. I didn't know," Jack said gravely. "He was a fine man."

As Abby walked in beside Jack, she wondered why his mother hadn't written him about that. Surely the death of an old family retainer rated a sentence in a letter.

They were shaking the rain off in the entrance hall when a blond vision carrying a small dog drifted past the open door that led into the house. Seeing the visitors, she paused. "Jack, how nice to see you. Were we expecting you?"

This was obviously the woman who had established Jack's taste for petite blondes. Helen, Lady Scranton, must be near fifty, but she was still slim, with shining bright hair and perfectly formed features. Across a crowded room, she could be confused with Celeste. Her small, chubby lapdog wore a dark blue ribbon that matched the trim on her ladyship's elegant morning gown.

"Mother!" For all his complicated feelings about his mother, Jack crossed the room and hugged her with pleasure, careful not to hurt the dog. "I wanted to surprise you. It's been too long."

"Far, far too long. And whose fault is that?" Her eyes were blue, not the hazel of Jack and Celeste. She turned to Abby, cradling the dog to her chest. "Who is this? Surely you didn't hire a companion for me! You know I don't need one, not when I have my dear Alfred."

Jack took Abby's hand and drew her forward. "Of course I did no such thing. Don't you remember that I wrote you about my marriage? Allow me to present my wife, Abby, the newest Lady Frayne."

Her ladyship's brows arched. "Really? I thought you'd marry someone prettier."

Abby flushed a deep, painful scarlet as the fragile confidence she'd acquired in London vanished. She felt like a great, ungainly cow. One who had been traveling for days, wore an old gown, and was wet from the rain.

Jack's hand squeezed Abby's hard. "That is an appalling thing to say to the new mistress of Langdale Hall," he said sharply. "I trust you will apologize for your slip of the tongue."

His mother shrugged, unrepentant, "I had thought your taste ran to elegant blondes, but of course I haven't seen you in so many years that I really don't know your preferences any more."

Was her new mother-in-law quite right in the head? Abby had trouble believing that any woman could be so indifferent to seeing a long-absent child. Trying to sound calm and gracious, Abby said, "Since Jack could never find a blonde as lovely as you and Celeste, he decided to marry a brunette. I'm pleased to meet you, Lady Scranton."

"Lady Frayne, if you please," the other woman corrected. "I have chosen to retain my title. With my dear Alfred's permission, of course. He says he likes being married to a viscountess."

Abby knew that it wasn't uncommon for women to retain the higher title when they married a man of lower rank, but having two Lady Fraynes under the same roof might be confusing. She hoped it wouldn't be for long.

Helen's lapdog struggled to get down, so she set her pet on the floor. The beast came over to Abby and started jumping on her. "Homer doesn't like you," Helen drawled. "He's very discriminating."

"I think he smells my cat." As the dog reared up, a low hiss came from inside the basket. Abby was about to check the basket's latch when the lid popped open to reveal Cleocatra, her white whiskers a quivering accent against her sleek black fur.

Homer began whining and jumping. Abby stepped back, but the dog managed to bang a paw against the bottom of the basket, setting it swinging. With a furious growl, Cleo leaped to the floor. Every ebony hair on her body was standing on end, making her look twice the dog's size.

Homer launched himself at the cat. Hissing like a dragon, Cleo slashed her claws across the dog's nose. Homer howled and raced away, escaping the entry hall as if pursued by demons.

"What a horrible beast!" Helen exclaimed. "You must get rid of it at once!"

As Abby scooped up Cleo and soothed her, Jack said, "Abby lives here now, and so does her cat. Homer could use training to improve his manners."

"Homer is *never* the least bit of trouble! That filthy cat is the problem."

"Like most cats, Cleo is immaculate," Jack said, suddenly amused. "I wish my soldiers had washed half as often."

As he and his mother talked, Abby studied Helen's aura. Under her polished exterior was monstrous self-absorption. Though she seemed glad to see Jack, her reaction was mild, more like greeting a distant cousin than her only son. She showed no interest in her new daughter-in-law. Even her insult had been casual. Was this Helen's true nature, or was her behavior another sign of Langdale's wrongness?

A dark presence entered the room. Helen turned and said caressingly, "Darling! Look who has come."

The tall, lean man with silver hair had to be Jack's wicked stepfather. Though Sir Alfred Scranton was conventionally handsome and meticulously well dressed, he felt *wrong.* It took her a moment to realize that he had almost no aura. Most people were swathed in subtly colored energy, but not Sir Alfred. Instead of radiating energy, he seemed to suck it from his surroundings. He was like darkness personified.

As she studied him, she felt a tug at her energy field. She strengthened her shields instinctively to prevent him from draining any of her life force. She wasn't sure if he was aware of how his negative energy pulled at everything around him. As was common with married couples, an energy bond connected him and his wife, but even that was colored by disturbing possessiveness.

Turning from Helen, he inclined his head politely. "Good to see you, Frayne. You should have let us know you were coming so we could prepare for your visit."

"This isn't a visit. I've come home for good, and I've brought my wife." As Jack performed the introductions, Sir Alfred's eyes narrowed. His expression was so serpent-like that Abby half expected to see a forked tongue flicker when he spoke.

Tired and uncomfortable with the tension in the room, Abby said, "Might I go to my room to refresh myself? It's been a long journey."

"That's a good idea." Jack put his hand behind her back. "Mother, could you order the servants to build a fire and make up the bed in the master suite?"

She looked shocked. "Those are *our* rooms."

His brows rose. "On my one other visit, you were in the blue suite. I'm surprised that you moved into my rooms without consulting me."

"You were never here!" She looked at her son with an air of tragic sadness. "Surely you wouldn't put your mother out of her own bed!"

Jack hesitated, and Abby felt him wavering. She glanced up at him, mentally trying to project the reminder that he had asked her to help bolster his resolve. He gave her a faint nod to show that he understood. "We shall discuss that and other matters over dinner," he said. "For now, my wife and I need a place to rest and refresh ourselves."

Abby returned Cleo to her basket, knowing that the first salvo had been fired. Larger battles lay ahead.

Chapter XXIX

J ack and Abby were assigned two guest rooms with a connecting door. Leaving Morris to unpack for him, Jack walked straight into Abby's room and wrapped his arms around her as Cleo, newly released from the basket, explored her surroundings. "I knew this would be difficult," he said as he absorbed her warmth and sanity, "but I didn't expect my mother to insult you to your face!"

Abby rested her head against Jack's shoulder. "Has she always been like this?"

The question helped him to regain his objectivity. "No, she was always flighty and perhaps a bit self-absorbed, like a shimmering dragonfly. But she had a kind heart. I never, ever heard her say something so rude."

"So she is also part of the estate's wrongness," Abby said thoughtfully as she left his embrace and removed her cloak.

"I wish . . ." Jack stopped. "I'd like to talk to someone knowledgeable about the situation, and I just realized I can. The vicar, Mr. Willard, was my tutor, and he has some magical ability as well as wisdom. It's still early afternoon. Do you mind if I call on him now? The village isn't far, just outside the estate. I'd like to speak with him before we dine with my mother and her husband. Assuming he's still here, of course."

"Take me, too." Abby made a face. "I would rather not be here alone."

He remembered the dream he'd had of soaring over the blasted fields of Langdale, his mate at his side. "If you're not too tired, I'd like you to come. I think it best that we be together as much of the time as possible."

"Strength in numbers?"

"Exactly." He could feel the blight pulsing around him like a poisoned fog, ready to move in and undermine his spirit. Mr. Willard might be an ally in the struggle.

They needed all the allies they could get.

The church's square Norman tower rose sturdily at the far end of Langdale's high street. The familiar sight eased Jack's heart. Next door stood the vicarage, the rambling structure constructed from matching gray Yorkshire stone. How many lessons had Jack received in the vicar's study? Hundreds, and they were some of the best hours of his childhood, even though at the time he'd complained bitterly about having to learn Latin and Greek and philosophy.

As they climbed from the carriage, Abby said, "The vicar's wife is a fine gardener. Her daffodils and crocuses are blooming and several trees are ready to leaf."

"Everything here is much healthier than on the estate," Jack agreed as he rapped on the door. "Mrs. Willard was a devoted gardener, but she died several years ago. She was a lovely woman who always had a ginger cake or piece of shortbread ready to feed a starving student of the classics."

The door was opened by a little maid. Her eyes opened wide when she saw that the visitors were gentry. "Sir? Madam?"

Jack said, "Lord and Lady Frayne are calling for Mr. Willard. Is he in?"

The girl invited them into the parlor, then left to summon the vicar. Jack felt a burst of happiness when Mr. Willard's familiar tall, thin figure appeared. He looked very much a vicar, but under his gentle, otherworldly air was dry humor and a shrewd mind.

Willard smiled at his visitors, and his aura was the clear, bright gold of spirituality. "Jack! Or rather, Lord Frayne. What a pleasure it is to see you again."

"Mr. Willard!" Jack crossed the room and caught the vicar's hands in both of his. "So much has changed. It's a blessing to find that you haven't." He grinned. "You will be pleased to hear that the Latin you pounded into my unwilling head proved useful. I found myself reading Caesar and Cicero and other Romans while on campaign in Spain."

"And did you read the Greeks as well?" the vicar asked with interest.

"Content yourself with your success in Latin." Jack beckoned Abby forward. "My wife is eager to meet you."

He was becoming better at reading energy; it was obvious as he performed the introductions that Abby and Mr. Willard were kindred spirits. His gray eyes lit up when his gaze met hers. "At last you've come. Welcome to Langdale, Lady Frayne."

"At last?" she said quizzically. "Do you have the ability to see the future?"

"I have a touch of the Sight. Usually it's more a nuisance than not." He gestured for them to sit on the sofa. "But for some time, I've felt that possible salvation was coming for Langdale, and it would take two people to bring it about."

"So there is hope." Glad they needn't waste time with social pleasantries, Jack leaned forward in his seat. "Tell me what has happened here."

The vicar tossed a scoop of coal on the fire. "The decline began with your mother's remarriage. As soon as Scranton moved into Langdale Hall, the estate began to fail. Many tenants and employees left, even though good jobs are scarce around here. Those who stayed there turned surly and suspicious." He sat in a chair opposite his guests. "Your mother changed most of all."

"She seems very different," Jack agreed. "Has the estate been cursed?"

"I don't believe so." The vicar frowned. "But I think your mother has been ensorcelled. I have known her a very long time. The woman living in the hall is like a frozen, glittering copy of her. The charm and sweetness that distinguished the lady gradually disappeared." He spoke as if an old, dear friend had died.

There was a break in the conversation when the young maid brought in a tray with tea and cakes. After the girl withdrew, Abby asked, "Mr. Willard, has anyone else with magical ability investigated the problems here?"

"Over the years, a number of skilled wizards have visited me and tried to detect the underlying problems, but none succeeded," the vicar replied. "One was a bishop with great experience in ghosts, curses, and spiritual possession. Even he could not find the cause of the dale's decline. There seems to be no magic involved, so most people have accepted the problems as natural, like the biblical plagues."

"Did anyone have a theory that might be a starting point for us?" Abby asked.

"I kept a journal of events and speculations, if you'd like to see that."

"I would." Jack's gut tightened at the knowledge that he would be reading a journal of his own failings. Even learning about the spell designed to keep him away from home could not relieve his ultimate responsibility. But maybe the journal would provide useful clues. "You have been the wizard closest to the estate's decline. What are your personal opinions about it?"

The vicar hesitated. "I suspect that the problem lies with the land itself. There is magic in the earth—magic and life. That magic has almost vanished from the estate. The amount remaining can barely sustain life."

"The problem isn't necessary magical," Abby said thoughtfully. "Sometimes estates go through periods of bad luck. If that's true here, Scranton's inherently negative personality might be making it worse, but not be the cause." She smiled a little. "Jack is known for his good fortune. Maybe his presence can turn Langdale's fortunes."

"Sir Alfred's presence might be amplifying anything else that is wrong," Mr. Willard agreed. "He never leaves the estate."

"Never?" Abby asked, startled.

"Possibly he goes to his own estate sometimes, crossing where the two properties touch. But I don't know for sure."

"What about my mother?" Jack asked. "I know she hasn't traveled to London in years, and she won't even visit my sister. But surely she must leave the estate even if only to come to the village."

"After her marriage, she stopped attending holy services." The vicar looked bleak. "I have offered to make pastoral calls at the hall, but she has refused."

Jack shook his head. "My mother always loved to be out and about. She enjoyed Sunday services as a chance to show off new clothes and visit the neighbors."

"I've known of cases where possessive men won't allow their wives out of their sight for fear of losing control," Abby said. "Often they beat the women to keep them obedient. If Scranton is that kind of man, it would explain why your mother won't even visit her own daughter at Alderton."

Jack swore. He'd heard of such cases, too. Sometimes they ended with the man killing his wife. "I'm not sure which is worse—my mother ensorcelled or beaten."

Abby flinched at his expression. Obviously she hadn't intended to incite Jack to homicide. "I didn't see any sign that your mother was being beaten. She seems very happy with her husband."

The vicar nodded agreement. "Your mother and Sir Alfred scarcely notice anyone except each other. No one else seems to matter."

That included long-absent sons. Her reaction to his hug had been tepid. "It won't be easy to dislodge Scranton from the hall," Jack said harshly. "But it must happen. That will be the quickest way of learning if he is the source of the problems at Langdale."

The vicar's brows arched. "You are going to ask your stepfather to leave? If you do, be very careful. He is rich and well connected and I fear that he will do almost anything to maintain his position in Langdale."

The more information they could pool, the better. Jack said, "Let me tell you some of what he has done already. Perhaps that will help us deduce what black magician he uses. That would help us in countering his wickedness."

The three of them together should be more powerful than one obsessive, negative man who could afford to hire black magicians. At least he hoped so.

Abby and Jack talked with the vicar all afternoon. By the time they returned to Langdale Hall, it was time to change for dinner. Abby took special care with her appearance as she prepared for her first meal at the hall. Even knowing that Jack's mother was probably ensorcelled didn't eliminate the sting of her words about Abby's looks. Despite the insult, Abby needed to keep the situation civil so that Jack wouldn't explode and kill his stepfather. She didn't think that was likely, but it was not impossible.

The sky blue gown she chose was one of Madame Ravelle's best, and just right for a family dinner in the country. She wore her sapphires because the jewels held some of her mother's protective energy. Having them around her neck made her feel safer.

A knock on the connecting door announced Jack's arrival. She turned and saw that he wore his uniform again. She was going to miss seeing him in it—and out of it!—when he finally packed his regimentals away. "You look wonderfully dashing."

"I wanted to remind my mother and Scranton what I've been doing for the last few years." His slow gaze moved over her. "You look splendid. How much time do we have before we have to go down?"

"Not enough time for that," she laughed, though his gaze was quickening her pulse. *Later.* She took a last glance at her reflection, glad that the corset concealed the effect his heated gaze had on her breasts. "I have determined not to allow either of them to irritate me again."

He grinned. "Refusing to anger will irritate Scranton, and probably my mother as well. I shall attempt equal control. If I don't keep a firm hand on my temper, I'll be tempted to bring my pistols to the dinner table."

Wishing that was a joke, Abby said, "If you have pistols with you, I trust you'll leave them in the room."

"I do, and I will. It's best I don't carry a weapon tonight."

"Use your magical perception," she advised, thinking he needed something to occupy his attention while they ate. "I don't suppose your stepfather is likely to poison us, but look carefully at your food, and don't eat anything that seems wrong in any way. Ideally, eat only from dishes that are shared by all."

Jack blinked. "What a very unnerving thought. I'm not physically afraid of Scranton—my instincts for avoiding murderous assaults are excellent. But I don't know if that extends to possible poisoning in my own home."

"There is risk all around us," Abby said soberly. "Our campaign must proceed with all due care and thought."

"I'm so much better at waving a sword and charging, but I shall strive for control." Jack offered his arm and together they descended to the small parlor to have drinks before dinner. He said quietly, "The house seems shabby. Not well maintained. Too many servants have left, maybe."

"And those remaining are dispirited." Abby frowned. "I suppose it's not surprising the house reflects the same problems as the land."

They stopped speaking when they entered the parlor to find Helen and Scranton already there. In the candlelight, the energy bond connecting the two was very clear. "Sherry?" Scranton asked, smoothly taking the role of host.

Abby saw the faint tightening of Jack's eyes at the recognition that his stepfather was acting like the master of the house, but he didn't challenge the older man. A veteran soldier learns to choose his battles. "Yes, thank you."

Abby also accepted a sherry. Scranton used the same decanter to pour all four glasses, and he made no attempt to influence which glass

Jack or Abby took. If there was poisoning tonight, it wouldn't be from the sherry. But just to be sure, she scanned it. There was nothing wrong about the wine.

Helen looked exquisite in a white and silver gown that was far too elaborate for the occasion. Though beautiful, it was also subtly out-of-date. The older woman's eyes narrowed with envy as she studied Abby's fashionable costume. "That looks like Madame Ravelle's work. She'll make dresses for anyone willing to pay her price."

"Yes, and a sensible philosophy that is," Abby said cheerfully. "Why work for someone who won't pay you?"

"You think like a tradesman."

"Why, thank you," Abby said, her eyes wide and innocent. Her determination not to let herself be baited worked, because Helen scowled and changed the subject.

It was going to be a long evening.

Chapter XXX

Conversation over dinner was stilted. The older couple talked mostly to each other and showed no interest in Jack's adventures or the background of his wife. Jack wasn't sure his mother even remembered that he had been seriously injured, though he knew Ashby had written her after the danger was over.

The second course had been served when his mother asked casually, "Are your rooms comfortable?" Her quick glance at Abby showed that she knew she was treating her daughter-in-law as a guest rather than as the new mistress.

"They're fine," Abby said, expression neutral.

His mother relaxed. "Good. I'd rather not move from my rooms."

It was time to speak up. Jack took a deep breath. "It would make no sense for you to change rooms when you'd just be moving again a few days later."

The statement gained him the full attention of Scranton and his mother. She looked baffled and vulnerable while Scranton glowered.

It would be easier to face a well-armed French brigade rather than his mother. He steeled himself. "There's no way to say this tactfully. While I'm glad that you've kept the house from sitting empty for years, now that I've returned with a wife, it's time for you to leave. Since the furnishings belong to Langdale Hall, you'll only have to move clothing and personal possessions. A week should be sufficient. Abby and I can stay in the guest rooms until then."

His mother gasped, "We can't leave the hall! Alfred, darling, explain to Jack how impossible that would be." Tears gathered in her eyes. "I can't believe that my only son would drive me from my home!"

It was an effort for Jack to keep his voice steady in the face of her tears. "If you were widowed and alone, of course there would be no question of your leaving, Mother. But you are not alone. You're married to one of Yorkshire's leading gentlemen, a man who owns a fine home only three miles away. The real question is why you have not long since taken up residence under your husband's roof."

His mother swung her head around to glare at Abby. "This is all your fault! You have poisoned my son's mind against me!"

Jack cut in before Abby could reply. "My wife has said nothing against you. The decision is mine. A fortnight from now, after you've moved and settled into Combe House, you'll be glad. It's a fine place, more modern and comfortable than here, and it would be *yours.*"

"She does not wish to go," Scranton said, his eyes glittering with anger. "I do not want your mother distressed, Frayne."

Reminding himself to be calm and tactful no matter what, Jack said, "You were most considerate to indulge my mother's sensibilities and not take her from the house that had been her home for so many years. But no house is large enough for two masters and two mistresses."

His mother was pouting like an adorable child. Though he was exasperated by her attitude, he could not despise her the way he did Scranton. He had too many fond memories of how she used to be. "The sooner you set up your own establishment, the better, Mother. You deserve to be mistress of your own home, and so does Abby."

"You don't understand. We *can't* leave." She rose from the table and darted from the room, weeping.

Scranton rose to follow her. "Don't do this, Frayne," he said ominously. "You will regret it."

Jack rose, his height allowing him to look down at the older man. "Don't make this any more difficult than it need be, Scranton. You have one week to leave peaceably. If you don't, I'll remove you bodily if necessary."

The expression in Scranton's eyes was chilling. His stepfather wanted him dead. "For Helen's sake, I will say it one last time—don't be a fool, Frayne."

"My decision has been made, and I can't think of any good reason why you shouldn't move back to your home."

"It is the bad reasons you should worry about," Scranton said with lethal softness before he stalked from the room.

Jack drew a shaky breath and sat again. "I can't say that went terribly well."

Abby reached across the table and took his hand. "It's hard to imagine how it could have gone smoothly. I'm curious why your mother is so sure they can't leave. It seems an unnaturally strong attachment to this property. Do you think Scranton might have had a geographic spell laid on her to create the belief that she can't go?"

"The opposite of the spell that made me stay away? It's certainly possible," Jack said, glad to have something to think about other than his mother's reproachful eyes. "Could you study her and perhaps remove any such spells if you find them?"

Abby frowned. "She carries a very powerful anti-magic spell. I would rather not force my way into her mind against that. Such tactics should be a last resort."

He squeezed her hand. "I think that we are rapidly approaching the last resort."

She sighed. "So do I, my dear. So do I."

•   •   •

After the confrontation with his mother and her husband, neither Jack nor Abby was in the mood to make love, but it was wonderful to cradle her warm body in the quiet of their bed. As she settled against him, she said sleepily, "I think we should redecorate the master and mistress's rooms before we move in."

"And maybe have them exorcised," he added dryly.

She laughed. "At the least, we can burn some incense and cast a circle of protection so that the energy will be clean and clear when we move in."

"Do you think they'll leave quietly, lass?"

She exhaled softly against him. "I think that Scranton will call on his black magician to create a really nasty spell aimed at one or both of us. Maybe more than one spell. We must be on our guard. Are you shielding yourself?"

He nodded. "I hope his black magician lives more than a week away so there won't be time to create trouble. I doubt we'll be so lucky, though."

"Much better to expect the worst." Abby yawned and drifted off while Jack stayed in the uneasy territory between sleep and waking. Scranton's words had been threatening, but what form would that threat take? The man had already driven Jack from Yorkshire and given him an attraction to risk, and there were far too many other possibilities. But now he had Abby beside him. Soothed, he finally dozed off.

In the deepest part of the night, Jack jerked awake, every fiber of his being saturated with despair. What was wrong?

Everything. His relentless mind spelled out all his failings in bitter detail. He had abandoned his family to become a middling army officer, one whose position could have been filled by better soldiers. Another officer who would have lost fewer men. In the horrors after midnight, the blood of Jack's lost troopers stained his soul.

There was more blood, a dark river of blood, from the men he had killed personally, and the men who had died as a result of his orders. Decent Frenchmen who had wanted to live, whose only crime had been the uniforms they wore. How many lay rotting in foreign fields because of him? More than he dared count.

Though he hadn't shot any of the inhabitants of Langdale, his betrayal of his people had surely caused deaths from misery and want. The knowledge of all the death on his hands was a tearing sorrow in his gut that could never be healed.

Agony swamped him, too excruciating to bear. His breath came in harsh pants and his heart hammered as if to burst from his chest. Frantically he wished for a way to end this anguish.

His pistols.

Knowing that he had a cure for his pain filled him with cool relief. He slipped quietly from the bed, taking care not to wake Abby. She was another of his failures, a lovely, gifted woman who had tied herself to a monster. She would despise him if he gave in to his violent nature and killed Scranton. She would be far better off without him.

He imagined her in London as the wealthy widowed Lady Frayne. Having been accepted by the ton, she could now have any husband she wanted. Yes, she would be better off without him, even though the thought of her with another man was like a saber in his belly. Lucky that they'd had a London lawyer draw up proper marriage settlements. Her future was secure, and Hilltop House would go to her outright.

The floor was icy under his bare feet as he padded into his adjoining bedroom. He knew exactly where to find his pistol case. He opened his trunk and bent over, finding the polished wooden box by touch. The pistols were French-made and very fine. He'd taken them from the tent of a dead French officer after the battle of Talavera.

Loading the pistols would be easier with light. He snapped his fingers over the bedside candle and the wick sparked into life. As he watched the flame catch and lengthen, he thought how the evil in his nature had surfaced. In the last weeks, Jack had managed to convince himself that magic was harmless, sometimes even good, but in the dark of night he knew it for wickedness. His father would be ashamed of him.

Dear God, what if the land's blight was because he had been drawing off power to preserve his worthless life during his army years? The thought was unbearable.

His fingers were numb with cold, and he dropped the metal ramrod after he poured the powder charge into the barrel. He had to kneel on the floor and feel around for the rod, since his vision was curiously hazed.

Ah, there it was. He rammed the ball into the chamber and primed the pan. He repeated the procedure with the second pistol, since a man always wanted a second shot available just in case.

Salvation was at hand.

Hoping his death would be enough to atone for his crimes, he raised the pistol to his temple. It was important that the weapon be aimed correctly. His hand shook so badly that the barrel jerked across his skin.

He sat down on the edge of the bed and raised his left hand to stabilize the weapon. Didn't want to miss the killing shot and end up a pathetic brain-damaged creature incapable of caring for himself.

"Jack! What are you doing?" a female voice cried out with horror.

He looked up. In the connecting door was a tall, nightgowned woman with wide, shocked eyes that pierced his soul. A woman—yes, Abby. His wife.

"I'm doing this for you," he tried to say, his voice a raw whisper.

He pulled the trigger.

Abby choked with terror when she saw Jack's finger curl to fire the pistol. Desperately she hurled energy at the weapon to disrupt the firing process. Yes, blow the priming powder away *now*.

The hammer slammed into the empty firing pan. Instead of an ear-numbing blast, there was only a metallic *click*. Misfire.

As she darted across the room, Jack lowered the weapon and looked at it with a puzzled frown. Then he set it on the bedside table and lifted an identical pistol.

Again she flicked the priming powder from the pan, but it seemed a chancy way to prevent the gun from firing. She snatched at the pistol, hoping to get it away from him, but he was too strong for her. As he wrestled to keep the weapon, his eyes were wide and staring, as if he was in a trance.

"Dear God, Jack," she cried. "What are you *doing*?"

"This is none of your affair!" The pistol wavered between them, and for an instant the barrel swung toward Abby.

"Abby?" Jack's expression changed as abruptly as if he'd been doused with ice water. He stared at her with horrified disbelief. "Abby!"

He instantly released his grip on the pistol, which sent Abby stumbling backward. As she struggled to keep her feet, Jack bent over and pressed his hands to his temples, gasping, "What madness is this?"

She set the pistol aside and laid her hands on the side of his head. Finding enough calm to channel healing energy wasn't easy, but after several long moments she managed to send him energy to reduce mental and emotional pain.

His expression smoothed out and the tension left his body. "There is heaven in your hands, lass," he breathed. "Was I under some kind of spell? I woke feeling the blackest despair I've ever known. All I could think of was ending the pain."

"It had to be some form of dark magic, though not one I recognized. Thank God a noise woke me. Since you weren't in bed, I came to investigate." Lightly she brushed his tangled hair as she took her hands away. Her heart still hammered from the terror of seeing the pistol pointed at his head. "Do you have any brandy here?"

He gestured at his trunk. "There should be a flask in there."

She found the well-worn silver flask without trouble and unscrewed the cap. Hoping to steady her shaking hands, she took a hefty swig before handing it to Jack. The brandy burn helped clear her thoughts. "Don't drink too much. We need to think about how this was done. The next attack might be more successful."

He swallowed a mouthful of the brandy, coughed, then took a smaller sip. "Let's do our thinking in our nice warm bed."

He got to his feet and capped the flask, then wrapped an arm around Abby as they returned to the other bedroom. As she stacked the pillows, he created a ball of light and attached it above their heads on the canopy of the bed. They settled against the pillow-stacked backboard and he pulled the covers up to their chests. Lord, his feet were icy cold! Bless Abby for putting her warmer feet on his. "Where do we start, apart from the fact that once more you've saved my life? How did that devil get into my mind?"

"I think we made a mistake in assuming that Scranton had hired a black magician to cast the earlier spells," Abby said slowly. "I think he must have created them himself. He isn't a regular wizard—I would sense that if he was. But my father's research has found references to odd magical talents that are not well known or studied. Given what we know about Scranton, I think that he has one of those twisted talents."

"Might he have the ability to draw life directly from the land?" Jack exclaimed. "That could be why the estate is ailing. He sucks up the land's energy for himself."

"I think you're right!" Abby sat up straighter. "When I met him, my first impression was that he drew energy from all around him. I even felt him tugging at me. His twisted talent might use that energy to create certain kinds of spells. My guess is that his power is inefficient, its range very limited. In the past he was able to drive you away from Yorkshire and make you reckless. Tonight he drained your sense of well-being and made you wish to end your own life. Those are inherently negative forms of magic."

"So he takes and destroys and never heals or builds," Jack said. "That odd magic may be able to get around my basic shields. Is there any protection that might be more effective against him?"

Abby bit her lip. "There might be." She slipped from the bed, crossed to her linen press, and returned with a needle. "I think this will help."

She stabbed it into the index finger of her left hand, then drew down the covers so she could raise the hem of his nightshirt all the way to his chest. Cold night air tickled his midriff. "I'll draw a symbol of protection on your solar plexus."

"Blood?" he asked warily.

"It sounds like the most dreadful hedge-witch flummery, doesn't it? But there is truth buried in the old superstitions. Blood has power. Particularly the blood of a wizard." With the bleeding tip of her finger, she drew a symbol that looked like three twisting spirals that joined at the center. He winced when she had to prick her finger again to renew the blood flow.

When she finished, she said, "This will be effective until it's washed off."

He took the needle from her. "You're stronger and more disciplined than I, but if this symbol protects me, I assume it will benefit you, also."

She shrugged. "I'm not likely to be the focus of Scranton's wickedness."

"We don't know that for certain, and I don't want to underestimate him again." He studied the symbol till he was sure that he could reproduce it, then uncovered her midsection and pricked his finger.

When he touched the smooth, pale skin of her midriff, she said, "That tickles!"

"Then I shall be quick." Trying not to be distracted by the lovely curves revealed by the magical light, he drew the three intersecting spirals. "Interesting. I can feel the protective shield forming."

"It's one of the most powerful of protective charms, but it's not used often because of the requirement for blood," she observed. "Plus, it's stronger if there is a bond between the person casting the spell and the one receiving it."

"So one couldn't hire a wizard to do this and get as strong a shield." He blew gently on the blood to dry it out, and a shiver passed through Abby. "Now, what else can I do while waiting for the blood to dry? Hmm." He bent and began kissing her belly, his tongue teasing the soft skin while his hand slid between her thighs.

She slid lower into the pillows, her hips pulsing in rhythm to his stroking hand. "We must take care not to rub off the symbols."

"If that happens, we'll draw more." His mouth followed his hands, tasting the hidden sweetness of her. She moaned and opened her legs to him as she buried her fingers in his hair.

After a brush with death, there was nothing sweeter than worshipping life.

Chapter XXXI

After making love to Abby, Jack slept soundly, but he awoke with reluctance. From the light, it was early and a clear, sunny day. Since Abby seemed awake, he asked, "Last night wasn't just a bad dream, was it?"

"I'm afraid not." Abby pushed herself up and studied his face, then nodded. "But we survived. What is on the schedule for today?"

Jack didn't suppose he could say, "Kill Scranton," since that would just upset Abby. But he didn't see another solution, since Jack wasn't up to a magical battle with the bastard. Abby's own positive, healing power was so different from Scranton's that she might be vulnerable to the man's twisted spells. "We should ride over the estate. I need to see the place for myself, inch by inch and tenant by tenant, and so do you. Are you up to a day in the saddle?"

"I look forward to learning the estate, and maybe finding some clues about how to heal it." She slid from the bed and reached for her robe. "Are your shields in place?"

He tested them. The symbol she'd drawn on his solar plexus pulsed with power. "Yes. I don't think that Scranton will be able to poison my mind again."

"I don't think he poisoned it," she said seriously. "Rather, he drew out everything good and positive in your nature, leaving the dark threads of fear and despair that haunt all of us on bad days."

"Even you?" he said quizzically as he climbed from the bed and retrieved his robe. "You seem so strong and calm and sure of yourself."

"Oh, Jack." She laughed a little as she poured water into the washbasin. "I suppose I must be glad that I conceal my doubts and fears so well."

He relaxed his eyes and studied her with inner vision as she splashed water on her face. Oddly enough, he'd never really looked at her like this, even after he had accepted that he had wizardly perception. Because she had always been strong, the rock he'd depended on when recovering from his accident, he hadn't thought about the fact that she must have her share of doubts and regrets.

Her shields were too strong for him to do more than dimly sense those shadows, but the knowledge that she was vulnerable invoked new tenderness. As he returned to his bedroom to wash and dress, he realized that even though she was his superior in wizardry, he could still be the knight to his lady.

After dressing in riding clothes, they headed downstairs. Abby looked splendid in a navy blue habit with gold military-style trimmings. The tenants of Langdale would be impressed by their new mistress, Jack knew.

As they reached the ground floor, she murmured, "Let's go to the kitchen and have bread and tea there rather than a formal breakfast."

"In other words," he translated, "you'd prefer to avoid Mother and her husband."

"That, and I haven't seen the kitchen yet since I haven't had a formal tour of the household."

She wasn't likely to get one from his mother, he realized. "The kitchen was my favorite place when I was a lad," he said fondly. "I spent more time there than anywhere but my bedroom. I wonder who rules there now? Not Mrs. Watson, I fear. If she was still cook, last night's dinner would have been better. She was the jolliest, kindest of women." Though he had doted on his mother, it was Mrs. Watson who'd hugged him when he fell from trees and listened while he chattered about boyish enthusiasms. And her pastries had been superb. He hoped she was alive and at another great house rather than dead. The world benefited from her existence.

Their plan to visit the kitchen unseen failed since they had to walk by the breakfast parlor. As they did, Scranton opened the door. His jaw hardened at the sight of them, and disappointment showed in his dark eyes. He must have hoped that the soul-sucking energy he had used on Jack would produce some permanent consequence.

With deliberate cheerfulness, Jack said, "Good morning, Scranton. It's good to be home. I haven't slept so well in years."

As the other man glowered, a savage blow struck Jack's energy field. Instinctively Jack deflected the attack. Scranton gasped, his eyes widening as negative energy rebounded on him. Jack found vicious satisfaction in the exchange, because it proved beyond doubt that Scranton had magic and was willing to use it against others.

Jack's mother emerged from the breakfast room, as polished and pretty as a goldfinch. Each time he saw her, she seemed younger and more childlike. Ignoring Abby, she said brightly, "Good morning, Jack. Darling Alfred said that surely you would reconsider about us leaving after sleeping on the matter?"

Darling Alfred had hoped his wife's son would be dead this morning, Jack thought dryly. "The night only confirmed my belief that it is time for you to leave." He turned to Scranton, his eyes narrowed with menace, thinking how strange it was to fight this silent battle behind polite words. "Will you be leaving six days from today, or sooner? I'd be happy to arrange for an estate wagon to move your goods."

"Your help will not be necessary." Scranton spat the words out like poison darts.

"True," Jack said heartily, since cheerfulness seemed to irritate the other man. "Moving personal possessions three miles is a minor matter."

His mother drew closer to her husband's side, her expression tragic. "Please don't do this, Jack. I can't bear the thought of leaving my home."

"I'm sorry, Mother, but unless you can give me a good reason why you can't move, you and your husband will have to be out in the next six days. Today I'm going to show Abby the estate. We shall see you at dinner." Shaking internally at being so implacable to his mother, he took Abby's arm and led her to the stairs that descended to the kitchen, glad to get away from Scranton's fury and his mother's accusing eyes.

When the door was closed behind them, Abby said thoughtfully, "I wonder if I shall always be invisible to them? It has certain advantages. I could conjure elephant illusions in the hallway and never be noticed."

Jack's laughter eased some of his tension. "I should like to see that. Never mind, in a few days they will be gone."

"But not without a fight," she predicted. "I wish I knew what battlefield will be chosen. Do they know I'm a wizard?"

"I don't believe so. I haven't told my mother, and I doubt that Celeste would have put such information in a letter."

"Then their ignorance is a weapon for us."

"A major weapon," he agreed. "If not for your power, I wouldn't be here."

They reached the flagstoned hallway at the base of the steps and walked back into the spacious kitchen. It was large enough to prepare a banquet for a king, and had done exactly that in days gone by.

The shape and layout of the kitchen and pantries were familiar to Jack, but as soon as he stepped inside he realized how much the spirit had changed. No longer was the room a warm sanctuary saturated with delicious aromas and the chatter of half a dozen people. The great kitchen contained only an aproned cook and a single drab scullery maid.

The cook was thin and gray and dispirited, but there was something familiar about the old woman. She glanced up from the bread she was kneading, her expression weary beyond imagining. Her eyes widened as if he was a ghost. "Master Jack, is that you?"

Dear God, it was Mrs. Watson! She had been nicely rounded and usually dusted with flour. Now her extra weight was gone, along with her smile.

"Mrs. Watson, how wonderful to see you!" He had always greeted her with a hug when he returned from school, so he stepped forward and embraced her, hiding his shock at her appearance.

She had once been soft and wonderfully comforting to hug. Now she was a collection of bones. She shook in his arms, and he realized that she was trembling with barely suppressed sobs. "I never thought to see you again, lad," she gasped.

"I'm home for good now," he said soothingly. "My mother never mentioned you, so I didn't realize you still presided here."

She patted him on the arm, as if needing to be convinced he was real. "Aye, 'tis me, lad, though all else has changed."

She looked ten years younger than when they'd entered the kitchen. He beckoned Abby forward. "This is my wife, Lady Frayne. She is your new mistress."

Mrs. Watson looked her over eagerly. "My new mistress, you say? It won't be Sir Alfred choosing the menus and giving the orders?"

So Scranton had taken over the household from Jack's mother. The news did not surprise him; the baronet would want to control every aspect of life at Langdale Hall. "Sir Alfred and my lady mother will be moving to Combe House in a few days."

"And it's past time they did, lad!" She wiped her hands off on a towel. "Now, will you be wanting some food? You never once showed your face here when you weren't hungry."

Abby laughed. "That's exactly why we're here, Mrs. Watson. Frayne told me that the kitchen was his favorite place in Langdale. We were hoping for a bite to break our fast, then perhaps some food to take with us as we ride over the estate."

"You'll be wanting eggs and bacon with your tea, and some nice fried potatoes, and maybe ham sandwiches and ginger cakes to take away. With more warning, I could do better." Mrs. Watson glanced at the scullery maid. "Annie, you make some fresh tea and set places at the table." She smiled, and looked younger yet. "My lord and his lady have come home."

Jack pulled Dancer to a halt when they came in sight of the crumbling stone cottage, surprised at the intensity of his disappointment. The day had deteriorated sharply after they left Mrs. Watson. He and Abby had ridden over much of the estate, and found mostly barren fields and unhealthy-looking stock. A handful of tenants and laborers were still in residence, but the majority of cottages had been abandoned.

"A shepherd named Maxon and his wife and four children lived here," Jack said bleakly. "The family has been in Langdale for generations, and I thought surely they would be among those who stayed. I wonder where they have gone?"

Abby got a faraway look in her eyes. "To a farm south of Leeds, with the oldest lad now in the army. The family remembers Langdale with fondness and regret. They would come back if the land was healthy again."

"It's disconcerting when you do that." Jack dismounted to take a closer look at the door and window framings of the cottage. "How often can you tell where people are and what they are doing?"

"It varies. The Maxons lived here happily a long time. Their thoughts are still tied to the place, which is why I received a strong impression of their current situation."

"If the estate is restored and this cottage repaired"—Jack frowned as he rapped the rotten wood of a window frame—"would you be able to locate them so they could be invited to return?"

"Perhaps. But first the land must be healed." She gestured. "We've been riding all morning and found only one in three cottages inhabited, and the people in them are a sad lot. The sun is out, but it's still winter here even though spring has come to the surrounding countryside. Scranton's damage runs deep."

"Are you *sure* I can't just kill him?" Jack asked wistfully.

"No!" she said emphatically. "That's much too dangerous, and not only because murder is a hanging offense. If it became known that you murdered a man and that you have magical power, it would put all wizards at greater risk." Abby's mouth twisted. "Even in communities where we're accepted, the line between safety and torches at midnight is a thin one. As a wizard, any crimes you commit reflect on all of us."

Jack hadn't thought of that. Reluctantly he accepted that he couldn't kill Scranton, even though the bastard deserved it.

He was about to remount when a skinny dog with matted black and white fur limped into the yard from behind the house. "That's a sheep-herding dog. I wonder if she was left behind when the Maxons moved."

"Perhaps. She looks as if she's been on her own for quite a while."

The beast approached Jack warily, as if unsure whether to wag or run. Jack offered his hand for her to sniff. "Maxon bred the finest sheepdogs in West Yorkshire. This poor old girl looks like one of his."

After the dog licked his hand, Jack scratched the unkempt head and was rewarded with an adoring, hopeful gaze. "Do you think you could do anything for that limp?"

Abby shook her head. "It's an old injury. She isn't bothered by it much now, but she can't herd sheep the way she once did. Or hunt hares for her dinner."

Jack took one of Mrs. Watson's thick ham sandwiches from his saddlebags and offered half to the dog. She grabbed the food eagerly, too hungry for manners.

As the dog wolfed down the sandwich, Jack said, "What I don't understand is why Scranton needs so much energy that he's stripped the estate of most of its life force. He would have been wiser to allow the place to run normally. Instead, Alderton and my London man of business have both visited to find out what was wrong. Granted, they found no malfeasance, but it would have been safer for Scranton if there had been no reason for them to come at all." He gave the dog the rest of the sandwich.

"The best wizards have absolute mastery of their powers," she said thoughtfully. "If Scranton is the exact opposite, it makes sense that he can barely understand or control what he's doing. Reading standard texts on magic wouldn't help him since his own talent works so differently."

"How do you think he learned his kind of magic?"

"By trial and error, I imagine. Even if the only spells he wanted to cast were the ones to keep you away, his negative magic is likely so inefficient that he had to drain massive amounts of energy from his surroundings to get results."

Jack pulled his second sandwich from his saddlebag and left it for the dog, then swung into his saddle again. "Why does he rob my land, not his own?"

"He probably wanted to keep his estate productive because that's where he gets his income. He wouldn't care what his depredations are doing to your income." She shook her head. "There's too much we don't know."

"If I can't kill Scranton, is there a way to cut off the flow of energy from the land to him?"

"There should be," Abby agreed. "If so, it's the single most effective thing we can do at this point. Even though we can't attack Scranton directly, Langdale will start to recover once he can no longer drain its life force. If we can find how he connects to the land, we'll be able to come up with a plan of attack. But the estate is so large that it's difficult to know where to start. I've been watching, and haven't seen anything that looks like it might be the link between the land and Scranton."

An image from one of his bad dreams floated through Jack's mind. "The well!"

"You've thought of a place?"

"There's a holy well with a reputation that goes back to the Druids and probably earlier," he explained. "I visited often to read Mr. Willard's magic books and daydream and practice spells. If the well is the source of the land's health, might Scranton work his wickedness there?"

"Let's find out. Which way?" Abby collected her reins. Despite the somberness of the atmosphere, she looked magnificent on horseback—like a warrior queen ready to lead her troops into battle.

"The well is located very near the border of Scranton's property. His land falls in the next dale and is separated from mine by a ridge. The well is in a hollow not far below the ridgeline." Jack gestured to the left and they set off. "When we get there, might I humbly beg one of your sandwiches, since I gave both of mine away?"

"Of course." Abby's gaze shifted behind him. "The sandwiches were a good investment. They seem to have bought you a dog."

Jack glanced back and saw that the ragged dog was following him, limping but determined. "I like her. Do you think Cleocatra will mind?"

"Cleo minds that animated fur muff of your mother's, but I'm sure she and this dog will learn to get along. Do you have a name for her?"

"Maxie, in honor of the Maxons." He snapped his finger at the dog. "Come along, my girl. It's soap and water and regular meals for you!"

They rode toward the holy well, which was in an isolated area of the estate they hadn't visited yet. As they turned down into the hollow where the well was located, he said, "Is it my imagination, or is the general sense of doom we've felt all over the estate getting stronger?"

"It's not your imagination," Abby said grimly. "I feel like I'm riding into a poisoned swamp that is trying to suck me under the surface."

He scanned the hollow, where a cluster of trees concealed the well. "This used to be a happy place—the heart and soul of Langdale. The closer I was to the well, the better I felt. Now the atmosphere is so heavy the horses are skittish."

She patted her mount's neck. "Even this old slug is nervous. Is the well close enough to walk the rest of the way? I'd rather not make the horses miserable."

"The well is in the middle of this grove, so we can leave the horses here." Jack reined Dancer in and dismounted. "I thought we could eat by the well, but unless the atmosphere improves greatly, we'll want to find another picnic spot." He scanned their surroundings, military habit causing him to note potential ambushes and danger points even though the struggle with Scranton would not be fought on this kind of battlefield.

After tethering his horse, he helped Abby dismount. She was quite capable of getting off her mount, of course, but helping was a good excuse to catch hold of her waist and lower her to the ground. Which left him well placed to steal a kiss.

Her return kiss was so luscious that he was able to briefly forget the tainted energy of the well. She ended the kiss, looking mischievously from under her lashes. "Make sure the place we find for our luncheon is very private."

He grinned. "Is it mere randiness that makes a kiss drive away some of the heaviness of the atmosphere? Or is it something more?"

"Something more." Her horse secured, Abby caught up the long skirt of her riding habit with one hand and took his elbow with her other hand. "Passion is positive because it's the essence of life. It creates a spark of light against the darkness."

They headed into the grove. Maxie, who had followed faithfully across the estate, began to whine. When Jack turned to look at the dog, she sat down on her haunches and gazed at him unhappily, a faithful servant being asked to do something impossible.

"She has good canine intuition," Abby observed as she bent over to ruffle the dog's ears. "Would I prove myself deeply clairvoyant if I predict that this scraggly beast is soon going to be moving into the house and growing fat at Mrs. Watson's hands?"

Jack laughed. "And you said you had no ability to see the future." He scratched the dog's ruff. "Go guard the horses, girl."

The dog turned and trotted back to where the horses were tethered as if she'd understood every word. Jack's amusement faded as they walked through the trees toward the well. Not only was the atmosphere increasingly menacing, but he felt physically heavier with every step, as if he was carrying a mountain on his back. From her set expression, he guessed Abby felt the same way.

They emerged in the clearing of the holy well. The spring that formed the well bubbled out of a crack in a large rock that bulged from the hillside. The water collected in a small pool a couple of feet below, with the pool draining into a brook. Even in the driest of summers, the water had always been sweet and abundant and thick vegetation grew around the banks of the pool and brook.

Now the spring had dwindled to a damp film on the face of the rock. The pool was a mere muddy puddle and the banks were bare, no longer lushly overgrown.

By unspoken agreement, they stopped at the edge of the little clearing. Abby drew a deep breath. "I find myself reluctant to approach any closer."

"I feel the same." The sense of danger and dark oppression had increased with every step, and now the desire to bolt was almost overpowering. "This is worse than the fear before battle, when there's a risk of being blown to bloody pieces."

"It's fear for the soul—a conviction that if we get too close to the source of evil, we'll be doomed forever. Which is nonsense, of course. Only God can choose what happens to souls. This is only a fear spell, but it's the strongest I've ever experienced."

"Since fear is the most negative of emotions, Scranton is probably a genius at creating such spells." Jack told himself that he'd visited here a thousand times before and there was nothing to be afraid of. His heart pounding as if crack French cavalry were charging down on him, he stepped away from Abby and began to walk the last fifty feet to what had once been a holy well.

"Jack, wait." A hand locked around his and Abby fell in at his side, her face bone white but determined.

Jack's fear diminished to a manageable level. "Together we can face anything Scranton can throw at us." This was the magical spell created by marriage, he realized. Together they were greater than the sum of their individual parts.

Side by side, they approached the spring. Though the sense of looming disaster increased, Jack managed to control his desire to turn and run.

By the time they reached the spring, negative energy was pounding them with almost physical force. It was like being inside a giant drum, assaulted from all sides. But endurable, barely. "Abby, I don't think one soldier in ten would have the courage to cross the clearing with me. You have the soul of a warrior."

"No, I just married one." She knelt and studied the stone where the spring emerged, leaning forward to explore the surface with her fingertips. "There are ancient runes carved into the rock. Do you know what they say?"

"Probably that the water is blessed. Below your hand is a Latin inscription that has been mostly worn away by the water. It says this is a sacred spring."

"Fascinating." Her voice showed that curiosity was driving out fear. "I'll copy the runes and send the inscription to my father. He might be able to interpret them."

"What about the well itself? Has it been poisoned beyond redemption?" He watched uneasily, worried that this place might hurt her.

Abby moved her attention from the runes and drew her fingertips across the moisture that seeped down the stone. "It's not poisoned, but terribly twisted and suppressed. You were right—this is the connection between Scranton and his theft of the land's life force. See this faint, grayish thread?"

She traced a line in the air about half an inch from the energy thread, which he could see easily now that she pointed it out. The connection was as thin as a strand of hair, and even less substantial. It spun away from them and became impossible to see within a few feet. "Such a small thing to cause such damage."

"With this connection, he has destroyed the natural balance of the dale." She glanced up at him. "Was Langdale once considered unusually fortunate?"

Jack nodded. "The crops and stock always did well. My family has been here since before records were kept. A Norman knight of my line married a daughter of the Anglo-Saxon owner, so the old blood was joined to the new. The family name, Langdon, was taken from Langdale, the name of our valley. Do you think that our centuries of good fortune are a result of this holy well?"

"The well surely helped, though other factors must have contributed." She smiled. "After all, your friends call you Lucky Jack."

"The well has been part of my family's history for centuries." He touched the stone, and an image entered his mind. Astonished by the power of his vision, he said, "How strange. I feel sure that distant ancestors were Druid priests who dwelled here and dispensed the healing waters to those in need."

"That would explain the magic that runs in your family." She seemed unsurprised by what he had seen, or the fact that he had seen it.

Wishing he could physically strike and destroy the dark energy that defiled this holy place, he asked, "How can we free the waters again?"

She flattened her palm on the rock face. "A healing circle might do it. Not as much power would be required as when you were healed because then we were working with a damaged physical body. For wizards, it's easier to deal with pure energy, which is what we would be doing here. I think that you, Mr. Willard, and I might be enough to dissolve the negative energy that has blocked the natural flow."

She stood and brushed off her hands. "In fact, that would be perfect. The healer, the divine, and the man who was bred to this land."

"Would a circle weaken Scranton by cutting off his supply of energy?" When Abby nodded, he continued, "Can we start the healing process by severing the thread?"

"Perhaps. I'll check the amount of power it's carrying." Delicately Abby stretched out a finger and touched the thread.

The world exploded.

Chapter XXXII

As Abby cried out, Jack was knocked backward in a maelstrom of warped light and searing madness that burned along his nerves and swallowed him in blackness. He had survived near hits by field artillery, but never anything like this.

He returned to consciousness in jagged pieces. From the position of the sun, very little time had passed, perhaps only a few moments. A dog was howling nearby. With painful effort, he remembered the dog they'd found. Maxie? That energy storm had been a trap, and by touching the trigger, they had been caught in its fury. Dark energy was boiling up from the pool, as frightening as lava spilling out of a volcano.

He lay sprawled on the hard ground. Abby lay motionless a yard away, one hand dangling limply into the empty pool. "Abby?"

It took all his strength to push himself up on one elbow. Hoping against hope, he asked hoarsely, "Abby, are you all right?"

She wasn't breathing. His heart almost stopped when he realized it. He felt for a pulse. Nothing.

She couldn't be dead, she *couldn't*. Dear God, what would he do without Abby? At the beginning, he had been ready to choose death over marrying a wizard. Now he couldn't imagine life without her. This glorious, intelligent, sensual woman was his—and now he had lost her.

He was in love with her. Why hadn't he realized that sooner? Maybe because he was a man and hadn't thought beyond how much he enjoyed bedding her and talking to her and riding with her.

And now she was gone.

A terrible grief seared through him. She was everything he could have wanted in a wife, and he had been too foolish to acknowledge it. By assuming her strength was equal to anything, he had lost her. He should have protected her better.

Tears burning in his eyes, he shouted up at the empty sky, "If there is a God in heaven, take my life and spare hers!"

His cry from the heart went unanswered. Dimly aware of the howling dog and the geyser of dark energy streaming up beside him, he bent and kissed her still lips. "I love you, Abby. Now and always." His voice caught. "Sleep well, beloved."

She coughed convulsively and her chest began to rise and fall. He caught his breath, paralyzed by hope. "Lass, you said that kisses were positive energy and they drove away the darkness," he whispered. "Maybe another will help."

And maybe magic would, too. After all, Abby had used it to save his worthless self. For the first time, he opened up and fully embraced the power that was part of him. Praying that he had a dash of healer in him, he touched his lips to hers again. At the same time, he imagined healthy, positive power cascading from him into her.

Under his lips he felt a faint, sweet response. Encouraged, he ran his hands over her body, checking for injuries from her fall. He found no blood or broken bones, though he guessed they'd both be bruised in the morning.

Though she was still unconscious, she gave a little sigh of pleasure when his hand brushed her breast as he checked her ribs. Experimentally he rested his palm on her right breast. Her lips curved into a smile.

If kisses and caring were positive energy, it was time for more of them. Once more he called on his magic, visualizing it as a river of health and well-being. When he kissed her again, her mouth opened and her tongue touched his with an unmistakable response. He whispered, "Abby, are you awake?"

Her eyes opened, looking soft and unfocused. "Jack, I had the most terrible dream, that I had gone away . . ."

"Don't think of that now, lass." He cradled her face in his hands and kissed her with body and soul.

As he concentrated on sending her healing energy, he recognized that his innate power was being enhanced by a greater power that was drawn from the earth itself. The earth was the source of life, and that vitality blazed through him. He asked for more and shared it all with her, offering life and passion and love without end.

She closed her eyes again, but her hands and mouth were urgent as her passion rose to meet his. She was his goddess, personifying the rich bounty of the earth. It was utterly natural to seek her secret places, to stroke and caress until she cried. "Jack!"

He entered her welcoming body, and their union was as fierce as a summer storm. Male and female, forever opposites and partners. Miraculously she had been restored to him, and as he climaxed, he gave her his heart as well as the seeds of life.

She clung to him, shuddering, until the rage of passion faded. He cradled her in his arms with the tenderness of love. When his heart had returned to a normal rhythm, he asked, "Are you well, lass?"

"Never better, despite what has happened." She opened her amazing eyes and smiled with a warmth that could have heated all Yorkshire. "What *did* happen?"

"When you touched the thread that connected the well with Scranton, you accidentally released a torrent of wicked dark energy that knocked us both out. I . . . I thought you were dead. No breathing, no heartbeat." He swallowed painfully. "So I kissed you good-bye, and called on whatever magic I could summon. I think that helped you come back. The more positive energy we generated, the stronger we both became."

Her eyes narrowed as she studied him. "Your aura blazes like a bonfire. You have connected with the earth energy of the estate. That is your special magic, Jack. This is your land, and it responded to you like a lover." She blushed. "Like I did."

"So together, we rekindled life here?" he said in wonder.

"We did indeed." She turned her head. "Look at the spring."

Water gushed lavishly from the crack in the rock and splashed into the pool. He hadn't noticed the sound because of all the other drama. "Has the well been healed? The energy coming from the spring looked like chimney soot."

She sat up and stretched one hand under the spurting water. After a moment, she said, "The spring is pure and healthy again." She scooped some water and drank greedily. "The negative energy that linked to Scranton was like a giant plug. When it was blasted away, the natural earth energy began restoring itself."

He splashed his face, then scooped handfuls of the cool, clear water into his mouth. It was the sweet taste of Langdale. "How does this affect Scranton?"

"He has to have noticed that he has been cut off from his supply of life force. Beyond that, I'm not sure." She got to her feet, wincing a little. "You have the power to protect the well so that he can no longer use it for his own twisted purposes."

He closed his eyes and knew she was right. The life force of Langdale pulsed through him like a torrent now that its natural vitality had been restored.

He spread his hands and envisioned white light cascading from the spring, then flowing outward over every hill and hollow until it encompassed the whole vale. He'd been a damned stubborn fool to resist his magic for so long, but now he and his land were united, and he was blessed with its strength. He gave a heart deep prayer of thanks that he had been given the stewardship of this place and its people.

Never again would Scranton be able to steal this precious life force. *Never.*

When he opened his eyes, Abby said in a hushed voice, "Look."

Greenery was sprouting around the bare rim of the pool. In the branches above, plump buds were starting to leaf, and around the tree trunk, a cluster of daffodils gave a golden shout. He bent to pick one of the flowers, half expecting it to be an illusion, but it was real. He inhaled the buttery scent, which was the essence of spring, then tucked the stem inside a buttonhole on Abby's jacket. "It's a miracle, lass."

She gestured. "Here's another."

Maxie, no longer terrified of the well's evil, had trotted over to join them and was busily lapping water from the pool. Appetite slaked, she looked up hopefully.

"There is a dog ready for another sandwich. And so am I—I'm ravenous." Abby brushed dried grass from her hair. "Shall we eat, then go confront Scranton?"

"It must be done," Jack agreed. "But not on an empty stomach. I hope there's enough food left for the three of us."

Amazing how quickly a dog could become part of the family.

Abby had always enjoyed the vibrant energies of spring, but never had she experienced anything like the revival of Langdale. "One can almost see the grass growing," she said with wonder.

"The vegetation on the estate will grow until it catches up with the rest of this part of Yorkshire." Jack seemed very sure. No wonder, given how the life force of the estate was pulsing through him. Occasionally she had seen such connections between farmers or gardeners and the land they loved, but never with such intensity. The dale had waited years for Jack to return, and they had healed and completed each other.

They stopped at a cottage that lay on the route back to the manor house. The housewife came out and greeted them with a beaming face, a toddler at her heels. "Welcome home, Lord Frayne!" She bobbed a curtsy to Abby after they were introduced. "I was beginning to think spring would never come, but when it comes, it does at a run, eh?" She wiped floury hands on her apron. " 'Tisn't much inside, but would my lord and lady join me for a bit of ale and bread toasted with cheese?"

Jack glanced at Abby, who nodded. "We'd love to, Mrs. Rome." He dismounted and helped Abby from her horse. The cottages they'd visited in the morning had been full of depressed, sullen people. There had been no smiles nor offers of hospitality.

The ale and toasted cheese were delicious, too. Since Maxie had received much of Mrs. Watson's packed food, Abby and Jack did full justice to the food offered. Abby admired the way her husband talked so easily with his tenant, completely at home. He discussed the land she and her husband farmed, bounced the toddler on his knee, and promised to have the roof repaired.

After they were mounted and on their way again, Abby said, "You've found your place in the world, Jack. A year from now, all the cottages will be inhabited again and the residents will be grateful they live at Langdale."

"It may take more than a year, but I hope such a day comes."

They were close to the manor house when they passed a fenced field containing a small herd of milk cows. The livestock milled around listlessly, too unwell to enjoy the springing grass. Many had sores on their shaggy hides. Jack frowned at the sight. "Would you mind waiting here with Dancer? I want to try something."

"Of course." Abby took his horse's reins, curious what her husband had in mind.

Jack climbed over the fence and moved among the cows, talking and laying hands on them. To Abby's amazement, the beasts improved before her very eyes. Sores disappeared, heads lifted and coats lost their dullness, acquiring a healthy sheen.

Though the cows were still scrawny, the way they began to apply themselves to the grass showed that they would be fleshed out and sturdy in no time. One heifer became so lively she almost knocked Jack down with a butt of her head.

Jack returned, beaming. Abby bent from her saddle to kiss him. "That was remarkable. I didn't realize that you were a healer. A healer of animals, perhaps?"

He shook his head as he mounted again. "I don't think it was healing so much as an extension of my connection with this land. They are my beasts, and I was able to . . . to channel some of the land's life force into them."

This was the man Jack was meant to be, she realized. Powerful, wise, kind, a nurturer of land and people and animals. He was like an ancient god of the harvest, one who could share his gifts all year round. She felt a pang at that recognition. She had healed him, then become his teacher as he learned to accept his magic. Now that he was fully realized in his own special kind of wizardry, he didn't need her in that way.

Regretful that he no longer needed her, she gave him her best smile. "We shall have to start looking for the people who left. Surely some would want to return."

"The Langdale steward and Mr. Willard can help us put together a list of departed tenants and laborers." The light died from his eyes. "But first we must deal with Scranton. How can we stop him from stripping the heart from other lands?"

"Perhaps my father will know a way." She'd been trying not to think of Scranton, but she forced herself to visualize him. She touched his energy, then gasped with horror. "We must return at once! Scranton knows that you've cut him off from his energy connection, and he is about to do something dreadful!"

Jack's expression froze, and she saw in his eyes that he also knew about his stepfather. "I'll go see. Stay away, Abby! I couldn't bear to see you hurt again."

He kicked his horse into a gallop and raced toward the hall at full speed. Abby followed, urging as much speed from her placid mount as she could. Foolish man, to think that she didn't belong at a confrontation with their enemy!

The hall was a furious five-minute ride away. She was two hundred yards behind Jack when he reached the stable yard and reined in his mount. "Take care of my horse," he shouted at a startled stable boy as he vaulted from the saddle.

He had disappeared into the house by the time Abby reached the stable yard. She dismounted in a fast tumble and tossed the reins to the boy. "Take care of my horse, too!" Catching up her skirts, she darted toward the house.

Maxie, limping hard, had galloped behind. When the dog reached the courtyard, she began to lap from the horses' watering trough. As Abby opened the door into the house, she called over her shoulder, "When you have time, give the dog a bath!"

Though Abby didn't know the house well, it took only a moment of stillness to locate the dark beat of trouble. Drawn by a sense of pending disaster, she ran through the corridors that led to the family parlor.

Jack stood in the open door, his body rigid. Abby found out why when she skidded to a halt beside him and looked into the room. Sitting on the fashionable Egyptian-style sofa was Helen, who was calmly knitting with narrow silver needles, ignoring the others in the room. She wore a magnificent low-cut silk gown and her golden hair was a stylish tumble of curls. A queen's ransom in jewels glittered on her throat, wrists, and ears.

Her glowering husband stood beside her, a double-barreled shotgun in his rock-steady hands. Scranton smiled chillingly as he aimed the weapon at the doorway. At this range, it would wound or kill both Jack and Abby. "You think you have won by breaking my connection with Langdale, but you haven't. The final power is in my hands."

Jack acknowledged Abby's arrival with a wry glance, as if he'd realized she would come. But he kept his concentration on his mother's husband. "This is not about winning and losing, Scranton. What I wanted was the control and health of my land, and I have that now. Yes, I'm angry about what you did, but I don't need revenge. You are free to leave. So is my mother, if she chooses to accompany you."

He took a cautious step into the room. "So why don't you put down that shotgun? There's no need for it here."

Jack stopped cold when Scranton's finger tightened on the trigger. "You don't understand," the older man said furiously. Beside him, Helen continued knitting. The narrow needles were creating something small and lacy. Her indifference to the drama playing out in front of her suggested that she was deeply bespelled.

"What don't we understand?" Abby asked softly, hoping that Scranton would feel less threatened by a woman than by a powerful man like Jack. "I want to know, if you'll explain. I do know that you have an unusual gift of magic."

The barrel of the shotgun jerked as his hands clenched spasmodically. "A twisted, nearly useless gift! Everything I have achieved with my magic has taken a dozen times the effort of an average wizard. But despite the obstacles, I learned how to use my power to get what I want. Behold my greatest treasure."

He touched Helen's shoulder with one hand. "My wife is my queen. The most beautiful woman on earth." His voice ached with emotion.

"She is a rare and precious prize," Abby agreed. "Why not simply take her and go? No one will stop you. You have the resources to live a full and happy life with your wife anywhere you choose. Combe House. London. Abroad, even."

"Because Langdale is the only place I can be with Helen!" Scranton's voice broke. "After living most of her life here, she is tied to this place, though not as much as *him*." He waved the shotgun at Jack. "Using Langdale magic, I can make her love me in Langdale. Here she is the perfect wife."

"Are you saying she married you because you ensorcelled her rather than from love?" Jack said, shocked.

"Of course she loves me!" The shotgun shook, though the barrels still pointed at the door. "But . . . but we are happiest here."

Abby gasped. "You've used your twisted magic to enthrall her! That's why you can't leave Langdale. Your spell would be too weak to hold her anywhere else."

From his expression, she saw that she had guessed right. Only at Langdale would Helen be the adoring wife Scranton wanted. His obsession had led him to learn how to drain the land's energy and twist it into the spell that bound her to him. No wonder he couldn't let her leave the estate, and why he stayed himself. He must have feared that if Helen ever escaped his control, she would be gone for good.

"You bastard!" Jack said in a low, menacing voice. "Until now I was willing to accept my mother's marriage because I thought she loved you. But if she has been your captive, I swear I will free her if I have to break your neck with my bare hands!"

He stalked forward. Scranton fired, the noise deafening in the small parlor.

Before Abby had time to panic, Jack flung up his hand and created a shield for himself and Abby. An invisible wall of force absorbed the velocity of the shotgun pellets and they fell harmlessly to the floor.

"You can't hurt me or Abby," Jack said as the vital energy of Langdale poured through him. "This is your last chance, Scranton. Surrender or face the consequences!"

"I cannot live without her! This is all your fault, Frayne. Remember that!" Eyes wild, Scranton turned and gave his wife a swift, desperate kiss. "Say good-bye, my beloved. Then do what I showed you earlier. No one else will ever have you!"

Helen raised her head and blinked vague blue eyes. "Good-bye, sweetheart. Good-bye, Jack." She pulled one of the narrow silver needles from her knitting, reversed it so the point was pressed under her breastbone and angling upward—and stabbed the metal shaft into her heart.

Chapter XXXIII

Abby gasped, scarcely able to believe what she was seeing. As Helen froze, her expression shocked, Scranton said brokenly, "We will be together in eternity, my beloved." He jammed the shotgun under his chin and fired the second barrel.

The blast knocked him backward and shattered his skull. As blood sprayed in all directions, Helen stood and stepped forward uncertainly. Slowly she crumpled to her knees, then fell onto her side. Abby saw the energy bond that had connected Helen and her husband dissolve. The dark magician's hold was broken at last.

"Mother!" Jack cried out in anguish as he dropped to his knees beside her fragile form. Gently he rolled her onto her back. The silver shaft of the knitting needle shivered from her midriff, a trace of blood staining her gown around it.

Abby swayed on her feet, closer to fainting than she had ever been in her life. So much blood . . . Her stomach roiled. Jack must have seen such sights on the battlefield, but even as a healer, Abby had experienced nothing so ghastly.

Several servants rushed into the room, then stopped, staring at the bloodshed with horror. Jack snapped, "Mark this sight well so you can bear witness that Scranton killed himself. Then get that . . . that *thing* out of here." He gestured toward Scranton's body. "Take the sofa away and burn it."

The young footman, Jenkins, swallowed hard. "Yes, my lord." His gaze went to Helen. From where he stood, the knitting needle wouldn't be visible. "What about her ladyship? Should we send for a physician, or did she just swoon from the shock?"

Jack shook his head. "She is gravely injured and a physician can't help her, but my wife is the best healer in England."

Jenkins looked relieved. Clearly he respected wizardry. Steadied by having something to do, he organized his fellow servants to obey Jack's orders.

Not looking at the ruined creature who had been Alfred Scranton, Abby forced her wobbly legs to cross to where Jack knelt beside his mother. Helen still lived, for she was blinking up at her son.

"Why, Jack, how lovely to see you! I had not expected you to come home this winter. It has been so long." She tried to raise a hand to his cheek but failed. "I . . . I feel very tired. Will you stay long?"

She spoke like a woman waking from drugged sleep. Even her voice had changed. This was the true Helen, Abby realized. The exquisite compliant doll who was Scranton's wife had been a creature of his dark obsessions, not a real woman.

Abby knelt beside Helen and studied the wound. Though the older woman had been splashed by her husband's blood, hardly any blood showed around the needle. Perhaps, God willing, there was still time for a miracle.

Helen looked up at Abby, blinking as if trying to focus. "Jack, you wicked boy, have you brought this young lady home to meet me?"

Voice choked, he said, "This is my wife, Abby, Mother. I wrote you about her."

"My foolish memory!" Helen gave a weak huff of laughter. "How could I forget a thing like that? Welcome to Langdale, child, and thank you for marrying this stubborn son of mine. Maybe now he'll stay home."

"Don't try to talk, Lady Frayne," Abby said. "You're very ill and need healing."

"I am . . . so cold. What's this?" Helen tried to focus on the shiny needle jutting from her body. "How very odd." Her lids fluttered shut and her face became slack.

"Can you save her, Abby?" Jack said, his eyes frantic. "To lose her like this!"

"I'll know better after I scan her."

"Should I carry her into the dining room so you can examine her better?"

"No, any movement might cause the needle to shift. That would be very bad." Abby spread her palms on Helen's chest, bracketing the needle but not touching it. Closing her eyes, she scanned deep into the other woman's body. "The needle has pierced several vital organs, but it's so sharp and the wound is so narrow that, so far, there hasn't been much internal bleeding. That could change at any moment. She's in shock, and her situation is precarious."

"What can be done?" Jack asked.

"With a healing circle, it might be possible to repair the damage to her organs, one by one." She shook her head. "I just don't know."

"If anyone can save her, it's you. What do you want me to do?"

"Summon Mr. Willard as quickly as you can. Since we can't move your mother, she must be treated right here. I will try to keep her stable until you can bring the vicar. I don't know if a mortal injury this deep can be healed, but because the wound is so narrow, it's worth trying. Otherwise, there is no hope."

Jack kissed his mother's forehead tenderly. "Be here when I return, Mother. Please." He rose and left the room, his expression grim.

Abby rested her hands on Helen's chest and concentrated on keeping the older woman alive. Though she was tempted to see if she could repair any of the internal wounds, she controlled the impulse. More power was needed for a real cure, and it would be foolish to waste her energy on futile attempts.

Helen's breathing steadied, shallow but regular. Abby rose and found a knee rug folded over the back of a chair. She shook it out and covered Helen, who was dangerously chilled by shock. Then she resumed her place by the older woman and rested a hand on her shoulder, hoping she had enough power to maintain Helen in this state until Jack and the vicar arrived.

The servants who had taken away Scranton's body returned. Working with quiet efficiency, they carried off the sofa. Before leaving, Jenkins spread a blanket over the bloodstained carpet. The men had overcome their initial shock at the violence. Abby sensed no sign of sorrow at Scranton's death, but they regarded Helen anxiously.

Since the servants were carrying a sofa, they left the door open and moments later clattering claws were heard. Abby looked up as Homer, Helen's fat little dog, galloped into the room. The dog skidded to a halt and began frantically nosing his mistress. When licking her face got no response, he sat on his haunches and howled with canine despair.

Abby had found Homer irritating before, but she couldn't bear to hear his heartbreak. She scooped the dog into her arms and stroked him soothingly. "I'm sorry, Homer. Your mistress is very ill. We'll do what we can. Why don't you lie down beside her and share some of your doggy warmth with her?" The unnerving howl faded into a whimper as the dog lay down alongside his mistress.

Then Cleocatra padded in. The cat had always had an instinct for people who were unwell. She'd slept with Jack regularly when he was recovering. Abby had a suspicion that cats could channel a form of healing energy invisible to humans.

Today there was no conflict between cat and dog. Cleo curled up against Abby's side, tucked in the angle between Abby and Helen. Her soft purr may or may not have helped the injured woman, but Abby appreciated it.

As she continued her efforts at maintaining her patient, Abby studied the other woman's face. Helen looked noticeably older than when they had met. She was still lovely, but she now showed the marks of half a century of living. Perhaps Scranton's enchantment had included an illusion spell to make her look younger. No wonder he had needed to draw so much energy from Langdale. It wasn't easy to turn an imperfect woman into a perfect wife.

Together Abby and her friends kept vigil until Jack could return.

Jack and the vicar were both tense with worry when they returned. They had a bonus with them, a calm older woman named Mrs. Neel, who was the village healer and midwife. When they were introduced, Abby said, "I was going to lead the circle, Mrs. Neel, but I will defer to your experience if you choose."

"Nay, lass, you're far more powerful than I." With visible effort, the older woman folded herself onto the floor beside Helen. "Och, I'm too old to sit like this. But I can add a good steady energy to the healing."

This circle would be less dangerous to lead than the one that had healed Jack because less power was involved, but less power also meant less healing potential. Abby closed her eyes for a moment and prayed they would be able to close this wound before it took Helen's life. Then she opened her eyes and briefly explained how the circle worked. Mr. Willard had participated in circles, but Jack's only experience was as a subject.

It was awkward arranging everyone around Helen's limp body—they would all have sore joints later—but they managed. There was even room for the two pets to stay in contact with the injured woman.

Abby explained, "I am going to remove the needle very slowly, and I will try to heal each damaged organ as the point comes free." She didn't need to add that if she removed the needle quickly, Helen would bleed to death.

Gently Abby grasped the shaft while Mrs. Neel rested a hand on her right shoulder and Jack on her left. Mr. Willard was between them. She tested their individual energies. Mrs. Neel, calm and experienced. Mr. Willard, whose gentle magic was augmented by his deep faith. And Jack, who burned with the vitality of all Langdale.

Feeling more confident, Abby set to work, starting at the tip of the needle, which was lodged in the heart. Her awareness explored the pulsing muscle around the sharp point. Then she began to rebuild tissue to block potential bleeding when the pressure of the needle was removed.

Fraction by infinitesimal fraction, she raised the needle. There was a little bleeding higher up along the shaft of metal, but the section she had repaired held.

She began to work on the liver. The needle was three quarters of its length out when she began to sway dizzily from the expenditure of energy. Instantly power poured into her from Jack. Now that the holy well had been restored and Scranton was dead, Jack had access to immense amounts of vital energy.

Steadied, she returned to her task. The closer she came to the end, the greater the temptation to pull the needle out and get the job over, but she forced herself to continue at the same slow pace.

"Thank God!" she said when at last the knitting needle was free of Helen's body. After closing the circle, she added, "I think she will be all right."

As she slumped down, weary to the bone, Jack exhaled with relief and the vicar said, "Truly, God be thanked."

Mrs. Neel patted Abby's hand. "It's a pleasure to meet you, Lady Frayne. I hope we work together again."

"So do I—but not soon!" She squeezed the midwife's hand gratefully before the other woman stood creakily and left.

Helen's eyes opened and she looked around in confusion. Her gaze settled on the vicar. "Jeremy! How lovely to see you. It's been so long." She frowned. "Too long. I've been very ill, haven't I? Am . . . am I dying?"

"You were gravely injured, but you're recovering now," Abby said.

"It's like a long dream. I keep seeing . . . Sir Alfred Scranton?" She shook her head in frustration. "I . . . I was married to him? Was he also injured?"

Abby exchanged a look with Jack. This was not the right time for his mother to learn the whole story. He said gently, "Yes. I'm afraid he is dead."

Helen's eyes drifted shut and tears leaked from under the lids. "Poor Alfred. He was a most devoted husband, but very limited in his interests. Perhaps I should not have married him. But I didn't want to be alone, you see."

"You need never be alone, Helen," Mr. Willard said huskily.

"Dear Jeremy." Helen opened her eyes and gave him an enchanting smile before drifting into sleep. Now that Helen was free of Scranton's spell, it was easy for Abby to see why men adored her.

"Can she be moved to her bedroom now?" Jack asked.

Abby nodded. "She is as well as we can make her. The rest is in God's hands."

Jack bent and lifted his mother as if she were made of fine porcelain. "I hope she can sleep away the bad memories."

Abby sat back on her heels and pushed a strand of hair from her face. "She needs to remember if she is to gain wisdom from what she had endured."

After a moment's hesitation, Jack nodded. "For most of her life, people have shielded her because she seemed too pretty to distress. The time for that is past."

As he carried his mother from the parlor, Mr. Willard offered his hand to help Abby up from the floor. She ached from sitting so long, and bruises were starting to make themselves felt from her earlier fall by the holy well. The vicar said, "I'd like to sit with Helen if I may."

"I shouldn't think Jack will mind. His mother is years behind in her prayers, so she needs her vicar with her." Abby cocked her head to one side. "Why didn't you marry her instead of letting Scranton have her?"

Mr. Willard looked away. "I considered making an offer when her year of mourning was done, but I am a country vicar while she was a viscountess. I was still debating the propriety of asking her to marry me when she wed Scranton. I was bitterly disappointed, but even so, I thought it was for the best. He was a wealthy man. What did I have to offer her?"

"Love instead of obsessive madness," Abby said dryly. "Though given Scranton's gift for negative magic, perhaps it's better that you didn't come between him and the object of his desire. You have a second chance, Mr. Willard. Use it well."

"I shall." His smile was wry. "I may only be a country vicar, but I do learn from my mistakes. More than anything on earth, Helen needs to be loved. Her first husband wasn't good at showing how deeply he cared. Her second stole her soul in the guise of love. I can do better than that."

He inclined his head and left the room. As he did, two maids entered the parlor. The older one asked, "May we clean in here now, my lady?"

Abby shuddered as her gaze went involuntarily to the bloodstained area concealed by the blanket. "Please do."

She left the room, feeling curiously empty. She had done her wizardly duty. Jack was healed in all ways and no longer needed her. His sister was happy and bearing a child for the man she loved. Helen was free from a hideous enslavement, and the dark magician who had caused it was dead by his own hand. What more was there for her?

Suddenly needing fresh air, she headed for the outdoors. Maybe that would salve her feelings of emptiness.

She paused a moment, startled, then continued on her way, her lips curving in a faint smile. Perhaps she wasn't entirely empty after all.

Chapter XXXIV

"There you are!" Jack strode along the path that led to the old gazebo. The structure was shabby, like so much of Langdale, but spring flowers bloomed exuberantly around the foundation and the little building commanded a glorious view of the dale.

Abby sat inside on the stone bench that circled the inner wall, Cleocatra on her lap and a damp but clean Maxie sprawled across her feet. There were circles under her eyes, and she looked ready to fall asleep where she was. A nod acknowledged him, but she didn't speak.

"It took time for me to remember that I could find you mentally," he explained as he settled on the bench beside her.

Her hand stroked the cat's black fur. "How is your mother?"

"Sleeping peacefully." Jack bent to scratch Maxie's neck. The dog looked up at him adoringly. "She woke briefly when I laid her on the bed. She says she is Scranton's sole heir, so she has inherited his property and fortune." His mouth twisted. "She is now a considerable heiress. It remains to be seen if she'll want to live in his house."

"Mr. Willard had best take care that this time another man doesn't steal her away before he can propose," Abby remarked.

"He won't make that mistake again. He's with her now. They've been friends for many years. I think they would suit admirably. He understands her, she respects him, and they're very fond of each other." Jack chuckled. "I wouldn't even mind admitting that he's my stepfather."

"So all is well." Instead of victorious, Abby looked sad.

"Except you. You look exhausted. Here, I stopped by the kitchen for food." He opened the canvas bag he'd brought and pulled out a meat pie. "After so much healing, you must be starved. This one is beef and mushroom, I think."

"I am hungry, actually." Abby bit into the pie, pastry crumbling onto her lap. "When I'm this tired, I don't even remember to eat."

Jack broke another pie into two pieces, using the smaller to lure Cleo from Abby's lap and the larger for Maxie. Then he bit into one himself. The pastries were warm and delicious. Mrs. Watson had recovered her skill along with her optimism.

He'd finished his meat pie before he noticed that Abby was still looking sad. "What's wrong, lass? It has been a terrifying day, and watching a man kill himself is disturbing, to say the least. But Scranton is no loss to the world, and together we have triumphed. Langdale is restored, and it couldn't have been done without you."

"Or without you. I've never been so frightened in my life as when he fired his shotgun at you." She stared down, crumbling the last edge of pie pastry. "When we agreed to wed, I said that I wanted children, but other than that, you needn't stay with me. I . . . I think I conceived today by the holy well."

"We're going to have a baby?" he exclaimed, stunned but delighted. "Are you sure?"

She nodded. "Celeste said that she felt sure that she was with child as soon as it happened. Now I know what she meant. The lad will be a strong wizard and a worthy heir to Langdale. I can return to Melton to bear the child. You are free to go back to the army if you wish now that the succession has been secured."

Jack was so shocked that he choked on his last bite of pie and began coughing. When he could speak again, he exclaimed, "What the devil are you talking about? I thought we were getting on rather well. Do you really want to leave me?"

"No," she said quietly, still not looking at him. "But we made a bargain when we married. It is not for me to change your terms."

This time he remembered to use magic much more quickly. Mentally he reached out to touch her emotions so he could understand her mood.

It was a shock to realize how she saw herself: as too large and plain and a wizard who was less than welcome except when her talents were required. "You really see yourself as undesirable? Despite all I have done to demonstrate otherwise?"

She bit her lip and didn't reply.

An insight struck him. "Lack of confidence runs deep, built up over many years. My being unable to keep my hands off you"—he took her hand—"is new. I suppose it takes a long time for doubts to fade."

Though she still gazed away, her fingers tightened around his.

He continued, his voice soft. "It's been such a busy day that I forgot to mention something rather significant that happened by the pool."

She glanced up at that, brief amusement in her eyes. "Creating a child together is certainly significant, but I haven't forgotten how it happened."

"Hush, lass, this happened earlier." He leaned over and scooped his large, lovely wife onto his lap. Caressing her hair, he said, "When I thought you were dead—the world stopped. I couldn't imagine living without you. I was devilish slow to realize it, but I love you, Abby. Now and forever, world without end, amen. Do you love me enough to stay with me? No man can hold a wizardly wife against her will, so I surely hope that you want to stay."

She began to sob uncontrollably. His first alarmed reaction lasted only a moment. She was increasing, all right. Even he knew that emotions ran high in a woman who was with child. Apparently that was true even if only a few hours had passed. "Are you going to tell me that you married me only for my title and entrée into London society?" he asked. "If so, I won't believe it. I've learned a thing or two from you, my lady."

She laughed a little through her tears. "It was never about your title, Jack. But I've suffered agonies of guilt about how I coerced you into marriage. Even though I gave you the opportunity to cry off, I've wondered ever since if you would have married me if you hadn't felt obligated."

He thought back to his chaotic emotions after his fatal accident. "Probably not," he admitted. "A wizard wife would have been unthinkable then."

"I knew I should let you go," she said with a hiccup. "But I'd been in love with you for so long that I didn't *want* to do the right thing. So I was selfish and let you be noble and marry me."

"You were in love with me?" he said, startled.

She nodded. "The first time I saw you in Melton Mowbray, I was just a schoolgirl. I was so struck by the sight of you that I followed you down the High Street. It was like being ensorcelled. Every hunting season, I prayed you would be back so I might see you again."

He caught her gaze, shocked. "Good God, lass, why? Surely not because I was so handsome!"

"No, most of your friends were more handsome," she agreed.

His mouth curved. "You didn't have to agree so quickly."

She laughed. "You were certainly well built and athletic and you drew the eye, but even more, you looked so very—agreeable. Like someone I would enjoy knowing." She ducked her head, but he could see her blush. "Like someone I would like to share my bed with."

"That's even better than if you considered me handsome." He thought of Lady Cynthia Devereaux and other petite, fluttering blondes he had admired. They were mere daydreams, with no more substance than a cloud.

The lush, sensual, wise woman in his arms was his reality. This amazing creature who was carrying his child. His heart full to overflowing, he said, "I didn't know what I wanted for a wife, so isn't it fortunate that you decided you wanted me? You really do have some ability to see the future, I think."

"I don't want you to regret what I did someday," she said seriously. "What if things work out badly between us?"

He kissed her hard, leaving no doubt what he thought about her desirability. "No regrets ever, Abby." He grinned. "And of course things will work out. It's not for nothing they call me Lucky Jack!"

Langdale was having its first harvest festival since the death of Jack's father, and a roaring success it was, too. Once Jack had done his duty in opening the festivities and greeting his guests, he went in search of his wife. She was easy to find. One of the first skills he'd mastered in his magical studies was how to locate Abby wherever she was.

He found her in the food pavilion, among tables piled high with made dishes and breads and jellies and sweets. When the sun reached its zenith and the whole pig and the side of beef now roasting over a fire pit were ready, the sides of the tent would be rolled up so guests could enter and feast.

"Hello, lass." He paused after the tent flap dropped behind him to admire his wife's splendor. She wore a fashionable blue morning gown, her height minimizing the effect of her pregnancy, even though she was seven months along. Abby was the kind of woman who became radiant when with child. Her skin was creamily perfect and her hair shone even in the dim light.

"Is all well?" She gave the special smile that was just for him, and stole a tart.

"Aha!" he said triumphantly. "Caught in the act. Mrs. Watson will be most displeased. She's very hard on food thieves." He used magic to tug at the pastry.

Abby resisted the tug and popped the rest of the tart in her mouth. "She gave me permission to indulge since I'm increasing," she said with a dignity that was undercut by the smear of gooseberry preserves on her chin.

"Increasing in wonderful ways." He stepped forward and kissed the gooseberry sweetness away while cupping her breasts. Pregnancy had made them even more magnificent than usual.

She purred and pressed against him. Desire flared like lightning. They were halfway to the point of no return when a child shouted just outside the tent. Blinking, Abby pulled away, saying huskily, "Later." She took two more tarts, giving one to him and biting into the other herself.

"Later," he agreed with a sigh. "I'm glad that you aren't letting the son and heir go hungry." It took major willpower to look away from the sensual sight of her teeth sinking into the flaky pastry.

"The daughter and heiress likes to eat," Abby said, expression grave but eyes dancing.

He gently spread his hand over the curve of her belly and felt a kick. There was a lot of activity there today. It awed him that this precious, energetic life had been created from their love and passion. "You still won't tell me if it's a boy or a girl?"

"It's good practice for you to learn on your own," she said with her best schoolteacher manner.

He closed his eyes and tried to discern the gender of that glowing, growing white light, but without success. Surely that reckless energy indicated a boy? Yet he sensed a sweetness that was so much like Abby that the baby must be a girl. He shook his head. "The only thing I'm sure of is magic. This will be quite a little wizard."

"And he or she will be raised to value that gift," Abby said seriously.

Jack couldn't agree more. No child of his would be beaten for showing too much interest in wizardry. Nor would any son be sent to Stonebridge Academy.

His gaze fell to her gown's fashionable décolletage, which was enough to rivet even a stone saint. "I will not be responsible for my actions if we don't go into a more public place." He offered his arm. "Will you join me as I stroll about in the role of gracious host? It will be even better if you're present as the gracious hostess."

"With pleasure, my lord." Abby took Jack's arm and they returned to the festival, which sprawled beside and behind the manor house. Children played games, adults waited their turn to view a peep show of the Battle of Trafalgar, and strolling players and puppeteers performed. Every few steps Jack and Abby stopped to exchange pleasantries.

As they moved away from the puppet show, Jack murmured, "You know almost as many people here as I do, and they all adore you."

She smiled, but shook her head in disagreement. "They're just glad to be part of a happy, healthy community again."

"They adore you," he said firmly. "As well they should. After all, I adore you, and I have impeccable judgment in this matter."

She blushed. Adorably. He loved watching the play of emotion in her expressive eyes. Every day she grew more beautiful.

Mrs. Watson, who had regained her good nature and her roundness, turned from the fire pit and announced in a carrying voice that it was time to eat. As she spoke, her minions rolled up the canvas walls of the pavilion and guests surged forward.

As Jack drew Abby away from the rush, a dusty but grand coach swept around the house and halted in front of the stables. Abby shaded her eyes. "Who can that be? I don't recognize the carriage, and all the local gentry are here already."

Jack narrowed his eyes, then set off toward the carriage, guiding Abby. "That's the Duke of Alderton's travel coach. Do you suppose my mother decided to return for the festival? I wrote her about it." After Scranton's death, his mother had gone to stay with Celeste, and the visit had been extended for almost six months.

"Oh, I hope she's back," Abby said, her step quickening. "Her letters are cheerful enough, but I'd like to see how she's doing for myself."

His wife was ever the healer, Jack thought affectionately. He wouldn't have her any other way.

They reached the carriage as his mother was being handed out. "Jack, Abby!" she cried as she skipped toward them. "Oh, come here so I can hug you both at once!"

The affection in her embrace made up for her coldness when Jack had returned to Langdale after his years away. After sweeping her from her feet with his embrace, he set her back on the ground and studied her critically as she hugged Abby. This was the laughing, sweet-natured mother he remembered.

Interestingly, she looked her age now. Beautiful, but as a mature woman, not as a girl. She had grown more thoughtful since Scranton's death.

"Don't I get a hug?"

Jack turned to see his sister stepping carefully from the carriage. Though she was only slightly further along in her pregnancy than Abby, her petite frame made it much more visible.

"Celeste, how wonderful that you came!" He hugged her, too, but more carefully than with his mother.

"Am I forgiven past transgressions, Frayne?"

Jack turned, and was startled to see that it wasn't a footman who had handed his mother and sister from the coach, but the Duke of Alderton himself. The duke looked a little wary, as if not entirely sure of his welcome after the unpleasantness in London.

"Piers! I'm glad you're here to see how much better everything is." He shook his brother-in-law's hand enthusiastically.

"We've brought you a present." The duke gestured behind the coach. Pulling to a stop in front of the stables was a large farm wagon filled with jumbled household goods and a family of five. Behind trotted several dusty herd dogs.

Not quite believing his eyes, Jack crossed to the wagon. That weathered face looked familiar. "Mr. Maxon, is that you?"

"Aye." The shepherd sucked on a blade of long grass, striving to conceal his nerves. "The duchess came to call and said that all was well at Langdale. That you'd settled in the hall and you wanted folk to come home."

Mrs. Maxon, the quiet woman sitting next to the shepherd, said softly, "It's true, isn't it? It . . . it has to be true."

Abby came forward and caught Mrs. Maxon's hand. "Bless the duchess for finding you! We have been looking for your family, but had not been successful. Welcome back to the dale, Mrs. Maxon. I'm Lady Frayne, and my husband has mourned your absence. He says that Mr. Maxon breeds the best sheepherding dogs in Britain."

The shepherd's face split in an unexpected grin. "Aye, that I do."

Maxie, who had been successfully begging for treats and attention all over the festival, trotted forward and began touching noses with newly arrived dogs. Jack smiled. "I repaired your old cottage, hoping you'd come back, and even added two more rooms. You'll be chief shepherd, but one thing you can't have is this dog. She's mine now."

One of the children, a boy of about ten, scrambled down from the wagon. "Our Lulu is alive!" He hugged the dog happily. "She'd gone missing, she had. Just before we moved. 'Tis good to see her, my lord."

"You must be hungry. Come and join the harvest feast," Abby suggested. "Your old friends and neighbors will be glad to see you again."

The Maxons climbed down from the wagon, the children tumbling headlong in their excitement. As the family moved off, Mr. Willard appeared, his expression blazing with happiness. "Helen!"

She caught the vicar's hands and looked up into his face, beaming. "I couldn't stay away any longer. Even with a letter a day from you, it wasn't enough."

"We'll have to wait six more months," he said softly. "Till you are out of mourning. If you're sure that you want to live in a vicarage . . ."

"I'm sure." She tightened her hold on his hands. "I was raised in one, and very happy I was. I'll be happy in any vicarage that has you in it."

Jack turned away, not wanting to intrude on their reunion. His mother would be in good hands with the vicar. He knew from Celeste that the two had been corresponding intensely while Helen was staying with her daughter, and he guessed that letters had brought them to a deeper level of understanding.

He and Abby escorted their guests to the house so they could freshen up. On the way out, he coaxed Abby into the alcove below the stairs for a bit of privacy. "It's a perfect day, lass," he said as he hugged her. "Did you know Celeste had found the Maxons?"

She settled her head on his shoulder with a happy sigh. "She said she was on their track and hopeful. She has a magical gift for finding, I think, and she loves practicing it. She said that her husband has even found it useful."

"And so magic enters the life of the noble duke." Jack held his wife tight, inhaling the rosemary scent of her hair. "Just like it entered my life the day I met you."

He placed his hand on her belly again, then caught his breath as a vision of two towheaded toddlers filled his mind. "Twins!" he exclaimed as the children of his vision each raised a hand. Magical light blazed from the small palms, meeting and swirling into one bright sphere. "You're carrying twins! A boy and a girl. Not one wizard, but two."

She laughed, her aquamarine eyes bright with joy. "I was wondering how long it would be till you realized that. We are doubly blessed. After all—you're Lucky Jack." She gave a smile that touched his heart. "And I'm lucky, lucky Abby."

About the Author

A *New York Times, Wall Street Journal,* and *Publishers Weekly* bestselling author, MARY JO PUTNEY is a graduate of Syracuse University with degrees in eighteenth-century literature and industrial design. The author of more than two dozen novels, Putney has been a nine-time finalist in the Romance Writers of America RITA contests, and has won two RITAs, four consecutive Golden Leaf Awards for Best Historical Romance, and the *Romantic Times* Career Achievement Award for Historical Romance. Her books have been listed four times by *Library Journal* as among the top five romances of the year. Putney lives near Baltimore with her nearest and dearest, both two- and four-footed. Visit the author's websites at www.mjputney.com and www.maryjoputney.com.

About the Type

This book was set in Garamond, a typeface originally designed by the Parisian typecutter Claude Garamond (1480–1561). This version of Garamond was modeled on a 1592 specimen sheet from the Egenolff-Berner foundry, which was produced from types assumed to have been brought to Frankfurt by the punchcutter Jacques Sabon.

Claude Garamond's distinguished romans and italics first appeared in *Opera Ciceronis* in 1543–44. The Garamond types are clear, open, and elegant.